The
Right
Hand of
Evil

The Right Hand of Evil

JOHN SAUL

BALLANTINE BOOKS

NEW YORK

A Ballantine Book
Published by The Ballantine Publishing Group

Copyright © 1999 by John Saul

www.randomhouse.com/BB/

ISBN 0-345-43316-5

Manufactured in the United States of America

Prologue

A live.

It was still alive.

She could feel it inside her. It was moving again, twisting and writhing in her belly.

She'd hoped it would die.

Hoped. And prayed. Since the moment she first felt it inside her, she'd fallen to her knees, begging God to deliver her from the evil within her—desperate prayers that continued through long days and longer nights. Sleep never came, for she dared not ever let down her guard, not ever relax her vigilance against the evil even for a few seconds of blessed release from the terror. Lying awake on dank sheets, listening to the whine of insects beyond the window, how many times had she gotten up from her bed in the meanest hours to stand at the window, gazing out into the black abyss, wondering if she shouldn't open the screen and let the predators in?

Once, she slashed through the mesh with ragged nails, ripping the screen to shreds, tearing open her nightgown as if to a lover, presenting her tortured body to the horde of tiny creatures that spewed forth from the night to settle on her skin in a thick and pulsating scum: clinging to her with piercing barbs; miring in the oily sweat that oozed from her; pricking with stinging needles. Producing a thrill of pain as she willed them to suck out her blood, and along with it, the evil that pervaded her every pore.

But the vileness within her had prevailed, as even against her own will she swept the insects away, slammed the window shut, and stood beneath a scalding shower for hours in a vain attempt to cleanse herself of the poisons.

She had returned to the bed, cursing herself and the man who lay beside her, but most of all cursing the disease that ruled her.

Disease.

Truly, that was what it was: an illness cast upon her in retribution for sins so vile that she had repressed even their faintest memory, leaving only the corruption inside, the monstrous horror that was metastasizing through her, consuming a little more of her every day.

"Dear God, why hast Thou forsaken me?"

The words—the cry of anguish that should have shattered the very air—dribbled from her lips like the mewling of a baby, a pitiful, weak sound, but enough to drive the life within her wild. It sent her screaming and stumbling from the house, where her balance deserted her and she dropped to her knees, skinning them on the harsh paving of the driveway. Moaning, she sprawled out, and for the tiniest moment of ecstasy thought she might be dying. Then the fury within her eased, and after a while her ragged panting mellowed into a rhythmic breath. Deliverance was not yet at hand. She struggled back to her feet and stood staring at the house.

She had thought it beautiful once, with its high-peaked roof and many gables, the broad veranda that wrapped around it with the fullness of a petticoated skirt, the shutters and gingerbread that decorated its face like the millinery of an age gone by. Now, though, she saw the fancywork for what it was: a veil that only barely covered the wickedness that lay within; a mask peeling back to reveal the slatternly face of a whore.

A whore like me.

The words rose unbidden from the depths of her subconscious, in a choking sob.

The evil within her tested its strength, and the woman's body convulsed.

She staggered forward, driven by pain. At the foot of the steps leading to the veranda—and the cavernous rooms beyond—she stopped.

Not inside.

The certain knowledge that something was different, had changed in the seconds since she'd fled outside, made her turn away.

Behind.

It's behind the house.

As if under the power of an unseen force, the woman slowly groped her way around to the back of the house. The sun, close to its zenith now, beat down on her, making her skin tingle and burn in an angry, itching rash that spread scarlet from her belly across her torso, down her arms and legs, like claws scraping at her from the inside, pushing to tear free from the confines of her body.

Then she saw it.

Her hands rose reflexively to her face as if to blot out the vision before her, or even to tear her eyes from her head. Then they dropped away, and she gazed unblinking at the specter beneath the ancient magnolia tree that spread its limbs over the area beyond the house.

It was the man.

The man she had married.

The man who had brought her to this house.

The man who had delivered the disease upon her.

The man who had lain unconscious beside her as she'd prayed for a salvation she knew would never come.

Now he was gone, his body, stripped naked of even the tiniest shred of clothing, hung from the lowest branch of the tree, a thick hempen rope knotted tightly around his neck.

His head hung at an unnatural angle, and his lifeless eyes were fixed upon her with a gaze that chilled the remnants of her soul.

The knife with which he'd slit open his own belly was still clutched in the stiffened fingers of his right hand, and his entrails lay in a bloody tangle below his dangling feet.

A swarm of flies had already settled on his disemboweled corpse; soon their eggs would hatch, releasing millions of maggots to feast upon him.

He had found his escape.

He had left her alone.

Alone with the disease.

Nearly doubled over by a spasm of terror and revulsion, the woman turned away and lurched toward the shelter of the house.

Muttered words, unintelligible even to herself, tumbled from her lips. By the time she escaped the brilliant noon sun, her entire body was trembling.

Hide.

Got to hide.

Hide from him.

Hide from *it*.

The corruption inside leaped to life again and, no longer aware of where she was or what she was doing, she obeyed the dictates of the foulness within.

A door opened before her, and she stumbled, then fell, plunging into the shadowy darkness, feeling blackness surround her, welcoming the release of death.

Her body slammed against the coldness of the cellar floor. She lay still. Against her will, her heart once more began to beat, her lungs to breathe.

And now the final agony—the agony she had always known would come.

It arrived as a point of white heat deep within, which spread and burned as it raced through her, igniting every nerve in her body into a fiery torment that sent a scream boiling up from her throat, instantly followed by a stream of vomit.

Every muscle in her body cramped. Limbs thrashing, hands and feet lashing out as if at some unseen tormentor, she was engulfed by the growing pain.

"NOOOooo . . ." The single cry of anguish burst from her, then trailed off into hopeless silence.

For a long time she lay unmoving, as the fire withdrew, leaving at last an absence of pain. A blank emptiness where the disease had been.

She pulled herself up and gazed at the tiny thing that lay between her legs.

Still covered with bloody tissue, the baby stretched its tiny arms, as if reaching toward her.

The woman stared at it, then reached out and picked it up.

She cradled it in her left arm, and with the fingers of her right hand she stroked its face.

Then, her eyes still fixed upon the infant, her fingers closed around its neck.

She began to squeeze.

As her fingers tightened, she heard herself say the familiar words that lifted her spirit and filled her soul with peace. "Our Father, who art in Heaven . . ."

The baby thrashed against her grasp, its fingers instinctively pulling at her own.

". . . Forgive us our trespasses, as we forgive those who trespass against us . . ."

The baby's tiny fingers fell away from hers; its struggles weakened.

". . . Deliver us from evil."

The movements stopped. The infant lay still in her hands.

"Amen."

They found her just after sunset.

She was still praying, but of the baby, there was no trace to be found. Indeed, it was as if the infant had never existed at all.

She offered no resistance when they lifted her to her feet, none as they led her from the house and put her in the ambulance.

As the ambulance drove away, she did not look back.

Her face was serene; she hummed softly to herself.

Deliverance, finally, was hers.

September

CHAPTER 1

Janet Conway felt the first flush of humiliation even before the clerk spoke. She was already calculating the amount of cash in her wallet as he picked up the phone and listened to what Janet had long ago come to think of as the Voice. The Voice was always the same. Perfectly pleasant. Perfectly reasonable. So familiar she could easily have limned a sketch of the face that belonged to it—a bland face, mostly round, with the kind of soft features that were the most difficult to draw, and devoid of any emotion whatsoever. The pronouncement of the Voice would be final: "The credit limit is exceeded."

She felt her face redden with embarrassment. *You should be used to it by now,* she told herself. *After all these years, you should expect it.* Unwilling to meet the clerk's eyes, she scanned the meager pile of supplies she'd put into her shopping basket: five tubes of paint, three of them shades of blue. She really needed only the cobalt. And she could do without two of the brushes, but the other one was absolutely necessary.

More necessary than food for tonight?

Her flush deepened, her humiliation turning into anger. Her gaze shifted from the artists' supplies on the counter to the young man—no more than two or three years older than her twins—who looked even more embarrassed than she felt. "It's not your fault," she assured him. *And it's not mine, either,* she could have added, but didn't. *"We don't air our dirty laundry in public,"* her mother's voice—stilled by cancer five years ago—echoed in her mind. "I'm sure it's just a mix-up," she told the clerk, forcing a smile that she hoped might cover her true emotions, and imagining her mother's nod of approval. "I'll pick these things up this afternoon." As she strode from the shop and out into the sweltering

Louisiana morning, she felt the clerk's gaze following her, and knew the young man didn't believe she'd be back any more than she did.

Maybe some afternoon next week, but certainly not this one.

She listened to the engine crank on her old Toyota, praying it would catch since there was no more chance her Visa card would be accepted at the garage than at the art supply store. Finally, she released the breath she hadn't realized she was holding as the motor sputtered into reluctant life.

Though the market was her next stop, and she knew the kids would be expecting her, she turned the car in the opposite direction, deciding it was more important to deal with the credit card issue right now than to put it off until Ted came home from work. *If* he came home, she thought, which was, as always, an everyday question in her life.

The Majestic Hotel might have been the pride of Shreveport—as its marquee proudly proclaimed—once upon a time, but once upon a time had been a long time ago. Parking in front of the ugly brick building in defiance of a GUESTS ONLY sign, Janet hesitated in front of the building, taking a last deep breath of fresh air against the stale cigarette odor she knew she would find inside, then pushing open the dirt-filmed glass door into the lobby. What next? she wondered as she stepped over a large tear in the threadbare carpeting. At least the last hotel in which Ted worked had managed to keep its lobby looking decent. Where would he wind up after this?

She didn't even want to think about it.

As she started toward the assistant manager's office, the desk clerk gave her a brief nod. "He ain't in his office, Miz Conway." He cocked his head toward the bar. "He's on break." Her anger, which had settled to a low smolder, flared up again. The desk clerk's lips twisted into a knowing smirk. "Been on break for about an hour now."

Once again Janet heard her mother's remembered voice in her head: *"Don't kill the messenger just because you don't like the message!"* She nodded a barely perceptible thanks to the clerk as she veered off toward the bar and a moment later stepped into its smoky interior. Half a dozen early drinkers littered the length of the bar. A bleached blonde of about forty, encased in a dress two sizes too small for her ample body, peered blearily at Janet just long enough to satisfy herself that she still had no competition in the room, then returned to her seduction of the shabbily dressed men sitting next to her. Apparently, she thought, the Majestic couldn't even attract a decent class of hooker anymore.

Spotting her husband on the second stool from the end of the bar, Janet brushed by the aging prostitute and took a stance in front of Ted with her arms crossed.

"It happened again," she said, lowering her voice so the bartender couldn't hear her. She could tell by Ted's expression that he knew exactly what she was talking about. To his credit, he at least didn't try to deny it.

"I ran short of cash," he told her. His eyes met hers, and, as always, the look of contrition on his face—the genuine sorrow in his chestnut eyes—chipped away at her anger. "All I put on it was a hundred."

"But it was a hundred more than we could afford," Janet objected, her voice rising more than she'd intended.

Tony, who was lazily rinsing glasses in the sink behind his bar, glanced their way. "And it's a hundred less than Ted owes."

Janet bit her lip, and Ted winced visibly.

"Look, honey, I'm really sorry. But you know how it is—"

"No, I don't know how it is," Janet interrupted, her anger flooding back in the face of his automatic expectation that no matter how bad things got, she would always understand. "I don't know why you keep on drinking up your paycheck every week when we barely have enough money to pay the rent and eat, let alone keep the car running and keep me in art supplies." She regretted the last words the moment they came out, for the look in Ted's eyes told her she'd offered him an escape.

"If you earned enough with your paintings, maybe I wouldn't have to pay for the supplies—" he began, but she didn't let him finish.

"The last three canvases I sold paid off the credit cards and bought the kids their Christmas presents. And if I have to, I can borrow some money from Keith at the gallery, since he's sure he won't have any trouble selling the two I'm working on." She hesitated, even tried to hold the next words back, but her anger won out. "And if I have to borrow money from Keith, you'd better believe I'm going to tell him why I need it. I'm not going to make up any stories to cover for you." Her voice was rising, and suddenly everyone at the bar was looking at her. She could hear her mother clucking with disapproval, but she ignored the warning. "Is that what you want, Ted? Do you want me to start telling everyone *why* the credit cards are maxed out and the checks are starting to bounce again?" She glanced around the seedy bar and shook her head in disgust. "Even the manager of this place won't want you working for him anymore."

The look of sorrow was back in his eyes. "I'll stop," he promised. "I swear to God, hon, I won't have another drink until every bill we have is paid off." He fumbled in his pocket, pulled out his wallet, and handed her all the cash he had. "Take it," he said. "Take it all. Maybe it'll be enough for whatever you need."

Janet gazed at him for a long time. Even in the dim light of the bar, she could see the pain in his expression. Beneath the erosion alcohol had carved on his features, the remains of the boyish looks that had first attracted her to him were still visible. She reached out as if to take the money, but her hand fell back to her side and she shook her head. "It's not the money, Ted," she said, her anger finally draining away. "It's you. I don't want your money. I want you." Turning away from her husband, Janet fled the dim bar, emerging into the light and heat of the morning.

At least I didn't cry, she told herself as she got back in the Toyota. *At least I didn't let any of them see me cry.*

But as she drove away, the tears she'd managed to control in the bar finally overcame her, running freely down her face.

Ted Conway watched his wife hurry out of the bar, then pushed his empty glass away, stood, and shoved his wallet back in his pocket. But before he could start back to his office, his eye fell on the empty glass.

He looked at it for a long time, knowing he should leave it where it was and go back to work. Instead he sat back down on the stool and nudged the empty glass toward Tony. "I guess one more won't hurt, will it?"

CHAPTER 2

Cora Conway had been awaiting death for more years than she could clearly remember. Long ago, she supposed, there must have been a time when she welcomed life, but memories of those times had long since faded away, disappearing into the gray fog that seemed to wrap itself more closely around her with every day that passed.

Not that Cora kept track of the days anymore, for each day was just like the day that had gone before, and would be just like the day that was to come. She would awaken in her bed, here in the room that was so familiar to her that if one morning she woke up blind, the image of her surroundings would be so vivid that the loss of her sight would make no difference.

The nightstand was on the left.

The table with the reading lamp and the music box was on the right.

If she got up from her bed and moved toward the door to the hallway outside her room—a door at the end of a short corridor that pierced the exact center of the north wall of her room—she would pass two other doors.

The one to the left led to the closet that contained her clothing.

The one on the right led to the bathroom she shared with the person in the room next to hers.

She had never seen the person in the room next to hers, had no idea if it was a man or a woman.

Nor did she care.

There was a window in the south wall of her room, but Cora had no need to look out of it: it faced another window a few feet away, beyond which was a room that she was quite certain was a mirror image of her own.

Once, long ago, she'd wondered if that room contained a woman who was a mirror image of herself, and the next time she'd looked in the mirror above the dresser that sat against the wall opposite the foot of her bed, she'd wondered if she might really be looking through a window into another apartment. She'd watched the woman in the mirror grow old, watched the face lose the beauty it had once had. She'd stopped touching her own face at all, clinging to the belief that the image in the mirror couldn't be hers.

That was why she never looked at her hands, or her feet, or any other part of herself.

That was why, day after day, she lay on her back on the bed and stared at the ceiling.

And waited as the days passed.

After Cora woke up, the woman with the breakfast tray would come, and then she would sit up, lean against the pillows, and eat her breakfast, careful not to glance at the woman in the mirror.

She would lie on her back until the boy brought lunch.

She would lie on her back until another woman brought dinner.

She spoke to no one; if she spoke, she would have to hear her own voice, which she had no desire to do.

She would go to sleep, and then wake up, and one day was exactly like the one that had passed, and the one to come.

She had no idea when the fog had begun to gather. She had merely become aware of it one day, a grayish mist at the far reaches of her consciousness. She hadn't thought much about it, but every now and then she'd noticed that the fog was creeping closer. Its gray was darkening, and it was beginning to blur the images of her world.

The fog, she thought, was death edging close, and so she began to prepare herself, begging forgiveness for sins grown so remote and indistinct that she had forgotten what those sins might have been. As the fog grew denser, she began to look for death, began to seek it out, searching the gray mists for the dark spirit she knew would soon emerge.

This morning she had finally seen it.

She'd caught her first glimpse of it by accident, for as she'd risen from her bed to make her way to the bathroom, she'd let her eyes stray toward the mirror over the dresser. Though she'd turned sharply away, something in the mirror had seeped into her memory, and when she came out of the bathroom a little while later, she went to the mirror and peered into it.

The woman she saw in the glass bore no resemblance to herself: the clouded eyes were sunk deep in a mass of wrinkled skin, and only a few wisps of whitish hair covered the blotchy scalp. But it wasn't the image of the dying woman that had caught Cora's attention; it was something that loomed behind her.

Though she'd never seen it before, she recognized it right away.

Death was finally emerging from the mist, coming for her.

In her mind, Cora had always seen the figure of Death clad in black, its eyes glowering coldly out from a skeletal face all but lost in the folds of its hood. But the angel who now approached her was nothing like the image she'd conjured in her imagination. This spirit wore no hood. The folds of its shroud flowed gracefully around it in shimmering waves of silver, and a radiant smile bathed its face in a golden glow. Its arms were spread wide as if to enfold her in a comforting embrace. The horror Cora had always felt toward death—the certain knowledge that whatever eternity might await her would be far worse than the years she'd already endured—began to crumble as the luminous figure approached.

Instinctively, her fingers moved to the tiny golden cross that hung from a thin chain around her neck, and she traced its delicate shape as she recalled for the first time in countless years the words of the person who had placed it upon her: *"This will protect you. Never let it go until the angel comes for you."*

Cora had not understood then, had never thought of Death as an angel who would deliver her from the weight of her years, but only as a harbinger of the punishment yet to come.

Now, as the figure moved closer, the swirling dark fog seemed to lift.

Returning to her bed, she sat on its edge and pulled open the top drawer of the nightstand. It was filled almost to overflowing with the detritus of a nearly forgotten life—scraps of paper with meaningless words scrawled on them, coupons torn from newspapers and magazines, small gifts brought by people whose names and faces had long since fallen from her memory. The drawer jammed halfway out, then crashed to the floor when Cora jerked it free. Falling to her knees, she rummaged through the litter on the carpet, her fingers searching for the single object that she knew—with sudden, piercing clarity—she must find.

When the nurse found her, Cora was still on the floor. She tried to explain what she was looking for, but the words wouldn't come, and when the nurse lifted her back onto the bed, Cora was unable to resist. She struggled against the straps the nurse bound her with, but they were too strong for her.

As she wrestled against the constricting bands, she caught another glimpse of Death in the mirror, and let herself sink into the familiar contours of the mattress, let the pillow cradle her head, and watched as the spirit drew closer.

The afternoon light faded as the spirit emerged from the glass, and Cora felt the comforting presence of Death so close by that had it not been for the straps restraining her arms, she might have reached out and drawn it to her.

Darkness closed around her. She thought she heard the spirit's voice, whispering that it was time for her to go.

Cora's lips worked, struggling to form words she hadn't spoken for years. "Ted," she whispered at last. "I want . . . please . . . Ted."

Drained by the effort it took to speak, a great sigh escaped Cora Conway's lungs, and she lay still.

For a moment the nurse thought Cora Conway had died, but then she saw that the old woman was still breathing, though shallowly. She seemed to have lapsed once more into the semicoma in which she'd lain for months; the nurse loosened the restraints. She would look in on her later, before her shift was over, to see how she was doing. Only then, if the patient seemed to be weakening, would she call the old woman's only relative.

Her nephew, Ted Conway, who hadn't visited his aunt in years. No reason to call, the nurse thought, unless some further change indicated that his aunt was dying.

Then, perhaps, he would come, if only to say goodbye.

Ted Conway glanced up as the five o'clock news came on the television behind the bar, and signaled Tony for one last vodka tonic before calling it a day. He was tired—despite what Janet had said, he hadn't just been "drinking up his paycheck" in the bar all afternoon. He'd been working, reviewing the file that lay open in front of him, but mostly keeping an eye on the bartender, whom he was all but certain was ripping off the Majestic. Ted still wasn't sure how Tony was doing it—he'd kept a careful eye on the way Tony poured the drinks, and even asked for a couple of straight shots, just to make sure the liquor wasn't being watered. Nor had he been able to catch Tony palming money, though he hadn't been able to rule it out, either. One thing he'd discovered in his twenty years in the hotel business was that bartenders learned lots of tricks, and sleight of hand wasn't the rarest of them. The trouble was, Frank Gilman, the general manager, wouldn't spring for the equipment they needed to keep their bartenders honest. All it required was a liquor meter, and a computerized cash register that wouldn't let the meter pour any booze that wasn't on a bill.

"We're not the Sheraton," Gilman had groused when Ted brought up the problem the previous week. "We can't afford that kind of stuff, and even if we could, I wouldn't put it in. A bartender should have the right to buy a customer a drink now and then. It keeps them coming back."

Well, at least Gilman was right about one thing: the Majestic was no Sheraton. Ted had worked in a Sheraton for a while, and it was a hell of a lot nicer than this dump. In fact, he thought, he'd still be there if the general manager hadn't been such an asshole. He still didn't understand what the big deal had been about his keeping a bottle of Smirnoff in his desk. After all, wasn't the hotel business based on hospitality? So he had a few drinks with the vendors who came in trying to sell him everything from linens to bar snacks. What was the big deal? That's how business worked. At least Frank Gilman understood that.

Tony put the fresh drink in front of him, and Ted was about to pick it up when he stiffened, knowing, even before he glanced up into the mirror behind the bar, that Frank Gilman was standing behind him. In the brief moment before he put on his best assistant manager's smile—the one that rarely failed to disarm even the angriest of hotel guests—he wondered why he could always sense the general manager's presence. And it wasn't just Gilman—it was every damn manager he'd ever worked for. It wasn't anything tangible; just a sixth sense he'd always had. But what was Gilman doing here? It was Friday—Gilman's golf day—and he'd left right after lunch, just like he always did. So what brought him back? If there'd been a problem in the hotel, someone would have called him. But the afternoon had been dead quiet, except for Janet coming in and hassling him about the credit card. Other than that, nothing had been going on. Nada. Then, as Gilman slid into the space next to him, he understood: his boss was finally taking his concerns about Tony seriously, and had dropped in to check up on him.

"I still don't get it, Frank," Ted said, keeping his voice low enough so Tony wouldn't be able to hear him. "I know he's doing it, but I don't know how."

Gilman's eyes narrowed. "Maybe we should talk in my office," he suggested.

Draining the vodka tonic Tony had set in front of him less than five minutes earlier, Ted stood up, steadied himself against the bar, then started after Gilman, who was already pushing through the door to the lobby.

"Don't forget your file, Ted," Tony said.

Turning back, Ted swept the file off the bar, swearing under his breath as half the papers fluttered to the floor. He knelt quickly, stuffed them back in the folder, then hurried after Gilman.

The bartender watched him go. As the door swung shut behind Conway, he turned back to his halfhearted polishing of the bar glasses, and the conversation he'd been having with the hooker perched two stools away from Ted all afternoon. "Don't think we'll be seeing him around much longer," he observed.

The hooker shrugged. "Too bad. At least he never hassled me like the last one."

Tony chuckled. "Think he was ever sober enough to notice you?"

The prostitute's laugh was just enough to carry through the door into the lobby, where Ted was about to step into Frank Gilman's office. Maybe when he was done with Frank, Ted thought, he'd go back to the bar and run the hooker out of the place. People like her could give the hotel a worse name than it already had. He moved through the door to the general manager's office, closing it behind him to shut out the whore's laughter. It wasn't until he was about to lower himself into the deep comfort of the worn leather easy chair in front of Gilman's desk that he realized that Gilman was still on his feet, leaning against his desk, his arms folded over his chest. Ted, his reflexes too slow to recover his feet, dropped gracelessly into the chair.

"You're drunk again, Ted."

Though Gilman hadn't stated it as a question, Ted shook his head vigorously. "I had a couple of drinks, sure," he admitted. "But how else am I going to nail that son of a—"

"Don't bother," Gilman cut in. "You've been sitting at the bar all afternoon, and by the last count, you'd had ten drinks."

Ted rose to his feet, his face reddening as his temper pounded at his temples. "Who said that? I had two drinks, and even those hardly had anything in them!"

Gilman's lips tightened and he shook his head. "It's too late, Ted. Tony doesn't short the drinks, and he isn't stealing from us."

Ted's eyes squinted into angry slits. "I can prove he is."

"You can't, because he isn't. Anyway, not what I call stealing. But looking at your expenses, I can't say the same for you."

Caught off guard, Ted hesitated. "Expenses?"

Gilman picked up a thin sheaf of papers from his desk. "You turned in a three-hundred-dollar bar tab last month, Ted. Three hundred dollars. I'd ask you how you did it, but I'm not sure I really want to know." As Ted started to speak, Gilman held up a hand to silence him. "I really don't want to know, Ted." Now he picked up an envelope and handed it to Ted. "This is your last paycheck. I put in a month's severance, and you can keep your medical for three months. Pretty generous, I'd say." His brows arched. "Frankly, if I were you, I'd use it to get some help with your drinking problem."

A vein in Ted Conway's forehead began to throb. "I don't have a problem," he began. "So I have a drink or two now and then. Who doesn't?" He gestured vaguely toward the expense report. "And most of that stuff's business." His voice took on a wheedling note. "C'mon, Frank, you know how it is! You used to do my job."

"And I was sober when I did it, Ted." He moved toward the door. "I'm going to need your keys."

Ted stared at his boss, reality finally sinking in. "You know what?" he said, fishing the heavy ring of keys out of his pocket and flinging them on the manager's desk. "You can't fire me, Frank. I quit! You run a crappy hotel here, and I can't believe how long I've hung around trying to clean it up. Well, the hell with it, Frank. The hell with it, and the hell with you! You can take this whole place and shove it." Snatching the envelope containing his last paycheck from Gilman's hand, Ted wheeled around and jerked the door open.

"On my report to the state, I'll say I laid you off, Ted," Gilman said. "That way you can collect your unemployment right away, and you won't have it on your record that you got fired. It's the best I can do for you."

Ted Conway ignored Gilman's words. Slamming the door shut behind him, he started across the lobby toward the bar, then remembered what Gilman had said about how many drinks he'd had that afternoon. Goddamn bartender must have been spying on him! Well, there were plenty of other places where he could get a drink.

And plenty of other hotels that needed a good assistant manager, too.

Who the hell needed the Majestic?

Goddamn dive!

It wasn't until he was a block away from the hotel, with the dank heat of the late afternoon sapping his anger, that he thought of Janet, and what she'd say when he told her he'd quit his job.

Automatically, Ted Conway turned into the first bar he came to.

CHAPTER 3

How much longer? Janet wondered. The unspoken question had seemed utterly innocuous when it first popped into her mind, relating to nothing more earthshaking than how much longer the reheated casserole in the oven might hold out before it would need the addition of a little milk to keep it palatable. But as she cracked the oven open to test the tuna and noodle concoction, the question that had posed itself in her mind kept coming back, each time attaching itself to another aspect of her life.

How much longer before Ted comes home?

How much longer until he gets fired again?

How much longer do the kids have to put up with the fights?

How much longer can *I* put up with it?

"Will you stop worrying, Mom?" she heard her son say, and for a moment she thought she must have spoken aloud. Then she saw the mischievous glint in Jared's eyes. "We'll just tell Kim and Molly that the mold is parsley, or blue cheese or something."

Janet took a mock swing at Jared with the mixing spoon, and he spun out of range with a grace she would have expected from a dancer rather than a football player. Not that Jared bore the bulk of most football players; at nearly sixteen, with only 160 pounds on his six-foot frame, he was considerably smaller and lighter than most of his teammates. Still, despite Jared's quick reflexes and lean agility, Janet always cringed when she saw those big, lumbering tackles charging toward her son. "I've never served you moldy food yet, Jared Conway, but if you keep that up, I just might start!"

"Want me to call Pa and see how late he's going to be?" Jared asked, ignoring her threat as he opened the drawer next to the sink and pulled out a handful of silverware. Though he'd tried to make the question sound casual, there was enough tightness in his voice to betray his true question: *Shall I see if I can find Pa at all?*

Janet hesitated, then shook her head. "Let's give him another half hour, then we'll go ahead and eat and I'll just save some for him."

Jared hesitated, too, and Janet thought he was going to say something else, but he picked up a bunch of paper napkins and began setting the Formica-topped table that she'd bought seventeen years ago at a garage sale. At the time, her mother had deemed it "perfectly acceptable for newlyweds." Janet suspected that her mother's words now wouldn't be nearly as charitable. In fact, she suspected her mother would be less than charitable about her whole situation. She glanced around the kitchen, which was even more in need of a coat of paint than the rest of the house, and wondered if there were any possibility of convincing the landlord to repaint the place, and fix the roof as well. Fat chance! She'd begged for new screens all summer, hoping that the kids wouldn't have to make the choice between sweating through the nights in airless bedrooms or opening the windows to clouds of merciless mosquitoes.

"Hey, they don't drink *that* much blood," Jared had replied last week when she'd wondered how he could stand the incessant buzzing in his tiny room at the back of the squat one-story bungalow. It was exactly the kind of response Ted would have made years ago, when they'd first been married and his alcohol intake was little more than an occasional extra drink at a party. There was so much of Ted in Jared, just as there was so much of herself in Jared's twin sister, Kim, that at times Janet wondered if she and Ted had somehow managed accidentally to clone themselves, rather than produce offspring that were an amalgamation of the two of them.

For Jared's sake, she prayed he wasn't too much like his father, just as she hoped that Kim wouldn't prove to have a weakness for the same kind of man she herself had married.

Which wasn't really fair, she reminded herself. When she met Ted Conway, he'd had an easygoing charm that was so unlike her own family's stiff formality, she'd fallen for him almost instantly. And for a long time the marriage had been fine. Ted had a knack for the hotel business, and both of them had assumed they'd wind up in Atlanta, or Miami, or even New Orleans, with Ted running one of the major hotels, and she showing in some of the better galleries.

But somewhere along the way his drinking had crossed a line neither of them quite noticed, and that was the end of their dreams.

Not that those dreams had completely slipped away: Janet still harbored fantasies of showing at the major galleries, though she'd long since stopped sharing her hopes with Ted, whose former appreciation of her talent had devolved to carping about the amount she spent on canvases, paints, and brushes.

His own dreams were still wildly alive, at least when he'd had a few too many drinks. Then she would hear about how bad the management was at whichever hotel had taken a chance on hiring him. Though there was a time when she might not have agreed with him, during the last couple of years, she'd had to admit he was at least partially right. After all, what manager who knew his job would hire Ted, given his reputation and his history?

So why had she stayed with him?

It was a question Janet had pondered more than once, and she was all too aware of the answer: she stayed with Ted because she didn't have the nerve to take the kids and strike out on her own. After all, how much worse could things get? She might not be able to make much money, but she suspected that whatever she could earn would stretch at least as far as Ted's paycheck, since she wouldn't be wasting a single cent of it on liquor. And the shock of her packing up the kids and leaving just might jolt Ted into taking an honest look at his own life. In the privacy of her own conscience, she knew she was at least as responsible for the conditions of her life as Ted was. But how much longer could it go on?

She was rescued from having to come up with an answer to that question by the sudden appearance of Molly, charging into the kitchen with far more energy than even a fifteen-month-old had the right to possess in the face of the heat and humidity that had settled thickly over the stillness of the evening. Right behind Molly came Kim, who swept her baby sister off the floor just as Molly was taking a desperate plunge toward the shelter of her mother's legs.

"Gotcha!" Kim cried out, raising the little girl high over her head and tipping her up so that Molly was peering almost straight down. Molly feigned outrage at being snatched off her feet, but her giggles got the better of her, and a huge grin spread across her face.

"Down!" she cried. "Wanna get down!"

"Oh, you do, do you?" Kim asked. "Okay, fine!" Releasing her sister, she let Molly drop in free fall before closing her hands around the little girl's waist once more.

"Don't do that!" Janet cried out as Molly uttered a shriek far more of delight than fear. "I swear, you'll give me a heart attack!"

"She loves it," Kim replied, swinging her sister around, then lowering her to the floor.

"Again!" Molly cried, trying now to shimmy up the legs of the very same person she'd been trying to escape only seconds before. "Do it again!"

"After supper," Kim told her. "And if you're very, very good, I'll let you help me wash the dishes." Giving Molly a gentle nudge toward the kitchen door, Kim opened the cupboard that held the luncheon china Janet's mother had given her for a wedding present. *"You don't need anything more formal for a few years, dear,"* Janet could still hear her mother saying, and she'd certainly turned out to be right. "Is Pa going to be here for dinner?" Kim asked.

Janet heard the same tension in Kim's voice that she'd caught a few minutes before in Jared's. "I'm not sure," she said carefully, maintaining the fiction that all was well within their family. "But let's set a plate for him. I know he'll be here if he can make it." Kim shot her a quick glance that Janet had no trouble reading: *You mean if he's sober enough!* But like Jared, Kim didn't push the issue. "We'll give him a few more minutes," Janet said.

B̲ut it was far more than a few more minutes before Ted came home that evening, and when he did—a little after eleven—his face was flushed, his step unsteady, and his eyes bloodshot from the long hours of drinking. Janet was alone in the living room, trying to concentrate on one of the books she'd gotten from the library that afternoon. Molly had been tucked into her crib hours earlier, and Kim and Jared had escaped the heat and uneasiness in the house by going to a movie. When Ted didn't call out to her as he came through the back door, Janet's suspicion that he'd been drinking all evening was confirmed. Steeling herself to cope with the argument that was surely coming when he finally appeared in the living room, she set the book aside.

"I quit that stinkin' job today," Ted announced without preamble as he confronted her, a beer clutched in his right hand.

Janet felt a sinking sensation in her stomach: she knew that whatever she said would be the wrong thing, but not saying anything at all would be even worse. "Did someone offer you something better?" she asked, choosing her words carefully, and keeping them free of any inflection that might trigger Ted's temper.

He dropped onto the sofa, his free hand landing on her thigh. "Just couldn't take Frank Gilman any longer. Man's a dumbass!"

"Well, I'm sure you'll find something else," Janet offered, but even through his drunkenness, Ted recognized her ploy.

His eyes narrowed to puffy slits, and his hand tightened on her thigh. "Don't patronize me."

Janet's mind raced, remembering the night two years ago when Ted came home even drunker than this, and decided he wanted to make love to her. She'd tried to put him off, but it hadn't worked, and rather than fight him, she'd given in.

It had been a horrible night for her. When she discovered she was pregnant, she'd toyed with the idea of getting an abortion, but only for a moment. And when Molly was born, Janet knew she'd been right. But she didn't want it to happen again. "I'm very tired, Ted," she began, but Ted only leered.

"Then let's go to bed."

She cast around in her mind for something else—anything to put him off—when the phone rang. The surprise of it startled Ted as much as Janet. His hand fell away from her leg as she stood up to answer it, thoughts of some accident to Kim and Jared already leaping into her mind.

"May I speak to Ted Conway, please?" a woman asked.

There was an official-sounding tone to the voice that raised Janet's apprehensions even further. But whatever news this caller possessed, Ted was in no condition to deal with it.

"This is Mrs. Conway," she replied.

"I'm sorry to call you so late," the woman said, and Janet's fear ebbed slightly. Surely no one would apologize if it was about her children, would they? "This is Lucille Mathers, from the Willows in St. Albans?" Janet felt the worst of her fears instantly abate. It wasn't the kids—it was Ted's aunt. "I'm calling about Cora Conway," the woman went on, confirming Janet's thought. "I think your husband should come down here."

Janet's mind raced. Right now? St. Albans was 140 miles southeast of Shreveport; even if they left right away, they wouldn't get there until three in the morning. And given Ted's condition . . . "How bad is she?" Janet asked. The last time she'd talked to the people at the Willows, Cora had been in a semicomatose state, and her condition hadn't changed in several months.

"I'm afraid it's not good," Lucille Mathers replied. Very quickly she added, "I don't think she can last more than another day." A pause. Then: "She wants to see your husband. If it's at all possible—"

"Tomorrow," Janet said, making an instant decision. "We'll leave early in the morning, and we should be there by eleven. Can you tell her that?"

"Of course," Lucille Mathers replied. "We'll look for you in the morning, then."

Hanging up the phone, Janet told Ted about Cora's request. As she talked she wasn't sure he was even listening, but when he spoke, his tongue thickened with the liquor he'd consumed, she knew he had.

And she knew it was the alcohol that was replying to her, not her husband. At least she hoped it was.

"Why the hell should I go see Aunt Cora?" he demanded. "She's crazy as a loon, and always has been. What am I supposed to do about her?"

"For God's sake, Ted!" Janet snapped. "She's dying, and you're the only family she's got!"

"So?" Ted replied. "What's she ever done for me?" Then, before Janet could answer him, his head dropped down onto the sofa and his eyes closed.

Janet was tempted to leave him exactly as he was and go to bed, but remembering that Jared and Kim hadn't come home yet, she changed her mind. Let them at least think he'd been sober enough when he came home to get himself into bed, she decided.

Shaking him hard, she finally got him to wake up just enough to let her guide him into the bedroom. A second later he was unconscious again, sprawled out on the bed in his clothing, snoring loudly.

No more, Janet thought as she lay beside him an hour later. Though Jared and Kim had come in and gone to bed and, undoubtedly, right to sleep, she herself was still wide-awake, listening to Ted's heavy breathing.

Something was going to have to change.

She couldn't live this way any longer.

None of them could.

CHAPTER 4

Jared and Kimberley didn't have to glance at each other over Molly's head to understand that both of them were thinking exactly the same thing: *How come we've never been here before?*

The long drive southeast from Shreveport had been made in silence, the kind of silence that strained everyone's nerves, as if a bomb were ticking somewhere in the car, and each of them was nervously waiting for it to explode. Both the older children had held their breath when their mother offered to drive so their father could sleep, but Ted contented himself with a deep scowl in his wife's direction, and the observation that "I drive better dead drunk than most people do stone sober."

Silence. No one was going to fall into *that* trap. Even Molly had somehow sensed that today was not a good one for fussing.

But now, as they drove into the town of St. Albans, the tension in the car finally began to ease, partly out of the simple knowledge that the long drive through the humid heat was almost over, but mostly because the scene unfolding before them was so completely unexpected, at least for Jared and Kimberley. Although neither of them had ever been there, they had both been aware of St. Albans for as long as they could remember.

It was where Aunt Cora lived, locked away in a sanatorium. Even when the twins were very small they'd imagined what it must look like. They'd whispered descriptions of it to each other in the bedroom they shared until they were five, vying with each other to describe the scariest place imaginable: a brick building with bars over the windows, surrounded by a high chain-link fence. "With barbwire on top," Jared solemnly assured his sister, "so the crazy people can't climb over and kill us all."

"I bet they keep them in cages," Kim had offered, but Jared, ten minutes older, and thus far wiser than his sister, shook his head.

"They keep the worst ones in pits," he told her. "With only a hole on the top that they drop food through, and a metal lid so they can't climb out."

The St. Albans of their fantasies was no less grim than their imaginings about the sanatorium. "I don't even want to talk about it," their father told them the few times they'd asked him what it was like. "My uncle threw my father out, and he never went back. Hated the place till the day he died, and hated my aunt and uncle, too. Said he'd rather burn in hell than live in St. Albans." The image the children conjured from this grim declaration was composed of bits and pieces of the worst things they'd ever seen—rotting shanties with no windows and sagging roofs, jumbled together on grassless tracts of worn-out land facing unpaved roads; a crumbling, heat-baked main street with a few stores with peeling paint and filthy windows displaying dusty, unwanted merchandise. In their minds, St. Albans was all but deserted—most of the population, of course, having been confined to the sanatorium, which they'd imagined as looming darkly in the center of the town.

What they now saw was even more surprising than their wild imaginings. The little town appeared almost out of nowhere as they came around a bend in the highway. Rather than narrowing, the road widened as it came into St. Albans, and became a boulevard with a broad median strip separating the two lanes. A row of ancient oak trees marched down the median, spaced widely enough when they were planted so that now their branches, dripping with Spanish moss, provided a perfect canopy for the street and the front yards of the homes that faced it. After half a mile the street opened into a large oak-shaded square that held a bandstand, some picnic tables, and a small playground for children. On one side of the square a row of shop fronts glistened from buildings at least a dozen decades old, but as freshly painted as the day they'd been built. Everywhere, the influence of New Orleans was clear, from the gated facades that promised sun-dappled courtyards hidden behind them, to the ornately worked wrought iron that decorated second-floor balconies. Jalousied shutters were closed against the morning heat, and only small windows pierced the thick walls of the shops, which were identified by ornately lettered signs hanging from curlicued iron brackets.

"It looks sort of like the French Quarter," Jared said as they passed through the center of town.

"But a lot duller," his father observed darkly, and a moment later turned right, away from the square.

The side streets appeared to be as well-kept as the main street and the area around the square, and were lined with houses that also echoed New Orleans, with French, Georgian, and Victorian styles jumbled

together in a pleasant mélange brought together by the moss-draped trees
that spread over the lawns and gardens. These offered shady respite from
the pervading heat that lay over the town even now, in early fall.

"It's beautiful," Kim breathed as her father turned left after driving
two more blocks. Here, the oaks gave way to willows, their branches
draping gracefully to within a foot of the ground. Then, in the next block,
placed in the center of a large lawn, she saw a sign:

> # The Willows
> ## At
> ## St. Albans

The sanatorium was not at all what she and Jared had imagined. A
white limestone structure whose core section rose two stories, it was fronted
by a broad porch with five Corinthian columns rising all the way up to support the roof. Single-story wings spread out from the center, also constructed
of white limestone. The windows, far from being barred, were flanked with
gray wooden shutters, held open with wrought-iron hooks. Bougainvillea
blooming in a profusion of scarlet, red, and pink was banked against the twin
wings, and a low fence of sculpted wrought iron surrounded a broad lawn
that boasted two of the largest willow trees Kim had ever seen.

Ted pulled the car to a stop in a parking area at the foot of the steps
that led to the wide front porch. But as his wife and children piled out into
the late-morning sunshine to stretch after the long ride, he stayed behind
the wheel, his eyes fixed on the building almost as if he expected some
danger suddenly to manifest itself.

Janet glanced nervously at the kids. "She's a harmless old lady,
Ted," she said quietly. "And she's dying. It's not going to hurt you to say
goodbye to her."

Ted's eyes narrowed, but he finally got out of the car. Together, the
family mounted the steps, crossed the porch, and pushed through the front
door.

Inside, they found a comfortable reception area, with several chintz-
covered, overstuffed chairs arranged around a large coffee table. A gray-
haired woman wearing a pale blue dress—and a small white badge that
identified her as Beatrice LeBecque—looked up from a computer termi-
nal, her smile of welcome fading into an expression of sympathy as she
recognized Ted and Janet Conway. "I'm so glad you were able to come,"
she said. "I think Mrs. Conway's been waiting for you."

"She didn't even know—" Ted began.

"She's awake?" Janet quickly asked, deliberately cutting Ted off, her glance darting warningly toward Jared and Kim.

"I believe so," the receptionist replied. She pointed toward a set of double doors at the far end of the reception area that led to one of the two wings. "The third room on the right, in East Two."

"Can the children wait here?" Janet asked.

"Of course," Beatrice LeBecque replied. "But if the two older ones want to see their aunt, I can look after the little one." Producing a bright red lollipop from the center drawer of her desk, she held it out toward Molly. "Look what I've got for you."

Molly immediately squirmed to be set free from her mother's arms, and Janet lowered her to the floor. In an instant she was around the end of the desk and climbing up into Bea LeBecque's lap. "I think we'll get along just fine." Bea smiled. "I like to think children like me, though I suspect it's more the lollipops."

As her youngest daughter picked at the wrapper of the lollipop, Janet turned to the older children. "Why don't you wait here until we find out if she's well enough to see you."

As their parents disappeared behind the double doors to East Two, Kim and Jared looked at each other.

None of it was anything like what they'd expected.

Not the town.

Not the sanatorium.

Once again the same thought occurred to both of them at the same time, and as always, both of them knew it. As if by some kind of silent communion, it was agreed that Jared would voice the question.

"Our aunt Cora . . ." he began uncertainly. "We've never met her, but we've heard—" He hesitated, but the words his father had invariably used finally fell from his lips. "Is she really crazy?"

Bea LeBecque stopped her gentle bouncing of Molly, and the little girl cocked her head, peering up into Bea's face as if she, too, were waiting to hear the answer to her big brother's question.

"She's very old," the receptionist finally replied. "And she's been very alone. But is she crazy?" She fell silent for a long moment, then her head moved in a slow nod. "Now that I think about it," she said softly, "I hope she is." She was silent again, then: "For her sake, I hope she is."

Janet laid a hand on Ted's arm just as he was about to open the door to his aunt's room. When he turned to look at her, she could still see the hangover in his eyes, but today the toll of his drinking appeared even greater than usual: the sharp planes of his cheeks and chin were blurring, and a network of veins was appearing on his nose. But more than that, there was an underlying anger in the grim set of his features that Janet hadn't seen before.

Or, more than likely, she thought, hadn't let herself see. But of course, she knew in her heart that the anger had been there for a long time. It wasn't as if Ted had tried to hide it. He'd even used it as an excuse for his drinking, shifting responsibility from one problem to another, shoring up one excuse with another until so much of him had disappeared into his defensiveness that she'd sometimes wondered if there was anything left of the man she had married.

Nobody, to hear him tell it, had ever given him a decent break; not his parents, who had split up when he was a baby, or any of the people he'd worked for. And certainly not his aunt Cora, who had been in this room through most of his life, becoming nothing more to him than a burden of guilt he'd always resented. But now it was almost over.

"She's dying, Ted," Janet repeated softly, her eyes meeting his. "I know how you feel about her, but all she wants to do is say goodbye." For a moment she wondered if he'd heard her, but then he gently stroked her cheek with a single finger, in a gesture she hadn't felt in years.

"Hey, I know I'm not always the easiest guy in the world to get along with, but I'm not a monster, okay?"

"Last night you said—"

"Last night I had a lot too much to drink. And I'm not going to pretend I didn't pay for it this morning, and made you and the kids pay for it, too." He forced a smile that Janet sensed was masking pain he couldn't let her see. "I'm not going to try to even any scores," he promised. "It's way too late for that."

The door to Cora Conway's room opened and a priest emerged. He was ancient, his face deeply creased, his shoulders stooped as if with the weight of the decades of confessions he'd heard. From the waist of his cassock hung the beads of a rosary, and in his arms he cradled a Bible that looked even older than he, the finish of its leather cover long ago worn away by the hands of those who studied it, the binding of its spine weakened—but not quite broken—from constant use. As he pulled the door closed behind him, almost as if to shut out his penitent's final visitors, his eyes fixed on Ted. His mouth worked as if he were about to speak, but then his lips closed and he turned away. With a step so halting he seemed about to fall, the priest made his way down the hall and disappeared around the corner.

Only when he'd vanished did Ted grasp the handle of his aunt's door. A moment later he stepped into Cora Conway's room, Janet closely following him.

Both of them smelled death in the air. It seemed they were too late; surely no life could remain in the still and shrunken figure that lay in the bed.

Cora's wispy hair was matted against her scalp, and her eyes were shut. Her left hand lay in her lap, but her right was closed on an object suspended from a chain around her neck.

There was a stillness to the room, a heavy silence that made Janet slip her hand into Ted's.

Another gesture that hadn't occurred in recent years.

Then, out of the stillness, there was a rasping gurgle.

Cora Conway's chest rose as she sucked air into her weak lungs, and her rheumy eyes opened.

She blinked.

Finally her eyes moved, slowly scanning the room, as if she were searching for something.

At last they came to rest on Ted Conway.

"Stay away," she gasped, her voice barely audible. "Stay away from here."

Instantly, Janet stepped around Ted and lay her hand on the old woman's shoulder. "It's all right, Aunt Cora. Everything is going to be all right."

The old woman's collapsed lips worked as she struggled to formulate words. "The children," she finally managed to whisper. "I want to see the children." Janet hesitated, gazing down into the ruined face of the dying woman, but Cora's eyes locked onto her own, and the old woman's left hand closed on her wrist. "Bring them," Cora whispered. The words, though barely audible, were not a plea. Rather, they were a command. "Bring them to me!"

Still Janet hesitated. In all the years she and Ted had been married, they'd visited Cora Conway only half a dozen times. The visits had been brief, for Ted's aunt had invariably commanded him to leave—just as she had today. The last two times Janet had come, she hadn't even tried to convince Ted to join her.

She had never brought the children, afraid that they would be terrified of the strange old woman, and that Cora would only become more agitated than she already was. Nor had Cora ever asked for them before; indeed, Janet couldn't tell if the old woman had even understood her when she talked about them. Now, though, it was clear.

Cora Conway wanted to see the children.

And certainly Jared and Kim were old enough not only to understand their great-aunt's condition, but the mental illness that had blighted so much of her life.

Making up her mind, she covered Cora's clutching hand with her own reassuring one, and bent low so she was speaking directly into Cora's ear. "I'll get them," she said. "I'll be right back."

"I'll stay with Molly," Ted said, following her back out to the reception area.

Janet nodded her agreement, relieved that at least this one time Ted's motives—which she suspected were primarily rooted in a desire to escape his aunt—coincided with her own needs. "It won't be long," she assured him. "It seems like she's barely hanging on."

On the way back to Cora's room, Janet tried to prepare Jared and Kim for the dying old woman who was their closest living relative, but the moment the twins stepped into the room, she knew she needn't have worried.

Showing no sign that they noticed the odor of disinfectant and death, the twins went directly to the bed. "Aunt Cora?" Kim said. "I'm Kim. It's so nice to finally meet you."

Cora Conway's eyes fixed on Kim for a fraction of a second, then shifted to Jared, fastening onto him with a burning intensity. For a long time she said nothing.

Finally, the boy extended his hand, as if to touch her. "I'm Jared—" he began, but Cora cut him off, shrinking from his touch.

"A Conway," she said. "I can see it. Stay away! Stay away from here!"

Jared, recoiling from his aunt's words, glanced nervously at his mother, then tried again. "It's all right, Aunt Cora," he said, this time reaching out and placing his hand gently on her shoulder.

Cora twitched away, as if she had been pricked by a needle. "Go!" she rasped. "Go now!"

Jared glanced at his mother, who tilted her head almost imperceptibly toward the door. "I'm sorry," he said softly. "I didn't mean to . . ." His voice trailed off as he realized his aunt Cora had already shifted her attention back to his sister. "I'm sorry," he repeated once more, then quickly backed away from the bed, turned, and hurried from the room.

As soon as Jared was gone, Cora pulled herself up in the bed. Her hands fumbled with the chain around her neck. "Wear this," she said, her voice croaking as she struggled with the chain's tiny clasp.

"Let me help you," Janet offered, moving closer to the bed.

Cora shook her head. "Kimberley. Kimberley must do it!" Exhausted by her efforts, Cora dropped back against the pillows and lay still as her great-niece carefully unfastened the clasp and lifted the chain from the old woman's neck. As the tiny golden cross hung before her, Cora reached out for it, almost as if to take it back, but then dropped her hand onto the coverlet. "Put it on," she told Kim. She fell silent again, but her eyes missed nothing as Kim carefully put the chain around her own neck, fastened it, then touched the small gold cross. "There is another one," Cora said when she was satisfied that the cross was in place. "In the drawer." She waited as Kim opened the drawer, searched for a moment, then found a second cross, identical to the one that now hung around her neck. "For the little one," Cora whispered. Her eyes flicked away from Kim, fastening on the place where Jared had stood a few moments ago. She smiled, as if recognizing some person unseen by either Janet or Kim, and both mother and daughter could see the tension draining from the old woman's body. "It will protect you," she whispered. "Just as it protected me. Don't ever take it off."

Suddenly, she extended both arms, as if to welcome an embrace. Her smile broadened, her eyes cleared, and the years seemed to fall away from her.

Before either Janet or Kim could move toward her, Cora's hands dropped back to her sides. With a long sigh she relaxed into her pillows, her eyes closing as if she'd fallen into a deep sleep.

Her breathing stopped.

Then, in a flash so brief Kim would never be certain it had actually happened, she sensed the light in the room had changed, muted into a golden glow that suffused the air.

Beautiful, she thought. *So beautiful.*

"I'll take Molly's cross," Janet said quietly as she led Kim toward the door a moment later. "When she's old enough, we'll give it to her together, and tell her where it came from."

Kim barely heard the words, and as she was leaving, she turned to look back.

The soft, serene light had vanished as utterly as if it had never been there at all.

The golden glow—like her aunt Cora—had gone and now the room seemed dark and cold.

So cold it made Kim shudder.

CHAPTER 5

"I'm so sorry, Mr. Conway."

The sympathetic expression in Beatrice LeBecque's eyes and the genuine sorrow in her voice told Ted what had happened far more clearly than the woman's words. He hadn't been too surprised when Jared came back into the reception area only a few minutes after he'd left with his mother and sister. Nor had his aunt's reaction to his son surprised him; indeed, it was her desire to see Jared at all that had caught him off guard. "Don't take it personally," he'd advised. "It doesn't have anything to do with you. It has to do with the fact that you're a male."

"If she's got a problem with men, how come she married your uncle?" Jared asked, relieving his father of Molly, who'd been squirming uncomfortably in Ted's lap.

"You got me on that one. Who knows? Maybe it was Uncle George killing himself that soured her in the first place. Anyway, she sure never got over it."

They'd fallen silent then, Ted leafing through a magazine as the last vestiges of his hangover finally lifted, while Jared played a game with Molly, the rules of which seemed far clearer to the toddler than to her big brother. When the phone on Bea LeBecque's desk rang, both of them looked up, sharply. Now even Molly was silent, sitting quietly on her brother's lap.

So, the old lady was finally gone. Ted tried to analyze what he felt:

Grief? How could you feel grief for someone you'd barely known, and from whom you'd never heard a friendly word, let alone a kind one?

Loss? Of what? Certainly not family, since he had no memory of ever having seen his aunt anywhere but here. The only family he knew—had ever known, really—was Janet. Janet, and their children.

Sympathy? A little. At least Cora Conway was finally released from whatever had tortured her for so long. And he felt relief. Relief that the ordeal was finally over. A twinge of guilt stabbed at him as he realized that most of the relief he felt was for himself rather than for his aunt. He tried to tell himself that he had no reason to feel guilty, that if she'd tried to be even halfway decent to him, he'd have come to see her more often, tried to do more to make her life a little easier. Except that now, with his hangover finally gone, he knew the truth: he could have ignored her treatment of him, could have risen above the invective she had poured over him. She'd been old, and ill in her mind as well as her body.

He'd ignored her very existence.

And now she was dead.

No loss, no sorrow, no sense that something valuable was gone out of his life.

Just guilt.

Well, at least I can take care of her now, he told himself. With his head finally clear—at least of alcohol—Ted's talent for organization, which had made him so good at his job before he'd started drinking, came to the fore, and he began making a mental checklist of things that would need to be dealt with.

As it turned out, though, all the arrangements had been made long ago. "She had some very good days, you know," Bea LeBecque explained as she gave him the letter in which all of his aunt's plans were laid out, and to which she'd attached the receipts indicating that Cora had paid her own funeral expenses in advance. "Really, all you need to do is contact Bruce Wilcox." The name meant nothing to Ted. "Your aunt's attorney," the receptionist explained. She picked up the phone on her desk and dialed the lawyer's number from memory, then handed the receiver to Ted.

Ten minutes later, with Janet and Kim back in the reception area, Ted repeated what the lawyer had told him.

"There's some kind of trust," he explained. "I'm not sure I understand it, but this guy Wilcox says Aunt Cora tried to break it a long time ago, and couldn't."

Janet's eyes clouded. "Why did she want to break it?"

"Wilcox said she wanted to get rid of the house. But apparently that was the whole point of the trust—to keep the house in the family."

"So we've inherited a house?" Janet asked.

Ted shook his head. "What we've got, the way Wilcox explained it, is the right to live in a house."

* * *

They gazed at it in silence. Their eyes moved over the massive structure that stood amidst an acre of land so overgrown with weeds that it was hard to tell where—or indeed if—gardens might ever have existed.

Besides the enormous gabled building that was the house, there was also a large carriage house—big enough for half a dozen cars, apparently with some kind of apartment above it.

Though most of the windows of both buildings were intact, the paint had peeled away from the clapboard siding, and the smashed roofing slates that lay around the perimeter of the house testified to the water damage they might expect inside.

Vines, unchecked by any hand, had threaded their way through the great willows, oaks, and magnolias that dotted the property and were banked against the house itself. Tendrils were creeping toward the eaves, and had established a hold on one of the half-dozen gables that pierced the steeply pitched Victorian roof three stories above them.

But more than the broken windows, the fallen slates, the peeling paint, and the kudzu, there was an atmosphere hanging over the house— a dark melancholy—that all of them felt.

It was Molly who finally spoke. "Wanna go home," she said plaintively, her tiny hand clutching her mother's.

Janet lifted her youngest child into her arms. "In a little while," she promised. "We just need to look around first. All right?"

Molly said nothing, but stuck a reassuring thumb into her mouth and began sucking. For once, Janet made no effort to stop her.

"I wonder what the inside looks like," Ted mused, starting to pick his way through the tangle of weeds toward the broad front porch. The broken remnants of the ornate gingerbread trim that had once graced the eaves and posts of the porch now looked like the jagged remains of broken teeth surrounding the gaping maw of some dying beast.

"Is it even safe to go up there?" Janet fretted, tentatively following him. "What if the porch collapses?"

"It's not going to," Ted assured her. "They built these old places to last. The frame's probably oak." He stopped and considered the looming mass of the house, a few yards away now. "When you think about it, it's not in such bad shape, considering it's a hundred and twenty-five years old and no one's lived in it for the last forty years."

"It doesn't look like anyone's even been inside it," Janet replied.

Ted winked at Jared. "What do you think?" he asked his son. "You game?"

Jared's reply was to start ripping his way through the tangle, tearing vines from the railing and steps before gingerly testing the strength of the old wood. "Dad's right," he called back to his mother and sisters. "It's fine!"

Ted tried the keys Bruce Wilcox had given him, and found a fit on the third one. The lock stuck, and he had to jiggle the key several times, until he felt it twist and the bolt slide back. Then the latch clicked, and the door itself—a huge slab of ornately paneled and molded oak hung from four tarnished brass hinges—swung slowly open.

Inside the front door was a large entry hall, with arched double doors leading into two enormous rooms—one of which had apparently been the living room. The other looked to Ted as if it must have been a reception room for the porte cochere that lay on the side of the house closest to the garage. At the far end of the entry hall was a graceful staircase that swept up to a small landing. The stairs split at the landing, leading in opposite directions to the symmetrical wings of a mahogany-railed mezzanine that provided access to the rooms on the second floor, as well as a clear view of the broad entry hall below. Suspended from the vaulted roof of the entry hall was an ornate chandelier, the sparkle of its crystal pendants dimmed by a thick layer of grime. Flanking the base of the staircase were two more corridors, leading to more doors.

From the front of the house there was no way even to guess what might be at the back.

For the next half hour they picked their way through the house, moving from one room to another. On the first floor, in addition to the living room and reception room, they found a dining room—easily large enough for a table to seat twenty-four—a library, a kitchen and pantry with a large service porch behind, and several smaller chambers that had apparently served as rooms for cards, music, sewing, and a variety of other activities. A conservatory constructed of three glass walls surmounted by an enormous glass dome extended out from the northern side of the house. Except for three cracked panes, the skylight was miraculously unbroken.

It was on the second floor, while her parents were exploring a large suite of rooms that lay above the library, that Kim felt it.

Suddenly her skin was crawling, as if a large insect were creeping across her neck. She jumped, reflexively brushing at the unseen creature, and the sensation vanished.

Steadying herself against the mahogany railing while her racing heart calmed, she glanced around for Jared, who had been with her only a moment before.

He seemed to have disappeared.

Then, a few paces away, she saw a door standing slightly ajar, and knew her brother must have gone into the room beyond it.

She started toward the door.

And felt it again.

This time it was an icy cold chill that fell over her, momentarily stopping her breath. She tried to call out to Jared, but the same paralysis that had fallen over her lungs had taken her voice as well. A terrible panic rose in her as the cold tightened its grip.

With no warning, the house itself had taken on a menacing quality, and she had a terrible feeling that she was about to die, that somehow this cavernous, decaying place was going to swallow her whole, and she would vanish, just as Jared seemed to have done a moment before.

"Kim? Hey, Kim! What's wrong?" The words startled her. She spun around to find Jared gazing worriedly at her. "What's wrong? How come you called me?"

For a split second Kim didn't trust herself even to speak, but then, as quickly as it had come over her, the strange sensations—the crawling skin, the icy chill, the strange paralysis—were gone.

Gone so completely that even her memory was fading with the rapidity of a dream vanishing in morning light, vivid one second, utterly gone only a moment later.

"I—I didn't call you," she stammered. Or had she? In the back of her mind she thought she felt a vague memory of wanting to call out to her brother. "D-Did I?" she asked.

Jared's concern congealed into fear. A second ago, in the bedroom a few feet away, he'd been positive he heard Kim's voice. And not just calling him, either.

She had been screaming—screaming in terror.

He had *heard* it!

Yet what could have caused her to scream? He glanced around, not knowing what he might be looking for. Could it have been a mouse, or even a rat? But Kim wasn't a sissy; some scurrying creature would only have provoked a surprised yelp.

What he'd heard—at least what he *thought* he heard—was the anguished cry of someone in fear for her life.

Now, though, she was staring at him, her head cocked, her eyes wide, her expression puzzled.

He remembered, then, something that had happened a few years ago, when they were eleven. Their mother had taken them for a picnic by a lake, and they'd gone swimming. He had hauled himself out onto a large wooden float, and was sprawled on his back, gazing up at the clouds floating overhead, when he'd heard exactly the same kind of scream from Kim as the one of a few moments earlier. He'd scrambled to his feet and scanned the water, but she was nowhere to be seen.

Then he'd looked down.

Kim, her eyes open and staring up at him, was lying on the bottom of the lake, under ten feet of crystal clear water.

She wasn't moving.

Without thinking, he'd dived for her, dragging her to the surface and wrestling her onto the float.

He'd started screaming himself then, calling frantically for help while trying to force the water from Kim's lungs. Others—grown-ups—arrived and took over, and after what seemed an eternity, but which he'd later been told was no more than a minute or two, Kim started breathing on her own again.

Afterward, when they asked him how he'd known his sister was drowning, it turned out that only he had heard her scream.

No one else heard anything.

Thinking about it, replaying those panicked moments in his mind, he knew his sister couldn't have screamed; even if she had, there was no way the sound would have carried out of the water.

It was, he'd finally decided, the Twin Thing, that strange, almost mystical connection he and his sister had always felt.

Today, though, he saw nothing that could have terrified Kim to the point of a scream. Not like that.

As if she'd read his mind—the Twin Thing again—Kim's eyes fixed on him. "Jared, what's going on? I swear, I didn't call you!" She paused, then spoke again, and he knew she truly had read his mind. "And I didn't even call you in my mind, like I did at the lake that day."

Jared hesitated, then shrugged. "Hey, if you don't remember, why should I?" he finally said. "And maybe it wasn't you at all—maybe it was a ghost!" He scanned the hallway, gave an exaggerated shudder, then fixed his sister with the most mysterious gaze he could muster. "Want to see if we can find one? If ghosts are real, this sure is where they'd be."

A moment later, the strange sensation she'd experienced all but forgotten, Kim set out with Jared to explore the second floor. Half a dozen bedrooms opened off the mezzanine—two of which had small parlors attached to them—along with three bathrooms. There were a few more rooms that were locked, but none of the keys their father had seemed to fit.

On the third floor, tucked beneath the huge oaken rafters that supported the slate roof, were half a dozen more rooms, each with a dormer window, those on the west side looking out over the town, the others over the wilderness to the east.

Finally, after they'd seen as much of the house as they could gain access to, the family gathered on the front porch.

"Well, what do you think?" Ted asked as they made their way back to the car. There was an excitement in his voice that immediately put

Janet on her guard. A thought had come to her fifteen minutes ago—a thought she had instantly rejected. The electric note in his question told her the same thought had also occurred to Ted. Before he even spoke, she knew what he was going to say. "It would make a great little hotel, wouldn't it?"

At least a dozen answers to Ted's question popped into Janet's mind, every one of them negative. Instead of voicing even one of them, she slowly turned around and looked back at the immense derelict of a house that had sat abandoned for the last forty years.

She thought about Ted, and what his future in Shreveport might be. Though neither of them had talked about it yet, she knew there would be no job offer, not for a very long time.

Which meant there was nothing to hold them in Shreveport; she had no family there, and neither did he.

In the last few years most of their friends had drifted away, unwilling to deal with Ted's drinking.

Even the kids' friends didn't come over anymore.

Though she had never been a particularly religious person, it occurred to Janet to wonder if it was truly a coincidence that Cora Conway had died and left them this house at the very moment when their own lives had come to a crossroads.

"I hate to say it," she finally replied as she got into the car, "but you might just be right."

From the backseat Kim, too, peered out at the house. Once again her skin began to crawl, and she felt a terrible chill.

And a single thought came into her mind:

No! Please, God, no! Don't make us live here!

Two pairs of eyes—each of them unseen by the other—watched as the dented and dust-covered Toyota disappeared down the road. When it was finally gone, and even the dust it kicked up had settled, both sets of eyes shifted back to the great hulking shape of the house that had stood empty for the last four decades.

Now, both of the watchers were certain, it was about to be occupied again.

Still unseen by one another, their gazes shifted once more, and fixed upon the huge magnolia tree. From its lowest branch George Conway had hanged himself.

One of the watchers began silently to pray.

The other—equally silent—began to curse.

CHAPTER 6

hree days later they were back in St. Albans. As their father pulled the car to a stop in front of the Gothic facade the church of St. Ignatius Loyola presented to the street, Kim and Jared looked at the school that stood across from it.

The school they would be attending, starting the next day.

"Maybe it'll be all right," Jared muttered, though neither he nor Kim had any real idea of what to expect. "I mean, how much different can it be?"

"It's going to be a lot different," he heard his father say, making Jared wish he'd kept silent. "For one thing, you'll get a decent education. They don't coddle the kids in parochial school the way they do where you two have been going. And they don't put up with any nonsense, either."

Jared knew it would be useless to remind his father that both he and Kim had always gotten straight A's, and that neither of them had ever been in any trouble. After all, his father hadn't listened to a word either of them had said for the last two days.

They were moving to St. Albans because some uncle who had died before he was even born had left them a house and enough money to fix it up and turn it into a hotel.

And he and Kim were going to parochial school because that same uncle had wanted it that way, including in the trust a clause directing that any children benefiting from it would attend St. Ignatius Loyola School.

"But we don't want to go to parochial school," he'd objected, speaking for Kim as well. "We haven't even gone to church since we were little kids. None of us have!"

Nothing they said had made a difference. For two days they listened

to their father talk about what a great opportunity they were being given,
and how much they should appreciate what they were being offered.

And they watched him drink.

Jared suspected that none of the great opportunities his father kept
talking about would materialize. Even if his father stayed sober long
enough to get the work done and actually open a hotel—and Jared was
sure he wouldn't—why would anyone want to stay there? And if the cus-
tomers stopped coming, his father would drink even more. The day before
yesterday—after his father had passed out—he'd talked to his mother
about it, and for the first time he heard exactly how bad the situation was.

"He's not going to be able to get another job," his mother explained.
"We have a little less than one hundred dollars in the bank. When that's
gone, I don't know what we'll do."

"I'll get a job—" Jared began, but his mother shook her head.

"For now, you'll go to school. If you keep your grades up, you'll be
able to get a scholarship for college. But if you get a job, your grades will
slip."

"But it won't work!" Jared protested. "Dad will just sit home and
drink all day!" The pain he'd seen in his mother's eyes made Jared wince,
and for a moment he thought she was going to cry. Instead, she'd taken a
deep breath and put both her hands on his shoulders.

"If that happens," she told him, looking steadily into his eyes, "I
promise we won't stay. I don't know how we'll do it, or where we'll go,
but I'll take you and Kim and Molly, and we'll leave. But we have to give
him a chance. We have to let him try."

So yesterday they had loaded a U-Haul with everything they owned,
and this morning they'd driven down from Shreveport, his father driving
the truck while the rest of them—including his dog and Kim's cat—
packed themselves into the Toyota. Fortunately, Scout was even more
placid than most golden retrievers, and had long since decided that Muffin, not being another dog, wasn't worth bothering with. While Muffin
curled up in Kim's lap, Scout had fallen asleep between them, waking up
only when Molly, strapped into her own seat, managed to grasp his tail
and give it a good yank.

They arrived at the church just ten minutes before the funeral mass
for Cora Conway was scheduled to begin. It had been almost ten years since
Ted Conway last attended a mass, and now, as he stood at the threshold of St.
Ignatius Loyola, he hesitated.

His eyes instinctively went to the face of the figure on the cross above the altar, and though he tried to look away, the agonized gaze of the martyred Christ held him.

Reproaching him?

Accusing him?

Superstition, Ted told himself. *None of it's anything more than superstition.* But even as he silently reassured himself that it was nothing more than his own rejection of the religion he'd been raised in that had kept him away from church all those years, the throbbing in his head refused to let him forget the real reason he'd stayed in bed so many Sunday mornings. *So what if I have a couple of drinks on Saturday night?* Ted asked the silent figure that peered steadily at him from its place above the altar. A knot of resentment hardened in his belly, and he wished he had a drink. He started down the aisle toward the waiting pews, but the reflexes bred into him in the first ten years of his life overtook him, and his fingers dipped into the font of holy water that stood just inside the door.

His knees bent slightly in an automatic act of genuflection.

He crossed himself.

Only then did the tortured eyes of the figure on the cross finally release him and let him start down the aisle of the nearly empty church.

Janet followed, holding Molly.

Kim and Jared glanced uneasily at each other, then quickly dipped their fingers in the holy water in imitation of their parents and walked down the aisle, taking seats next to each other in the front pew. They stared at the coffin that stood in front of the altar, its lid closed.

Three sparse floral remembrances—along with the emptiness of the church—gave testimony to the loneliness of the years Cora Conway had spent at the Willows. As an unseen organist began playing softly in the background, Janet sighed and wished that she'd come to visit the old woman more often. Why had she assumed that her husband's aunt had friends who were visiting her? Obviously she hadn't. As the priest came in from a side door, signaled them to rise, and began the opening prayers of the mass, she quickly scanned the church and saw that it was still all but empty.

In fact, besides the five of them and the priest who was conducting the mass, there were only two other people present.

A middle-aged woman clad in a navy blue suit—her face veiled—stood in the very last pew, nervously twisting a pair of gloves in her hands.

And in one of the alcoves—barely visible from the church—Janet caught a glimpse of another priest. Had he come to the mass for Cora, or was he merely tending to his own private devotions, silently offering prayers to one of the saints, oblivious to the memorial service taking place only a few feet away?

The officiating priest finished his opening prayer, gestured to them to sit, then turned his back to them so he faced the coffin and the altar beyond. Raising his arms in supplication, he began to speak. To Janet's surprise—and for the first time since she was a little girl and had attended the funeral mass of her own grandmother—she heard the rhythmical cadences of the Latin mass.

"Jesus," she heard Ted whisper beside her. "If we'd known this was the deal, we wouldn't have bothered to come!"

Janet shot him a warning look. "She must have wanted it," she whispered back. "And it won't hurt us."

Ted's eyes rolled scornfully, and a few minutes later his head dropped forward onto his chest as he fell asleep.

An hour later, as the last phrases of the prayer of benediction rolled from the priest's tongue, Ted came awake and, responding to childhood memories similar to those stirring in Janet, straightened in the pew and dropped automatically to his knees. He crossed himself once more, then made his way past his wife and children to perform the single act his aunt had required of him.

Joining five men from the undertaker's who entered the church from one of the side doors, he took his position at the head of his aunt's casket to bear her out of the church to her final resting place. Janet, holding a sleeping Molly, stood with Jared and Kim as the casket passed, followed by the priest. As she started up the aisle, Janet glanced into the side chapel where she'd seen the elderly priest just as the service was beginning.

He lay prostrate on the stone floor, his arms spread wide. He seemed oblivious to the tiny procession passing behind him.

J anet blinked as she stepped out of the cool gloom of the church into the sultry heat of the Indian summer afternoon. As she followed the coffin toward the open grave that waited in the far corner of the small cemetery adjoining the church, she had the uncomfortable feeling that she was being watched. She tried to ignore it at first, telling herself that of course anyone who happened to be passing by the graveyard would glance in; perhaps even linger long enough to watch the burial. Surreptitiously, she glanced around, but before she could spot whoever might be watching, her eyes were caught by the inscription on a weathered bronze plate affixed to the door of a small mausoleum that stood by itself, set off from the rest of the cemetery by a rusting wrought-iron fence.

```
┌─────────────────────────────┐
│      GEORGE CONWAY           │
│    BORN JULY 29, 1916        │
│    DIED JUNE 4, 1959         │
└─────────────────────────────┘
```

But how was that possible? Janet wondered. George Conway had committed suicide, hadn't he? Then how could he be buried here in sanctified ground? But when she saw the utter neglect the area around the mausoleum had suffered, she understood.

The ground upon which George Conway's mausoleum stood had been deconsecrated; the rusting fence had been erected not to protect the structure, but to shut it away from the rest of the cemetery, and all those who had died in a state of grace.

There was another crypt in the mausoleum, next to the one in which George Conway's body lay, and Janet assumed it had been George Conway's intention to have his wife buried there.

But the little procession passed it by. When the pallbearers stopped several yards farther on and set the coffin on boards that had been laid across an open grave, Janet saw that there were no other Conways buried nearby.

No two of the graves surrounding Cora Conway's bore the same last name.

Here, in the corner of the cemetery farthest from the church, was the final resting place of those who had apparently died as they'd lived—alone. Janet felt a great wave of sadness for her husband's aunt. As she struggled against the lump rising in her throat and the tears blurring her eyes, she felt a gentle hand touch her arm.

She heard a voice then, so soft that for a moment she thought she might be imagining it. "She wasn't crazy. She wasn't crazy at all."

The hand dropped away; the voice went silent. With Molly still asleep in her arms, Janet turned, but did not see who had spoken. Forcing herself to concentrate on the priest's words, she stared down at the open grave.

And once again she felt herself being watched.

The final litany done, the coffin was slowly lowered into the ground. Following Ted, Janet stepped forward, stooped to pick up a clod of the soft soil, then straightened up. Whispering a final goodbye to the woman she'd barely known, whose death three days ago had so totally changed her life, she let the lump of earth go. And then, as she looked up, she saw him.

She couldn't be certain how old he was—he might have been anywhere between forty and sixty. A thin black man in worn, nearly threadbare clothing, his face covered with a grizzled stubble. He stood on the cobbled sidewalk outside the fence, in the shade of one of the huge magnolias that spread over the cemetery. He was watching the little group gathered around the grave, and although deep shadows concealed the expression on the man's dark-skinned face, Janet could feel the emotion radiating from him like heat waves.

Hatred.

Hatred, and anger.

For a moment she froze, caught in the strength of the man's silent fury, but then he turned and moved away, shambling slowly down the street.

"Jake Cumberland," the same soft voice that had spoken to her only a few minutes earlier now said.

Startled, Janet turned to find a woman of about seventy watching the retreating figure of Jake Cumberland.

"Do you know him?" Janet asked.

The woman nodded. She was small and neat, wearing a pale lavender dress with a matching sweater thrown over her shoulders, despite the warmth of the afternoon. "Oh, yes. Everyone knows who Jake is. He lives in a cabin out by the lake. Just him and his dogs, and he hardly ever comes to town." She smiled brightly and offered Janet a tiny gloved hand. "I'm Alma Morgan. I worked at the Willows until they told me I was too old." She glanced down at her dress. "I hope you don't mind me wearing this," she went on. "It was Cora's favorite, and I thought she'd like it much better than black. Besides, black is much too hot for this weather, don't you think?" Without waiting for an answer, she plunged on. "You're Janet, aren't you?"

Janet nodded. "Actually, she was my husband's aunt—" she began, but Alma Morgan was already speaking again, this time leaning forward and clasping Janet's arm tightly.

"She wasn't crazy, you know. Don't pay any attention to what anyone says." Then, before Janet had a chance to respond, Alma Morgan was gone. Janet was still trying to decide what the woman's words meant when someone else spoke.

This time it was the middle-aged woman who had been sitting at the back of the church. Now that the service was over, she'd pulled her veil back, revealing warm blue eyes that watched with amusement as Alma Morgan scurried out of the cemetery. "Now, the question—as I see it, anyway—is this: What is the exact state of Alma Morgan's sanity?" She smiled. "I'm Corinne Beckwith. My husband is the sheriff here."

Moving close to Janet, Ted extended his hand toward Mrs. Beckwith. "I'm Ted Conway. This is my wife, Janet. And this," he added, releasing Corinne Beckwith's hand to lift Molly out of Janet's arms, "is Molly, the true ruler of our house. Can you say hello to the nice lady?" he asked Molly.

Molly, just waking up, happily mumbled something, then demanded to be let down. A moment later she was darting off among the headstones, already lost in some game she'd made up in her own mind. And Ted, freed of his youngest daughter, set about charming Corinne Beckwith.

How can he do it? Janet marveled as she listened to Ted chat with the woman as if they'd been friends for years. *How can he be so nice when he's sober, and so—*

She cut the thought short, refusing to tarnish the moment by anticipating what the rest of the day might hold if Ted started drinking. Instead, she tuned into what Corinne Beckwith was saying.

"Just because what happened in that horrible old house took place forty years ago doesn't mean everyone's forgotten about it, you know." Corinne had fixed her attention on Ted as if she suspected he might be trying to hide something from her. "This is a small town, and people talk about things forever. And now with your aunt gone, we'll probably never know what really did happen that day."

"What 'really did happen'?" Janet repeated, frowning. "She had a nervous breakdown when she found her husband, didn't she?"

Corinne Beckwith's brows rose a fraction of an inch. "There was the question of the baby, too."

"The baby?" Janet echoed. "What baby?"

"The one Cora Conway gave birth to right after she found her husband hanging from the magnolia tree."

Janet's eyes shifted to Ted, and she could see that he was as mystified by Corinne's words as she. "I'm sorry," she said. "I'm afraid neither one of us knows what you're talking about."

The other woman's eyes widened in surprise. "You mean no one ever told you your aunt was pregnant?" she asked.

Ted held up his hands as if to fend the question off. "Hey, I was hardly even born when all that happened."

Corinne Beckwith had the grace to be embarrassed. "Oh, Lord, what am I doing?" she said, disconcerted. "Why *would* you have known about it? It's probably nothing more than small-town gossip anyway," she went on in a rush. "And of all the places to bring it up—" She was still floundering when the priest stepped easily into the breach.

"And since we don't know what the truth was, maybe we shouldn't speculate about it." He gave Corinne a reproachful look, then extended one hand to Ted, the other to Janet. "I'm Father MacNeill. I'm so sorry about your aunt."

"It was a lovely mass," Janet began, automatically mouthing the words she knew were expected of her. But even as she made conversation with the priest, her mind was whirling. A baby? Aunt Cora had a baby? But surely Ted would have heard of it, wouldn't he?

"I understand you'll be moving to St. Albans," she heard Father MacNeill say. "We're looking forward to having the children in our little school, and all of you, of course, in our congregation."

How did he know the children were going to parochial school? Janet wondered. They hadn't told anyone. But then she understood—St. Albans wasn't Shreveport. Here, obviously, everyone knew everyone else's business. Which meant, she realized with a sinking heart, that everyone in town would know about Ted's drinking problem the first time he got drunk.

"Well, I'm not exactly sure all of that will be happening," Janet heard her husband say, and she instinctively braced herself for what might be coming next. *Please, Ted, not here,* she silently begged. *Don't make a scene here.* But it was already too late.

"I'm afraid I'm what you call a 'lapsed' Catholic," Ted went on. "In fact, I haven't been to mass more than half a dozen times since I was a kid."

Father MacNeill's smile faltered. "Perhaps I can change that—" he began.

"Don't count on it," Ted said flatly. "I just don't hold with religion. Never have. I don't mind my kids going to your school, but don't count on any of us showing up for church on Sundays."

The last trace of Father MacNeill's smile faded away. "Have you found a place to live yet?" he asked, and Janet relaxed as the priest seemed to shift the conversation away from Ted's lack of religious convictions. But as she listened to Ted explain that they would be moving into his uncle's house and converting it into a small hotel, Janet saw the priest's expression darken. "A hotel?" he repeated when Ted had finished. "Well, I hope you're prepared for a fight on that one!"

"A fight?" Ted asked. "Why would there be a fight?"

A veil dropped behind the priest's eyes. "Perhaps I'm wrong," he said quickly. Too quickly, it seemed to Janet, thinking that Ted had made a mistake in airing his religious views so freely. They'd barely arrived in St. Albans, and already he'd made an enemy. "It's just that in a small town, there are always objections to change, aren't there?" Father MacNeill said smoothly. He glanced at his watch, a gesture Janet interpreted as an excuse to cut the conversation short. "Good Heavens, look at the time," he said, betraying himself by putting a little too much surprise into his voice. "I'm terribly sorry, but I'm afraid I'm running late."

An uncomfortable silence spread over the little group as the priest hurried back into the church. Then Ted said, "Well, I guess I put my foot in it with him, didn't I?"

I guess you did, Janet thought, but bit back the words before she spoke them.

Corinne Beckwith, though, nodded. "Father MacNeill doesn't like having his toes stepped on. Not about religion, or anything else. But it isn't just what you said. I think it's your house, too."

"Our house?" Janet repeated. "What could be wrong with fixing up our house? I'd think everyone would be thrilled."

"Not around here," Corinne Beckwith replied. "That area's zoned residential, and I have a feeling there will be a lot of opposition to giving you a variance."

"But why?" Janet pressed. "If we're bringing money into the town—"

Corinne shook her head. "Money has nothing to do with it." She hesitated, then went on. "It's your family. There are a lot of people here who simply don't have much fondness for anyone named Conway." Her lips twisted into an apologetic semblance of a smile. "Welcome to St. Albans."

Father Devlin slowly emerged from his trance of prayer.
The church was silent; Cora Conway's funeral over.

Slowly, every joint and muscle protesting, he pulled himself to his feet and haltingly made his way back to the tiny cell he occupied on the top floor of the rectory. The cell was his penance, a penance he had assigned himself forty years ago, on the day he knew he'd failed. He'd resigned his ministry that day, turning over his church and his authority to young Father MacNeill, and retreated to his cell to spend whatever remained of his life contemplating his own sins.

And offering comfort to the only penitent he would hear.
Cora Conway.

The years had slowly ground by, each seeming longer than the one before, and he slowly came to understand that even death was to be withheld from him.

He even understood why: his failure to find a way to absolve Cora Conway, to release her from the torture that gripped her mind. Even three days ago, when he'd administered the last rites of their faith, he'd still been unable to cast out the demons that haunted her.

"Take this," she'd breathed, her clawlike fingers stroking the worn leather of her Bible. "It's in here. Everything is in here." Then, just as he was about to leave, she'd spoken one more time.

"And this," she'd whispered, her shaking fingers grasping the music box that sat on the table by her bed. He'd brought her the music box himself, on the day she'd been brought to the Willows, but he'd never heard it play. "Take it," Cora had whispered. "Listen to its voices."

He'd slipped the music box into the pocket of his cassock, pronounced a final benediction upon Cora's troubled soul, and then departed, the weight of her Bible—and her troubles—almost more than he could bear.

Until today he hadn't opened Cora's Bible, but now he carefully lowered himself onto the straight-backed chair and reached for the Bible on the table nearby. Chair, table, and narrow cot comprised the only furnishings of his cell. He pulled the Bible close and, holding it by its cracked spine, allowed it to fall open to whatever page upon which God might place His finger.

The Bible opened to the division between the two testaments, where lay the history of the generations through which the ancient Bible had passed. The page that lay open in front of Father Devlin was filled with careful, cursive script of a time gone by, but despite the clarity of the letters, Father Devlin still had to strain to read the faded words.

A date had been inscribed: April 16, 1899.

Beneath the date there was a smear of ink, but then the entry began:

I shall not survive this evil day,

the first line said. The beat of his ancient heart quickening, Father Devlin read on . . .

LORETTA VILLIERS CONWAY SAT AT HER DESK, HER BACK AS RAMROD STRAIGHT AS HER MOTHER HAD TAUGHT HER WHEN SHE WAS A GIRL, BUT DESPITE THE PERFECTION OF HER POSTURE, FOR WHICH SHE WAS FAMOUS THROUGHOUT ST. ALBANS AND THE COUNTY, HER HAND QUIVERED AS SHE DIPPED HER PEN INTO THE POT OF INK AND SET IT TO THE BLANK PAGE OF THE BIBLE SHE KEPT WELL-HIDDEN FROM HER HUSBAND. A DROP OF THE BLACK FLUID FELL FROM THE PEN'S POINT AND SPLASHED TO THE PAGE, BUT SO DISTRAUGHT WAS LORETTA THAT SHE HARDLY NOTICED IT. SHE CONTINUED WRITING.

I had thought it was the crowing of the cock that woke me. But it was not the cock, as I found out when I stepped out onto the mezzanine of the house that Monsignor Melchior built for us. The cry was louder there, and I recognized it at once as coming from the servant girl, and knew her time had come. Even now I remember thinking that perhaps today Bessie would confess the name of the man who invaded her. But when the babies were born, I needed no confession from Bessie, for the image of the father was clear on the faces of each of the tiny babes. Bessie, who is very strong, took the second one to her breast immediately, and called her Francesca. But Francis—who was my son until I saw the faces of his Negro children—took the second child away. When I came down from Bessie's room—having tended her as best I could—I heard noises coming from the cellar below the house. It did not matter, though, for already I knew what I must do. The curse that has befallen this family will not be lifted, and I know now that there is but one escape. I know not whether Heaven or Hell awaits me at the end of the noose I shall place around my neck when this paragraph is done. It matters not. It will be enough that I have finally escaped this house.

AFTER NEATLY WIPING ITS POINT, LORETTA VILLIERS CONWAY SET THE PEN ASIDE. WHEN SHE WAS CERTAIN THE INK HAD COMPLETELY DRIED, SHE TOOK THE BIBLE TO BESSIE DELACOURT, WHO STILL LAY IN HER BED, HER REMAINING DAUGHTER CRADLED AGAINST HER BREAST. SHE SLIPPED THE VOLUME INTO THE TOP DRAWER OF BESSIE'S SCARRED DRESSER, THEN TURNED TO THE SERVANT.

SHE BORE BESSIE NO MALICE, FOR IT WAS HER SON WHO HAD BETRAYED HER, NOT THE IGNORANT GIRL.

"I HAVE PUT A BIBLE IN YOUR DRAWER," SHE SAID. "WHEN MY SON MARRIES, YOU MUST GIVE IT TO HIS BRIDE."

SHE STARTED TOWARD THE DOOR, THEN TURNED BACK AND LOOKED ONCE MORE INTO THE FACE OF HER GRANDDAUGHTER. SHE REACHED OUT, ALMOST AS IF TO TOUCH THE TINY CHILD, BUT THEN DREW HER HAND AWAY. HER BACK AS STRAIGHT AS EVER, SHE LEFT THE SERVANT GIRL ALONE WITH HER BASTARD CHILD.

IN HER OWN ROOM, LORETTA VILLIERS CONWAY PUT ON THE DRESS SHE HAD WORN THE DAY SHE MARRIED MONSIGNOR MELCHIOR CONWAY.

SHE TOOK THE VELVET BELT FROM HER FAVORITE DRESSING GOWN.

STANDING ON HER WRITING CHAIR, SHE TIED ONE END OF THE BELT AROUND THE CHANDELIER THAT HUNG FROM THE CENTER OF THE CEILING.

SHE TIED THE OTHER END AROUND HER OWN NECK.

SHE CHECKED BOTH KNOTS CAREFULLY.

SATISFIED THAT THEY WOULD HOLD, LORETTA VILLIERS CONWAY STEPPED OFF THE SEAT OF HER WRITING CHAIR.

NO SOUND, NO CRY OF FEAR OR PAIN DISTURBED THE SILENCE THAT
FILLED THE ROOM AS LORETTA VILLIERS CONWAY DIED.

Father Devlin's eyes remained fixed on the last words Loretta Villiers Conway had written a century earlier. So George Conway was not
the first of his family to commit the mortal—irredeemable—sin of suicide. There had been rumors, of course. In his younger days, when he'd
first arrived in St. Albans, Father Devlin had heard the stories, but he'd
refused to credit them, preaching instead against wagging tongues. But
now, as the words on the page imprinted themselves on his mind, the old
priest finally understood that the stories had been more than mere gossip;
that the horror that had befallen George and Cora Conway had somehow
happened before. " 'For I the Lord thy God am a jealous God,' " he muttered softly to himself, quoting the fifth verse of the twentieth chapter of
Exodus, " 'visiting the iniquity of the fathers upon the children unto the
third and fourth generation.' " But how had it begun?

He reached for the Bible once more, then stopped, his fingers trembling in midair. Did he really want to know? Loretta Conway had died a
century ago—there was nothing he could do now except pray for her soul.
But even that would do no good, for by her very act, Loretta—like George
Conway—had condemned herself to eternal damnation.

The exhaustion of the day, along with his nearly ninety years,
caught up with Father Devlin, and his hand dropped back to his lap.

Some other day.

Perhaps some other day he would pursue the matter further. But for
now his energy was gone, and his cot beckoned to him. Putting Cora Conway's Bible away, he surrendered himself to the oblivion of sleep.

CHAPTER 7

"You guys really gonna live here?"

The voice startled Jared so much he dropped his end of the mattress he and Kim were wrestling out of the rented U-Haul, eliciting a howl of outrage from his sister. As she struggled to get a grip on the mattress, she looked up in annoyance at the boy who had just spoken. He looked to be about the same age as Jared, but was a couple of inches shorter, wiry almost to the point of scrawniness, and had a thatch of light brown hair falling over his forehead. The boy grinned at her and grabbed one corner of the unwieldy object. He was wearing torn jeans and a sweatshirt that had had the sleeves torn off. "I'm Luke Roberts," he said. "You want me to help you get this up on the porch?"

"How about all the way up to my room?" Jared countered. When Luke cast a quick glance at the house before answering, Jared asked, "What's wrong? You're not scared, are you?"

" 'Course I'm not," Luke replied a little too quickly.

"You ever been inside the house?"

Again Luke glanced at the looming shape of the huge Victorian. He shook his head. "I got an uncle who says he was in it once," he offered.

"You want to see it?" Jared put just enough of a challenge in his voice to be certain Luke would be unable to refuse.

"Sure," the other boy replied.

Together, the three teenagers wrestled the mattress up to the second floor, where they dropped it onto the box spring that Kim and Jared had already brought up.

"How many rooms does it have?" Luke asked.

Jared shrugged. "I don't know—maybe twenty, I guess. We're going to turn it into a hotel."

They were back out on the landing, and Luke gazed down into the vast entry hall below. "Who'd want to stay here?"

"Well, it's not going to look like this," Kim replied. "Dad says it won't be ready for at least six months."

"I still bet nobody'll stay," Luke said. "Not after everything that's happened." Jared and Kim eyed each other uneasily, reading each other's thoughts: *Do we really want to hear?* But before either of them could reply, Luke was already telling them, "Sometimes you can hear a baby crying. And lots of people have seen that guy who hung himself."

"That was my dad's uncle," Jared said.

If Luke heard the hint of warning in Jared's voice, he chose to ignore it. "They say he's still here. Looking for the baby."

Kim and Jared exchanged another quick glance, both of them remembering the words they'd overheard at the funeral that morning. "Father MacNeill says nobody knows if it was even true that my dad's aunt was pregnant."

Luke Roberts rolled his eyes scornfully. "Father Mack wouldn't even admit his own mother was ever pregnant! And he sure wouldn't ever believe a woman would kill her own baby."

Kim's fingers flew involuntarily to the cross that hung from her neck, clutching it tightly. "How do you know Aunt Cora did that?" she asked.

"Everybody knows it," Luke Roberts replied. "Just because they never found the baby—"

The cross suddenly felt hot, and Kim jerked her hand away. "If they never found it, how does anyone know she killed it? How does anyone know there even was a baby?"

For the first time, a look of uncertainty clouded Luke's face, but he answered: "If there wasn't a baby, how come you can hear it cry at night? And how come it cries if its ma didn't kill it? I'm telling you, everybody knows what happened. My uncle says—"

Kim felt a surge of anger. How could this boy know what had happened here? He hadn't been here! And how come he kept saying "everybody knows"? "I bet *none* of it happened," she cut in before Luke could repeat whatever his uncle had said. "What have you ever seen yourself? What have you actually *heard*? And if you were close enough to see or hear anything, what were you doing? Just because nobody was living here doesn't mean it wasn't private property!" Luke Roberts's face flushed scarlet, and Kim could see his right hand clench into a fist. "What are you going to do, hit me?" she asked, her eyes locking onto his as if daring him to raise his fist.

Luke, shocked into silence by Kim's outburst, lurched back against the balustrade, lost his balance, and tumbled over. As he screamed with terror, the fingers of his right hand grabbed onto the railing. For a second he hung suspended from one arm, his left hand groping wildly before closing on one of the posts that supported the banister, but he quickly began to lose his grip, and for an instant that seemed to stretch into an eternity, his eyes—glazed with fear—fastened on Kim.

She knew that if he fell, the image of his eyes, terrified and accusing, would be burned into her memory forever. The horror of the moment paralyzed her, but in her mind she screamed out to Jared to help Luke.

As if he'd heard her, Jared darted to the railing, his own strong hands closing on Luke's wrists before the other boy's grip gave way. Then he hauled Luke back over the balustrade.

"I—I'm sorry," Kim stammered. "I didn't mean—"

But now that he was safe, Luke's terror was transmuting into anger. "What the hell did *I* do? I was just telling you what I heard! Christ—I coulda broken my neck!" As he started down the stairs, he glowered back at Kim. "Maybe your aunt wasn't the only *crazy* one around here."

Before Kim could reply, he had slammed the front door behind him.

CHAPTER 8

The silence that fell over the old house that night was far deeper than any of its occupants had ever experienced before, and except for Molly—who fell asleep almost the moment Janet laid her in her crib—each of them lay awake for a long time.

They listened to the silence.

No insects chirped.

No animals rustled in the darkness outside.

Even the ancient frame of the house itself uttered no sound to disturb the quiet.

Yet each of them heard echoes of voices in the silence; each of them found eyes watching them from the darkness.

For Janet, it was the eyes of Jake Cumberland, reaching out to her from the deep shadows of the magnolia tree outside the cemetery. They held her in thrall. And the voice was Alma Morgan's, telling her that Cora Conway had been perfectly sane. But Corinne Beckwith's voice, too, echoed softly in the night, whispering of a baby who would have been her husband's cousin—if it had lived.

If it had ever existed at all.

Her eyes open, Janet scanned the darkness, as if somehow the truth of what might have happened in this house forty years ago might be hidden in the black folds of the night.

But the darkness, like the silence, kept its secrets.

As the night crept on, and sleep continued to elude her, Janet felt an urge to reach out to Ted, to slip her hand into his if for no other reason that to feel the comfort of knowing she wasn't alone in the silence and the darkness. But it had been so long since she'd welcomed his touch that she could no longer bring herself to reach out to him. When sleep finally embraced her, she lay with her back to her husband.

For Ted, it was the darkly penetrating eyes of Father MacNeill that glowered at him out of the darkness, the priest's voice that echoed in the silence. *"A hotel? . . . I hope you're prepared for a fight on that one!"* But far more than the threatening words, it was the look he'd seen in the cleric's eyes that kept Ted awake in the silence and darkness of the night. The look flared up the moment Ted told him he wouldn't be coming to his church, wouldn't be listening to him preach every Sunday morning, and though the priest only let him see it for a few seconds, it was a look Ted had seen before.

It was the same look he'd seen in Frank Gilman's eyes the day he'd lost his job.

The same look he'd seen in Tony's eyes just before he'd walked out of the bar to go to Gilman's office.

The same look he'd seen in the eyes of so many people.

All the men who'd ever fired him.

All the others who'd refused to hire him.

All the bartenders who'd poured him drinks.

All the men who once had been his friends.

He'd seen it in the eyes of his father.

He'd even seen it in the eyes of his son.

It was a look he'd learned to recognize long ago, when he was still a boy. A look that told him he did not belong, that there was something everyone else knew, something everyone else shared, that they would never share with him.

For a while, in the first years of his marriage, he hadn't noticed it in Janet's eyes. She'd hidden it well at first, but as the years went on he'd started catching glimpses of it. She tried to hide it, but he'd seen it clearly enough.

A look of superiority.

No understanding, nor pity, nor even sympathy.

Only superiority. And something else.

It rose up out of the darkness, and though he'd never let himself recognize it before, in the silence of the night he finally knew exactly what it was he'd seen so clearly in the priest's eyes that afternoon.

And not just the priest's eyes, but everyone else's as well.

Contempt.

Their eyes had always said it all:

You don't belong here.

You're not part of us.
We don't want you here.

It had been that way all his life, for as long as he could remember. From the time his mother left him when he was only a baby, until his father died while he was still in school.

Through all the places he'd never fit in, all the jobs where they'd found reasons to fire him.

Never, ever, had he felt like he belonged.

But here—in this house—he did belong. This house had been his uncle's house, and his grandfather's house, and his great-grandfather's house. And now it was his house.

And he belonged!

A burning fury at the injustices he'd suffered began to glow inside Ted Conway. As he lay in the quiet of the house—*his* house—he swore he would never let it happen again.

This time, he would show them all.

He would restore this old wreck—make it more beautiful than it was when it was built. And he would have his hotel.

He would have it, no matter who tried to stop him, and it would succeed. It would succeed so well that no one—not the priest, not his wife, not his son, not *anyone*—would ever dare hold him in contempt again.

Reaching out in the darkness, he slid open the drawer of the nightstand. His fingers closed on the pint of bourbon he'd hidden away that afternoon.

Now, in the silence and darkness of the night, he opened it and held the bottle to his lips.

I'll show them, he swore to himself once more as the warmth of the fiery liquid fueled the rage inside him. *I'll show them all!*

It was Luke Roberts's eyes that kept Kim awake that night, for every time she closed her eyes, she saw them again. Saw the terror, and the accusation.

And heard his words in the silence that the darkness had brought: *"If there wasn't a baby, how come you can hear it cry at night? And how come it cries if its ma didn't kill it?"*

Could any of it be true? Of course not! He'd just been trying to scare her. But still she found herself listening, straining to hear . . .

What?

She didn't know.

As the night stretched on and the silence grew heavier, she strained to listen for the sounds that had always lulled her to sleep at night: crickets chirping, frogs calling for their mates.

Even the whine of mosquitoes or the bark of the dog next door—the barking that Scout had instantly echoed, waking everyone in the house—would have been welcome this night.

So would the droning of traffic in the street, or the eerie hoot of an owl hunting in the night.

But to hear nothing at all . . .

She tossed and turned restlessly until Muffin, curled on the pillow beside her, angrily swiped her, then moved to the foot of the bed. And finally, blessedly, she fell into sleep.

And heard it.

It was a scream such as she'd never heard before; an unearthly wail that tore the mantle of sleep from her with enough force to jerk her upright in bed.

Her heart was pounding and her skin was clammy with a cold sheen of sweat.

But the night was still so silent that she knew at once the scream she'd heard existed only in her mind.

She lay back down, curled tightly on her side.

And saw it.

A creature, blacker even than the night, crouched on the far side of her room, as if about to lunge for her.

She froze, too afraid even to breathe, and then, out of the silence, she heard the words whispered to her by her dying aunt: *"It will protect you . . . Don't ever take it off."*

Her fingers closed around the cross, and she felt her terror begin to ebb.

A shadow, she thought. It's only a shadow!

Propping herself on her side, she saw that the moon was just beginning to rise, its silvery glow barely seeping through the windows, whose years of accumulated grime had yet to be washed away.

And on the windowsill stood Muffin, her back arched, her tail sticking straight up.

As Kim watched, the cat paced the length of the windowsill.

"Muffin," Kim called out quietly. "Come on, Muffin. Come back to bed."

The cat hissed in the darkness, then turned and stalked back the other way.

"What is it?" Kim asked, getting out of bed and going to the cat. "What's wrong? What's out there?" Kim pressed close to the window, straining to see through the heavy smudges that coated them, at the same time reaching out to soothe Muffin with a gentle stroke.

The cat hissed, and took another swipe at her. This time, its claws left three stinging welts on the back of her hand. Then, as if to make its desires crystal clear, the cat struck hard at the windowpane.

"Now?" Kim whispered. "Why do you have to go out now?" She reached out as if to stroke the cat again, but when Muffin hissed a warning, she quickly snatched her hand back. "All right," she said as she fumbled with the window latch, struggling to work it loose. "If it's that important—" The latch came free, and she jerked the window open.

In an instant the cat was gone.

Kim pulled the window wide and peered out into the night, searching for some sign of her pet. "Muffin?" she called. "Muffin, come back!"

But the silence of the night swallowed her words as thoroughly as if she'd never spoken them.

And then, just as she had when she'd awakened a few minutes earlier, she froze, her heart beating with cold terror.

Nothing had changed—nothing she could see or hear, at least.

The night was still silent, and even the light of the moon could barely penetrate the darkness.

But there was something out there.

Kim could feel it.

Something—or someone—was out there.

Out there, watching her.

CHAPTER 9

Every muscle in Jake Cumberland's body tensed.

He hadn't moved in nearly six hours, not since nightfall had let him steal out of the woods on the east side of the property and move close to the old carriage house, where he hid himself so completely in the deep shadows that even someone passing within a few feet of him would never have known he was there.

There he'd remained, keeping his silent vigil, watching the house.

He hadn't really believed it when he'd first heard someone say people were gonna be moving back into the old house. After all, everyone knew there weren't any more Conways, not since the old woman had died. But it had turned out that everybody was wrong.

There *were* still Conways around—five of 'em, anyways.

Right after he'd heard the talk—the same day the old lady died—he'd made his way along the path through the bottomland to a place where he could keep a watch on the house, and sure enough, there they were. He'd recognized them the minute he saw them—'specially the man. Everything about him had Conway written all over it.

It wasn't just the dark hair and blue eyes.

It was the way he moved, too, and held his head.

Jake could practically smell it on him.

He'd watched while they all went into the house, never moving, just like when he was out hunting and had to hold stone-still for hours at a time, less'n the game would get scared off. He'd waited until they'd come back out of the house and gotten back in their car and gone away, but even as he watched the car disappear, he knew they'd be back, knew it the same way he always knew just where to set his traps, even on nights when it was so dark he couldn't hardly see a thing.

Then, when he'd gone to the funeral this afternoon, he'd seen them again. 'Course, he hadn't gone inside the church or the cemetery—his mama had warned him about churches when he was still so small he didn't even go to school—and he hadn't never liked cemeteries. Sometimes you had to go into them, though, but only when you needed something, and even then you only went in the middle of the night when the moon was high and its silvery light made everything look like it was made out of pewter, like the mug his grandmama had left him. It still stood on the windowsill above the sink in the cabin. Though he didn't really remember his grandmama, he thought about her every time he used the mug, peering through its glass bottom while he drank.

"It's so you can see your enemies, even when you're drinking," his mama had told him. *"Your grandmama always said it was important to keep an eye on your enemies, so they won't catch you by surprise."*

Sometimes, when his mama was working her magic, Jake watched her peering into the mug, and knew that even when she wasn't drinking from it, the window in the bottom of the mug let her see what her enemies were doing, no matter where they were. *"They can't hide, Jake,"* she'd said. *"Not as long as you got the mug."* Even now, whenever Jake drank from the mug, his eyes stayed open as he searched for any threat that might lie beyond the glass.

But never had he seen any Conways through the bottom of the mug. In fact, he'd almost wondered if maybe he'd been wrong before. But when he'd hung around outside the fence of the cemetery this morning, there they were, the man helping carry the old lady's coffin, and the rest of them following after.

He stayed and watched them bury the old lady, and tried to work some of his mama's magic on them, but knew it wouldn't work. You couldn't just work the magic—you had to have a lot of stuff first, but he'd still tried. And he was pretty sure the woman, at least, felt him give her the eye, 'cause she'd looked straight at him a couple of times. But he hadn't flinched. No, sir. He'd stayed right where he was.

Then, after they all left the cemetery, he'd come around through the woods and kept right on watching.

They'd come back here and started taking their stuff out of the truck and putting it into the house. Only then had he decided that it was true, they really were planning to stay.

Shoulda burnt that place down, he thought. *Shoulda burnt it down years ago.*

Finally he'd gone home and waited for nightfall, when it would be safe to creep back to the house and search for the things he'd need to make his mama's magic work.

Jake knew what he needed—knew exactly what he had to do.

And ever since night had fallen over St. Albans, he'd been there, hidden by the shadows, holding perfectly still in the darkness, waiting.

The hours crept by. He could feel the people inside the house, almost see them tossing in their troubled sleep.

His ears, sharpened by a life spent tracking the creatures that roamed the night, could almost hear them breathing, and when, in the small hours of the night, the cat leaped from the windowsill, he heard it clearly, even though its paws struck the ground so lightly they made almost no sound.

As the cat moved through the darkness, Jake tensed, waiting.

His ears and eyes tracked it as it moved through the area, exploring the wilderness that had closed around the house as the years had passed. He waited patiently, knowing that soon it would move in his direction.

Perhaps it would even sense him.

But if he held still—if he made no sound at all—

Yes!

It was coming toward him now.

Jake held his breath as the cat stopped, tensing as it caught his scent. For an instant he thought it was going to bolt, but then, as he silently willed it forward, it dropped low to the ground and began slinking nearer.

Jake waited, every muscle in his body vibrating with the strain of holding perfectly still.

The cat crept closer, its tail twitching.

It paused once more, when it was still just beyond his reach. But then, its curiosity overcoming its caution, it moved still closer.

Closer . . .

Close enough!

So quickly the cat had no time to react, Jake's arms snaked through the darkness.

His huge hands closed around the cat's neck.

CHAPTER 10

"You promise you'll look for Muffin?" Kim asked when Janet pulled the Toyota to a stop in front of St. Ignatius School the next morning.

"Will you stop worrying?" Jared said as he slid out of the backseat. "She's a cat. They do what they want to do. She'll come home when she feels like it."

"But what if she tried to go back to Shreveport?" Kim fretted.

"I'm sure she didn't do that," Janet assured her. "Jared's probably right. But I promise I'll keep an eye out for her." She looked at her watch. "Now let's get you two enrolled so I can get back to the house before your father—" She cut her words short, but it was too late. She saw Kim and Jared glance at each other and was certain they were supplying the words she hadn't uttered: *starts drinking.*

But maybe, just maybe, he'd really meant what he said about making this work, about starting over again in St. Albans. When she woke up this morning, Ted was already out of bed, and for a fleeting moment—and it had only happened because she wasn't quite awake yet—she felt the same despair that had washed over her at least half a dozen times in the last few months when she woke up to find that Ted hadn't come to bed at all.

Mostly, she'd found him passed out on the sofa in the living room.

Once, she found him in the bathtub.

And once he hadn't come home at all. That morning, she'd been on the verge of calling the police when he'd phoned her with a story—which she chose to believe, although she knew it was undoubtedly a lie—about having worked most of the night and finally collapsing in one of the rooms at the Majestic.

But this morning, Janet had found him downstairs ripping up the worn carpet that covered the dining room floor, in order to expose the intricately inlaid hardwood hidden beneath it. "Will you look at this?" he crowed. "It's incredible! Oak inlaid with cherry, walnut, and God only knows what else. All it needs is sanding and refinishing." He kept working while she put together a makeshift breakfast, and when she left to enroll Jared and Kimberley at St. Ignatius, he was still at it. Molly, in her playpen, had been watching her father work and happily played with a scrap of carpet he'd given her. And for the first time in years, Janet allowed herself to hope that maybe this time things really would change. But even as she let that tiny ray of hope into her consciousness, she reminded herself that he'd made dozens of promises before. None of them had ever been kept.

"Come on," she said now, starting up the steps to the school. "No matter what's happening at home, I still need to be there. I'll keep an eye out for Muffin. I promise."

The moment he stepped through the door, Jared's worst fears about what St. Ignatius might be like were instantly validated. The front door opened onto a long, narrow corridor lit only by a few old-fashioned glass globes that hung at the intersections where other hallways led off to the right and left. The walls were wainscoted, but the wood and plaster had been painted the same color—a sort of beige that looked yellowish and dirty. The floor was covered with a dark linoleum unbroken by any pattern, unless you could count a worn strip down the middle through which the wood of the floor beneath was starting to show. Jared decided the worn strip didn't count.

As they made their way to the office, Jared and Kim glanced uneasily at each other, but neither said anything.

Half an hour later, after their mother had left, the twins started up the stairs to their new homeroom. "You'll like Sister Clarence," Father Bernard, the priest who ran St. Ignatius, had assured them. "She's one of our best teachers, and all the children love her."

"Not exactly like Shreveport, is it?" Jared observed as they emerged from the stairwell onto the second-floor landing. Ahead of them stretched a duplicate of the corridor on the first floor, except this one contained a bank of lockers, two of which had been assigned to them. "They'll need to have locks, of course," Father Bernard had told Janet. "We require combination locks, and the combinations must be on file in the office." He'd fixed Jared with a hard look, as if he expected his charges to try to get away with as much as they could. "We do spot checks, and if the combination has been changed, it is an automatic one-week suspension."

Now, as Jared eyed the lockers, he grinned at his sister. " 'Spose if

I put a padlock with a key on my locker, I could get kicked out completely?"

Kim resisted the urge to laugh. "Let's just make the best of it. Mom's got enough problems without having to worry about us."

Jared sighed. "I know. But I'd still like to see the look on Father Bernard's face if he found a lock he couldn't open."

They found their room halfway down the hall, and Jared pulled the door open for Kim. As they stepped through, the black-clad figure who had been writing on the blackboard turned and impaled them with a stare that knifed through steel-rimmed glasses.

"I am Sister Clarence," she said.

"I'm Jared Con—" Jared began, but the nun cut him off.

"I know who you are." She indicated two seats in the second row with the slightest nod of her cowled head. "We are discussing the role of the Vatican in World War Two," she went on. "You've already missed the first two weeks of school. I'll expect you to have caught up with the reading by tomorrow."

As she turned back to the blackboard, Jared and Kim slipped into their seats at the old-fashioned school desks. Directly behind Jared sat Luke Roberts, who slipped Jared a note. Jared unfolded the note and read the scrawled message.

Welcome to St. Ignoramus.

Suppressing a smile, Jared refolded the note and passed it across to Kim. A nearly inaudible giggle escaped her lips. She silenced it a moment too late.

"You will share that note with the rest of the class, Kimberley," Sister Clarence pronounced, her eyes boring into Kim, whose face reddened.

"I—It doesn't really—"

"Stand up," Sister Clarence ordered. "In this school, we always stand when we are spoken to, or when we wish to speak."

Her knees trembling, her flush deepening, Kim got to her feet.

"Read the note," the nun ordered.

Kim bit her lip, and her eyes darted to her brother, who winked at her. " 'Welcome to Saint Ignoramus,' " she read, her voice barely audible.

"I can't hear you," Sister Clarence said, each word a chip of ice. Kim's face burned. The nun certainly hadn't had any trouble hearing her a minute ago, when all she'd done was utter an almost silent giggle.

She read the note again—more loudly—into the hush that had fallen over the room.

"And you think that's funny," Sister Clarence said, her voice making it clear that her words were not a question.

Kim said nothing.

"Does anyone else think it's funny?" Sister Clarence asked.

Though Kim dared not even glance around, she knew that no one else in the classroom had so much as moved a finger, let alone raised a hand. Then, from the corner of her eye, she saw Jared stand.

"I do," he said. Kim saw the surprise—and cold fury—in Sister Clarence's eyes as they shifted to Jared.

"Both of you think it's funny to mock the school?"

"It's just a pun," Jared said. "I bet lots of people call it that."

"It is disrespectful, and it will not be tolerated. Is that clear?"

Jared hesitated, then bobbed his head a fraction of an inch. "Yes."

" 'Yes, *Sister Clarence,*' " the nun corrected him.

Kim could almost feel the anger rising in her brother. *Don't,* she silently begged. *Just let it go!*

The quiet in the room stretched out as Jared and the teacher confronted each other.

Everyone waited.

Once again Kim reached out with her mind and begged her brother not to say anything more.

Sister Clarence's eyes behind the steel-rimmed glasses glittered dangerously.

Jared's jaw tightened. Kim saw his lips starting to form words she knew would only dig him in deeper than he already was. *Don't, Jared!* she pleaded a third time, praying that this time he would pick up her thought and heed it.

Just let it go! The moment seemed to stretch out endlessly, but then, as clearly as if he'd spoken aloud, Kim heard Jared's voice inside her head.

Okay, he said. *But I hate this. I really hate it!*

A split second later Jared spoke aloud, his voice betraying none of the anger Kim had heard in his unvoiced thought. "Yes, Sister Clarence," he said softly.

Sister Clarence's gaze shifted back to Kim. "I've decided to overlook this, since this is your first day. But in the future such things will not be overlooked. Is that clear?"

"Yes, Sister Clarence," Kim said, her chastened voice little more than a whisper.

Sister Clarence's response stung like the lash of a whip. "Speak up!"

"Yes, Sister Clarence," Kim repeated, her face burning as tears welled in her eyes.

For the rest of the hour, Kim and Jared sat silently at their desks, trying to concentrate on the lesson the nun was teaching. But for both of them, their humiliation kept replaying itself in their minds.

It doesn't matter, Kim finally told herself. *It's just different here, and I'll get used to it.*

Jared, though, was absolutely sure he'd never get used to it. Never.

Janet Conway climbed down off the ladder, automatically arching her back and stretching first in one direction, then the other. As the ache in her spine and burning knots in her shoulders eased, she surveyed the results of her two hours at the top of the ladder, where she'd twisted herself into contortions to which her body had been mounting increasingly strenuous objections. But already she knew that no matter how much pain she had to put herself through for the next day or two, in the end it would be worth it. Already, light—the clear, clean light of the fall morning—was streaming through the glass roof and the upper third of the conservatory's northern and eastern walls. When she was finished, the room would provide her with the studio that until a few days ago she had only dreamed about. With sunlight coming in from three directions as well as from above, there would never be a time when she wouldn't be able to get exactly the illumination she wanted on her canvas. Just the thought of spending hours here with her paints and brushes, her easel and canvas—bringing to life the visions she'd always seen in her mind—quickened her pulse and made her fairly tingle with excitement and anticipation.

But as her eyes moved beyond the windows to the view outside the enormous glass walls, her excitement gave way to dark trepidation.

She told herself there was nothing ominous here. Just the tangle of vegetation, the thick, creeping kudzu that snaked out of the forest to slowly engulf the property, banking up against the carriage house, swallowing up the shrubs that had once had their own distinctive shapes and colors but were now slowly being strangled under the thick tentacles of twisted vines. Even the enormous oaks, willows, and magnolias were on the verge of succumbing to the tendrils, which had reached all but their highest branches; soon they, too, would be choked by the invader.

Yet even the devastation brought by the kudzu couldn't completely erase the vision in Janet's mind. Despite the decades of grime that still fogged the lower portion of the windows, she could see the possibilities. Tomorrow—maybe even this afternoon—she would start hacking away at the encroaching foliage. She'd start with the trees; once she cut through the thick stems of the vines, cutting off their connections to their roots, they would quickly die off, and pulling them down would be much easier. She would cut those that were climbing over the house, too. And this weekend Jared could begin clearing off the rest of the property, stripping the kudzu away. The lawn, of course, had been ruined years ago, but some of the larger shrubs might yet be saved. And halfway between the conservatory and the woods, she could just make out the shape of what looked like a fountain. In her mind's eye she stripped away the tangle of vines to reveal . . .

What?

Marble! Yes, of course. It would be made of marble—though limestone would be almost as good—carved into some wonderful pattern over which the water would shimmer and ripple as it flowed. She could almost see the plumes of water that would rise from the restored fountain, nearly hear the gentle sound of its spray splashing back into the catchment basin. Perhaps they could even put some goldfish in it.

The vision took on more details, and Janet could see the beginnings of a painting. Or better yet, a trompe l'oeil mural big enough to cover an entire wall of one of the house's huge rooms. It would depict the grounds as they would have looked when the house was new, when Ted's ancestors had first built it. The gardens would have been formal, she was sure, with perfectly manicured box hedges bordering beds of azaleas and roses. A profusion of flowers, in every color of the rainbow. There would have been furniture, too—white-painted wrought iron, upon which graceful women holding parasols would lounge.

Pointillism. That was it. And perhaps she would give it a French cast, to fit with the New Orleans influences of the town. She would do it in the style of Georges Seurat, filling it with light and texture and—

A sudden sharp rap on one of the French doors leading to the terrace outside the conservatory jerked her out of her reverie, startling her so badly she almost knocked over the ladder upon which she'd been so precariously perched only a few minutes before. "Hello?" a voice called from outside. "Is anybody here?"

Steadying the ladder, Janet went to the French doors, fumbled with the lock, then pushed the handle down. When she pulled on the door, the upper corner stuck fast, the frame warped so badly that the glass threatened to break.

"Stop!" the voice from outside called. "Let me push from out here!"

Janet let the door go fully shut. Then, as she tried to ease it open again, the person outside struck the upper corner sharply and the door came free.

"I hate these old French doors," Corinne Beckwith announced as she stepped into the conservatory. "The frames always stick. This fancy stuff might have been okay a hundred and fifty years ago, but give me something nice and modern, preferably in anodized aluminum. No paint, no rust, no upkeep." She gazed around at the interior of the conservatory, and Janet could practically see her adding up the hours it would take just to clean this one room.

"The others are just as bad," Janet said.

The other woman shook her head slowly. "I don't know." She sighed. "I guess it's nice that there are people who want to take on projects like this, but if you want to know the truth, I've got a feeling that folks around here are only going to take your trying to restore this place as proof that they're right."

"Right?" Janet echoed, unsure what the sheriff's wife meant. "Right about what?"

Corinne Beckwith grinned. "That all the Conways are crazy!"

Corinne's words touched a nerve in Janet. "If that's why you came over here—" She bristled, but Corinne raised her hands as if to fend off her words.

"I'm sorry—I was just trying to make a joke." Her smile disappeared. "I really am sorry. It wasn't a very good joke, and I suspect you're not really in the mood for jokes anyway. Actually, the real reason I came over was to talk about your project. If you're really going to try to turn this place into an inn, you're going to need all the help you can get. And Father MacNeill's just going to be the beginning, although frankly I'm not sure exactly how you're going to get around him."

"But all he said was that there'd be some people who'd object."

Corinne's brows rose in a cynical arch. "That's code, Janet." Her eyes darted around as if searching for an unseen eavesdropper, and her voice dropped a notch. "Ray—that's my husband—would kill me if he knew I was telling you this, but Father MacNeill never does anything up front. He doesn't have to, since practically everyone who's anyone in this town is Catholic, and if they didn't go to St. Ignatius School themselves, then their kids are going there now. And they do what Father Mack wants them to do. If he said there would be objections, it's because he's planning to make very sure that there are."

Janet cocked her head quizzically. "I gather you're not Catholic?"

Corinne shrugged. "I still go to St. Ignatius because Ray does. But I like to think for myself." Once again she glanced around as if searching for invisible ears. "Ray doesn't always like it, but that's the way I am."

Janet decided she liked Corinne Beckwith. "May I get you a cup of coffee?"

"If I can drink it while you give me a tour of this place. I've been dying to see it ever since I was a little girl and heard all the stories."

For nearly an hour the two women wandered through the house, stopping briefly to play with Molly and pet Scout, who seemed to have appointed himself the little girl's baby-sitter.

When they were finally back in the kitchen and Janet had split the last of the coffee between them, Corinne Beckwith offered up her opinion of the house, and there was no trace in her voice of the enthusiasm expressed by her words. "Well, your husband's right. This place would make one hell of an inn."

"If you agree with him, why doesn't it sound like it?"

Corinne's lips pursed thoughtfully. "It's none of my business, but does the trust have enough money to pay for everything that needs to be done?"

Janet nodded.

"And your husband can run a hotel right, as long as he—" Corinne cut her words short, and looked as if she wished she could recall them.

She knows, Janet thought. *She knows about Ted's problem.* Janet felt a flush of anger. Who had told her? Or had she gone digging around, snooping into things that weren't any of her business, looking for something—Janet cut off her thoughts as sharply as Corinne Beckwith had stopped her own words a moment ago, reminding herself again that St. Albans wasn't Shreveport; here, everyone knew everyone else's business. There was no point in denying what everyone already knew. "As long as he stays sober?" she asked, finishing Corinne's question. When Corinne nodded, Janet took a deep breath, then let it out in a sigh. "As long as he stays sober, yes, he can run a hotel. And I hope he does stay sober. So let's assume he does. And let's assume we can get the variances we need. What else is there?"

"The house itself, and your husband's family," Corinne told her, deciding to match Janet's honesty with her own and confirming Janet's suspicions about the St. Albans grapevine. "I can tell you that since yesterday the phones have been ringing off the hook. And apparently what I told you about your aunt being pregnant wasn't just gossip. There must be half a dozen people who remember that she was pregnant when her husband died. But when they found her, she wasn't. The assumption was the shock of finding her husband's corpse induced labor, and she delivered the baby that morning." When Janet said nothing, Corinne went on. "The problem, as far as I can tell, is that no trace of the baby was ever found. There is no record of it having been born."

"Perhaps it was stillborn," Janet suggested.

"Even with a stillbirth, there should be a record. And there's something else. You remember the man outside the cemetery yesterday. Jake Cumberland?"

Janet almost shuddered. "I'll never forget him. The way he was looking at us. It was like he hated us, even though he's never met us."

"He probably does," Corinne replied. "His mother was the house-keeper for George and Cora Conway. And she disappeared that day, too."

"Disappeared?" Janet repeated. "I'm not sure what you mean."

"I'm not sure what I mean, either," Corinne told her. "I heard a lot of things, and I don't know what to make of it all. Apparently Jake's mother—her name was Eulalie—was some kind of voodoo priestess."

"Oh, come on," Janet began, but Corinne held up a hand.

"Let me finish. From what I've heard, Eulalie thought there was something 'evil'—that was the exact word she used, according to everyone I talked to—going on here, and she decided to put a stop to it. Apparently she made a doll."

"A voodoo doll?" Janet echoed, her voice incredulous. "Come on, Corinne, nobody believes in that stuff!"

"Actually, a lot of people believe in it," Corinne replied. "And certainly Eulalie Cumberland did."

Janet's lips tightened. "I can't believe anyone would think—"

"Just let me finish," Corinne interrupted. "Nobody I talked to knew the details, but apparently the doll was found. And there had been a fire in the yard the night before. And after George and Cora Conway were found, Eulalie and Cora's baby were both gone."

"If people think Eulalie took Cora's baby, why would they blame Ted's family for anything?"

"Nobody thinks she took it," Corinne replied. "Everyone I talked to says that Eulalie would never have left Jake. He was just a child, and she was all he had. It's the one thing everyone agrees on—that Eulalie wouldn't have left Jake. If she'd gone anywhere, with or without the Conways' baby, she would have taken Jake with her."

"So what do they think happened?" Janet asked, though in her heart she already knew what the answer was going to be.

Corinne hesitated. Then: "All anyone would say was that they're sure George and Cora did something to Eulalie, and that ever since the Conways left this house, nothing bad has happened here."

Janet's eyes met Corinne Beckwith's. "And they think that now that we're here, bad things will start happening again?"

Corinne nodded.

"I don't believe it!" Janet said, trying to contain her anger. "What are they going to do, come after us with pitchforks, like the villagers in *Frankenstein*?"

Corinne Beckwith's lips curved into a tight smile. "I suspect it will be a little more subtle than that, but I think you've got the general idea."

Janet's outrage coalesced into cold determination. All the doubts she'd had about Ted's ability to do what he'd promised vanished. If Corinne Beckwith—or anyone else—thought they would simply pack up and leave, they were wrong.

Dead wrong.

"That's not going to happen," she said quietly. "If we leave, it will be because of our own failures. But nobody's going to drive us away. Nobody."

CHAPTER 11

T ed sat in the comforting darkness of the bar, staring at the drink in front of him. Straight vodka, with just a twist of lime for flavor. In the back of his mind a tiny voice whispered to him to leave the drink where it was, and go home.

Shut up, he silently whispered back. *It's just one drink, and I deserve it. Anybody would!*

He lifted the glass and stared at the clear liquid for a long moment, as if daring the voice in the back of his mind to challenge him again.

It remained silent, and Ted raised the glass to his lips, drained it, then lowered it to the bar and nudged it toward the bartender, who immediately responded to the unspoken request. As the bartender—another Tony, for Christ's sake—refilled his glass, Ted studied himself in the mirror behind the bar. What the hell had everyone been staring at all day? There wasn't anything wrong with the way he looked—in fact, he looked a hell of a lot better than most of the jerks who'd been staring at him. But it wasn't just the way they looked at him that pissed him off. It was the way they acted, too.

It started that morning, right after he'd left the house. He'd been on his way to the Home Depot to pick up some wood stripper and a sander and the other supplies he needed to restore the dining room floor, but as he was going around the square in the middle of town, he passed a small brick building whose columned entry and small dome had immediately identified it as the St. Albans Town Hall. And with that identification had come the echo of the words he'd heard at his aunt's funeral.

". . . there will be a lot of opposition to giving you a variance."

"I hope you're prepared for a fight on that one . . ."

If there's going to be a problem, I might as well know about it right now, Ted told himself. He slid the Toyota into an open slot half a block past the brick building. As he walked back, he nodded to the two people he passed. One was a woman about his own age who was clutching the hand of a little boy who was perhaps a year older than Molly. The other was a man of about sixty, clad in overalls, with a fringe of gray hair sticking out from beneath a stained baseball cap.

Neither the man nor the woman replied to his greeting, though he was certain they'd both heard him. And he'd also had the distinct impression that they knew who he was.

The funeral, he told himself. *They saw us at the funeral, and they've heard all the stories about Uncle George and Aunt Cora.* Well, there were bound to be small people with small minds in small towns. But there would be just as many other people who wouldn't hold his family against him.

Entering the Town Hall—which at first glance appeared completely deserted—he looked around for a building directory and saw a sign on a door identifying it as the office of the Town Clerk. Inside, there was a long counter, behind which were two desks, one occupied by a young woman with short blond hair and a look of efficiency about her, the other by a man who looked to Ted as if he should have retired a dozen years earlier. A small plaque on his desk identified him as Jefferson Davis Houlihan.

The words TOWN CLERK followed his name, in letters just as large as the name itself.

"May I help you?" the efficient-looking blonde asked, offering Ted a polite if not quite warm smile. The plaque on her desk—much smaller than Houlihan's—informed him that her name was Amber Millard.

"I'd like to check the zoning on a piece of property," Ted replied. Was it his imagination, or did Amber Millard and her boss exchange a quick look? When he gave her the address of the house and saw the smile on her face turn brittle, he knew it hadn't been his imagination.

"That would be residential," she told him so quickly that Ted was certain she'd already looked it up. Her next words confirmed it: "Here's a copy of it. Someone else was just asking about the same property." Getting up from her desk, she came to the counter and handed Ted a single sheet of paper.

He scanned it carefully, though he was already certain of what it said. "Would you mind telling me who was asking about my house?"

This time, Amber Millard deferred to her boss.

"Well, now, that would be a breach of confidentiality, now wouldn't it?" Jefferson Davis Houlihan drawled.

Ted's first impulse was to ask Houlihan how many lawyer shows he'd been watching on television lately, but he checked the impulse; it would only anger the man. Studying the document in his hands again, he returned his attention to Amber Millard. "I'm going to need an application for a variance."

This time Houlihan didn't wait for his assistant to defer to him. "Not sure we have any. Haven't had any call for one in maybe twenty years."

Ted felt his temper rise. "Would you mind looking?" he asked, making no attempt to soften the edge in his voice.

"Don't mind looking," Houlihan drawled, lazily getting to his feet. "Just not sure where to start." His eyes fixed on Ted. "Maybe if you came back in a week or two . . ." he suggested, letting his voice trail off in an unmistakably deliberate way.

As he was leaving Town Hall a few minutes later, the first urge for a drink came over Ted, an urge that only grew stronger as the day went on. Everywhere he went, it was the same as at the Town Clerk's office.

No one was rude to him.

No one turned away as he approached.

Most people even smiled at him.

At first he tried to pretend it was just the way small towns worked: everybody here had known everybody else all their lives, and nobody knew him. It would take a while, but once they got to know him, they'd accept him. Especially once he got the inn open and his guests started spending money in the restaurants and shops strung neatly along the south side of the square. *It's money that talks,* he reminded himself, *and mine's as good as anyone else's.*

Nobody refused to sell him anything.

By lunchtime, when he'd hauled the first load of supplies back to the house, he'd already spent close to five hundred dollars, and in the afternoon—after Janet told him about Corinne Beckwith's visit—he made sure he spent a lot more.

He ordered paint and wallpaper, new slate for the roof, and new fixtures for every bathroom in the house. He spent an hour at the one furniture store in St. Albans, searching through catalog after catalog, finally putting half a dozen of the best—and most expensive—into the car to take home to Janet.

He talked to the plumbers and electricians and roofers, and anyone else he could think of who might be able to help him on the restoration. "I'm not worried about money," he assured every one of them—and made certain they all had Bruce Wilcox's phone number so the lawyer could confirm that the money was, indeed, there. "I'm interested in getting the job done right."

All of them listened politely.

All of them sold him whatever he wanted.

But all of them—the plumbers, the electricians, the roofers, and everyone else—told him the same thing: "I don't know. It's pretty busy right now. Don't see how I can fit you in. And that house is in pretty bad shape. Be better just to tear it down."

By the end of the afternoon, Ted was sick of hearing it. His last stop was at the market, where he picked up everything on the list Janet had given him. Then, he decided to make another stop to add a few things of his own.

Some bourbon. Some gin. A lot of vodka.

He'd had a rough day. He deserved a drink.

The girl at the cash register passed the bottles across the scanner without saying anything, but he'd seen the look in her eye, and had no trouble reading its meaning: *Go away. We don't want you here.*

Now, sitting in the bar, he met his own gaze in the mirror. *To hell with you,* he said silently. *To hell with all of you. I'm here, and I'm not leaving.* Draining the second drink in a single gulp, Ted dropped enough money on the bar to cover the bill and a tip and walked out.

After he was gone, the bartender scooped up the money, dropped part of it in the cash register and the rest of it in his tip jar, then picked up the phone.

"He was here," he said. "And he's drinking."

There was a short silence, and then the recipient of the call spoke. "That's good," Father MacNeill said softly. "Maybe he'll drink himself to death."

Evening lay like a shroud over the house. Janet tried to tell herself that her dark mood was just a result of the weather—the heat and humidity, unseasonable even for mid-September that wrapped St. Albans like a sodden blanket. The iron determination that Corinne Beckwith's visit instilled in her that morning had begun to erode as soon as Kim and Jared came home from school. Jared tried to put a good face on it, but Kim made no effort to hide her feelings. Her unhappiness, Janet was certain, was heightened by the fact that there hadn't been any sign of Muffin all day.

"Something's happened to her," Kim said as she finally gave up trying to call the missing cat. "She wouldn't just run away."

"Cats can be pretty independent," Janet told her, trying to offer Kim hope for her pet, but at the same time wanting to prepare her for the possibility that the cat might never come back. "Maybe she just didn't like it here, and has found somewhere else to live."

"But she wouldn't do that," Kim protested. "Not Muffin!"

"Well, perhaps she'll come back," Janet told her, and changed the subject. "How was the first day at school?" she asked, and immediately wished she hadn't.

Kim moaned. "It was awful," she said. Opening the refrigerator, she rummaged around for a couple of Cokes, one of which she tossed to her brother. For the next twenty minutes Janet listened to her oldest daughter's account of the twins' humiliation in the first ten minutes they'd been in class at St. Ignatius. "And it wasn't even Jared's fault," she finished. "Sister Clarence never even asked if he wrote the note, and of course he wouldn't tell her he didn't."

"Look how she treated us," Jared said. "And it was our first day in school. If I'd told her Luke Roberts wrote the note, she'd have probably had him expelled, or made him stay after school and say two thousand Hail Marys or something."

Kim rolled her eyes, wondering once again how it was that Jared never seemed to get mad about anything—even someone else getting him in trouble—and always managed to make it sound like he hadn't done anything special. He didn't even seem to be angry at Sister Clarence. "Will you at least admit Sister Clarence is a total creep?"

"Kim!" Janet did her best to glare at her daughter, but as she'd listened to Kim recounting their day at school, a dark suspicion had been growing in her mind that there was more to it than Kim knew.

Father MacNeill.

But surely he wouldn't go so far as to turn a teacher against her own students? Or would he? For the rest of the afternoon the problem gnawed at her, nibbling away at the resolve that had come to her only a few hours earlier.

Then Ted came home, and even before they saw him, they knew what he'd been doing. It was nothing visible; nothing they could hear or smell, taste or touch. But all of them had been living with it for so long that they recognized it the instant he entered the house.

It was the aura of alcohol.

Janet, testing the roast she'd fixed for dinner, caught the look that passed between Kim and Jared. Though neither said a word, she could read their common thought as clearly as if they'd spoken: *He's drunk!*

Molly began to cry, as if she, too, had picked up the thought—or perhaps detected her father's condition with some internal radar of her own.

Then he came into the kitchen, confirming their unspoken thoughts.

His step was a little too careful, his speech a little too precise.

"Why are you all looking at me that way?" he asked, and the tension in the house notched up as they heard the paranoia in his voice. Neither

Kim nor Jared replied, and did their best to neither look at their father nor appear to be trying not to look at him.

Molly's wail rose to a scream.

"Does that child have to howl every time I come into the room?" Ted demanded.

As Janet scooped Molly up from the floor and tried to comfort her, she had to repress the angry words that threatened to spill from her lips: *She only does it when you've been drinking!* "Dinner will be on in a few more minutes," she made herself say instead.

"Then Jared can unload the car," Ted said, his eyes fixing on his son. "If it's not too much to ask." The last words were spoken with biting sarcasm, warning Janet that an explosion wasn't far away.

"Not a problem," Jared said, already on his feet. Kim, grabbing at the opportunity to escape the ugliness in the kitchen, quickly followed her brother.

"What's wrong with her?" Ted asked. "Do I look like I have some kind of disease or something?"

Once again Janet forced herself to hold her tongue, but when Jared carried inside a large box filled with bottles of liquor, she turned furiously on Ted.

"You said you were going to stop drinking." She struggled to keep her voice under control, and wished she'd found the strength to hold her anger in check until later, when she and Ted would be alone. But it was too late. Ted was already glowering at her.

"Just because it's here doesn't mean I'm going to drink it."

This time Janet did stifle the words that came to mind. But it didn't matter. She'd already set Ted off.

"You all make me sick," he rasped. "Can you blame me for having a drink every now and then, the way you all act?" He picked up the box of bottles, nearly lost his balance, then managed to recover himself. "You want dinner, go ahead and eat it. I'll take care of myself." He disappeared through a doorway that led to a butler's pantry and the big dining room beyond. Jared made a move to follow, but Janet stopped him.

"Don't. Just leave him alone. Maybe at least the rest of us can enjoy our dinner."

But of course they couldn't. The pall over the house grew heavier, and though Janet kept telling herself it was just the dank heat of the evening, all of them knew its real cause.

Somewhere in the house, Ted was drinking.

When dinner was finished and the dishes cleared and washed, Kim and Jared retreated to the second floor, pleading homework to be done and a few more boxes still to be unpacked. But when Jared lifted Molly

into his arms—"Come on, small fry, if we have to work, so do you!"—
Janet got the message loud and clear.

We don't want to deal with him.

After they left, Janet lingered in the kitchen. At first she told herself
she simply wanted to be alone, wanted to put off dealing with her husband
for as long as possible. But it was more than that.

Once again she was hearing her mother's voice, and this time it was
saying something it had never said before: *Leave him. Take the children,
and leave him. He's a liar, he's a drunk, and whatever his problems are
have nothing to do with you. Don't let him destroy you. Don't let him
destroy the children. Get out now, before it's too late.*

The words, so clear it was as if her mother were sitting at the kitchen
table, shook Janet. Not because they were unfamiliar words.

She'd said them to herself a hundred times.

But always before, there had been qualifications.

And always before, fear had followed immediately on the heels of
the thought. Fear of trying to raise the children alone. Fear of trying to put
a roof over their heads, and food on the table, and clothes on their backs.
But this evening, in the heavy heat of the Louisiana night, all the fears had
fallen away.

Now she was far more afraid of staying. She stepped to the back
door and looked out. The sky was a leaden black—a thick cloud blotted
out whatever light the stars might have provided—and in the inky darkness she saw all the forces that suddenly seemed to be arrayed against her.

The priest, whose words of warning at the funeral seemed far more
menacing in the dark of night than they had in the bright light of morning.

Jake Cumberland, who had stood glowering from the sidewalk as
they buried Cora Conway.

All the people whom Ted had told her about over lunch, people
who—for whatever reason—didn't want them here, and made no effort to
hide their feelings.

Sister Clarence, who had chosen to humiliate her children on their
very first day at St. Ignatius.

And what was keeping them here?

A free house, and an income that would allow Ted to drink all he
wanted.

Why had she let herself believe that he'd really intended to stop
drinking? Stupid! That's what she was—just plain stupid, like all the
women she'd seen on those television talk shows who stayed with men
who beat them, and cheated on them, and humiliated them every chance
they got. So how was she any different from them?

Just because Ted didn't beat her, or cheat on her?

So what?

He lied to her—had lied to her hundreds of times over the years! Why had she believed him this time?

Stupid, stupid, stupid!

Well, no more!

Stepping back into the kitchen, she closed the door, shutting out the darkness. As she started through the lower floor of the house, her mood began to lighten. A flood of relief told her she'd made the right decision far more strongly than the purely intellectual knowledge that she had no other choice.

If she and the children stayed here, something terrible would happen.

To all of them.

She found Ted slouched on the single tired sofa they'd brought with them from Shreveport and installed in the small den behind the living room. He was clutching a glass, and on the floor next to the sofa was a fifth of vodka, half drunk.

"I'm leaving tomorrow," she told him. "I'll take the kids and Scout—and Muffin, if she's back—and the car."

Ted lurched to his feet and took a step toward her, lost his balance and grabbed at the mantel over the small fireplace to steady himself. "You're not going anywhere," he growled, this time making no attempt to conceal the slur in his speech.

Janet refused to be drawn into a fight. The decision she'd finally made was giving her a serenity she hadn't felt in years. "It's over, Ted," she said, her voice so quiet it riveted her husband's attention. "All the years of lies, all the years of broken promises. I don't want to deal with it." Her glance took in the room; the reality of the life around her. Now, instead of the possibilities she'd seen through Ted's eyes a few days earlier, all she saw was the peeling wallpaper, the stained plaster, the filthy and broken chandelier that hung from a sagging ceiling. And every room in the house was just like it. "Look at this place," she went on. "It's just like our marriage—everything about it is rotten, and it ought to have been torn down years ago." Ted's fist clenched spasmodically, but Janet didn't so much as flinch. "Don't bother," she said. "It won't work. Don't bother to threaten me, don't hit me, and for God's sake, don't make me any more promises." She turned away, but at the door she looked back at him one more time. "And don't bother coming upstairs tonight, either. The bedroom door will be locked." She left the den and walked through the living room into the foyer, then started up the stairs. She was halfway to the landing where the staircase split when Ted's voice thundered through the house.

"You won't leave me!" he bellowed. "You'll never leave me!"

The calm she'd been feeling was shattered by her husband's fury. Racing up the rest of the stairs, she fled into her room, locking the door behind her. The thick oak slab would keep him away from her for the rest of the night, but it wasn't thick enough to protect her from the sound of his rage.

"Do you understand?" he roared from downstairs, his voice echoing through the ruined rooms. "You'll never leave me!"

CHAPTER 12

I t was time.

Even though he'd been deep in sleep since just after sunset, something inside Jake Cumberland knew it was time. He came awake in an instant, throwing off the ragged coverlet he'd slept under since he was a boy and swinging his feet to the bare wooden floor in a single smooth motion. As he pulled on his pants there was a faint scratching at the cabin door; his hounds, too, had sensed that the time had come. "Give a body a chance," Jake muttered. At the sound of his voice the two yellow dogs fell silent. Slipping his arms into the frayed sleeves of a shirt so old that its plaid pattern had all but disappeared, Jake lit a candle, then moved to the door and opened it just enough to let the animals inside. The dogs— so thin their ribs were clearly etched beneath their scarred hides— slithered into the cabin's single room, their noses already seeking out the food their master might have provided. "Maybe later," Jake said as he shut the door against the darkness outside.

The dogs dropped to the floor, their muzzles resting on their paws. Their bloodshot eyes, glowing like burning embers in the candlelight, fixed on Jake. As he lit four more candles, lining them up on the scarred pine counter by the sink, their bodies tensed and a faint whimper crept from the throat of the smaller one. "Quiet," Jake commanded. The dog flinched and cowered, but emitted no further sound.

As smoke from the five candles filled the room, Jake went to the trunk in the corner—his mother's trunk—and opened it. Just under the lid there was a shallow tray, divided into half a dozen sections, each of which contained an assortment of small jars and vials. His mother's altar cloth lay beneath the tray, but Jake knew better than to touch it until he was certain which of her charms and potions to use.

"Soon's you unfold it, the magic starts to work," she'd told him when he was a boy. *"So you got to be ready. Got to know what you want to do, and what to use to do it."*

"But how do you know?" Jake had asked, his eyes wide as he watched his mother—whose own eyes were tightly closed—pass her hands over the tray, her fingers plucking out some objects, leaving others untouched.

"It's the magic," she'd told him. *"The magic will tell you."*

Now Jake knelt before the trunk, and just as his mother had done when he was a boy, he held out his hands, suspending them just a fraction of an inch above the tray. He closed his eyes and lifted his face toward the ceiling.

"Help me," he implored. "Help me, Mama."

The dogs, unseen by Jake, raised their heads, then stood. As the fur on their hackles rose, each of them lifted a forepaw off the floor.

Their tails extended straight back.

They held their perfect point as steadily as Jake held his hands above the tray in the open trunk.

Jake's right hand moved, hovering above the jars and bottles, drifting first in one direction, then another. In the beginning it seemed to be nothing more than random movement, but slowly a pattern emerged, as time after time his hand stopped, suspended over the same five objects.

His eyes still closed, his face still raised toward the ceiling, he began plucking objects from the tray.

The dogs, their bodies tense, kept their eyes fixed on their master's right hand.

When all five objects had been lifted from the tray and placed on the floor beside the trunk, Jake finally opened his eyes again. Gently, almost reverently, he lifted the tray itself from the trunk and set it upon the bed. Then, his hands trembling, he reached for his mother's altar cloth. Never before in his life had he removed it from the trunk—never even so much as touched it. Even now, as the candlelight flickered around him, he hesitated.

The dark bundle, tightly bound with ribbon of a purple so dark it was nearly lost in the black of the cloth itself, seemed to throb in the flickering candlelight as if some unknown life were struggling to free itself from the confining folds.

The magic.

His mama's magic.

His fingers vibrating, Jake lifted the bundle out of the trunk. Carrying it to the table, he carefully untied the ribbons, pressed them flat, then rolled them up the way he'd seen his mama do. Loosened from its bonds, one edge of the cloth fell free, its finely embroidered border dropping into Jake's hands as if inviting him to shake it open. Jake's fingers closed on the soft velvet. Its inky blackness seemed to swallow up the candlelight like a feeding beast. Suddenly Jake's arms were lifted high, his wrists snapped, and he brought the cloth back down. In an instant the bundle unfurled, the folds of velvet spreading across the table like the mantle of darkness that had fallen over the cabin a few hours earlier. A second later the cloth dropped to the tabletop. As it fell into place, the creases of its folds disappeared and the rusty stains of age faded away. The corners of the cloth dropped perfectly, each of them hanging an inch above the floor.

In the center of the cloth a golden star had been embroidered, its points formed by five triangles whose bases, together, inscribed a perfect pentagram. Jake placed a candle on each of the star's five points, and as he set the last one in place, their combined light grew far brighter, washing the shadows from the dark corners of the cabin. Then, as if some unseen being had turned down the wick of a lamp, the light faded once more.

But something in the cloth had changed.

The space within the pentagram appeared to have opened, and as Jake stared into it, he felt as if he were peering into a bottomless abyss.

A wave of dizziness swept over him; Jake felt as if he were teetering on the brink of the abyss, about to plunge over into the darkness— darkness that would swallow him up as surely as the conflagration he'd watched forty years ago had swallowed up his mama.

Uneasy growls rose in both dogs' throats, but as Jake turned away from the altar he'd created, the guttural sounds died away.

One by one Jake picked up the items he'd taken from the tray. There were three small jars and two vials. Removing the lid from the first, he took a pinch of the ground tusk of a wild boar and rubbed it into one of the triangles.

As the candle at the triangle's point flared brighter, Jake murmured a quick prayer: "May your belly be torn, and your entrails spilled."

From the second jar he took the curved thorn of a wild rose. "Let your skin be ripped, and your blood ooze from your wounds." The second candle flared.

He removed the stopper from one of the vials, and the stench of skunk oil filled the room. As he poured a single drop of the oily fluid in front of the third triangle, feeding its struggling flame, another incantation fell from his lips: "May your lungs burn and pus fill your throat."

The broken quill of a porcupine came next, and now four of the candles were flaring up. "May your eyes be pierced and blackness fall over you."

Finally Jake opened the second vial and let flow a single drop of the clear liquid within. As the flame of the last candle swelled and the acid from the last vial ate into the velvet's surface, he uttered one last prayer: "May your flesh be stripped away, and your bones be consumed by dogs."

The two yellow dogs edged closer, as if anticipating a meal.

Once again the combined flames of the candles filled the cabin with a luminous golden glow. Now Jake went to the far corner and picked up one of the tattered canvas bags in which he carried home the fruits of his trap lines. Tonight, though, it wasn't a nutria the sack contained, or the carcass of a weasel or otter or possum.

Tonight the bag contained the prize he'd captured the night before.

Carefully, respectfully, he lifted the carcass of Kimberley Conway's cat from the folds of the canvas. The animal's eyes were open, and it seemed to watch him as he laid it in the center of the pentagram.

From a rack above the kitchen counter, he took a filleting knife whose blade was worn thin from years of honing.

In the brilliant light of the flaring candles, Jake Cumberland set about his work.

In half an hour it was done.

He'd divided the entrails of the cat into four equal portions, and each of the portions had been seared by the flame of one of the first four candles.

The cat's hide, scraped free of every scrap of flesh, was held over the fifth candle. The flame consumed a patch of its fur as quickly as the acid had eaten through the velvet on which the candle stood.

The ritual complete, Jake packed away the entrails, and the hide and head, in his canvas bag and blew out the candles. As their light died away, the smoke in the room began to clear, taking with it the foul odor of the skunk oil.

The white powder of the boar's tusk vanished into the nap of the velvet, along with the rose's thorn and the porcupine's quill.

The hole eaten through the cloth by the acid disappeared, and as Jake lifted the velvet from the table, it fell once more into the folds from which he'd shaken it loose an hour ago.

As the distant toll of the church bell striking midnight sounded, Jake rebound the cloth with the purple ribbons and returned it to his mama's trunk. He placed the tray back on its supporting rails and closed the lid.

Just before leaving the house with the canvas bag, Jake Cumberland fed his two yellow dogs. They fell hungrily upon the skeleton of the cat, growling and snarling as they ripped the tendons apart and crushed the bones in their jaws.

* * *

The huge clock in the corner of the cavernous living room—an ornately carved piece that had a distinctly Germanic look to it—began tolling the hour as Ted was tearing the plastic seal loose from a fresh bottle of vodka.

The second one, or the third?

He couldn't quite remember, but decided it must be the second. If it was the third, he should have been sound asleep by now, and he wasn't.

He wasn't even close.

His fingers stopped working at the bottle's seal as he counted the hours the clock was striking.

. . . ten . . . eleven . . . twelve . . . thirteen.

Thirteen?

What the hell . . . ? There wasn't any such thing as thirteen o'clock—everyone knew that.

As the seal broke, he gave the cap a twist, then lifted the bottle to his lips and took a healthy swig. The familiar warmth of alcohol flowed comfortingly down his throat and spread through his belly.

And Janet's words—the words that had been slamming at his head all evening—quieted for a few seconds.

She didn't mean it—couldn't mean it! Without him, what the hell would she do? Besides, he'd heard it all before. Wasn't she always whining that she couldn't stand it, that if he didn't stop drinking, she was gonna leave? But she never did—never would. She loved him.

Couldn't live without him.

But what the hell was going on with the clock? Come to think of it, how come it was running at all? He didn't remember winding it. 'Course, Janet or one of the kids could've done that. But he didn't remember hearing it chime before, either.

What the hell kind of clock only struck once, and then struck the wrong time?

Ted struggled off the sofa and lurched over to it, staring up at its etched brass plate. There were dials all over it—one that showed the time, and another that showed the seconds ticking by, and a big one with the moon on it. The clock was running, all right. He could see the pendulum moving. His gaze shifted to the dial that showed the seconds. There was something about it that appealed to him, the way it ticked a notch forward every time the pendulum swung.

It was . . . His mind groped for a word, then found exactly the right one.

Tidy. That's what it was.

Neat and tidy.

The way things should be.

Except that they weren't. Reaching out to steady himself against the bookcase built into the wall next to the clock, he peered around at the room. Even through the haze of alcohol, he could see the curling wallpaper and peeling paint, and the stains in the carpet. What the hell had Janet been doing all day? Couldn't anybody but himself do anything?

His eyes shifted back to the clock.

A couple of minutes past midnight.

Not thirteen o'clock at all.

Stupid. Stupid idea, thinking it could be thirteen o'clock. Musta just miscounted. Reaching up to the glass door that protected the face, he fumbled with it for a second, then managed to pull it open.

He pushed the minute hand forward until it pointed at the three.

But instead of striking the quarter hour, the clock once more began chiming the hours.

Once again, Ted counted.

Again the clock struck thirteen times.

Ted backed away from it, though his eyes remained fixed on its face, as if held there by some unseen force.

As he watched, the hands began to move, and once again the clock began to strike.

A trick! It had to be some kind of trick!

The hands couldn't be moving as fast as it looked like they were—it was impossible.

But as the minute hand came around to the nine, the clock once again tolled thirteen times.

Still unable to tear his eyes from the clock's face, Ted watched as the hand moved inexorably toward the twelve. Unconsciously, he held his breath as the clock began striking for the fifth time. As the deep chord reverberated through the house—once, twice, then thrice—Ted realized that something else was wrong.

The clock still read midnight.

But the minute hand had made a complete revolution! He knew it had! He'd watched it!

—five, six, seven times the clock struck.

Broken. That was it—the thing was just broken!

—ten, eleven, twelve—

Ted waited, his breath still trapped in his lungs, as the note faded away and silence descended. Finally, when he could hear it no more, he slowly exhaled. Turning away, he raised the bottle once more to his lips.

And once more the clock began to strike.

The bottle dropped from his hand. "Janet?" His wife's name slipped unbidden from his mouth. Then he whispered it again: "Janet, help me."

The last tolling of the clock died away. Before it could start again, Ted snatched up the bottle—half of the contents had already drained out onto the carpet—and stumbled out of the living room, pulling the doors closed behind him.

He moved across the huge foyer and into the dining room, pushing its doors tightly closed.

Safe.

Even if the clock started to strike again—

Even before the thought was fully formed he heard it again. But not muffled—not like it was coming from another room at all.

He whirled around.

And there was the clock! Standing against the opposite wall, between the two windows that looked out toward the wilderness behind the carriage house. Ted's heart raced as he told himself it wasn't possible, that the clock was still in the living room, that there wasn't any clock in this room, at least not one like this.

Its tolling grew louder, echoing through the room. Once again Ted dropped the bottle and clamped his hands over his ears, but the striking of the clock grew ever louder—so loud that with every chord it felt as if spikes were being driven into his ears.

Crazy!

He was going crazy!

Fumbling with the latch on the heavy dining room doors, he finally threw them open again, and fled back into the huge entry hall. But the sound followed him, and he realized his mistake—now he was hearing both clocks.

"Janet?" he called out again, instinctively invoking the name of the one person he'd always been able to rely on. "Janet, where are you?"

Upstairs. She was upstairs, in their bedroom.

Got to get there! Got to get upstairs!

He started up the flight, stumbling on the first step and barely catching himself on the mahogany banister. A wave of dizziness swept over him as he pulled himself back upright. His stomach felt queasy.

Drank too much. Drank just a little too much.

Hanging onto the banister with both hands, he pulled himself up a few more steps.

And the tolling of the clock struck him again.

Sagging to his knees, he peered up into the gloom, and there, on the landing, he could see it.

The clock!

The same clock that had been in the living room and the dining room.

"Nooo . . ." he wailed, his voice cracking as a sob of fear choked his throat. Turning away from the tolling clock, he stumbled back toward the foot of the stairs, but missed his footing completely on the third step, reached for the banister, missed again, and tumbled down the stairs, his right shoulder wrenching painfully as he sprawled out on the floor of the entry hall. Ignoring the pain in his shoulder, Ted scrambled to his feet, stumbling from one room to another, searching for some place—any place—that would be free of the terrible striking of the clock. Everywhere he went the clock was there, tolling the impossible hour time after time until it felt as if every part of his body was being subjected to the blows of the hammer.

Finally there was only one door left, and Ted stumbled through it.

He was at the top of a steep flight of stairs leading into the basement. The darkness below him yawned like the gaping mouth of some great beast, and Ted fumbled for a light switch, found one, and flipped it on.

The darkness below was pierced by a beckoning light. His heart still pounding, the terror of the impossible chimes still battering at him, Ted lurched down the stairs until he came to the bottom.

And still the terrible tolling found him.

"Stop it," he whispered, jamming his hands against his ears, but now the sound seemed to come from inside his head itself, throbbing inside his skull, falling into rhythm with his heart.

A stroke!

That was it!

He was having a stroke!

The pain in his head ballooning, he stumbled through another door. Once again he tripped, and this time when he fell to the floor an agonizing knife-twist shot through his right wrist. Screaming, Ted clutched at his wrist.

Another wave of dizziness hit him, and his belly heaved. As the contents of his stomach shot from his mouth, he dropped to the floor and felt the heat of his own vomit on his cheek.

The rancid fumes caused him to puke again, and then, rolling over onto his back, he began to sob.

"No—" he pleaded, his voice breaking and choking.

"Don't want to die. Don't want to."

But he was going to die—lying in the dark chamber with only a few rays of light leaking through the door. He knew it.

With Janet asleep upstairs, he was going to die.

Die alone, die drunk.

Dead drunk.

"No. No. Nooo." A whisper. A sob. "Help me . . . please, help me. Someone, please help me."

He retched again, and then again. He struggled to move, at least to slither away from the pool of vomit in which he lay, but any movement he made was pure agony.

Then, from somewhere deep in the darkness surrounding him, he saw something.

From somewhere hidden in the darkness a mist was rising. A mist that seemed to be illuminated from within, as if a thousand candles were burning unseen in the strange fog. As he stared at the fog, a face began to take shape.

A powerful face, with glowing eyes that bored into the depths of his soul.

A hallucination.

That had to be it—he was hallucinating.

Or dying.

That was it—his life was ebbing away, and this was a spirit come to lead him into the mists of death.

"Help me," he whispered once again. "Please help me."

The mist itself seemed to reach out to him, and he felt a touch—a burning touch—on his cheek.

A voice spoke. A whisper. Neither a woman's voice nor a man's, something unearthly yet distinct. "Will you give me whatever I ask?"

Ted stared up into the glittering eyes. "Yes," he whispered. "Oh, God, yes."

The terrible tolling in Ted's head eased.

The nausea in his belly calmed.

"Anything," he pleaded once again. "I'll do anything. Just help me."

Once again he felt the searing touch.

In an instant the pain in his wrist and shoulder were gone.

In the sudden silence Ted Conway fell into sleep. But just before he surrendered to blankness, he knew that something inside him had changed.

Nothing, he knew, would ever be the same again.

CHAPTER 13

"Jared?"

The sound faded into the silence that surrounded him. At first Jared wasn't really sure he'd heard someone calling his name. But then it came again, faint, barely audible. "Jared!"

His father's voice.

Though he could barely hear it, Jared recognized it immediately, rasping with the anger that was always there, even when his father was sober.

Was he sober now?

Jared couldn't tell.

Then the voice came again, and this time it carried a note of command. "Jared!"

He sounded nearer now, and Jared tensed. His eyes flicked first one way then the other, trying to catch a glimpse of his father. But he saw nothing. Then, as his father called out to him yet again, Jared realized he was lost. But that was crazy—he knew exactly where he was: in the big house in St. Albans, in his room on the second floor. Except now he wasn't. He was in a room—a big room—but there was nothing in it. No furniture, no carpets, nothing hanging on the walls. One of the walls, though, was pierced by two windows. Jared moved close enough to the glass to look out.

Nothing.

It was as if a thick fog had fallen beyond the window, and when he tried to peer into it, his eyes found nothing to focus on. A weird disorientation fell over him, causing him to lose his balance. Staggering, he instinctively reached out to steady himself against the window frame.

His right hand plunged through it, disappearing into the gray morass beyond the boundaries of the room. Jared froze in shock.

He jerked his arm back, and for a single terrible instant thought his hand was gone. But no! It was there, and it didn't hurt, and—

What the hell had happened?

For several long seconds he stood perfectly still, his eyes fixed on the spot where his hand had disappeared. Then, as if drawn by some unseen force, his hand started moving once again toward the same spot.

"No!"

The word jabbed his consciousness like the stinger of a hornet, and Jared jerked back to life. He sprung around, certain his father was standing right behind him. The room was still empty.

He whirled around again. Now the gray fog beyond the window had vanished. Instead there was a blackness that seemed to go on for all eternity. But it was a blackness that was not empty.

As he gazed into it, his heart pounding, he felt something reaching out to him.

Something that wanted to touch his soul.

A strangled cry rising in his throat, Jared backed away from the window, then turned and fled through the room's single door.

He found himself in a corridor, a long, broad passage that seemed to stretch on forever in both directions. He looked one way, then the other. Which way should he go? Panic began to rise in him. One way looked exactly like the other.

But he had to make up his mi—

He stopped.

Something was close to him. Very close.

He held his breath, listening.

Silence.

Yet it was there. He could feel it; it was edging closer.

The hairs on the back of his neck stood on end, and a shiver passed through him.

Behind him! It was behind him, and now he could almost feel its touch.

If it touched him, he would die.

Die, and disappear forever into the terrible blackness he'd glimpsed beyond the window.

Then, once more, he heard his father calling to him. This time Jared followed the voice, racing down the hall, for a moment certain he'd escaped.

Then he felt it again. Still there—the unseen thing that had emerged from the darkness beyond the window crept across the room and reached out to him.

It was behind him again.

He tried to run faster, but no matter how fast he ran, or how far, the passageway stretched endlessly away. Then it forked, and forked again, and again Jared felt a surge of hope. He turned and started down a new corridor. Abruptly, out of nowhere, his way was blocked.

Sister Clarence, pointing at him accusingly, her eyes flashing with daggers of fury.

Turning back, Jared ran in the other direction.

But this time Father MacNeill blocked his path, screaming curses at him and holding a crucifix high, as if trying to ward off the Devil himself.

He whirled again, but now a huge black man, grinning wickedly at him, reached out to grasp his throat. Once more Jared spun away and ran. He dodged in one direction or another, but everywhere he turned the nun was waiting for him, or the priest, or the black man who wanted to strangle him.

Then, once more, he heard his father's voice. "This way! Come this way." Again he dodged this way and that, always following his father's voice, his unseen pursuer drawing ever closer. Urged on by his father's voice, Jared ran until finally he could run no longer. Lungs burning, heart pounding, he collapsed to the floor, his breath coming in gasping pants. Terror and exhaustion overwhelmed him, and he began to sob.

Then, through the overpowering fear, he felt the force from the darkness encircle him, grasping and enclosing him in the dark, suffocating despair he was too tired to resist.

Couldn't run.

Couldn't hide.

Couldn't escape.

It was over.

After what might have been a second or an eternity, Jared heard his father's voice once more.

"Open your eyes, Jared."

He obeyed, but saw nothing at all. It was as if he'd been drawn into the blackness beyond the window of the room he'd fled, been sucked so deep into its vortex that no light would ever again penetrate his world. Then, deep in the blackness, twin embers began to glow. At first they were no more than pinpricks of light, but as Jared watched, they grew larger and larger, burning brighter, moving toward him. Slowly, they began to take on form.

Not lights, but eyes.

Glittering, golden eyes, their pupils not round, but slitted. They seemed to be lit from within, and as they drew closer, the light grew bright enough to show him the face from which they peered.

The face was dark, and covered with scales, and from its mouth— an angry gash between the two dripping holes that were its nostrils—a slithering tongue darted forth. As if hypnotized by the terrible visage, Jared remained where he was, immobile.

The face drew closer yet. Now Jared could feel the tongue flick against his cheek, then move across his jaw and down his body.

Everywhere it touched him, it felt as if a razor had sliced his skin. But instead of blood oozing forth from his wounds, an icy chill crept inward.

The tongue kept moving, creeping over every part of him, and slowly the cold took hold, reaching into him through every pore, like the tendrils of some vile plant growing within him. As it spread he knew there was nothing he could do to throw it off. For the first time since the nightmare began, Jared opened his mouth to scream.

But it was too late.

The ice had already captured him, the darkness taken possession of his soul.

It was as if an electric charge had shot through Kim. She jerked awake, her body convulsing, throwing off sleep like a dog shaking water from its coat. "Jared?" she heard herself cry out. "Jared, what's wrong?"

Why did I do that? The question popped into her mind even as the reverberation of her words died away, and for several seconds she sat perfectly still in her dark room, listening.

Nothing.

Nothing, at least, except the sound of an owl hooting in the distance, some insects chirping, the normal creaking of the house, and the comforting ticking of the old-fashioned wind-up alarm clock she kept by her bed.

Nor could she find any remnants of dreams clinging to the corners of her consciousness. One moment she'd been sound asleep, and the next wide-awake. Wide-awake, and worried about Jared.

The Twin Thing.

But that didn't make sense. Why would it have happened now, in the middle of the night? She picked up the clock and tipped it toward the window, where a little moonlight was seeping in. A little after three-thirty in the morning. Usually, when the Twin Thing happened, she and Jared were both awake. In fact, most of the time, they were together when that sudden understanding passed between them. But she'd read about other twins who had experienced powerful connections. Like knowing when the other was in some kind of trouble. Hurt, or sick, something like that. Could it happen when you were asleep?

Getting up, Kim pulled on the old cotton bathrobe she'd appropriated from her brother when he outgrew it, and went to her door. She listened again, but this time it was for her father. What if he hadn't passed out yet and was still drinking? If he spotted her, he'd yell at her, or want her to stay up and talk to him. Except he wouldn't want her to talk at all—he'd want her to listen while he went on and on about how unfair everything was.

Like anybody ever said life was supposed to be fair. At least she and Jared had figured that one out a long time ago.

Finally, she opened her door a few inches and peered out through the crack. There was enough light coming up from one of the rooms downstairs so she could see all the way across the broad entry hall to Jared's room, opening off the opposite wing of the mezzanine.

His door was closed, and no light showed from the crack beneath it.

Kim paused to listen again. Hearing no sounds drifting up from the floor below, she quickly padded around the mezzanine to her brother's door. "Jared?" she whispered. "Jared!"

She heard a soft whining.

Scout?

But Scout always slept at the foot of Jared's bed, and it was Jared who had to wake the dog up every morning, not vice versa. She twisted the knob, felt the latch come free, eased the door open and peered inside. Instantly, Scout jammed his muzzle in the gap, demanding to be scratched. "What is it, boy?" Kim asked. She pushed the door open wider and knelt down to rub Scout's neck, massaging his shoulders the way she knew he liked it. But a second later Scout pulled away from her and darted to the open window, where he reared up, braced himself on the sill with one paw, and scratched eagerly at the screen with the other. "Oh, no," Kim whispered. "That's how Muffin got—"

Muffin!

Maybe that was it! Maybe it wasn't Jared at all! Maybe Muffin was trying to get back in, and somehow she'd known it!

She crossed to the window and looked out into the night. "Muffin?" she called. Then, trying to keep her voice soft, so only the cat would hear it: "Here, kitty, kitty, kitty. Come on, Muffin!"

"Kim?"

Startled by her brother's voice, Kim whirled around to find Jared glaring at her.

"Jesus, Kim," he said, "what are you doing in my room? What time is it?"

"Three-thirty," she told him. "Something woke me up. I was worried about you—"

"Yeah, right," Jared said, his voice harsh with anger. "You were so worried about me you came in and started hollering for your damn cat."

Kim's mouth dropped open in surprise. Jared had never spoken to her like that—never! "I *was* worried about you," she protested. "But when Scout went to the window, I—"

"Will you just go back to bed?" Jared cut in.

"Well, sor-*reee*," Kim shot back. "Next time I get worried about you, I'll just go back to sleep!"

"Fine!" Jared said, flopping back down onto his pillow and turning his back on his sister. "Just leave me alone, okay?"

Well, if that's how you feel, fine! Kim said to herself as she moved toward the door. But before leaving his room, she turned back. "Jared?" she said. "Are you sure you're okay?"

Jared emitted an exaggerated sigh. "What do I have to do, take a physical? Just shut the door and leave me alone!"

Kim slammed it hard enough to make him jump.

"Jesus," he complained to Scout, now at the side of the bed, pawing at him. "Like it was my fault or something!" But as he turned over to go back to sleep, he had a vague memory of a dream he'd had—a nightmare, in which he'd been running through the halls of the house, trying to get away from Sister Clarence, and Father MacNeill, and a big, black guy who looked kind of familiar but whose name he couldn't quite remember.

But it hadn't been Kim who finally came to his rescue. It was his dad.

His dad! Yeah, like that would ever happen! If he was ever really in trouble, his dad would probably be too drunk to do anything but watch him die. Then, remembering what he'd overheard earlier, when his parents were fighting, he wondered if his mother really meant it this time about leaving. Probably not—she'd said it all before. Jared turned over in bed again, and Scout scratched at him again. "What's with you, boy? Just lie down and go to sleep, okay?"

But instead of lying down, the big dog ran to the window and scratched at the screen. Realizing the dog wouldn't leave him alone, Jared moved to the window and crouched next to Scout, looking out. "What is it, boy?" he asked. "What's out there?" Scout bounded to the bedroom door, whimpered eagerly, and scratched at it. "Okay, I get the message," Jared groused. He pulled on his jeans and a T-shirt, and shoved his feet into a pair of sneakers.

When he opened the bedroom door, Scout raced for the stairs. The dog disappeared through the dining room, toward the kitchen, long before Jared reached the landing. He paused halfway down the stairs, listening for any sign of his father. Chances were he'd passed out hours ago, but you never knew.

Jared decided he didn't even want to think about it.

He hurried down the rest of the stairs, made his way through the dark dining room and into the kitchen, where Scout stood at the back door, scratching and whimpering to be let out. Jared peered through the window, searching for whatever Scout was upset about, but he couldn't see anything.

He was about to open the door and let the dog outside when he remembered what had happened to Muffin. According to Kim, the cat had just gone out the window and disappeared.

More likely, he thought, a raccoon got her, or a bobcat, or something.

Dumb cat.

Still, if there were something out there, and Scout went after it . . .

Sighing, Jared poked around in the service porch until he found an old piece of clothesline. Giving it a couple of yanks, he decided it would hold, and tied one end of it to Scout's collar. Then he let the big retriever out the back door, expecting the dog to move a few steps out into the overgrown yard and lift his leg. Instead, Scout raced off toward the carriage house, the rope burning across Jared's palm as the dog pulled it through his fingers. Throwing a couple of quick loops around his wrist, the boy reined the dog to a stop, but when Scout continued to pull, Jared started down the back steps into the yard.

Scout led him around to the back of the carriage house, then reared up, placing his forepaws on the building's siding.

And in the moonlight, Jared saw it.

Hanging with head down, its tongue lolling out of its mouth, was Muffin.

Or at least what was left of Muffin.

The cat's hide had been nailed neatly to the wall, the legs spread, even the tail tacked in a curve so it looked as if Muffin were trying to climb down the wall.

It was just out of Scout's reach, but the dog kept stretching, as if trying to touch the cat's head.

Jared stared at the hide for a long time, then reached out and tore it loose from the wall. He was about to throw it into one of the garbage cans when he changed his mind. What if Kim came out in the morning and found it? Better put it somewhere else. He cast about in his mind and remembered the packing boxes he'd stowed inside the carriage house.

Leaving Scout whimpering next to the wall where the hide had been nailed, Jared disappeared into the building. A moment later he was back. "Okay, Scout," he said, his voice low but hard. "Who did it? Show me who did it, Scout. Find him!"

In response, the dog began sniffing around the area. Then, catching a scent, he headed for the scrubby woods that edged the eastern boundary of the property. Pulling in most of the clothesline, Jared followed Scout to the edge of the woods, where he stopped.

Maybe he should go back and try to find a flashlight, he thought. But who even knew which one of the cartons to look in? Besides, the moon was still high, and the night was clear.

And Scout could see anything, even in the dark.

"Okay, boy," he said softly, making up his mind. "Let's go."

Following close behind the dog, giving him no more than six feet of rope, Jared made his way along the path through the woods. The dog kept his nose to the ground, moving quickly, taking them farther and farther from the house. Then, just as Jared was about to pull Scout off the scent and start back toward him, the retriever froze, one foot off the ground, tail extended.

Jared crept forward and dropped to his knees next to the big dog. He peered through the darkness, and at first saw nothing. Then, barely visible in the gloom, he made out the silhouette of a cabin. "There?" he asked. "Is that where he came from?"

Scout trembled, whining eagerly. Then he tensed.

Feeling the dog's muscles harden, Jared, too, held perfectly still, listening.

Off to the left he heard something.

Not much. Just the softest rustling, as if something were moving in the bushes.

Something, or some*one*?

Jared's heart began pounding, and for a second he was certain that whatever—or *who*ever—was out there must surely hear it.

The rustling came again, and then something else.

The snap of a twig?

He heard it again.

Closer this time.

Much closer.

His fingers tightening on Scout's collar, he pulled the dog back. "Come on, Scout," he whispered. "We'd better—"

Before he could finish his sentence, or move away, the night was rent by a howling sound that exploded out of the cabin. A second later the howling dropped into the steady baying of hounds. The cabin door

opened. An oil lamp was held high, casting a yellowish glow a few feet
from the ramshackle structure. "Who's out there?" a rough voice yelled.
"I'm warnin' you! You get away right now, or I'm turnin' these dogs
loose!"

Under the cover of the hounds' baying, Jared scurried back down
the path, pulling Scout with him.

Twenty minutes later, he crept back into the house and up to his
room. Stripping off his clothes, he slipped back into bed. Though he'd
been out only an hour, he felt as if he'd been up all night. But it didn't
matter how he felt—he'd found out what he needed to know.

He'd found out, and he'd do something about it.

CHAPTER 14

I'm leaving him. This time, I'm actually going to leave him.
     It had been the last thought in Janet's mind last night, and it was still there as the alarm dragged her out of sleep that morning. She started to get out of bed, then stopped.

Something had changed.

She listened.

Nothing in the house sounded different. A mockingbird was singing in the yard outside, not quite drowning out a rooster crowing in the distance, and when she went to the window, she saw only a sunny morning, the soft blue of the sky broken by a few fluffy clouds. Her gaze dropped to the landscape around the house, and as she focused on the kudzu that had wrapped itself around every growing thing in the yard, a wave of claustrophobia broke over her. She felt as if she couldn't breathe, and her arms—no, her whole body—were wrapped in layers of cloth from which she couldn't free herself. Dear God, what was happening to her? She was suffocating; she could hardly move—

No! She wasn't suffocating. It was only the kudzu. And once the house and the yard were free of it— She cut off the thought, refusing even to finish it.

Out, she reminded herself. *I'm getting out.* She turned away from the window and surveyed the room. Most of her clothes were still packed in the boxes they'd brought from Shreveport. Most of the kids' things were still packed as well. Would all those cartons fit into the Toyota? And she'd have to repack some suitcases . . .

The Toyota! Where was it?

She whirled back to the window and gazed down at the empty space where Ted had parked the car when he'd finally come home yesterday.

Had he put it in the carriage house?

Of course not—he'd left it outside, and spent the rest of the evening drinking. By the time she'd finally told him she was leaving, he'd been barely able to stand up, let alone—

Abruptly, she understood.

If he took the car, she couldn't take it herself. Her moment of panic when she'd seen that the car was gone dissolved into anger. How drunk must he have been to think that taking the car would keep her here?

Far too drunk to drive.

A stab of fear jabbed through her anger, and she sagged back down onto the bed, her roiling emotions draining the energy out of her. Automatically, she reached for the phone by the bed. How many times had she done this? How many times had she called the police, called the hospitals, even called the morgue, looking for her husband?

She couldn't even count them.

It wasn't until she'd started dialing the old-fashioned Princess phone on the nightstand that she remembered it wasn't hooked up. The telephone man was supposed to come today.

This morning, or this afternoon?

She couldn't remember.

And suddenly she didn't care.

Get through it, she told herself. *Just get dressed, fix some breakfast, get the kids off to school, and get through it. He'll come back. He always does. And when he does . . .*

When he did, she would be ready. She'd have a suitcase packed, and one for the kids, and as soon as he showed up, she'd take the car, and that would be that. She'd put Molly and Scout in the backseat, pick up the kids at St. Ignatius, and they'd be gone.

Pulling on her robe, she lifted Molly—who was rubbing her eyes sleepily—out of her crib, unlocked the bedroom door, and carried her youngest daughter down to the kitchen. Kim had already started a pot of coffee and was getting cereal and milk out of the refrigerator.

But there was no sign of Jared, who was usually up even earlier than Kim.

"Where's your brother?" she asked.

Kim's eyes clouded and she shrugged her shoulders. "Still asleep, I guess," she said. The listlessness in her voice spoke far more clearly than the words she had uttered.

They'd heard it all, Janet thought. *They both heard the whole thing.* "I guess you know I've decided to leave your father," she said carefully.

Kim turned to look at her. "You mean we're going back to Shreveport?"

Janet hesitated, then nodded. Now that Kim had spoken the words out loud, she realized that this time she really did mean it. She bit her lip, trying to hold back tears, but couldn't hold them back any longer. "I just can't take it anymore," she said, crying softly now. "I can't, and you and Jared can't, either. I don't know what we're going to do, but I don't know what else to do. I—" Janet sank into one of the kitchen chairs as Molly began crying, too.

Kim lifted her little sister out of her mother's arms. "It'll be okay, Mom," she said as Molly calmed down. "We'll figure it out. Jared and I can get jobs after school—"

She stopped abruptly, and Janet realized someone else had just come into the room. *No*, she said silently to herself. *Don't let it be Ted. Not now. Not right now. Just give me a little time.* But when she turned, she saw that it wasn't Ted, it was Jared.

Her son stood in the doorway, his worn denim jacket slung carelessly over his shoulder. His head was cocked and his eyes were fixed on Kim.

"What do you mean, we'll get jobs after school?" Jared asked.

Janet opened her mouth, but it was Kim who spoke. "Mom says we're going back to Shreveport. After last night—"

"Yeah, right," Jared cut in, rolling his eyes scornfully. "Mom's not going anywhere. None of us are." With a derisive toss of his head, he turned away. "See you at school."

He was gone before either Kim or Janet could speak. The front door slammed. As Molly began crying again, Janet once more struggled to control her own tears. "Oh, God," she said, her voice breaking as the turmoil of emotions she'd been through since she'd awakened overwhelmed her. "I'm sorry. I'm so sorry. How could I have put you both through all of this?" She buried her face in her hands, sobbing.

"It'll be all right, Mom," she heard her daughter say, Kim's hand on her shoulder. "As soon as we get out of here, everything will be all right."

Fifteen minutes later, after cleaning up the kitchen, Kim left the house for St. Ignatius.

It wasn't until she was halfway there that it hit her.

Not once had she walked to school alone, she realized. Always before, until this morning, Jared had been with her.

But not today.

Today she was walking by herself.

But it was more than that: today she couldn't even find Jared in that strange corner of her mind where, for as long as she could remember, she'd always felt his presence, always felt a connection to her twin.

Today, that connection was gone.

Today, she was truly by herself.

CHAPTER 15

The problem with being mayor of St. Albans—or anyplace else, for that matter—was that you had to be nice to everyone, whether you liked them or not. And with the man who now sat across from Phil Engstrom, who had held the office of mayor for ten years, and fully intended to hold it for at least twenty more, the problem became a double-edged sword. Mayor Engstrom's visitor that morning was Father Mac-Neill, who was not only a constituent—though the priest regularly assured him that the Church was *always* above politics—but was Phil Engstrom's confessor, as well. The cleric invariably provided the extra emphasis to the word *always* in his disclaimer of any church interest in local politics, as if somehow that would convince Engstrom of the statement's veracity. The fact that Phil had never particularly liked MacNeill only added to the problem, but at least this morning nothing so important as his soul was at stake. Of course, his dislike of the priest had long ago made him less than candid in the confessional. That, he thought, combined with his recent yearnings to skip mass entirely in favor of putting in eighteen holes at the new course up in Valhalla, had undoubtedly already condemned him to an eternity in purgatory, or worse. Now, as the priest finally came to the point after ten minutes of small talk to which Engstrom had made all the proper responses, he put on his best look of concerned interest.

"It just doesn't seem that the old Conway house is the right place for a hotel," the priest said. "It's always been a residential area, and if we allow one commercial enterprise to take root there, how can we protect the integrity of the neighborhood?"

Engstrom leaned back in his chair, tenting his fingers over a belly that had lately been suffering from a little too much of his wife's perfectly fried chicken. "I'm not ezactly sure I'm followin' your interest in all this," he said, sweetening his voice with a little extra drawl and putting on a look of vague confusion. "Sort of seems like fixin' the old Conway place up would be good for the community. Pretty old house like that— seems a shame to just let it go to the kudzu, now doesn't it? And now's I think about it, it's not really in any specific neighborhood, is it? Not too many houses out there on Pontchartrain, and it's at the end of the street, kinda set off by itself, so it doesn't hardly seem like much of a variance would have to be made." Something flashed over the priest's face that Phil Engstrom couldn't quite put his finger on. "'Course, if there's somethin' I don't know about, I'm sure here to listen." He gave the priest a smile. "Just like you're always there to hear me out when I been less than the man I'd like to be, right?"

Father MacNeill returned the smile, but Engstrom felt no warmth from it. "It *is* a lovely old house," the priest agreed, but something in his voice warned the mayor what was coming next. "But I'm not sure the Conways are the kind of people we want to encourage."

Aha! Engstrom thought. *Now we get to the grits.* "An' why might that be?" he asked. "Ya'll know somethin' about 'em that the rest of us don't?"

Father MacNeill's lips pursed and his expression tightened, a sign that he was about to confide in the mayor.

Sure enough, the priest leaned forward slightly, and his eyes darted around the office as if seeking some unseen person who might be eavesdropping. "If I might speak confidentially . . . ?" he began, letting his voice trail off in an invitation to Engstrom to reassure him that his confidence would not be violated.

"Ya'll can think of this office as my own personal confessional," the mayor said, picking up his cue. "You'd be surprised the things I've heard in here, and I'm happy to tell you there's not a single soul in St. Albans ever regretted talkin' to me."

Father MacNeill still hesitated, as if trying to make up his mind, though Engstrom suspected the man paused only to decide how much poison to throw in the well. "He's . . . evil," the priest finally said. "Whenever there have been Conway men living in this town, there has been trouble." For the next five minutes he detailed the death of George Conway, as if Phil Engstrom had never heard the story before. "As the spiritual guardian of our community, I simply don't believe I can countenance his presence here," Father MacNeill finally concluded.

Phil Engstrom leaned back in his chair and nodded in satisfaction. "I do appreciate your comin' down here to fill me in on all this, Father Mack. I purely do. And I can tell you I'll give everything you've told me every consideration if Conway ever tries to bring a variance up before the council." He glanced at the clock on the wall with a practiced manner that would ensure that his visitor not only saw him, but thought he was trying to check the time surreptitiously. "It's people like you who make this town what it is," he went on, launching into what he and Marge called his Exit Speech. Sure enough, the priest was already getting up from his chair, so Engstrom quickly got to his own feet and strode around the desk to walk his visitor to the door. He went through the rest of the speech, putting a genial arm around the priest's shoulders as he opened the door. "I know how busy you are, and I can't thank you enough for cuttin' into your schedule."

When Father MacNeill had left, Phil Engstrom went back to his desk, sat down in the big black-leather executive chair the council had approved for him only last year, and swiveled around to gaze out the window. It was a view he never tired of. The town square was spread out across the street, and beyond that lay a neighborhood of generously proportioned old houses, most of them sitting on lots of at least half an acre, shaded by huge spreading oaks and magnolias that seemed to throw a comforting green quilt over the whole town. But in the midst of that neighborhood, its steeple poking through the leafy canopy like a needle through the quilt, was the church of St. Ignatius.

It was also a needle in Phil Engstrom's side, a constant reminder that his was not the only power base in St. Albans, and that if he wanted to keep his office, he'd better pay more than simple lip service to Father MacNeill.

Not that there could be anything to what the priest had told him; the very idea that Ted Conway was "evil" was ridiculous on the face of it. Still, if a man wanted to remain in that big black-leather chair—and Phil Engstrom very much liked being mayor of St. Albans—he had to choose his battles carefully, and Ted Conway's battle was one he didn't need to fight. Maybe it might be just as well to put a few well-placed words in certain of the town's ears, he thought. Of course, if he let Father Mack have his way on this, he'd have to find another issue—something trivial, preferably—upon which to thwart the priest, so MacNeill didn't start getting any ideas about who was really in charge. Sighing, and wondering if maybe he could trade off his support for the priest on this hotel deal for a few Sundays on the golf course, he reached for the phone. A few well-placed calls would get "a groundswell of public opinion" rolling against whatever plan this Conway person might have in mind. But just as his fingers touched the receiver, the instrument came alive, and he heard Myrtle Pettibone's voice float over the intercom.

"There's a Mr. Conway here to see you," his secretary said. "A Mr. Ted Conway?"

Phil hesitated, but only for a moment. Might as well at least have a look at the chicken whose head he was about to chop off. "Well, send him on in," he boomed, already preparing his warmest smile of welcome. "Don't keep him waiting, Myrt. Just send him on in!"

Half an hour later Phil Engstrom was once again alone in his office, but when he picked up the phone, it wasn't to start torpedoing Ted Conway's plan. In fact, sometime in the last thirty minutes he'd completely changed his mind about where he stood on this particular deal. Ted Conway, it turned out, wasn't the man he'd been expecting at all. In fact, he'd turned out to be a downright fine fellow—"charming" was the word his wife would have used—and everything he'd said had made perfect sense to Phil Engstrom. By the time the half-hour meeting had ended, he knew Conway was not only a man he could work with, but a man he could be friends with, as well. But if he was going to go against Father Mack on this thing—and he surely was—he would have to be subtle.

Dialing his home number, Phil drummed his fingers impatiently on the desk while he waited for Marge to answer, meanwhile steeling himself to keep even the slightest trace of annoyance out of his voice when she finally did. He'd learned years ago that there wasn't any point in riling up a horse you were planning to break. "I think we ought to be havin' those new people to a dinner party," he said after his wife had finished repeating every word she and her mother had exchanged that morning. "Maybe on Saturday night."

"*This* Saturday?" Marge fretted. Phil read her intonation perfectly: Marge always worried that if she called people for dinner less than two weeks in advance, it might look as though the Engstroms' calendar wasn't full. "Don't you think it's awfully late to be—"

"Now, honeychild," Phil cut in smoothly, "you know people always love your fried chicken. I can't think of a single person in this town who wouldn't drop whatever they're doing for one of your dinners. And I want you to invite the new people—the Conways." There was a long silence, and for a moment Phil was afraid Father Mack might already have talked to his wife. But when Marge finally spoke, he relaxed.

"You're up to something, aren't you?" she asked.

"Who, me?" Phil countered with exaggerated innocence. Home free.

"Don't you try to fool me," Marge scolded. "I know how you stay mayor of this town."

"And how you stay Mrs. Mayor," Phil replied. "Here's what I want you to do . . ." As he talked, he could almost see Marge making quick notes, already planning the menu, the flowers, the seating plan, and every other detail that would make the evening perfect.

Marge would set the stage.

He would introduce the cast.

But the rest would be up to Ted Conway; the man would have to sink or swim on his own.

Either way, nobody would ever be able to accuse Phil Engstrom of having taken a stand.

Still, he'd go this far. After all, Ted Conway had struck him as a hell of a nice fellow, and it couldn't hurt just to introduce the man to a few people.

Could it?

CHAPTER 16

The clouds gathering in the sky were a perfect reflection of Janet's mood—dark and angry, promising that before the day was over a major storm would rage over St. Albans. But there would be no storm in the Conway house that day. No matter what Ted's condition might be when he eventually came home—*if* he came home—she would ignore it. Her suitcase was already packed and waiting by the door next to the boxes she'd packed for the children. She would simply put Molly in the Toyota, pile the boxes in, and leave. If school wasn't yet out, she'd wait for the twins in front of St. Ignatius, and they'd leave from there.

No more arguments.

No more fights.

No more scenes.

But what if Ted didn't come home?

What if he'd wrecked the Toyota?

That won't happen, she told herself.

But what if it did?

She tried to come up with a list of people she might call to come and rescue her and the children from St. Albans. Only there wasn't a single person she felt she could ask to come down and pick them up.

And that, she thought morosely as she gazed out at the gathering thunderheads, was something she should have thought about years ago, when she first realized Ted's drinking was eroding her friendships. In those days, she'd told herself her friends were wrong about Ted, but now, nearly twenty years later, she knew they hadn't been.

And now, when she'd finally decided it was over, there was no one left for her to call.

Janet was about to turn away from the living room window when she saw a car pull into the driveway. A moment later a woman picked her way through the tangle in the front yard—a woman whose bearing marked her as someone who counted, at least in St. Albans. Though her dress was linen, she was the type who could wear it all day without a single wrinkle daring to show. Her hair was ash-blond and framed her face in the simple blunt cut that seemed never to go out of style for a certain sort of woman.

"I'm Marge Engstrom," the woman said as Janet opened the door. She was smiling easily, her hand extended. "For the last half hour I've been trying to think of some clever reason why I'm here, but I'm afraid I'm not very good at dissembling. My husband is the mayor of St. Albans, and he sent me. It seems you have a problem. May I come in?" Somehow, Marge Engstrom managed to slip through the door before Janet really thought about whether she wanted to invite her in or not. "This is a terrible intrusion, isn't it? But since you don't have a phone yet, what could I do?" She scanned the expanse of the huge entry hall and her smile faded. "Oh, my, this *is* a mess, isn't it?" As she heard her own words, she reddened. "Oh, Lord, listen to me. Phil always says I talk before I think, and there I go. I'm so sorry. I—"

"It's all right," Janet assured her. "It is a mess. In fact, it's a horrible mess!" *Stop!* she told herself. *Whatever the reason she's here, it isn't to hear about your marriage.* She took a deep breath, then started over. "Would you like a cup of coffee?"

"Actually, I'd like to see this house," Marge told her. "And maybe you can tell me just what it is that has Father MacNeill in such an uproar?"

By the time they entered the kitchen half an hour later, Janet had decided she liked Marge Engstrom's directness and the warmth the woman exuded like a comfortable old blanket. Marge had told her exactly why she was there, and what the purpose of her proposed dinner party was. For her part, Janet had held back from unburdening herself to this woman she barely knew.

Still, she had to say something. But what?

That she was going to be out of town for a few days and they would set something up when she got back? *"Don't ever lie, Janet,"* she heard her mother admonishing her from the dim reaches of her childhood. *"Lying only makes a bad situation worse."* If she told the truth—that her husband was a drunk, and she was planning to leave him that very day— what chance would Ted ever have—

Ted!? Why was she worrying about him? Besides, didn't Marge Engstrom—and everyone else in St. Albans, for that matter—deserve to know the truth? Before she could say anything, though, she saw their old Toyota pull into the driveway, towing a trailer filled with more building supplies—at least five times as much as Ted had brought home the day before.

Who was going to unload it all, with Jared at school? she wondered. Unless she did it herself, she was sure the supplies would remain in the open trailer to be ruined as soon as the steadily building storm broke. And when Ted heard about Father MacNeill's visit to Phil Engstrom, she knew exactly what would happen.

First he'd get mad.

Then he'd get drunk.

Then he'd start feeling sorry for himself.

Then he'd start blaming her, or the kids, or anyone else he could think of. And given the hangover he was still undoubtedly nursing after last night, she suspected he'd probably already had a couple of drinks this morning. She braced herself for the scene to come, wishing there were some way to get Marge Engstrom out of the house, or at least to warn her. But it was too late. Ted was already coming through the back door.

"Do I smell coffee?" he asked. "Boy, would a cup of that taste good right now!" Janet, already on her feet, started toward the stove, but Ted waved her back to her chair. "Sit, sit! I can get it myself." Picking a cup out of the sink, he rinsed it, and, as he filled it with coffee, offered one of his dazzling smiles to Marge Engstrom. "I'm Ted Conway," he said. "And you'd be Phil Engstrom's wife, right?"

Janet stared at him, bewildered. After last night, his eyes should be bloodshot, his face haggard, and his mood even nastier than it had been yesterday afternoon. But his eyes were clear, there was a buoyancy to his step, and he was treating Marge Engstrom to the brilliant white smile Janet hadn't seen in years.

A smile she knew would darken into black rage as soon as Marge explained why she'd come, to invite them to a dinner party she was proposing for Saturday evening.

But Ted's smile didn't darken. It simply softened into an expression that looked more like sympathetic regret than anything else.

"Well, I guess I can't expect everyone to think my idea's as terrific as I do," he said. "I'm just glad we're not going to be totally on our own." His eyes shifted to Janet. "Do we have any plans for Saturday night?"

As if we've had plans for any Saturday night in the last ten years, Janet thought bitterly. She shook her head.

Ted turned back to Marge Engstrom. "Then we'll see you on Saturday. Can we bring anything?"

Bring anything? Janet silently echoed. *The only things Ted had ever*

*taken to a party were the half-dozen drinks he'd belted down before they
got there.* But what did it matter, really? With her and the kids gone, the
odds of Ted even remembering the dinner party were next to zero, and the
chances of him showing up sober were far less than that. And whatever
chance he might have had at enlisting the mayor's support would vanish.

But it wasn't her problem anymore.

"I'll have to check the calendar," she said. She'd been covering up
for Ted for so many years that her voice betrayed none of her emotions.
"Perhaps I'll call you tomorrow?" But when Marge left a few minutes
later, the neutrality vanished from her tone. "Where have you been?" she
demanded. "Do you have any idea what it's like to wake up and find that
your mate—who was so stinking drunk he couldn't stand up straight the
last time you saw him—has taken off in the car?" Ted opened his mouth
to reply, but Janet didn't give him the chance. "Of course you don't! And
you never will, as long as you're married to me. But that's going to end,
Ted. I've had it! Do you understand? I've finally and forever had it!" She
paused, her breath momentarily spent, and braced herself for the explosion.

"I'm sorry," he said softly. "I don't know why you've put up with it
all these years."

The genuine contrition she heard in his voice threw Janet totally off
stride. She'd been prepared for the usual scene: a fight, building until she
was finally reduced to tears. Only then, after he'd shouted her down, battering at her defenses until she had none left, would he finally gather her
in his arms and promise that things would be different. But never, not in
all the years since the drinking had started, had he suggested that she
shouldn't have put up with his drinking at all.

But even now she was certain that whatever he said, his motivations
were simple—to keep her with him, to keep her taking care of him. Her
eyes narrowed suspiciously. "Why would you know?" she asked, her
voice reflecting the exhaustion she suddenly felt. "You've been too drunk
to know anything, haven't you? Too drunk to know why you lose your
jobs, and too drunk to know how frightened your kids are of you. And
way too drunk to know what you've done to me."

Molly, standing up in her playpen and clutching at the netting with
her tiny fingers, began to cry, and Janet reached down to scoop her up.
"It's all right, baby," she cooed. "Mommy and Daddy aren't going to
have a fight. We're not ever going to fight again." Her eyes shifted back
to Ted. "I'm leaving this afternoon," she told him, "as soon as I get the
few things I'm taking with me into the car." Scout, who had been curled
up on the floor, suddenly rose, whining almost as if he knew what she was
saying. "Don't worry, boy," she told the big dog. "We'll take you, too."

Once again she braced herself against the attack Ted might mount on her determination, marshaling her grievances like an army, ready to repel anything he might say. Once again, he surprised her.

"Let me tell you what happened last night," he said so quietly it commanded her full attention.

But she didn't lower her guard an inch. "You mean you remember?"

Ted nodded. "Every bit of it. After you left, I kept drinking, and started wandering around the house. And everywhere I went, all I saw was a mess." A painful smile twisted his lips. "It was like looking at myself," he went on, his gesture sweeping over the kitchen and beyond, to the tangled mess of the grounds surrounding the house. "Everything about it's been let go, just like I've let myself go. Another few years, and it's literally going to fall apart." He turned back to Janet and met her gaze steadily. "Just like me," he went on. "Last night it finally came to me. I'm not just killing our marriage, and my relations with my kids, and my career. If you can call that job at the Majestic a career," he added derisively, but without even a hint of the self-pity Janet had always heard in his previous pleas. "I'm killing myself, too. I decided I didn't want to die."

Janet felt the first tiny crack develop in her defenses, and fought against it. "And," she asked, deliberately edging her voice with sarcasm, "having stumbled drunkenly upon this great truth, what exactly did you decide to do about it?"

Ted flinched, but didn't try to turn away. "I made myself sick," he replied. "I went down in the basement, and I threw up more than I've ever thrown up in my life." For the first time since he'd begun to talk, a genuine smile played around the corners of his mouth, and a sparkle of humor lit his eyes. "And you have to admit, I've thrown up some doozies in my life." When Janet failed to respond to his stab at a joke, his smile fled. "Look at me," he said softly. "Just look at my eyes."

Don't do it, Janet told herself. But she could feel the cracks in her resolve widening, and finally she allowed herself to look into his eyes.

Something *had* changed.

It wasn't just their clarity, which was surprising enough, given how much he'd been drinking last night. Still, if he'd really thrown up most of it, it might be possible that he'd slept it off.

It was as if he read her mind: "When you drink as much as I've been drinking, it takes a hell of a lot to bring on a hangover."

Janet made no reply, but still she gazed into his eyes. There was something familiar there, something dimly remembered.

And then she knew. It was as if she were looking into Ted's eyes when they'd first met, and she'd felt as if she could sink right into him through his eyes, or float in their blue clarity forever, needing nothing else but him, and his caress, and the look in his eyes when they beheld her.

"Come with me," he said now. Lifting Molly out of her arms and settling her gently back into the playpen, Ted took Janet's hand and led her out of the kitchen, through the entry hall and the living room, to the small room in which she'd found him last night.

The empty bottle still lay on the sofa, and the box of full ones still sat on the hearth, just as it had last night. As Ted lifted a bottle of vodka from the box, broke its seal, and opened it, Janet felt a cold emptiness in her stomach. Was he planning to prove that he'd changed by having a drink? But instead of raising the bottle to his lips, he held it over the sink in the wet bar that had been built next to the fireplace and tipped it up.

Its contents flowed down the drain.

He reached for another bottle, and drained it, too.

And then another, and another, until every bottle in the box was empty. "Have you ever known me to do that before?" he asked.

In her mind, all the assurances and all the promises he'd ever made echoed.

"I don't have to drink—I like to drink."

"Just because it's here doesn't mean I'll drink it."

"I won't touch a drop, but we have to have something to serve company, don't we?"

How many times had she heard it? How many variations had there been? And the couple of times she'd simply poured out his liquor herself, he'd only replaced it, usually within the hour. He'd even had a rationalization for that: *"Even if I decide to have a drink—which I won't—wouldn't you rather I had it here?"*

No! she had wanted to scream. *I don't want you to drink at all!*

But no matter what she'd said, it didn't do any good. There had never been a time—unless they ran completely out of money—when there wasn't any liquor in the house. Then she remembered the trailer behind the Toyota.

Again it was as if he'd read her mind. "And I didn't buy any more," he said. There was a flash of lightning, a crash of thunder shook the house, and the first drops of rain began to fall. "Oh, Jesus," Ted cried. "I've got to get all the stuff in the trailer into the carriage house before it gets ruined!" Dropping the last of the bottles into the sink, he raced through the house and out the back door. By the time Janet caught up with him, he was already digging deep into the trailer's depths. "There's some plastic drop cloths—" His hand closed on something and he pulled it out. "Here!" he cried. Ripping a plastic bag open, he pulled one of the polyethylene sheets out and began shaking it open. A minute later he and Janet had it stretched out over the trailer, protecting its contents from the storm. But already the wind was starting to pull at it; in a few minutes it would be gone. "Get in the car," Ted told her as the rain came down harder. "I'll open the carriage house doors, and you can pull it in."

"The garage isn't big enough," Janet protested.

"Back it in," Ted replied. "I'll guide you." The rain was pouring down in sheets now.

"But you'll get soaked—" Janet began, but Ted was already pulling the double doors of the carriage house open. She got into the Toyota, and a moment later Ted was calling out instructions to her.

Janet edged the trailer back, twisting the wheel first one way, then another, trying to maneuver the trailer through the doors into the shelter of the carriage house. Twice she had to pull all the way forward and start over again.

Meanwhile the rain came down harder, until she could hardly see Ted, even with the windshield wipers going full blast.

On the third try, she managed to ease the trailer—and the back half of the Toyota—into the carriage house, and cringed when she felt the right rear fender scrape against the doorframe. Getting out, she dashed into the shelter of the structure, where she found Ted adding another sheet of plastic to the trailer, and tying both sheets down with a length of clothesline. "I wondered why I bought this," he said as he secured the last corner. "Now I know." He looked up through the rafters at the badly leaking roof. "Maybe I ought to get up there and fix that right now."

"Are you crazy?" Janet demanded. "You'd slip off and break your neck!"

"But—"

"No 'buts,' " Janet said. "Let's get in the house before it gets any worse."

Together, they sprinted across the yard to the back door, ducking into the kitchen just as another bolt of lightning ripped at the clouds, followed by a crash of thunder that sent Molly into a fit of terrified screaming. This time it was Ted who plucked her out of the playpen.

"It's okay," he crooned. "Just a little thunder. Can't hurt Daddy's little sweetheart."

As she watched him soothe their youngest child, Janet tried to decide whether this was just another performance designed to keep her here.

But if this were an act, it would take a far better actor than Ted had ever been.

Soaking wet, he was gently soothing Molly's fears away, and when the little girl was finally quiet again, he actually smiled at Janet. "I think it went pretty well out there, all things considered," he said.

Janet looked straight at him. "You do know I hit the doorpost with the right rear fender, don't you?" she asked.

Ted shrugged. "With that car, who's going to notice? I'm amazed you were able to do it at all, the way that rain's coming down." After a moment's silence he said, "I know you have to go." His voice was very quiet. "I'll get the trailer unhitched." He hesitated again, and she could almost feel him searching for the right words. But it was as if he knew it was too late, that there weren't any right words anymore. Once again his eyes—as blue and clear and deep as on the day she'd met him—found hers. "I'm sorry," he said softly. "I'm sorry for all of it." He started toward the back door, and she knew—knew deep in her soul—that he was telling her the truth.

Something inside him had, indeed, finally changed.

"Ted?"

He paused, then turned to look at her.

"Maybe one more day," she heard herself say. "Maybe the kids and I can stay one more day, and see what happens."

CHAPTER 17

The jangling of the bell signaling the end of the school day startled Kim so badly she almost jumped out of the cramped school desk at which she'd been trying to unsnarl a seemingly unsolvable quadratic equation. With each period of the day, she'd felt more and more as if some terrible mistake had been made and she'd been put in the wrong classes. But all the rest of the kids were her age, and none of them appeared to be as unprepared as she felt. Was it possible that the public school she and Jared had gone to was as far behind the Catholic school as it seemed? But it must be, to judge from her classmates, at least as far as math, science, and French were concerned. The rest of it wasn't so bad—she'd always been good at history and English. But the hard classes—or those that had always been difficult for her—were nearly impossible. As she stuffed her books into her backpack and headed for her locker, she wondered if Jared felt as lost. If he did, they were both going to be in trouble. At least in school they'd always had different talents and were able to help each other out.

At her locker, halfway along the narrow main corridor on the second floor of the building, she worked the combination, and had a sinking sensation in her stomach when the handle refused to budge. It wasn't until the third try that she realized what was wrong—she was using the combination from the old school. As her fingers rotated the dial one more time, she sensed someone standing behind her.

Someone who made her feel oddly nervous. She tried to concentrate on working the combination, but after the first number her mind went blank.

How many turns was it? Two? Three?

And what number was she supposed to stop at? Then it came to her: twenty-six!

Or was it eight?

No! Eight was the last number!

She started over again, but could sense that whoever was behind her had moved closer, and now the hairs on the back of her neck were standing up.

What did he want?

He was very close to her now. So close she could hear him breathing, almost feel his breath on the back of her neck.

He was going to touch her!

Her skin crawled. At any moment she would feel his fingers on her. Unable to stand it any longer, she whirled around to confront the person behind her. "What do you—" she began, and abruptly stopped. Jared! It was just Jared! "My God," she breathed, sagging against her locker. "You scared me! How come you didn't say anything?"

His eyes darted in one direction and then the other. Was he looking for someone? Kim scanned the corridor, seeing several faces she recognized, even some she could put names to. But who would Jared be worried about? "Who are you looking for?" she asked.

He frowned. "No one. But I think some of the nuns are looking for me," he said, his voice barely audible.

Kim stared at her brother. First he'd walked out without eating breakfast, not even waiting for her. Then she'd hardly seen him all day. She'd looked for him at lunchtime, but he hadn't been in the cafeteria, and so finally she sat with a girl named Sandy Engstrom and some of her friends. But she'd spent most of the hour keeping an eye out for Jared, and hadn't been able to concentrate on anything they were saying. "Why would they be looking for you?" she asked now. "Did you do something wrong?"

Jared shook his head. "They just don't like me."

Kim rolled her eyes impatiently. "What do you mean, they don't like you? They act like they don't like anyone."

Jared's expression hardened. "I'm telling you, they don't like me! All day, they've been watching me."

"Watching you?" Kim echoed. Why would the nuns be watching him? But then she thought she knew—he was feeling the same thing she was, that everything was going to be harder here. For some reason he was taking it personally. "It doesn't have anything to do with you," she protested. "It's just different here, that's all." She turned back to her locker, her fingers once again working at the combination, and finally the lock snapped open. "I've been feeling like some kind of retard all day, but it doesn't have anything to do with the sisters. It's just—"

But Jared wasn't listening to her anymore.

In fact, he wasn't even behind her. As she closed her locker, she saw him disappearing down the stairs at the end of the hall. She stared after him.

What was going on? Why was he acting so strange today?

But it wasn't just that he was acting strange. It was something else—something more.

It was the Twin Thing. She remembered noticing it this morning, when she felt the odd sensation of being alone, as if the mental connection she and Jared had always shared had suddenly been severed. At first she'd attributed it to Jared's moodiness, and was certain that by the time she got to school, their link would be mended. But it hadn't been, and all day she'd felt an unfamiliar loneliness, which she'd never experienced before.

Just now, when he was standing right behind her—less than a foot away—she'd had no idea it was him. That had never happened before. All her life, she'd always known when Jared was nearby, always known when he came into a room she was in. When they were really little, they'd even made a game of it, trying to fool each other, to sneak up on one another, each hoping to catch the other off guard. But neither of them had succeeded.

Until today.

And then she understood why Jared was feeling so strange. The same thing had happened to him! Of course! That had to be it. She hurried after her brother, threading her way through the crowd of students that milled in the hallway, then skipping down the stairs two at a time. Bursting out the front door, she looked around for Jared and spotted him half a block away, talking to Luke Roberts. She hurried toward them, calling out his name. But as she approached, both boys went silent, and when Jared looked at her, she had the impression that he wasn't glad to see her. His words confirmed it: "Can't you just leave me alone?"

Kim stopped short. "I—I just—" She floundered, unable to find the words she was looking for. Jared continued to stare at her, and now, in sunlight that seemed even brighter than normal in the wake of the storm that had passed through that morning, she saw that something in his eyes was different. Where before she'd always felt that she could see right into her brother through his eyes, now she sensed a curtain between them, as if there was something he didn't want her to know.

Something he was hiding from her.

Muffin! That must be it—he must have found out what happened to her cat, and didn't want to tell her. Which meant . . . Kim's heart sank when it occurred to her why Jared wouldn't tell her if he'd found her pet. "It's Muffin, isn't it?" she asked. Jared's face remained impassive. "You found her, didn't you?" She thought she saw something flicker in his eyes, but it was gone so fast she wasn't sure she'd seen it at all. And once again the Twin Thing was telling her nothing. But somehow, even though Jared had betrayed nothing, she was certain she was right.

Muffin wasn't coming home. She felt her eyes sting with tears, but managed to hold them back. "I—I just thought we could walk home together," she finally stammered, for the first time in her life feeling unwilling to share her emotions with her brother. Before he spoke, she knew what he was going to say, and this time it didn't have anything to do with the Twin Thing, or with Muffin. This time she could read it in the expression on his face.

"I'm gonna hang with Luke for a while," he told her. "You go ahead."

Suddenly all the uneasiness, all the worry Kim had been feeling, coalesced into something else.

Anger.

If that was the way he felt—if he just wanted to cut her off—fine!

Without another word, she turned and walked quickly away, her head high, her back straight, determined that Jared wouldn't see the tears that glistened in her eyes.

When his sister was gone, Jared turned back to Luke Roberts. "Well, what about it?" he asked. "If I show you where the cabin is, will you tell me who lives in it?"

Luke uneasily shifted his weight from one foot to the other. "How come you want to know?" he hedged. "When'd you see this place?"

Jared's voice hardened. "Someone killed my sister's cat," he told Luke. "He nailed its skin to the back wall of our carriage house." Luke's eyes narrowed. "My dog tracked him back to a cabin, but there were a couple of hounds guarding it."

"Maybe you oughta just forget about it," Luke suggested. "Can't your sister just get another cat?"

Jared's gaze fixed steadily on Luke. "You chicken?" he asked, his voice low, his eyes boring into Luke's. The other boy's jaw tightened and his right hand clenched into a fist. But Jared held his gaze steady on Luke, and finally the clenched fist relaxed.

"Okay," Luke said. "Let's go."

Kim was so totally preoccupied with the confrontation she'd just had with Jared that she barely noticed the pungent scent of smoke in the air. But when she turned the corner, she saw it—a great cloud of smoke was billowing up from—

The house!

Her heart pounding, she broke into a run, then slowed as she realized it wasn't the house that was on fire at all. There was a huge bonfire burning behind the house, a fire that was sending up clouds of steam and smoke so large they all but hid the building from her view. As she approached, her father came around the side of the house, into her line of sight. He was stripped to the waist, his skin glistening with sweat, as he pulled kudzu off the magnolia tree. As she came into the yard, he hurled a great armful of the tangled vines onto the fire. The flames leaped upon the leafy offering like a voracious beast, spitting new plumes of smoke and steam into the sky and filling the afternoon with hissing and crackling as it devoured the tangled green mass. Kim stopped and hung back, staying well away from the ravening flames. Even when the fire began to die back, she still watched the scene warily.

Was her father drunk? But he didn't look like he was, and when she scanned the area for the drink he invariably had with him whenever he was home, she saw no sign of anything—not even a beer. But the kudzu had all but vanished. The carriage house had been stripped of it, as had the house, and even the mounds of it that had overgrown the yard were all but gone. Where this morning the grounds had been an almost unbroken sea of the invading vine, now she could recognize the remnants of what had once been a lawn, along with the skeletons of shrubs that the kudzu had long since choked to death.

"It's not quite as bad as it looks," she heard her father say. Startled, Kim turned to find him standing only a few feet away from her. Instinctively, she drew back to distance herself from the alcoholic fumes he usually exhaled. "Take it easy, Princess," he said, smiling at her and using the pet name she hadn't heard for years. "Believe it or not, I'm not drunk."

His words startled Kim almost as much as the way he'd addressed her. She tried to remember the last time he'd even admitted to drinking too much, let alone being drunk, and the answer came to her almost as quickly as she asked the question.

Never.

In her entire memory, Kim could not recall her father doing anything but insist that he didn't have a drinking problem. "I didn't think you were," she blurted out so quickly he couldn't help but know it was exactly what she'd been thinking. She braced herself against the wave of fury she was certain was about to break over her. But to her amazement, her father kept smiling.

"Of course you were," he said. "Let's face it—it's been a few years since you've seen me when I wasn't drunk."

Kim's mind spun. What on earth had happened today? "I—I didn't mean—I mean, I meant—" she stammered.

Her father reached out as if to pull her close, but stopped himself. "Consider yourself hugged," he said, eyeing his own filthy hands and sweaty torso. "If I really did hug you, I think you could consider it absolute proof that I've been drinking. But I really haven't. At least not since last night." Kim's eyes flickered toward the house, and her father's next words told her he again had guessed what she was thinking. "Your mother's giving me one last chance," he said. "We had a long talk this morning—not a fight," he added quickly, reading the expression on her face. "A real, genuine talk." He hesitated, and Kim had the feeling he was trying to decide how much to tell her. Then he went on, and again his words surprised her. "I know I haven't been the best father," he said. "And I'm not going to make up any excuses. I'm not going to try to blame my failures on anyone but myself . . ."

He continued to talk directly, honestly, to her for five minutes, and concluded, "I'm not asking you to forgive me, and I'm sure not asking you to forget. All I can do is apologize for what I've put you and everyone else in this family through. I know there's no way I can make it up to you, but I'm going to be better from now on." As Kim's eyes flooded with tears, her father smiled, his face lighting up. "Of course, practically anything would be better than what I've been, wouldn't it?"

Kim hesitated, then nodded. Part of her wanted to throw her arms around her father's neck and feel him wrap her up in the kind of hug she hadn't felt since she was a little girl. But another part of her—the part that had learned not to trust what her father said—held back. As she was sorting out her emotions, trying to decide what she wanted to say, her father seemed to read her mind the same way her brother always had.

"Don't say anything," he said. "In fact, if I were you, I think I'd be pretty suspicious right now."

She looked up at him, gazing into his eyes for the first time in years. Was he telling the truth? She wanted to believe him, wanted more than anything to trust what he was saying. Unconsciously, her fingers went to the small golden cross her great-aunt had given her, as if somehow the amulet might guide her.

"It's okay," her father told her. "Why don't you go in and talk to your mother?" He glanced up at the sun. "I've got about three more hours to get this mess cleaned up, and if I hurry, I just might make it."

Kim watched as her father went back to work, hacking at the thick vines that were still wound around a few of the old oak and willow trees that shaded the grounds, and hauling the vines down from the lower branches. The kudzu fought him, reluctant to give up its hold on the trees, but in the end it crashed in a jumble around his feet and was fed to the consuming fire. Watching until the flames had devoured the vines, Kim finally turned away and went into the house.

She saw the change as soon as she entered the kitchen: the boxes stacked against the far wall this morning were gone; their contents, she would discover, had been put away in the cupboards above the long counters. The kitchen itself was scrubbed clean, the rust stains gone from the sink. The tired refrigerator they'd brought from Shreveport was gone; in its place was a gleaming new one, and the old-fashioned range on which her mother had somehow managed to cook dinner the night before had vanished as well, replaced by an immense double-ovened, six-burner affair that looked like it should have been in a restaurant.

"Mom?" she called out. "You here?"

"In the studio," her mother called back.

The studio, too, had been transformed since yesterday. The rest of the windows had been cleaned, and everything unpacked and put away. Molly was in her playpen, playing with a doll. Her mother was perched on a stool, a stick of charcoal in her right hand, carefully eyeing a canvas on the easel before her. When her mother turned to look at her, Kim instantly understood that the changes she'd already witnessed weren't confined to the yard, the house, and her father.

The strain, the misery, she'd seen in her mother's face was gone. Everything about her was different. Her eyes, which had looked so exhausted this morning, were sparkling, and she seemed somehow to have gotten younger.

"Come and look," her mother said before Kim could speak. "Tell me what you think!"

Almost warily, Kim approached the canvas, not sure what to expect. As she gazed at it, she realized that whatever she might have guessed her mother was working on, it would not have been what she was looking at.

It was a sketch of an outdoor scene, but it bore no resemblance to the ruined landscape that lay beyond the windows. Drawn onto the canvas was a formal garden. Although it was still little more than a charcoal sketch, the composition her mother had limned gave Kim the eerie feeling that she was somehow looking into the past. It was as if her mother had imagined the garden as it might have looked a century ago. There was only one human figure in the garden, and even though it, too, had been realized with a few quick strokes, Kim recognized it as her father.

But not the father she'd known most of her life.

This was the father she'd met outside a few minutes ago, his expression open, his eyes seeming to smile though the image was barely developed.

So it wasn't just toward her that he'd changed, Kim thought. Her mother had seen it, too. "What happened?" she asked quietly, her eyes remaining on the figure as she waited for her mother to answer. "Would you please tell me what's going on? This morning—"

"This morning seems like a lifetime ago," Janet replied. She moved closer to Kim, looking at the image of Ted over her daughter's shoulder. "Something happened to him last night," she said. "It's like—" She hesitated, searching for the right words. "It's like he finally woke up," she said. Choosing her words carefully, she related the day's events. "He's been working all day," she eventually finished. "A truck showed up with the new stove and refrigerator, and after he helped me with the kitchen, he went to work outside, and—well, you saw for yourself what he's been doing."

When she went up to her room a few minutes later, Kim tried to pull it all together in her mind. Only this morning the house had been filled with tension.

Her father had been gone.

Her mother had been ready to leave him—had even told her she was going to.

And now everything was different.

But how long would it last?

Despite what her mother and her father had both told her, she still wasn't ready to believe it.

Something, she was sure, was wrong.

Very wrong.

CHAPTER 18

"How much farther?" Luke Roberts asked.

Jared glanced around, uncertain where they were. When they left the school half an hour ago, he'd thought about going back to his house and following the same trail Scout had led him along in the early hours of the morning. But as they started out, he had the idea that he could find the trail just by heading east from the edge of town into the woods. As they made their way along the labyrinth of paths, though, everything started to look alike. A couple of times he'd caught Luke eyeing him suspiciously, and at one point could see that Luke was about to ask him if he even knew where he was.

Despite his uncertainty, Jared silenced him with a look, unwilling to admit that they might be lost. Then, fifteen minutes ago, they came to a place where two trails crossed, and he'd known.

This was it, he thought. This was the trail.

But how had he known?

He'd scanned the area carefully, looking for something that stood out, that he might have remembered from his predawn foray with Scout. But there was nothing. And besides, when he was here before, he'd made his way through the darkness with nothing but moonlight, just following where Scout led.

And yet he knew. This was the right trail.

"This way," he announced.

"Yeah, sure," Luke drawled, hitching up the jeans that threatened to slide off his hips. "This don't look any different than any of the . . ." His voice died away as Jared fixed him with the same look that had silenced him a few minutes earlier.

Now, though, Jared slowed.

Close.

They were very close.

Once again he scanned the forest, looking for any sign of a cabin. Off to the left, barely visible through the tangle of kudzu that was spreading everywhere, he could make out the glimmering of sunlight on water.

A lake. Had the cabin he'd seen early this morning been close to a lake? He didn't know.

"Ahead," he said softly. "It's right up ahead."

Luke's brows arched skeptically. "I don't know," he replied. "Maybe we oughta just go back to town and go get a Coke or somethin'."

But Jared was moving along the trail again. A slight breeze had come up, and he stopped. "You smell anything?" he asked, sniffing.

Luke shook his head. "Do I look like some kinda hound or something?"

That was it! The dogs he'd heard last night! He could smell them! "Come on," he said. "We're almost there."

Once again Luke hesitated, but in the end gave Jared no argument. Leading the way, Jared crept forward, waiting for the dogs to begin baying.

This afternoon, though, they were silent, and suddenly Jared knew why. If he could smell them, he was downwind. They couldn't smell him.

He came to a bend in the trail. Though there was still no tree or rock that he remembered, he knew that as soon as they rounded the bend, they would see the cabin huddled in the small clearing. And a moment later, there it was.

Now, in the bright sunlight, Jared could see the lake. It lay only a few yards beyond the cabin. The bank was low and muddy, and there were a couple of old wooden rowboats—so worn they didn't look as if they could even float—lying on the shore, tied uselessly to a tree with rotting cotton rope.

Curled up in the shade of the cabin were two dogs.

"That's it," Jared said softly. "You know who lives there?"

Luke said nothing, but Jared knew immediately that he'd seen this cabin before. "Come on," he said, his voice rising. "Tell me!"

"Jake Cumberland," Luke Roberts finally said. "This is his place."

"Who is he?" Jared pressed.

Luke's expression turned wary. "Just a trapper," he replied. "He's always lived out here."

Jared's eyes narrowed. "You're scared of him, aren't you?"

Luke paled, but shook his head.

"Bullshit," Jared said. "Tell me the truth."

"There's . . . stories," Luke admitted. "About his ma."

"What kind of stories?"

"She was supposed to be some kind of voodoo queen or something." Luke's eyes shifted away from Jared. "An' they say she worked for your uncle before she disappeared."

"Disappeared?" Jared repeated. "What do you mean, disappeared? You mean she just took off?"

Luke shrugged. "Nobody knows. Leastwise, nobody I ever talked to knows. But my ma says the last time anyone ever saw her was the night before your uncle hung himself." He reddened slightly. "My ma says she heard your uncle might have killed her. She says there was all kinds of talk about him and Jake's ma. Like maybe they were gettin' it on, and she was gonna tell. So he killed her." As Jared's fists clenched and his jaw tightened, Luke held up his hands. "Hey, don't get pissed at me. All I'm tellin' you is what I heard."

But Jared was no longer looking at Luke. His eyes were fixed on the cabin. It cowered in the humid afternoon heat like an exhausted, dying dog. Every one of its windows was cracked—several panes were missing entirely—and whatever paint the weathered boards might once have worn was long gone. There was a sagging front porch with no railing, and most of the roof was covered with corrugated metal, badly rusted by the Louisiana heat and rain.

Though he wasn't certain why, Jared knew the cabin was empty.

His eyes shifted from the cabin itself to the two hounds.

As if sensing his gaze, both dogs scrambled to their feet, tensing. As they caught sight of him, they went on point, tails held straight back, eyes fixed on him. As Jared took a step toward them, the wind shifted and the two dogs caught his scent.

He moved a step closer, and now the dogs lunged forward, the wail of their baying ripping the quiet of the afternoon.

"You nuts, Jared?" Luke Roberts demanded. "What if Jake's in there?"

"He's not," Jared said. "He's nowhere around here."

"How the hell do you know?" Luke asked, but Jared didn't bother to reply.

He moved closer to the two dogs, now struggling at the end of their chains, their teeth bared, their baying dropping to low snarls as they tried to get at him.

He stopped a foot beyond the reach of the nearest dog—the one whose chain was a foot or so shorter than the first, who leaped and thrashed as it struggled to get closer.

"You want me?" Jared asked, squatting low and extending his right hand out toward the snarling animal. "That what you want? You think you want a piece of me?"

The dog howled with rage and threw itself against its chain, lost its balance, and skidded in the mud the morning's rainstorm had left. Writhing for several seconds, it regained its footing and lunged at Jared once more.

Jared extended his fingers until they were within inches of the dog's snapping teeth. "That it?" he taunted. "That what you want?"

"Are you crazy?" Luke called. "If he gets loose—"

But Jared wasn't listening. "Try it," he whispered. "Go on, just try it. See what happens."

He darted his fingers out, and the dog's jaws snapped shut on them. Luke howled as if he himself had been bitten. "Jesus!"

"Got a taste?" Jared whispered, his eyes fixed on the dog. Abruptly, the dog dropped back to cower on the ground. While the other animal continued its baying, still twisting to get at Jared, he reached down and put his fingers around the cowering dog's neck. "Not gonna do that again," he said softly. "Not ever gonna do that again!"

His fingers tightened around the animal's neck, and then he gave it a fast, hard jerk.

The animal screamed once, a high-pitched shriek of pain that was cut off as its neck snapped. It dropped back into the mud.

Luke stared mutely at the limp animal. "You killed him," he whispered.

Jared turned to look at him. "He bit me," he said, his voice reflecting no emotion. "What did you expect me to do, pat him on the head?"

The second dog, silent now, sniffed at its litter mate's lifeless corpse. Then it slunk back until it was huddled against the wall of the cabin.

Removing the chain from the dog's neck, Jared picked it up.

"What are you going to do with it?" Luke asked, his voice trembling.

Jared made no reply. Instead, he turned and carried the dead dog into Jake Cumberland's cabin.

The door closed behind him.

Jake Cumberland had been out on the lake most of the afternoon. The battered bucket that served him as a makeshift creel held half a dozen catfish—plenty for him and the two hounds. After he'd caught the last fish, about an hour ago, he thought about heading back home and taking the hounds out for a while. Check a few traps, maybe even do some hunting. But after being up most of last night, he felt tired; what his ma would have called bone-weary. It would've been okay if he'd slept through once he got home last night, but after the dogs had set to baying long before dawn, he'd been unable to get back to sleep. Just sort of lay there, trying to figure out what might have spooked them.

Probably just some critter, he'd told himself over and over again. A possum, maybe, or a 'coon. Except he'd known right away it wasn't a critter. The hounds had a different sound to them when they were on the scent of something they wanted to hunt. And this morning, when they jerked him awake with their first howl, he'd recognized it right away.

They were warning him.

That was why he'd lit the lantern and gone to the door.

He hadn't seen anybody.

Hadn't even heard anything.

But he'd still known someone was out there.

Out there, watching his cabin.

As he'd stood in the doorway, peering out into the darkness, trying to catch a glimpse of whoever was hiding in the night, he heard an echo of his ma's voice whispering to him when he was just a boy: *"You can feel him, child. When he's around, you can feel him. And you gotta be careful, real careful. 'Cause he's stronger'n you, child. Never forget that. He's stronger."* So even after the dogs finally quieted, Jake had stayed awake, the lantern turned low, waiting for the dawn to come. When the eastern sky began to brighten, he didn't go to bed, but instead set about his usual chores. He tidied up the cabin and fed the dogs. Checked the traps he'd baited the day before, then spent the hour when the thunderstorm tore through skinning and cleaning the three rabbits that were all the traps had produced.

Finally, after frying up some of the rabbit meat to tide him over till supper, he'd headed out in the rowboat, telling himself he was going fishing, but knowing he'd probably spend most of the afternoon just dozing in the sun. But he hadn't really dozed, because even in the daylight his ma's words kept rolling around in his head like the last few beans in a coffee can.

"When he's around, you can feel him."

Who'd she been talking about? When he was a little boy, he always figured it must have been Mr. Conway. But even back then, he'd never really been sure what his ma was talking about, because he never felt much of anything at all when he saw his ma's boss. Not until that night.

That last night, back when he was only a boy . . .

*J*ake woke up to the smell of smoke and the flicker of candlelight, and *knew before he even saw her what his mama was doing.*

Getting ready to work her magic.

That was what she called it—workin' her magic. "But don't you be tryin' it," she'd warned him the first time he'd awakened in the middle of the night and found her sitting at the little table in the corner of their cabin. "Little boys got no business with this kind of magic." She sent him back to bed that night, but he stayed awake, peeking at her from beneath the folds of the single thin blanket that was all he had to keep him warm, even on the coldest nights.

And ever since, whenever he awakened to find his mama hunched over the scarred table, her hair wrapped in the blue bandanna he himself had saved up to buy her for Christmas one year, he tried not even to stir in bed, so she wouldn't know he was awake. Tonight, though, he slipped out of the bed and went to stand by his mama, watching worriedly as she prepared the effigy.

That, he knew, was what it was called.

An effigy.

To him, it looked like nothing more than a doll—and not really a very good one—but his mama had explained to him that it wasn't really a doll. "With an effigy, you can make things happen to people," she'd told him. Now, as he watched her fingers stitch the material around the stuffing, he remembered what his teacher had said in school a few days ago.

"Sister says magic's wrong," he said worriedly. "She says if you try to work voodoo on people, you'll go to Hell."

His mama looked up from her work, her dark eyes glittering in the light of the single candle that illuminated the table. "Sister don't know everything."

Jake stared at the dead frog that lay on the table close by the effigy, its belly slit open all the way up to its mouth. "But I don't want you to go to Hell," he pressed, his voice quavering.

His mama reached out and laid a gentle hand on his head. "Don't you worry," she crooned. "I'm not goin' to Hell." Her eyes flicked toward the doll. "But that don't mean others won't. Now, you get on back to bed and go to sleep. You have to go to school in the morning."

Jake slid back under the blanket, but a few minutes later, when his mama went out into the night, he pulled on his clothes and followed after her.

First she went down to the edge of the lake and squatted down amongst the reeds that grew there, hiding the frogs and turtles Jake liked to hunt.

A low sound—exactly like the ones the frogs themselves made—rumbled from her throat, and she cast the carcass of the dead creature he'd seen on the kitchen table into the murky water. As ripples spread from the spot where she'd thrown the frog into the water, she stood up, muttering so softly that Jake couldn't make out the words. Then, carrying *the effigy doll with her, she walked slowly through the night, pausing here and there to whisper a muttered prayer, break a twig from a bush, or pick up some object—once a feather, another time a pebble—from the path.*

"All of them have magic," she'd explained to Jake one afternoon when they came across the clean-picked bones of a dead crow, and stooping down, she'd picked up the bones—even the beak and the feet—and slipped them into her pocket. "Every living thing has magic, and every dead thing, too. You just have to know how to use it." Tonight his mama had gathered so many things that Jake was sure she was planning to use the most powerful magic she knew.

As he followed her through the darkness, he remembered the words his teacher had spoken, meanwhile staring right at him, just like she knew what his mama did sometimes. "Christ is the Savior, and only through Christ can we be saved. All the rest is evil. All other paths lead only to Hell." As Jake followed his mama along the twisting paths, he silently prayed for her to turn around and lead him back to their little cabin. But then, after what seemed to him to be a very long time, they stepped out of the woods, and Jake knew where they were.

The huge house—the house where his mother worked every day, cleaning the floors and doing the laundry and cooking the meals and whatever else she was told—loomed before him, and it dawned on him what magic she was practicing tonight. As he cowered in the deep shadows by the carriage house, his mother stepped out into the light of the rising moon. She paced slowly, her head down, as if searching for something. Then, a soft chant welling up from somewhere deep inside her, she began circling, pacing around in an ever-tightening spiral until at last she was slowly spinning over a single spot.

Her spinning slowed further, then stopped. She lowered herself until she was sitting cross-legged on the ground. Her eyes fixing on one of the second-story windows, she began removing things from the deep pockets of her dress.

First came the effigy doll, which she lay before her, its head pointing toward the great house.

Then a knife, its blade glinting in the moonlight.

Some bones, picked clean of flesh, she laid in a circle around her.

Then came stones, and bits of moss. Some leaves, and a handful of dust.

She spread it all before her, her incantations growing ever louder, until it seemed to Jake they might summon up the dead from their very graves.

A light went on inside the house, a light that spilled out of the sec-

ond-story window to catch his mother like a fly in a spider's web. A few minutes later a door opened and a man stepped out.

"Eulalie, is that you out there?"

Jake recognized the voice—it was George Conway. The man who owned the house.

The man his mama worked for.

When his mama didn't answer, George Conway left his house and came out into the yard. Then he was standing above Jake's mama, and the boy could see the anger in the man's face as he studied all the things Eulalie Cumberland had spread around her.

"Take your junk and go home, Eulalie," George Conway commanded.

Jake held his breath, waiting for his mama to grab all her things and scuttle away. But instead she lifted her face until her eyes fixed on Conway's. Then, her right hand outstretched, she pointed to the great house silhouetted against the night sky. "Evil," her voice intoned. "Evil everywhere. Evil in your house, and evil in you!" She held up the effigy doll then, and shook it in his face. "It's in here now. It's all in here." She snatched up the knife, holding it close to the doll. "Soon I'm cutting it out. Cutting it all out!"

George Conway glowered down at his mama. "Don't threaten me, Eulalie Cumberland. Don't you dare to threaten me."

Jake saw his mama's chest heave as she straightened up to face George Conway's rage. "Ain't a threat," she said, and though her voice was barely above a whisper, it carried perfectly through the stillness of the night. "I'm promisin' you. By the next moonrise, the evil will be gone from this place!" As she went back to muttering her incantations, George Conway turned away from her and strode toward the carriage house.

He'd been seen! Jake's heart pounded and his eyes searched the darkness for some means of escape. But the woods were too far away, and there was no other shelter to protect him. A frightened cry rose in his throat, but just as it was about to slip from his lips, Conway disappeared through a door into the building against which he was huddled.

Safe! He hadn't been seen at all; he was safe.

Still, Jake held his breath; any sound he made would betray him. After what seemed an eternity, George Conway reappeared, carrying something in his right hand. As the man started back toward his mama, Jake finally let out his breath and took another.

"I'm telling you for the last time, Eulalie," he heard Conway say. "Go home."

But his mama didn't budge, and when George Conway used both

his hands to raise the object above her head, Jake was certain he was going to smash her with it. But instead he tipped it, and water began to flow over his mama's head.

Another second went by, and then the acrid odor hit Jake's nostrils.
Not water.
Gasoline.

"Last chance, Eulalie," Jake heard George Conway say.

Jake's mama peered up at the man who loomed above her. "I ain't afraid of you, and I ain't afraid of what you been messin' with." As her incantations began again, the flare of a match illuminated the face of George Conway. The man gazed down at his mama for another second or two, then stepped back a pace.

With no change in his expression at all, George Conway tossed the match into the puddle of gasoline that surrounded Eulalie Cumberland. There was a strange whooshing sound as the gasoline exploded into flames, and George Conway stepped back two more paces as the first flash of heat struck him.

Jake's eyes widened in horror and his hands clamped over his mouth. He wanted to race forward, wanted to jerk his mama out of the fire, wanted to rescue her from the flames suddenly dancing around her, but his muscles wouldn't work.

As he stared numbly at the horrifying spectacle before him, he was vaguely aware of a hot wetness spreading through the crotch of his jeans. But even as he lost control of his bladder, he could do nothing to free himself from the paralysis that held him, couldn't even bring himself to tear his eyes away from the fire consuming his mother.

Eulalie Cumberland made no sound at all as her clothes caught fire and the flames began eating away at her flesh. Nor did she make any effort to save herself. But her hands reached out of the flames and closed on two of the objects she'd spread around her.

In her left hand she held the effigy doll, suspended from a noose she'd tied around its neck.

In her right hand she held the knife.

While Jake and George Conway watched her, she plunged the knife deep into the body of the doll, then jerked it downward. As the thin cotton from which she'd made the doll ripped open, the entrails of the frog poured forth from its belly.

The flames, higher now, engulfed her head, but still she held the doll high. The bloody guts hanging from its belly glimmered in the firelight, and as George Conway stared at them, his own eyes widening in terror, Eulalie Cumberland began to laugh.

It was an unearthly sound, erupting from her throat in peal after

*peal, and even after she finally pitched forward into the flames, her laugh-
ter still seemed to hang in the night air.*

*Jake, transfixed by the horror of watching his mother burn, trem-
bled in the darkness as the flames died slowly away.*

*Even when the fire had finally burned itself out, he couldn't bring
himself to leave. He watched from the shadows as George Conway dis-
posed of the remains of his mama, wrapping them in a thick blanket, then
disappearing back into the great dark house, carrying his burden with
him.*

*All through the rest of the night, Jake Cumberland stayed by the
carriage house.*

*He tried to tell himself that what he'd seen couldn't have happened,
that it had to be some kind of terrible nightmare.*

*Pretty soon he'd wake up and be back home in the cabin, and his
mama would be at the stove, frying up the grits she always fixed for breakfast.*

*Only when the sun finally crept over the horizon did Jake finally go
home. He stayed in the cabin as long as he could, not coming out for three
days and three nights. And when finally the sister came looking for him
and asked him where his mother was, he didn't tell her what he'd seen
that night.*

He didn't tell anyone, ever.

*But when he heard that they'd found George Conway the afternoon
after his mother died, hanging from the magnolia tree behind his house,
still clutching the knife he'd used to tear his own belly open, Jake heard
something.*

He heard his mama laughing.

He'd known right away why she was laughing. It was because even
though Conway had killed her, she'd still won. But he'd still never understood what she meant when she talked about feeling the evil.

Not until last night when the hounds started up.

For the first time, he'd known exactly what his mama had meant.

He *had* felt something.

Something evil.

Something outside in the darkness, lurking somewhere just beyond
the circle of yellow light cast by the lantern.

Usually, he would have turned the dogs loose, but not last night.
Something held him back, something whispered to him to keep them
inside the cabin.

This afternoon, though, when he'd left the cabin to take the little boat out, he chained them up outside—couldn't keep them inside all day long. But even as he'd tossed his fishing pole, bait, and bucket into the boat and shoved it out onto the water, he wondered if maybe he shouldn't put them back in the cabin.

Or maybe even take them along.

In the end he told himself that whatever had been skulking around the cabin last night was long gone. And in the bright light of the afternoon sun, he was pretty sure he'd just imagined it anyway. Probably just feeling jumpy after his own midnight outing. Not that he'd done anything wrong—in fact, he'd been doing that whole family a favor. If they had any smarts at all, they'd pack up and move themselves right back to wherever they came from. And there sure wasn't any way they'd know who it was nailed the cat skin on the back of their carriage house. Even if anyone suspected, they couldn't prove it.

No, he'd just been jumpy.

Finally letting himself relax for the first time since he'd opened his mother's trunk last night, Jake lay back on the bottom of the boat, holding his fishing pole loosely in his right hand, his feet propped up on the bench across the middle, his head resting comfortably in the bow. He tipped his straw hat down over his face and closed his eyes.

And then the dogs began baying.

Jake jerked bolt upright, recognizing the sound at once. It was his hounds that had set to wailing, no question about it—even from a mile, maybe two miles away—he could recognize the sound of his dogs. And they were letting out with the same howling they'd set up last night—not all excited, like when they caught the scent of a 'coon or a rabbit. Just like last night, they sounded mad.

Worried, and mad.

Jake reeled in his line, stowed the pole, and started rowing back toward shore. He'd been drifting quite a while, and the cabin looked to be nearly a mile away now, though the dogs' baying carried so clearly over the water they sounded like they weren't more than a couple hundred yards away.

He'd only pulled a few strokes on the oars when the baying died away. He stopped rowing, shipping the oars for a minute while he listened.

Nothing but a fish jumping off to the left, and the whining of a mosquito as it zeroed in on his neck. Then, just as he slapped at the mosquito, he heard it.

Jake knew what the sound meant the second he heard it. A high-pitched howl of pain, cut off so quickly that Jake knew exactly what had happened.

One of his dogs had died.

The mosquito forgotten, Jake lowered the oars back into the water and began pulling hard in a steady rhythm that sent the boat slicing through the water.

Twice he paused, feathering the oars over the lake's rippled surface as he listened, but it wasn't until he was within a few yards of the shore that he finally heard it.

A single dog—he was almost sure it was Lucky—was whimpering.

The boat slid up onto the beach, and Jake jumped out of the bow, pulling the craft out of the water until half of it rested in the hard-packed mud that formed the bank. Leaving everything in the boat, he hurried up to the cabin.

At first glance, nothing looked different. But then, when he got around to the back, he saw that he'd been right. Lucky was at the end of her chain, whimpering as she sniffed the ground around the end of the other chain.

Red was gone.

Jake strode forward and dropped down on one knee. "What happened, Lucky?" he asked. "What's been going on around here while I been gone?"

The dog whimpered eagerly, and wriggled under Jake's touch, but then went back to sniffing the ground around the end of Red's chain. Frowning, Jake picked up the chain and tested the clasp he'd attached to Red's collar.

Nothing wrong with it.

Nor was there any sign of the collar.

"Where is he, Lucky?" he asked. "Where'd he go?"

Snapping the chain off Lucky's collar, Jake stood up. "Find Red," he instructed softly. "Show me where he is."

The dog dashed around the corner of the cabin, and a moment later Jake found her sniffing and scratching at the door.

Mounting the porch, Jake hesitated. Why would Red be inside the cabin? If something had killed him—

Then he remembered. Not some*thing*. Some*one*. An icy chill came over Jake, but he crossed his sagging porch and opened the door to his house.

And there was Red.

The dog lay on the table, its belly slit, its entrails spilling over and hanging nearly to the floor.

At Jake's feet Lucky whined softly and pressed close.

"Oh, Jesus," Jake whispered. "Oh, Jesus Lord, who did this?" His stomach heaving, Jake moved closer, reached out and gently stroked the dog's muzzle, as if to comfort it. Then his eyes fell on the dog's right fore-leg.

The paw was missing, severed neatly, leaving the leg to end in a bloody stump.

Too late, Jake thought.

It's already too late.

CHAPTER 19

J anet glanced fretfully at her watch for what must have been the dozenth time. Quarter to six.

Fifteen more minutes.

She'd give Jared fifteen more minutes, then—then what?

Call the police? Call the hospital?

"There's nothing to worry about," Ted had assured her an hour ago. "He's almost sixteen." Then, reading perfectly the thought that had popped unbidden into her mind, he grinned. But it wasn't the kind of ridiculing sneer that had so often twisted his lips in the early stages of his binges. This time it was just a friendly grin, and when he spoke, his voice held no hint of sarcasm. "Hey, Jan, come on. He's not me—he's not out getting drunk somewhere. He's probably just hanging out with a buddy or something." He'd put his arms around her then, and nuzzled her hair the way he had years ago.

But hadn't for how long? Five years? Ten? So long ago, anyway, that she couldn't even remember. But his breath had no trace of alcohol now, and when she felt his arms around her and he ruffled her hair, the years fell away and it was as familiar as if he'd held her like this yesterday. "Let's not go looking for trouble until we know it's out there, okay?"

The tension had drained out of her, and she'd gone back to work, peeling the potatoes that were now simmering on the stove while Ted played with Molly, both of them sitting on the kitchen floor, pushing Molly's favorite red and yellow ball back and forth.

Scout was curled up in the corner by the refrigerator.

Kim was up in her room, struggling with her homework.

Like a normal family, Janet thought. *We look like a normal family.*

But as the minutes crept by and Jared didn't come home, her worries had once more started to build. *Habit. It's just habit,* she told herself. *I'm so used to worrying about Ted that if I don't have to worry about him for even one day, I find someone else to worry about.* But it hadn't even been one day since Ted came home, she reminded herself. Tomorrow, even tonight, it could all change. For all she knew, he might have a case of vodka hidden away in the house. And yet, all day, as she watched Ted work—and work far harder than he had since they were first married— she'd seen the change in him. Even when he didn't know she was watching, when she stood far back in one of the upstairs rooms so he couldn't possibly see her, he'd kept at it, his torso glistening with sweat, his muscles straining with the unaccustomed labor. And when he finally finished in the backyard, he hadn't rewarded himself with a beer. Instead, he poured himself a glass of the iced tea she'd made before lunch, then taken a shower and played with Molly.

Like a normal family.

"If he doesn't get here by six, we'll just go ahead and eat without him," Ted said, once again reading her thoughts. He winked at her. "After all, it wouldn't be the first time this family had been a member short at the dinner table. And I promise," he went on when his words didn't erase the worry from her eyes, "if he's not home by seven, I'll go look for him. Okay?" Getting to his feet, he began setting the kitchen table, with Molly tagging after him. Again, years of habit came into play, and Janet moved to scoop her daughter up before Ted could brush her aside. But once again her husband surprised her. "Let her be, hon. She's just trying to help."

Ted called Kim down exactly at six, and the four of them—with Molly in her high chair—started eating.

At five after six Scout stood up and a low growl rumbled in his throat. All of them except Molly stopped eating as the big dog moved toward the kitchen door. They heard the front door open then, and close.

"Jared?" Janet called out. "We're in the kitchen! Supper's on the table." She got up to serve her son's plate, but when she tried to gently nudge Scout aside so she could get to the stove, the big retriever didn't move. Instead, the dog stood rigid, his eyes fixed on the kitchen door, his hackles up. And when Jared appeared in the doorway, another low growl of warning reverberated in the dog's throat. "For heaven's sake, Scout, it's only . . ." The words died on her lips as she saw that Jared wasn't alone. Behind him was the boy she remembered from the day of the funeral, when they'd been moving into the house. Mark? No. *Luke.* That was it. Luke. Her eyes shifted back to her son. "You should have called," she told him. "If I'd known you were bringing a friend home, I'd have made enough to feed him."

"It's okay," Jared replied. "We got some pizza downtown. We're just gonna go up to my room and listen to some music, okay?" Without waiting for a reply, he and his friend disappeared back through the dining room.

But Scout, instead of following Jared as he always had before, remained on the alert until the sound of the two boys' footsteps on the stairs faded away. And when the retriever returned to his spot next to the refrigerator, his head stayed up.

"See?" Kim said. "I told you Jared was acting weird. Even Scout can tell."

"Don't you think Scout might have been reacting to Jared's friend?" her father asked.

Before Kim could reply, a thunder of music rolled through the house—a hard-pounding rap whose lyrics, even if they hadn't been muddled by the ceiling above the kitchen, were all but drowned out by the pounding rhythm of the synthesizer that accompanied them. Molly, who'd been happily playing with her food a moment before, wailed, and Janet, reacting to the habits inculcated in her over the years, rose from the table, already anticipating her husband's anger. "I'll make him turn it down—" she began, but Ted was already on his feet.

"You take care of Molly," he told her. "It's going to be bad enough having me tell him to keep it down. If it's you, he'll die of embarrassment."

As Janet lifted Molly out of her high chair to soothe the screaming child, Ted headed upstairs. A few seconds later the music was cut short, and shortly afterward, Molly's anguished howls settled into quiet sniffling. Then the little girl rubbed her eyes with her fists and struggled to get back to her dinner. Janet slid her back into the high chair, and Molly scooped a handful of potatoes toward her mouth, getting most of them onto her face and bib.

When Ted returned, Janet waited for the music to start up again.

But the silence held.

"Would you mind telling me how you did that?" she asked.

"Simple," Ted replied, dropping back into his chair. "I made a deal."

"A deal," Janet repeated. "What kind of deal?"

Ted grinned at her, his eyes glinting with mischief. "Probably shouldn't tell you," he said. "Guy thing. But since you're bound to find out anyway, I might as well confess. I gave him one of the rooms in the basement."

Janet stared blankly at her husband, then shook her head. "Sorry, but I'm afraid you'll have to explain. I don't get it."

Ted shrugged. "Think about it—Jared's almost sixteen, right? Just the age when kids like that kind of music."

"*I* don't," Kim interjected. But before either of her parents could correct her, she quickly modified the statement. "At least I don't like it so loud it hurts your ears."

"But your brother obviously does—or at least his friend does, which amounts to the same thing. So, since with any luck at all we're going to be having a lot of paying guests around here in a few months, I'm moving Jared into the basement. I told him he could fix it up any way he wants, as long as he makes it soundproof so that no one up here has to listen to whatever he's listening to. He winds up with his privacy, and we wind up with one more room to rent and one less teenager hogging a bathroom upstairs."

"I don't hog the bathroom," Kim protested. Before her mother could object, she changed direction. "What if *I* wanted a room downstairs?"

Her father looked at her blandly. "Do you?" he asked, his voice betraying nothing of what he might be thinking.

Kim thought about the dark cavern downstairs, with the rabbit warren of dusty rooms lit only by a few bare lightbulbs. God only knew what might be down there, creeping around in the darkness. Unable to hide the shudder that ran over her, she shook her head. "No!"

"Didn't think so," her father replied, winking at Janet.

Half an hour later, when Kim had gone back up to her homework and Jared and Luke had disappeared into the basement to start making plans for his new room, Janet stood at the sink washing dishes.

Washing the dishes, and trying to fathom what had happened that day.

How was it possible that she could have gotten up this morning with the decision to end her marriage finally made, and now actually be looking forward to settling down to spend the evening with the very same man she'd been intending to leave?

Except he wasn't the same man.

Whatever had happened to Ted—whatever truth had finally come to him in the midst of his drunkenness—had, indeed, changed him. And the Ted who came home this morning wasn't a total stranger—he was the Ted she'd met years ago, before the drinking had begun.

He was the Ted she'd always wanted, not the Ted her friends warned her against marrying.

Finally, she'd been proved right. *Maybe,* her mother's voice interjected. Janet wanted to reject her mother's silent warning as soon as it came into her head, but knew she couldn't.

Ted, after all, had made promises before.

And every time, every single time, he'd broken them.

So why would this time be any different? In the quiet and solitude of the kitchen, she admitted to herself that it might *not* be any different. She would just have to wait and see.

But for now, for the first time in years, she felt married again.

For as long as it lasted, she was going to enjoy it.

"You sure this is a good idea?" Luke Roberts asked as he scanned the room. Perhaps a dozen feet square, its walls were made of thick oaken planks nailed to the huge twelve-by-twelve posts that supported the main joists of the house. It was lit by a single naked bulb hanging from a wire that had been strung along the beams beneath the floor. High up on one wall there were two small windows opening into light wells that, though they might brighten the room a little bit during the day, wouldn't let anyone inside see out, except for maybe a tiny slice of sky. Just the idea of moving into this place was enough to make Luke shudder, and if he'd been given the choice between this dungeon and the big room on the second floor—which was at least twice this size—he knew which one he'd have gone for. In fact, he'd have gone for a room half this size if it had a real window you could open up to let some air in.

There was a funny smell in the room, too. It seemed to be coming from the floor, which was made out of concrete that was starting to rot, with pits Luke was certain must be full of mold and mildew. "What's that?" he asked, pointing to a grate in the middle of the floor.

"It's the sump," Jared replied. "If it gets real wet, and water starts collecting down here, it all runs in there. Then when that gets too full, a pump goes on, and pumps all the water outside."

The room, already close to a complete zero on Luke's list, dropped another notch. "You mean you want to sleep in a room that might flood?"

Jared shrugged. "Even if it floods, it's not going to be that bad." Then he grinned, his eyes glinting in the bright glare of the bulb that hung from the rafters. "And I'd sure rather be down here than upstairs where everyone'll know what I'm doing."

"There isn't even a bathroom," Luke said sourly.

"Sure there is," Jared countered. "It's over in the corner, near the stairs."

"So what are you gonna do if you have to take a leak in the middle of the night? There's gotta be all kinds of spiders and stuff down here."

"Jeez," Jared groaned. "Haven't you ever heard of a bug bomb? You just set it off and close the place up for a few hours."

"Your dad's gonna love that idea," Luke observed.

"It was my dad's idea in the first place," Jared retorted. Then: "You got a joint?"

Luke's expression clouded suspiciously. "What if I do?" he asked, his voice carefully neutral.

Jared's eyes rolled. "If you do, we can smoke it."

Luke stared at him. "With your folks right upstairs?"

Jared shrugged. "Why not? That's the great thing about being down here—nobody's gonna walk by, so they won't even smell it if it leaks under the door a little."

Luke's eyes narrowed. "Bet you wouldn't," he said, with just enough challenge in his voice to tell Jared he did, indeed, have a joint.

"I'm gonna go up and get some food and Cokes," Jared said. "Then we'll smoke it, and figure out how to fix this place up."

In less than five minutes he was back, bringing not only Cokes and potato chips, but the radio from his room as well, along with a couple of candles. Plugging the radio into the single socket jury-rigged onto one of the walls the same way the light had been hung from the rafters, he turned it on, but kept the volume low enough so it wouldn't bring anyone down from upstairs. "So how about it, Luke?" he said. "You gonna share the joint?"

Luke frowned. "How'd you know I had one?"

Jared's lips curved into a mysterious smile. "I know all kinds of stuff," he said.

Luke reached into his pocket and pulled out a red tin box just like the ones that practically everyone Jared knew carried. Opening the lid, Luke carefully lifted the paper that cradled the peppermints inside. Underneath were three neatly rolled joints. After taking two of them out and placing them on the floor, Luke slid the box back into his pocket.

Silently, Luke handed one of the joints to Jared.

Jared struck a match, lit the joint, and sucked the smoke deep into his lungs. Holding his breath to keep the fumes in his lungs as long as possible, he passed the joint to Luke. "See?" he said after they'd each taken three tokes. "No big deal." Both of them sank down onto the floor, leaning against the oak wall.

"Good shit," Luke muttered as he sucked a fourth toke into his lungs.

Jared got up and lit the candle, pulled the string that shut off the glare of the naked lightbulb, and settled down against the wall opposite Luke. "Not so bad, is it?"

"Can't see anything," Luke groused, temporarily blinded.

But as the joint took effect and his eyes grew accustomed to the glow cast by the candle, the whole look of the room seemed to change.

The rough surfaces of the planks that formed the room's walls softened, and the ceiling seemed to rise above them until it seemed there was no roof at all.

"Cool," Luke breathed.

"Shhh," Jared hissed. "Just let your mind go." He picked the second joint off the floor, lit it, and passed it to Luke.

The light in the room began to flicker and swell.

So, too, did the texture of the walls. No trace of the planks was left at all. Instead, the walls seemed to have turned translucent, with rainbows of color rippling through them. Then the walls—like the ceiling a few minutes ago—began to recede.

It seemed to Luke that they were in a chamber as huge as a cathedral, with a ceiling vaulted so high they could barely make it out. The walls were gold, set with stained glass in swirling patterns that made the light appear to move as it flooded through from somewhere beyond. In front of Luke something that looked like an altar appeared, above which—apparently floating in the air—was a woman.

A woman more beautiful than Luke had ever seen before.

She moved toward him, a silvery robe flowing around her, and as her feet touched the floor, she reached out, her fingers stretching toward him.

She knelt, and gently caressed his cheek.

"Touch me," she said in a voice that sounded like the most beautiful music he'd ever heard. "Touch me."

Hesitantly at first, Luke reached out to the perfect woman.

Her robe fell away, revealing the perfection of her firm flesh and her golden skin.

Luke's fingers touched the woman's flesh, and he trembled.

"I want you, Luke," the woman breathed, "like you want me. . . ."

The vision of the woman blotting everything else from his consciousness, Luke Roberts let himself sink into an ecstasy such as he'd never felt, and knew that when it was over he would be changed forever.

"Yes," he breathed. "Oh, God, yes . . ."

As Luke surrendered to the pleasures of the perfect woman, Jared Conway watched.

Watched, and smiled.

October

CHAPTER 20

Sandy Engstrom eyed Kim Conway anxiously. Over the last few weeks—ever since Kim had asked if she could sit at Sandy's favorite table in the St. Ignatius cafeteria—the two of them had become best friends. Sandy had been surprised that first day, because only the day before Kim had hardly spoken to anybody but her brother. *Her gorgeous brother,* Sandy amended to herself, though she'd been careful not to let Kim know that she'd developed a crush on Jared Conway the minute she saw him. In fact, the main reason she'd been friendly toward Kim was in the hope of meeting Jared. But by the end of that first lunch, she knew she'd found someone to replace Melissa Parker, her best friend since kindergarten, until Melissa moved to New Orleans just before school started. As for Jared, Sandy's crush on her new friend's brother had faded almost as quickly as it had come over her. Maybe if he hadn't started hanging out with Luke Roberts . . .

But he *had* started hanging out with Luke, and as far as Sandy was concerned, anyone who was a friend of Luke's was off her list, if for no other reason than the way Luke had dumped Melissa Parker last year. He hadn't even had the guts to tell her he was breaking up with her himself. Instead, he'd invited Dawn LaFrenier to the homecoming dance, and by the time Melissa found out, it was too late to get another date. Sandy hadn't had a date, either, so the two of them went to the movies that night, and struck Luke—and all his friends—off their list of boys they'd have anything to do with. And just because Melissa was gone, Sandy wasn't about to reinstate Luke Roberts to her list of friends.

Fortunately for Kim, the stigma Jared carried because of his new friend didn't extend to her. Since that first day almost six weeks ago, the two girls had been having lunch together every day, and studying together at Sandy's nearly every afternoon. So far, Kim hadn't invited her over to the Conway house, and although Sandy was curious about it, she still wasn't sure she actually wanted to set foot in it. In fact, she'd even wondered out loud a few times if Kim wasn't afraid to live there.

"Why should I be?" Kim had asked. "I mean, it's not like it's haunted or something." The look on Sandy's face had given her away, and Kim groaned. "You don't believe all those stories about my dad's aunt and uncle, do you?" When Sandy reddened, Kim sighed in exasperation. "It's just a house! And it's been empty for a long time, but just because Luke Roberts thinks it's haunted doesn't mean it is."

The invocation of Luke's name had been enough to keep Sandy from repeating all the old rumors, but she wasn't convinced there was nothing to them. Of more concern to Sandy, Kim appeared oddly distracted at times. Sandy was convinced that there was something Kim wasn't telling her.

"Kim?" she said now. "Are you okay?" They were sitting in the pizza parlor around the corner from St. Ignatius, having sneaked away from the cafeteria rather than face the nuns' macaroni and cheese one more time. "You look like you're worried about something."

In fact, Kim was. Worried about what would happen if the sisters caught them out of school. But even more than that, she was worried about Jared. She knew, though, how her friend felt about her brother—or anyone else Luke Roberts knew—so she shook her head. Besides, even if Sandy might be sympathetic, she didn't know exactly what to say. She'd felt more cut off from Jared as the days passed until now it seemed she didn't have a brother anymore, let alone a twin.

"I'm fine," she replied, but seeing that Sandy wasn't convinced, she cast around in her mind for something that might satisfy her. "Actually, I was sort of wondering what excuse you were going to give me when I invited you."

Sandy cocked her head. "Invite me to what?" she asked. "And why would I say no?"

"A sleep-over on Friday," Kim said casually. She waited, then added: "At my house." As she'd been sure it would, a shadow of apprehension clouded her friend's face. "You're not scared, are you?" Kim asked with exaggerated innocence.

"N-No," Sandy answered, a little too fast. "I just—"

"We'll rent horror movies and pretend it's Halloween, even though it'll be two nights early. We can . . ." Her words died on her lips at the look on Sandy's face, which was enough to tell Kim who must have come into the pizza parlor. Luke Roberts's voice confirmed it.

"Hey," he said, coming up the aisle on one side of their table and sliding onto the banquette next to Kim, while Jared crowded in next to Sandy on the other side of the table.

"What's going on?" Jared grinned at his sister. "How come you guys didn't invite us along when you snuck out?"

Kim saw Sandy's eyes fix coldly on Luke Roberts, and realized, to her horror, that she was staring at her brother exactly the same way. She looked at him carefully, studying his face. His features—everything about him—looked exactly the same as ever. But it just didn't *feel* the same. All her life she'd felt the Twin Thing—that deep link with her brother—which had always let her know that no matter what else happened, he was always there.

Now he wasn't.

She just didn't *feel* him anymore. Kim sighed inwardly. Maybe it was just something she had to forget about. Maybe it was just that they were both growing up.

She was jerked out of her reverie by . . . what?

Something had touched her leg! Then she felt Luke Roberts's thigh pressing against hers. She turned and glared at him. "Could you just move over?"

Luke rolled his eyes scornfully, but he pulled away.

"And keep your hands on the table," Kim told him.

"Jeez," Luke groaned. "What is *with* you?"

Kim gave him a cold smile. "Not you!" she said.

Across from Kim, Sandy Engstrom was acutely aware of Jared Conway's presence next to her. She'd seen him when he first came in, and when their eyes met, the strangest feeling had come over her.

As if he'd looked right inside her.

But not just looked in. It seemed he'd reached into her, actually touched her. She'd felt a rush of heat and her skin broke out in goose bumps. And right away—even before he'd started toward her—she'd known he would sit next to her.

Now, with his body pressed against hers, the goose bumps were back, and she could once again feel that delicious heat.

What if Jared asked her out?

Should she go?

Sandy shivered with excitement as she began to think about the possibilities.

*   *   *

I don't believe it! Kim thought as once again Luke Roberts's fingers touched the skin on her leg. Giving Luke a hard enough shove that he almost fell off the banquette onto the floor, she slid out of the booth. "Let's get out of here," she told Sandy. "We've only got ten more minutes, and I have to stop at my locker."

"What's the big hurry?" Luke protested. "Come on—we just got here!"

"Maybe you don't care if we get caught, but I do," Kim snapped. "This was a stupid thing to do in the first place!" She headed toward the door, refusing even to glance back.

Sandy followed her, but at the door, turned to look back at Jared. His eyes locked on hers, and once more she had the strange feeling that he was reaching right inside her, sending a warmth through her that made her almost tremble with pleasure.

Like he's making love to me, she thought. *It feels like he's making love to me.* Doing her best to control her emotions—and praying no one would notice her deep blush—Sandy hurried after her friend.

Suddenly, she could hardly wait for the sleep-over at Kim's house.

The pizza parlor had emptied out twenty minutes ago, but so far Jared showed no sign of being ready to leave. Luke Roberts was starting to get nervous. Very nervous. For ten years—ever since he'd started at St. Ignatius, when he was five years old—he'd lived in fear of the wrath of the sisters. He'd first learned to fear their swift brand of retribution when Sister Katherine rapped his knuckles with a ruler for passing a piece of chewing gum back to one of his friends, sitting behind him. His hand had bled for the rest of the day, but Sister Katherine wouldn't even let him go put a Band-Aid on it. "If Jesus didn't ask for Band-Aids on the Cross, I think you can stand a little cut on your knuckles, Luke," she'd told him. The rest of the class giggled at the way she talked about Jesus on the Cross, but a single look from the nun silenced them, and Luke burned with shame when the pain in his knuckles made him cry. If Jesus hadn't asked for Band-Aids, he sure couldn't have cried, either. But he'd learned his lesson, and never tried to pass another piece of gum.

He'd also learned not to talk during class, and to stand up next to his desk when he answered a question.

And he'd learned not to be late.

He made that mistake in sixth grade, when Sister Michael was his teacher. Sister Mike—the only nun who let the kids shorten her name—had made him stay after school and write on the blackboard.

I waste my time when I'm late.

I waste the class's time when I'm late.
I waste Sister Michael's time when I'm late.

He'd written the three sentences a hundred times, and when he was done, he vowed never to be late to class again.

And he hadn't, until today. Now he glanced at the clock, trying not to let Jared Conway see him doing it. But Jared seemed almost as good as the sisters at knowing what he was doing.

"What's the matter?" he asked now. "Afraid Sister Clarence is going to make you stay after school?"

"No," Luke replied, knowing he'd spoken a little too fast.

Jared's eyes clamped mockingly onto his own. " 'I waste my time when I'm late. I waste the class's time when I'm late. I waste Sister Michael's time when I'm late,' " he parroted, as if reading the words off the blackboard.

Or out of his own mind, Luke thought.

How? How'd he know? He thought back over the last few weeks, when he'd been spending almost all his time with Jared Conway. Had he told Jared about that afternoon when he was in Sister Mike's class?

He must have.

But he hadn't—he was almost sure of it!

How had Jared known?

"I can read your mind," he told Luke the day after they'd smoked the joints in Jared's basement room, when Luke had the weird hallucinations.

Hallucinations that were still so vivid, even weeks later, that he could hardly believe they'd been hallucinations at all. Just last night, before he went to sleep, he'd even imagined he felt the touch of the woman who appeared that night, stroking his cheek and letting her fingers trail down over his neck and chest, caressing his stomach, then reaching lower and lower until—

"Maybe you better go into the men's room," Jared drawled, slouching back in the booth and leering suggestively at Luke.

Luke felt his face burn, and shoved the memory out of his mind. Then he looked at the clock again. *Sister Clarence is gonna kill us*, he thought. *This time she's really gonna kill us.*

Jared grinned at him, and winked. "Well, we wouldn't want Sister to kill us, would we?" he said. Laughing, he slipped out of the booth and headed for the door.

As Luke followed, he found himself wondering again if it was really possible that Jared could somehow read his mind.

* * *

Sister Clarence stopped speaking as the door to her classroom opened and the two boys walked in, led by Jared Conway. A cold knot of anger formed inside her as she gazed at her newest student, and—not for the first time—immediately begged her savior for forgiveness for her failings. *I know I should love all the children*, she silently prayed, *but I cannot love Jared Conway.*

She'd thought about it many times over the past six weeks. Late at night, when she was alone in her tiny cell on the third floor of the convent next door, she occasionally blamed herself for the change in the boy. Perhaps she'd been too hard on him that first day, when he passed the note to his sister, but she'd learned years ago that when children arrived at St. Ignatius from public school, it was never too early to begin challenging the laxity of their habits. That nothing was demanded of the children was the worst failure of the public schools. Not that their parents were much better than the teachers, for the most part. But at St. Ignatius, lack of discipline—mental, physical, or moral—was simply not tolerated, so when she'd caught the Conway twins misbehaving on their very first morning, she hadn't hesitated to discipline them. And Kimberley had certainly responded well. The girl settled right into the routine of the school, and immediately made friends with exactly the right sort of girl—Sandy Engstrom was one of Sister Clarence's favorites.

But the boy was another story entirely. On the surface, Jared seemed unchanged. He was still the handsome boy who had walked into her classroom with his sister, a friendly smile on his lips, a strand of his dark curly hair falling over his forehead.

But something about him had certainly changed. It wasn't something Sister Clarence could quite put her finger on—and her inability to identify the difference troubled her. She found herself dreading his arrival in her classroom, and upbraided herself for it, but despite her efforts to exorcise the demon of anger, it still resided within her. In fact, it was growing stronger every day, and as she saw the effect that Jared was starting to have on Luke Roberts, the demon's strength increased. Now, as her class fell silent waiting to see how she would deal with Jared Conway, she struggled with the demon.

She wished to be fair.

She wished to be just.

He knows what I'm thinking. He knows, and even though it doesn't show in his face, he's laughing at me! The demon anger raged inside her, but she held it firmly in control. "Don't bother to sit, Jared," she said as he moved toward his seat. He stopped as her words struck him, but showed no sign of feeling the sting she'd injected into them. "Or you, either," she added as Luke Roberts slouched toward his desk. Though her words were directed at both the boys, her eyes remained on Jared Conway, held by his gaze like—

Like a mouse staring into the eyes of a coiled cobra.

For the first time in all her years of teaching, Sister Clarence had to struggle to keep her voice steady. "Both of you will report to Father Bernard's office at once." She waited, and for one terrible moment had the feeling that Jared Conway was somehow taking her measure. That he was thinking of defying her. Then he turned away and led his friend out of her classroom. But before he released her from the grip of his gaze, Sister Clarence saw the tiniest hint of a smile playing around the corners of his mouth.

The cold knot of anger within her congealed into hatred.

Hatred, and something else.

Something she'd never felt before, at least not in the presence of one of her students.

She felt fear.

For some reason she couldn't quite fathom, Sister Clarence realized she was dreadfully afraid of Jared Conway.

CHAPTER 21

J anet climbed down off the ladder and stepped back to survey her work. When it was finished, the mural would cover most of one wall of the dining room.

When she first told Ted her idea of doing the trompe l'oeil, making the long dining room wall opposite the French doors appear to open out onto another, far more formal garden from a time long past, she confessed that she'd almost given up on it before she even started. And it hadn't been simply the vastness of the wall that deterred her. "It's a whole different technique," she'd explained. "You have to know everything about perspective, and lighting, and—"

"And mostly, you have to have the ability to put what you see on the canvas," Ted had interrupted. They'd been in her studio, where she'd shown him the first sketch she made of the imaginary garden from the past. "I might not know much about art," he'd gone on, "but even just in black and white I feel as if I could walk right into that garden."

She eyed the image on the canvas as objectively as she could, and knew he was right—it was good. But still, the task of expanding it to fill the dining room wall seemed all but impossible. What if she couldn't do it?

"The worst that can happen is that you make a mess, and we paint it over. What have you got to lose?"

"Time," she'd reminded him. Just that morning, she'd tried to make a list of everything that needed to be done in the house, but gave up when the job began to look so staggeringly huge that she didn't see how they could ever succeed. But Ted had had an answer for that, too.

"Time is the one thing we're not lacking. Don't forget—there isn't any deadline for opening the hotel. I'd love to be ready by spring, but if it doesn't happen, it's not going to kill us. All the trust says is that I have to be living here. It's *my* idea to turn it into a business. And there's plenty of money in the accounts to hire people if I need to. So why not give the mural a try?"

He'd taken her hand—something he hadn't done in years—and led her through the house to the cavernous dining room. He had stripped the walls of their peeling wallpaper only the day before. "Maybe it's just the way you did the drawing, but I keep seeing a night scene." His eyes left the wall and scanned the vast, empty room. "And I keep seeing this room done in white—with fresh flowers everywhere—on the tables, on the sideboards, everywhere. I want to make it really romantic, with lots of candles, and tables for two—maybe a few for four, but mostly deuces." His eyes shifted back to the huge blank wall. "And when people look at that wall, they'll see what it must have been like here a century ago, with all those perfect formal gardens no one can afford to keep up anymore. Maybe with a reflecting pool, and moonlight . . ." He stopped, and looked worried. "Am I biting off more than you can chew?"

Janet shook her head. "If I could do it right, and it were lit right, it could be gorgeous at night. But what about breakfast and lunch?"

"We build a breakfast room," Ted had told her, and for the next hour he led her from room to room, describing the visions in his head. As she listened, Janet, too, began to see the elegant little hotel he wanted to build.

"I don't know if I can do it," he admitted when they were back in the dining room. "But I figure I'll take it one step at a time, and when I come to something I can't do, I'll find someone to help me out. So how about it? What's wrong with you trying to do something wonderful with that wall?"

She started the next day, elaborating on that first sketch she'd made. She worked through the morning, and Ted stopped by now and then to look over her shoulder at the drawings. But he never said anything unless she asked him what he thought. By the end of the morning, she'd finished a drawing that he assured her was a perfect depiction of exactly what he'd had in mind.

And Janet, after studying the drawing as objectively as she possibly could, decided that whether or not Ted was simply humoring her, the drawing was *good*. Right after lunch, she set to work expanding it onto the huge expanse of the dining room wall.

Within a couple of days—after she'd transformed the wainscoting into a faux-marble balustrade—she realized that Ted was right. She *could* do it. Slowly, the image took form, and as she worked, new ideas came to her. The painting seemed to take on a life of its own.

Now, even though the mural was still far from complete, the illusion was starting to emerge. She moved from the base of the ladder to the double doors opening from the entry hall, and was trying to gauge the mural's overall effect when she heard Ted come up from the basement, where he'd been working most of the day on the plumbing. For a moment she felt all the automatic responses that had become almost instinctual in her over the years:

The flush of apprehension as she waited to see how much he'd had to drink.

The reflexive shrinking away from the alcohol on his breath, and the roughness of his touch.

The measuring of the anger he always carried with him, which increased in proportion to the number of drinks he'd consumed.

But since that morning six weeks ago when he rid the house of the alcohol he'd bought only the day before, all of that had changed. Slowly, Janet had lowered her guard. Now, as she felt him behind her, she found herself looking forward to his touch rather than dreading it. She snuggled back against his chest, her fingers stroking the thick curly hair on his forearms as he slipped his arms around her and nuzzled her neck with his lips.

"I must smell like a pig," he growled into her ear.

"You smell wonderful," Janet murmured, her whole body responding to the musky odor emanating from his skin.

"Where's Molly?"

"Sound asleep," Janet replied. "I put her down half an hour ago."

Ted's fingers gently caressed her breasts. "How long will she sleep?"

"Maybe an hour." Janet twisted in his arms, and put her own around his neck. "Think that'll be long enough?"

"Not by half," Ted whispered. His lips moved from her neck and ear to her mouth, and his arms tightened around her. "Want to go upstairs?" he asked when their lips parted again.

Janet thought of the paintbrushes she'd left on the tray at the top of the ladder.

She thought of the mess in the kitchen that she hadn't cleaned up since lunch.

She thought of the hundred other things that needed to be done.

"I can't think of anything I'd rather do," she said.

He swept her up in his arms and started across the foyer toward the stairs.

"What are you doing?" Janet cried. "Ted, for God's sake, put me down! You'll cripple yourself!"

"Quiet, woman!" he commanded. He started up the stairs, and Janet's struggles gave way to giggles.

"If you drop me, so help me I'll—"

The front door opened then, and they heard Kim's voice. "Mom? Dad? What's wrong? How come you're carrying Mom?"

"Damn," Ted swore. Janet froze, waiting for the explosion. But when he spoke again, his voice was low enough that only she could hear him. "There goes a perfectly good ravaging. But just wait until later, when the children are locked in their rooms . . ." His voice trailed off seductively, then he kissed her and lowered her to the stairs. "Nothing's wrong," he told Kim, starting back down to the first floor. "How was school?"

Kim's face clouded. "Okay, I guess," she said, her voice giving the lie to her words.

"What happened?" Janet asked, also back in the foyer now.

Kim's eyes flicked from her mother to her father, then back to Janet. "Just Jared and Luke. They were acting like jerks."

"Anything special, or were they just being adolescent boys?" Ted asked.

Kim's gaze shifted uncertainly back to her father. It had been so long since he'd wanted to talk to either her or Jared that she still wasn't used to it. "Well, Sandy thought they were being jerks, too."

"Sounds like teenage boy stuff," Ted said.

The clouds in Kim's face turned stormy. "Why do you always defend him?" she demanded, glaring at her father. "What's going on around here? It seems like anything Jared wants to do is just fine with you, even when he's acting like an—"

"Hey, I'm sorry," he said with no trace of anger, holding up his hands as if to ward off Kim's attack. "I guess sometimes your old dad can still be a chauvinist pig. So what exactly did he do?" Kim hesitated, and Ted thought he knew what she was thinking. "Come on," he urged her gently. "I'm not going to bite your head off. And I promise I'll listen. Okay?"

Kim, mollified, first told them what had happened at the pizza parlor, then the aftermath in Sister Clarence's classroom. "I don't know what's going on with him," she finished. "But something's wrong. He's just not like himself. He—"

"He's growing up, honey," Ted told her. "Just like you are. Neither one of you is like you used to be. But that's not a bad thing. It's just—"

The phone rang, and he stopped as Janet picked it up. A moment later she mouthed *Father Bernard* at him. The conversation was brief.

"Father Bernard wants to see us," she said as she put the phone down. "Jared won't be home for a while."

Ted's brows rose. "What's he doing?"

"Cleaning the church," Janet said. "Father Bernard decided that if they didn't see fit to get to class on time, they might as well find out how they would enjoy being janitors, since, as he put it, 'that's about all either of them will be fit for if they don't straighten up.' "

Ted's eyes flashed with the sudden fury of his drinking days. They cleared quickly, but when he spoke, his voice was harsh. "Well," he said, "I suppose Father knows best, doesn't he?"

Clean the church.
Clean the freakin' church!
What kind of crap was that? Jared wondered, though he was careful to say nothing out loud until he and Luke were safely out of the school building. So they'd been a few minutes late getting back from lunch. What was the big deal? It wasn't like they were going to miss out on learning the secret of life, for Christ's sake. So they didn't get to hear Sister Clarence discuss the proper use of the subjunctive tense, or whatever the hell she'd been talking about. Who cared? But the thing that had pissed Jared off most was that Father Bernard left them waiting outside his office all afternoon. It wasn't like he'd been doing anything important—Jared was sure that most of the time he'd just been sitting there, inside. But they'd had to stand and wait, with everyone else in the school staring at them during the breaks.

No one had spoken to them, as if they were afraid they might catch some dread disease.

Bunch of kiss-ups, that's all they were, he thought.

Then, when they'd finally been called into Father Bernard's office, the priest made them stand at attention, like they were in some kind of military academy or something! And he'd even given them the "this hurts me as much as it hurts you" line of crap, like he really cared what happened to either one of them.

The way the priest had spoken, Jared assumed they would be suspended, but in the end he told them they were going to have to clean the church. "Perhaps if you see what it's like to work as a janitor, you might appreciate your classes a bit more."

More likely it was free labor that Father Bernard wanted, Jared decided.

"I bet he finds some reason to make a kid clean the church every single week," he said when he and Luke left the school. Sometime during the afternoon the weather had shifted, and the heavy mugginess in the air made Jared wish he could just go home and maybe sprawl out and take a nap. "What do you 'spose he'd do if we ditch it?" he asked.

Luke scuffed at the sidewalk, his hands shoved deep in the pockets of his jeans. "You can do whatever you want. But if I don't show, my mom'll find out, and she'll kill me."

Jared eyed the church that loomed across the street. The last time he'd been inside was for his aunt Cora's funeral. He remembered thinking it had been kind of pretty, with the light coming through the stained-glass windows. But now it seemed forbidding, and as he came to the steps, he suddenly didn't want to go inside.

But why should I want to? he wondered. Going inside meant spending the next three hours scrubbing the floors, polishing the brass railing in front of the altar, and cleaning all the statues. But even as he silently ticked off the list of chores Father Bernard had assigned them, he knew there was more to his reluctance to enter than just that.

As he stared at the high limestone facade of St. Ignatius, a deep anger took hold inside him.

"Come on," he growled. "Let's get it over with."

They walked into the vestibule, and Luke automatically dipped his fingers into the font of holy water that stood just outside the doors to the sanctuary, and genuflected.

Jared reached toward the water himself, then stopped. *Why should I?* he asked himself. *I'm not here to pray. I'm here because I'm being punished.* "Where do they keep the cleaning stuff?" he asked.

"Downstairs," Luke told him. "I know where it is."

He started up the aisle toward the altar, with Jared trailing after him. But halfway up the aisle, Jared felt a strange queasiness in his gut, as though he was getting the flu. He stopped. Now, he felt a cold sweat break out, his whole body feeling clammy, and a shiver passed through him. "Hey, Luke," he said. "Where's the bathroom?"

Luke spoke without turning around. "You either have to go next door to the parish hall, or use the one downstairs."

"What do you mean, downstairs? Where're we going?"

"Will you just come on?" Luke countered. "Jesus, what's wrong with you?"

"I—I just don't feel so good," Jared replied.

Luke turned to look at him, his eyes narrowing suspiciously. "Well, you don't look like anything's wrong," he said. "You trying to stick me with all the work?"

Jared glared at him. "I just need to use the can. No big deal."

As he followed Luke down the aisle, his queasiness getting worse, he prayed that he wouldn't puke or have an attack of diarrhea right here in the middle of the church. Luke would never let him forget that. Everything inside him was churning by the time they got to the sacristy, and when he saw the stairs at the back of the small chamber, he hurried down them. At the bottom, there were three storage closets and the rest room.

"Start getting the stuff," Jared said. "I'll be out in a minute." Going into the rest room, he groped around until he found a light switch, turned it on, then closed and locked the door. As his guts continued to churn, he pulled down his pants and sat down on the toilet.

A plume of vomit spewed from his mouth, and as he turned to throw up the rest of the contents of his stomach into the toilet, the diarrhea struck.

Jared was drenched in a cold sweat and thought he was going to pass out. But a moment later the attack began to pass. His vision cleared, the pain in his stomach eased, and the chill that had seized his body released its grip. Easing himself back onto the toilet, he lowered his head between his knees.

There was a knock at the door, and Luke said, "Hey, Jared—you okay?"

"Yeah," Jared grunted. "I'll be out in a minute."

He sat up straight. The last of the queasiness had faded, and he didn't feel any different than he had before the attack had hit him. Using most of the roll of toilet paper that hung from the wall of the one stall, he cleaned himself up, then pulled up his pants. As he was washing his hands, he looked at himself in the mirror, and for a moment he didn't recognize his own face.

His complexion was chalk white, and his eyes were bloodshot and looked as if they'd sunk deeper into their sockets.

Dead, he thought. *I look dead!*

But then the color began to creep back into his face and his eyes cleared.

Still, he didn't look quite right. In some weird way he couldn't describe, he looked different.

On the other hand, why wouldn't he? Hadn't he just puked and shit his brains out? It was a wonder he could stand up at all!

Turning away from the mirror, he set to work with the paper towels he found on a shelf over the sink, cleaning up the mess on the floor. When he was done, he looked at himself in the mirror. He was still pale, but he thought he looked better.

"Jeez, Jared, what took you so long?" Luke asked when he finally came upstairs ten minutes later.

"The runs," Jared said. "Never had anything like that happen before."

"You still trying to get out of this?" Luke asked suspiciously.

Jared glowered at Luke. "Let's just get it done and get out of here, okay?" His eyes wandered over the church, and again he felt the sickness building inside him. "I think I'm starting to hate this place."

They worked steadily for the next two hours, alternately scrubbing, polishing, and dusting until at last there was nothing left to be done.

The brass gleamed; the statues shone.

Luke shook his head. "I never want to see another can of Brasso in my life."

Jared, though, said nothing, for while Luke was surveying their work, he'd been staring at something in one of the niches set into the sanctuary's walls. It was a shrine to one of the saints, the altar on which the statue stood constructed of ornately carved marble. Surrounding the statue were more than a dozen crosses of various sizes.

"What's the big deal with that one?" Jared asked, tipping his head toward the statue.

Cocking his head, Luke gazed at it. "I don't know. I guess maybe she was someone's favorite saint or something."

Jared moved closer to the statue, which now seemed to be looking straight at him.

Looking at him, and accusing him of something. "She looks like she thinks she's better than the rest of us," he said. His eyes swept over the rest of the figures that adorned the church. "They all do."

"So?" Luke countered. "They're saints. They *were* better than the rest of us. Whatcha gonna do about it?"

Jared smirked. "Oh, I've got a couple ideas." Stepping over to the altar on which the figure stood, he reached out and broke off one of the crosses.

"Jeez, Jared," Luke breathed. "What are you doing?"

Jared's eyes locked on Luke's. "What does it look like I'm doing? I'm taking one of these things. There's so many of them, they'll never miss one. Bet they don't even notice it's gone."

"But what are you going to do with it?" Luke asked.

"Just wait," Jared said softly. "You'll see."

Monsignor Devlin rose slowly to his feet, his joints aching from the hours he'd spent sitting motionless within the confines of the tiny confessional. Although it had been years since he'd last heard any confession but Cora Conway's, the closeness of the partitioned booth still offered him a peace of spirit he found nowhere else. With the shutters to the grille closed against any penitent who might wander into the other side of the stall, he often sat the whole afternoon, following the wanderings of his mind wherever they led, knowing nothing would disturb his peace.

But today his peace *had* been disturbed. While he'd tried his best to close his consciousness to the sound of the two boys cleaning the church, their profanities destroyed his contemplation. Momentarily, he'd felt an urge to drive them from the sanctuary, but quickly thought better of it—a sanctuary from which two such obviously troubled souls could be driven was no sanctuary at all. In Monsignor Devlin's mind, the church should be as fully dedicated to the profane as to the devout, so he kept his silence, and quietly prayed for the boys' salvation.

Once, as he'd been silently repeating his rosary, he'd felt a draft seeping through the confessional's grillwork, and glanced up to see one of the boys passing his retreat.

Though he'd never seen the boy before, he recognized him at once—he had the features of all the Conways, so that even the tiny glimpse of the nephew reminded him of the great-uncle.

The great-uncle, and all the Conways who had gone before.

After Jared Conway passed his way, Monsignor Devlin was unable to concentrate on his devotions any longer, for no matter how hard he tried to keep his mind on his prayers, the words written in the Bible that Cora Conway had entrusted to him kept rising up from his memory, chilling his soul. After finishing Loretta Villiers Conway's last words, he'd put the Bible aside, feeling he'd somehow violated the privacy of the long-dead woman, never intending to open it again. Yet today, after glimpsing Cora Conway's great-nephew, he had come to realize that Cora must have wanted him to read the words her husband's ancestors had written, wanted him to understand something about her family. Why else would she have entrusted the family Bible to him?

Leaving the boys alone in the church and returning to the rectory, he climbed laboriously to his room on the top floor, opened Cora Conway's Bible, and set to work. The entry after Loretta Villiers Conway's was written in a hand so unsure it was barely legible. He had to decipher the words one at a time, but after an hour he was done. Rubbing his rheumy eyes and stretching against the pain that had settled into his back, the old priest reread the laboriously inscribed message, the text only slightly easier to decipher this second time. A date, almost obliterated by an ink blot, was scrawled at the top of the page . . .

August 22, 1912

Miz Loretta give me this Bible the day she died. I coud not reed or rite then, but I lernd some in the yeers sinst becuz this is the famly Bible and my girl Francy is part of the famly. It dont matter what Mister Frank says. My girl Lucy was part of it to, but she died birthin. Anyways, thats what Mister Frank said but I dont beleeve him. I think maybe he kilt her. Ifn he did, I hope he dies like Miz Loretta did! Anyway, I did not tell him about this like Miz Loretta said I should not. I guess this is just for the women folk.

BESSIE DELACOURT STARED AT THE WRITING SHE'D PUT IN THE BIBLE FOR SEVERAL LONG MINUTES. MAYBE SHE SHOULDN'T HAVE SAID WHAT SHE DID ABOUT MISTER FRANK KILLING LUCY THE DAY SHE WAS BORN, BUT IN HER HEART, SHE KNEW IT WAS TRUE. BUT IF MISTER FRANK EVER SAW WHAT SHE'D WRITTEN, HE'D PROBABLY KILL HER, AND MAYBE FRANCY, TOO.

EVERY YEAR SINCE FRANCY WAS BORN, BESSIE HAD SWORN SHE WOULD TAKE HER LITTLE GIRL AND MOVE NORTH, BUT SHE NEVER HAD. SHE DIDN'T KNOW ANYONE OUTSIDE OF ST. ALBANS, AND WHEN IT CAME RIGHT DOWN TO IT, SHE WAS EVEN MORE SCARED OF GOING THAN SHE WAS OF STAYING. SO ALTHOUGH THE FLAME OF HOPE FOR A BETTER FUTURE BURNED LOWER WITH EVERY PASSING YEAR, IT STILL FLICK-ERED—MAYBE THEY'D LEAVE NEXT YEAR, WHEN FRANCY WAS FOUR-TEEN AND DIDN'T NEED SO MUCH TAKING CARE OF . . . .

FOR NOW, THOUGH, THERE WAS TOO MUCH TO DO TO WASTE TIME ON SOMETHING SO FLEETING AS HOPE. WITH MISTER FRANK GETTING MAR-RIED TOMORROW, THE HOUSE HAD TO BE CLEANED AND THE FEAST PRE-PARED. THE UPSTAIRS WAS ALREADY SWELTERING IN THE AUGUST HEAT, AND BESSIE WOULDN'T EVEN LET HERSELF THINK ABOUT WHAT IT WOULD BE LIKE IN THE KITCHEN. AND OLD MONSIGNOR MELCHIOR—WHO DIDN'T LOOK ANY OLDER THAN MISTER FRANK, EVEN THOUGH HE WAS SEVENTY-EIGHT—HAD ORDERED ALL THE SILVER AND ALL THE CRYSTAL TO BE POLISHED FOR THE WEDDING, WHICH MEANT BESSIE AND FRANCY WOULD BE UP ALL NIGHT. BUT EVEN BEFORE SHE STARTED ALL THE WORK, THERE WAS ONE THING SHE HAD TO DO. CLOSING THE BIBLE—EVERY PAGE OF WHICH SHE'D FINALLY MANAGED TO READ IN THE YEARS SINCE MISS LORETTA HAD ENTRUSTED IT TO HER—BESSIE WRAPPED IT IN A TOWEL, THEN LISTENED FOR ANY SOUND OUTSIDE THE DOOR OF HER ROOM IN THE ATTIC'S EAVES.

SILENCE.

SHE STOLE OUT INTO THE NARROW CORRIDOR THAT LED TO THE BACK STAIRS, THEN MOVED ALONG THE MEZZANINE UNTIL SHE CAME TO THE ROOM IN WHICH MISTER FRANK'S BRIDE WAS STAYING. GLANC-ING AROUND ONCE MORE TO BE CERTAIN SHE WASN'T BEING WATCHED, BESSIE OPENED THE DOOR AND SLIPPED INSIDE.

THE ROOM'S OCCUPANT WAS LYING ON A CHAISE NEAR THE OPEN WINDOW, HER EYES CLOSED, A BOOK OPEN ON HER BREAST. BESSIE CROSSED THE ROOM AND BENT DOWN. "MISS ABIGAIL?" SHE ASKED. "MISS ABIGAIL, ARE YOU AWAKE?"

STARTLED OUT OF THE DOZE THE SOMNOLENT SUMMER AFTERNOON HAD BROUGHT HER, ABIGAIL SMITHERS SAT UP TOO QUICKLY AND THE VOLUME OF POETRY SHE'D BEEN READING FELL TO THE FLOOR.

IN AN INSTANT, BESSIE SNATCHED IT UP AND RETURNED IT TO ITS
OWNER.

"CAREFUL," THE MAID CAUTIONED. "BOOKS ARE VALUABLE."

"IT'S ONLY SOME VERSE," ABIGAIL SAID, SMILING AT BESSIE.

BESSIE'S EYES REMAINED SERIOUS. "ALL BOOKS ARE VALUABLE,"
SHE SAID. "ESPECIALLY THIS ONE." SHE UNWRAPPED THE BIBLE AND
PLACED IT IN ABIGAIL SMITHERS'S HANDS. "I BEEN HOLDING THIS," SHE
SAID. "I BEEN HOLDING IT FOR NEAR ON TO FOURTEEN YEARS. IT BE
YOURS NOW."

HER BROW KNITTING IN PUZZLEMENT, ABIGAIL STARTED TO OPEN
THE THICK VOLUME, BUT BESSIE LAID HER HAND GENTLY ON THE OTHER
WOMAN'S, STAYING IT.

"IT'S FOR LATER," BESSIE SAID SOFTLY. "YOU DON'T WANT TO BE
READING IT NOW, NOT THE DAY BEFORE YOUR WEDDING."

ABIGAIL'S EYES FIXED ON THE SERVANT. "THEN WHEN SHOULD I
READ IT?" SHE ASKED.

BESSIE DELACOURT STRAIGHTENED UP. "YOU'LL KNOW," SHE SAID
QUIETLY. "YOU'LL KNOW WHEN TO READ WHAT'S WRITTEN IN IT, AND
YOU'LL KNOW WHEN TO WRITE IN IT YOURSELF. BUT IT BELONGS TO
THE WOMEN OF THIS FAMILY. IT HOLDS ALL THE SECRETS. THE MEN
DON'T KNOW ABOUT IT, AND THEY DON'T NEED TO KNOW ABOUT IT!"

AS BESSIE DELACOURT LEFT THE ROOM, ABIGAIL SMITHERS GAZED
APPREHENSIVELY AT THE BIBLE, HER FINGERS STROKING ITS ALREADY
WORN LEATHER. SHOULD SHE OPEN IT?

BUT NO—BESSIE HAD SPECIFICALLY TOLD HER SHE SHOULDN'T
READ IT NOW. AND SHE WAS CERTAIN SHE KNEW WHY. UNDOUBTEDLY,
THE PAGES CHRONICLED ALL THE INEVITABLE TRAGEDIES THAT HAD
BEFALLEN FRANK'S FAMILY OVER THE YEARS, AS WELL AS THE JOYS
ALL FAMILIES SHARED, AND THE SERVANT DIDN'T WANT HER TO CLOUD
THE HAPPINESS OF TOMORROW BY READING THE SAD PARTS TODAY.

CARRYING THE BIBLE TO THE TRUNK SHE'D BROUGHT WITH HER
LAST WEEK FROM BATON ROUGE, SHE BURIED IT DEEP BENEATH THE
LINENS AND LINGERIE THAT WERE HER TROUSSEAU.

THE SERVANT WAS PROBABLY RIGHT—SHE WOULD KNOW WHEN
TO READ THE ENTRIES IN THE BIBLE, BUT IT CERTAINLY WAS NOT
TODAY.

OR TOMORROW, EITHER.

BESSIE DELACOURT POLISHED THE LAST SMUDGE OFF THE LAST PEN-
DANT OF THE IMMENSE CHANDELIER THAT HUNG OVER THE GREAT
MAHOGANY TABLE IN THE DINING ROOM. THE CLOCK IN THE LIBRARY

WAS TOLLING THE HOUR OF MIDNIGHT, AND EVERY MUSCLE IN HER BODY PROTESTED AS SHE CLIMBED DOWN OFF THE LADDER.

BONE-WEARY, THAT'S WHAT SHE WAS.

JUST PLAIN BONE-WEARY.

BUT THE WORK WAS DONE—LEASTWAYS THE HARD WORK WAS. SHE AND FRANCY WOULD STILL BE UP UNTIL DAWN POLISHING THE SILVER, BUT THEY COULD DO THAT AT THE WORKTABLE IN THE KITCHEN, WHERE AT LEAST SHE WOULDN'T HAVE TO STRETCH HER BACK AND TWIST HER NECK EVERY WHICHWAY LIKE SHE'D HAD TO DO WHILE STRAINING TO GET A GOOD LOOK AT EVERY FACET OF THE CRYSTALS ON THE CHANDELIER.

SHE WAS JUST LEANING OVER TO PICK UP THE BUCKET WITH THE AMMONIA WATER SHE'D USED TO CLEAN THE CHANDELIER WHEN SHE HEARD THE VOICE.

"LEAVE IT!"

THE TWO WORDS STUNG BESSIE LIKE THE STING OF A WASP, AND SHE JERKED UPRIGHT, STARTLED. FRAMED BY THE DOUBLE DOORS THAT LED TO THE HOUSE'S CENTRAL HALL WAS FRANCIS CONWAY.

MISTER FRANK.

FRANCY'S FATHER.

"IT'S TIME," HE SAID AS THE LAST TOLL OF THE HOUR DIED AWAY. "COME WITH ME."

A COLD KNOT OF FEAR FORMED IN BESSIE'S BELLY, AND SHE WANTED MORE THAN ANYTHING ELSE IN THE WORLD TO TURN AWAY FROM FRANK CONWAY, TO RUN AWAY FROM THIS HOUSE, TO TAKE FRANCY AND FLEE BEFORE IT WAS TOO LATE.

BUT SHE KNEW SHE COULD NOT, BECAUSE THE MOMENT FRANK CONWAY HAD SPOKEN, BESSIE HAD LOOKED INTO HIS EYES.

SHE HADN'T MEANT TO.

SHE WISHED SHE HADN'T.

BUT SHE HAD, AND NOW, JUST AS THEY HAD SO MANY TIMES BEFORE, FRANK CONWAY'S BLUE EYES HELD HER. IT WAS LIKE THEY COULD JUST REACH OUT AND TAKE HOLD OF HER, MAKING HER DO THINGS SHE'D NEVER DO IF IT WAS LEFT UP TO HER.

THINGS SHE COULDN'T EVEN THINK ABOUT, LET ALONE TELL ANYONE ABOUT.

AND NOW, THE NIGHT BEFORE HE WAS GOING TO MARRY THAT NICE MISS ABIGAIL FROM BATON ROUGE, HE WANTED TO DO IT AGAIN.

AND SHE KNEW SHE WOULDN'T BE ABLE TO STOP HIM, NOT ANY MORE THAN SHE'D BEEN ABLE TO STOP HIM IN ALL THE YEARS THAT HAD GONE BEFORE.

NOW SHE FOLLOWED HIM THROUGH THE DOOR THAT LED TO THE BASEMENT STAIRS.

DOWN THE STAIRS.

THROUGH THE DOOR THAT WAS ALWAYS LOCKED, THAT ONLY MISTER FRANK AND MONSIGNOR MELCHIOR COULD OPEN.

INTO THE DARKNESS THAT WAS PIERCED ONLY BY THE LIGHT OF A FEW CANDLES . . .

BUT EVEN IN THE LIGHT OF THE CANDLES, BESSIE DELACOURT COULD SEE THE COUNTENANCE OF MONSIGNOR MELCHIOR GLOWERING AT HER.

AND SEE THE GLINT OF LIGHT THAT REFLECTED FROM THE BLADE OF THE KNIFE HE HELD IN HIS HANDS.

INSTINCTIVELY, BESSIE KNEW WHAT WAS ABOUT TO HAPPEN TO HER.

THE SAME THING THAT HAD HAPPENED TO LITTLE LUCINDA—HER PRECIOUS LUCY, WHOM SHE'D BARELY SEEN BEFORE MISTER FRANK HAD TAKEN HER AWAY.

AS MISTER FRANK PICKED HER UP AND LAID HER ON THE TABLE BEHIND WHICH MONSIGNOR MELCHIOR STOOD, BESSIE FELT NO FEAR, FELT NO URGE TO SCREAM OUT.

BUT SHE KNEW, AS SHE WATCHED MONSIGNOR MELCHIOR RAISE THE KNIFE ABOVE HER, THAT SHE WOULD NOT RUN AWAY WITH FRANCY NEXT YEAR.

INSTEAD, SHE WOULD GO—THIS VERY MINUTE—TO JOIN LUCY.

AS THE KNIFE SANK INTO HER CHEST AND PIERCED HER HEART, BESSIE DELACOURT FELT A GREAT PEACEFULNESS COME OVER HER.

SHE, LIKE MISS LORETTA BEFORE HER, AT LAST WAS FREE OF THE CONWAY FAMILY.

Monsignor Devlin once again closed the Bible. Was it possible that Frank Conway could have killed his own child, as Bessie Delacourt said? But of course it was—a hundred years ago a child born of a servant in St. Albans was less valued than a hunting dog.

But even so . . .

The old priest flipped back, searching for an entry in the Bible that might have predated the one made by Loretta Villiers, but found none. Then, as he examined the ancient Bible more closely, he saw something: deep in the crevice between the two pages, cut so close to the binding as to be all but invisible, was the remainder of a page that had been removed from the volume.

Had Cora taken it out before giving him the Bible?

Or had it been someone else, someone who had gone before?

Sighing heavily, Monsignor Devlin put the Bible aside. Later, when his eyes were up to it, he would continue reading the rest of the entries made through the years by the women who had kept this strange journal of the family they had married into. But for now he turned to the histories of his own church—the parish of St. Albans—searching for some clue as to who this Monsignor Melchior could have been, this man who by the title associated with his name must once have been a priest.

A priest who had broken his vows and abandoned his vocation, yet kept his title?

Why?

He gazed dispiritedly at the thick journals filled with the scribblings of all the priests who had preceded him in St. Albans. Most of their hands were no more legible than that of the semiliterate servant, Bessie Delacourt. If he were truly going to find the answer to what might have been written on the pages that had been torn from the Conway family Bible, he would need help.

Father MacNeill!

Of course! He would talk to Father MacNeill, whose mind was much younger and sharper than his own.

Feeling as if a burden had been lifted from his back, Monsignor Devlin let his tired eyes close, and quickly drifted into the quiet of sleep.

CHAPTER 22

The phone call from Father Bernard hadn't taken Ellie Roberts entirely by surprise. In fact, she'd been expecting it—or at least one very much like it. She'd seen it coming ever since Luke started hanging around with Jared Conway. Ellie herself, of course, knew all about the Conways, even though she hadn't been born until a few years after George Conway hanged himself from the magnolia tree behind his house. Even now she could remember the first time she and her friends had snuck over to the big house on Pontchartrain Street. She'd only been five years old, and she'd stood on the edge of the road—none of them had dared set a foot on the property itself—and listened, wide-eyed, as Rudy LaFrenier, who was two years older than her, and knew everything—told them the story of what had happened here.

"Father Fitzpatrick says they was voodoos," Rudy had said, and even now, thirty years later, Ellie could remember the fear the words had instilled in her. "Father Fitzpatrick says this whole place is full of voodoo, and anybody who even walks on the lawn will go to Hell!"

The story had been enough to keep Ellie and her friends away from the Conway house, and even when she was old enough to realize that whatever tale Father Fitzpatrick—who had retired when Father Bernard came to St. Albans—might have told Rudy LaFrenier probably wasn't entirely true, she'd been unable to shake off her fear not only of the house, but of the Conways as well. After all, even if there wasn't anything to the voodoo story, George Conway must have been crazy to hang himself from the magnolia tree, and everyone knew what had happened to his wife when she found him. While Ellie didn't believe in ghosts, there'd always been something about the old Conway Victorian. Which was why she'd told Luke right off that she didn't want him hanging around with

Jared Conway. "There's just something about that place," she said. "And the Conways, too. Whenever there've been Conways in this town, there's been trouble."

Luke had rolled his eyes scornfully. "It's just a house, Ma," he replied, his voice taking on a stubborn note that reminded Ellie of his father. "Besides, I like Jared."

For perhaps the millionth time, Ellie wished Luke's father were still alive to deal with Luke, but there was nothing to be done about that. Big Luke had been a good man, doing a good job as a deputy sheriff, and when his motorcycle skidded out from under him that day, Ellie had wondered how she'd ever make it without him, let alone raise Little Luke by herself.

"The Lord works in mysterious ways," Father MacNeill had explained to her, "and the Lord will provide for you and young Luke."

And He had. She found a job working in the rectory. It didn't pay much, but it was enough. It also meant that Luke could go to St. Ignatius School for free, and during the first few years, the Sheriff's Office helped out, too. Ellie tried to bring Luke up right, doing her best to be both mother and father to him. It hadn't been easy, but she always tried to figure out what Big Luke would have told his son, and all in all, she thought, Luke was turning out all right.

Until he started hanging around with Jared Conway.

Father MacNeill suggested she forbid Luke to spend time with Jared, but she knew that wouldn't work. Times weren't like they used to be, when whatever your parents told you was law, and you didn't even think of disobeying them. Nowadays, kids did pretty much what they wanted to do, and even if Father MacNeill didn't understand it, she did. After all, even in St. Albans a lot of the kids were growing up with only one parent, or even if they had two, both parents worked. You just couldn't keep an eye on them as in the past. But it had helped that Luke was at St. Ignatius, because at least the sisters didn't put up with the kind of nonsense the public school teachers did.

And Luke hadn't caused any problems.

Not until today.

Mortified. That's how she'd felt when Father Bernard called to tell her about Luke's misbehavior. Just plain mortified. She'd sat at her desk in the rectory, the phone pressed so hard to her ear that it hurt, as if she were trying to keep Father Bernard's words from leaking out, so nobody would hear them but herself. But of course that wouldn't happen. Not in St. Albans, and certainly not within St. Ignatius parish.

What if Luke got expelled from school?

What if she lost her job because of it?

Finally, knowing she had no choice, she'd gone to see Father Mack about it.

When he looked up from the homily he was working on, she could tell he'd already talked to Father Bernard. So at least she was saved from the humiliation of having to confess Luke's sins herself. Then, when Father MacNeill began talking to her, Ellie realized that the situation wasn't as bad as she'd feared.

"Nobody blames Luke," the priest assured her. "We all know him, and know what a fine young man he is. But even the finest young men can fall under . . ." Father Mack hesitated, and Ellie could see him searching for exactly the right words. "Let's just say all of us sometimes fall under the wrong influences, shall we?" He smiled at Ellie, and her fears began to abate. "The problem isn't Luke himself." He pursed his lips, and tented his fingers in front of his chest as if he were about to begin praying. "It's the Conway boy I worry about."

"I know," Ellie quickly assured him. Father MacNeill had not only offered her a job when she was most in need, he'd also become her adviser in everything else in her life as well. "I've been worried ever since Luke started hanging around with that boy." She shook her head. "I wish they'd just go away. I know it isn't charitable of me, but I just wish the entire family would go away."

Father MacNeill's expression eased. "Then perhaps you might want to come to the hearing about the hotel Jared's father is planning to open."

Ellie had heard about the plan to turn the old place into a hotel— everybody in town had. But it hadn't occurred to her that there might be something she could do to prevent it from happening. She'd never paid much attention to politics, and Big Luke had always told her it was best to stay out of it. *"All you can do is get folks mad at you,"* he'd explained. *"So the best thing is just to keep your mouth shut, and let other people make the decisions."* But now, as Father MacNeill spoke, she saw that if she was going to pry her son away from Jared Conway, she would have to take a stand.

In the years since her husband had died, she'd done a lot of things she never would have thought herself capable of doing.

She could do this, too.

When Luke finally got home from cleaning the church, Ellie was waiting for him. She was sitting in Big Luke's chair, which still dominated the living room of the little house on Court Street, and which she never sat in unless she had to lecture Luke. "I want to talk to you," she said as he started toward his room at the back of the house.

"I got homework," Luke countered. "I stayed after school to—"

"I know why you stayed after school," Ellie interrupted. "Father

Bernard called me. At work," she added, her eyes fixed accusingly on her son. "How could you have done that? After everything I've done, after everything I've sacrificed—"

"Jesus Christ, Ma," Luke groaned. "All that happened was that me and Jared were a little late getting back from lunch."

"Don't take the Lord's name in vain," Ellie said, quickly crossing herself. "Your father—"

Luke's eyes flashed with anger. "Aw, come on, Ma. Dad's dead, remember? He's been dead since I was a baby! And I bet he swore!"

"He didn't!" Ellie flared. "Never!" *Well, at least he didn't swear in front of me,* she silently compromised. Certainly when Big Luke was working on the car, he'd used some words she didn't approve of. But never in front of her. "But that's not what I want to talk to you about."

Luke's eyes clouded suspiciously. "So what is it? If it's about being late—"

"It's more than that." Ellie hesitated, then decided to face the issue head on. "It's Jared Conway. I don't want you to see him anymore."

"Why?" Luke demanded. "What's wrong with Jared?"

Ellie rose from her dead husband's chair, trying to summon up the words Big Luke would have used. "He's a bad influence and I don't approve of him. So you won't see him anymore. Is that clear?"

Luke's jaw tightened and his eyes smoldered. "Yeah," he finally said. "That's clear. It's bullshit, but it's clear."

"And you will obey me?" Ellie pressed.

Her son eyed her, and for the first time in her life, Ellie found herself frightened by the way Luke was looking at her. It was almost as if he was taking her measure.

"Maybe I will," Luke said, "and maybe I won't."

CHAPTER 23

It was nearly six when the back door opened and Jared entered the kitchen. Janet looked up from the salad she was making, wondering what he would say about his lateness. Until recently, she wouldn't have wondered about it—Jared would have told her. But recently, especially since he'd moved into the basement room, he'd been disappearing downstairs as soon as he came home from school, and staying there until suppertime. And after supper, unless he went off to meet Luke somewhere, he'd vanish back downstairs.

"What's he doing down there?" she'd asked Ted a few days ago.

"It's all right, Janet. Let him have his space," Ted told her. "He's growing up. And no matter what the politically correct view might be, boys and girls are different. You can't expect Jared to be like you." A mischievous sparkle lit his eyes. "Of course, we don't want him to be quite like me, either, do we?"

"Lord, no," Janet replied without thinking, and then old habit had brought up her defenses as she waited for him to bristle at what she'd implied. But he only smiled at her.

"Every day I thank my lucky stars that you put up with it as long as you did. And don't worry—whatever Jared's doing down there, I'm sure he's not drinking. Believe me, I've had enough experience, so I'd know. I'd see it in him even faster than you'd see it in me if I fell off the wagon."

"But why does he need a lock on his door?" she pressed. "*Kim* certainly doesn't seem to need one."

"Territorialism," Ted had told her. "It's like an animal marking the boundaries of its hunting grounds."

Janet sighed. "Well, I guess a lock on the door is better than that."

But nothing Ted told her helped: a gulf had formed between Jared and the rest of the family, and it seemed to be widening every day.

Now, as Jared passed through the kitchen on his way to the butler's pantry and the dining room beyond, he didn't even speak to her, not even to say hello, much less offer an explanation of why he was so late coming home.

"Jared?" When her son didn't even slow down, she spoke more sharply. "Jared!"

He stopped, but didn't turn around.

"Look at me, please," Janet said, her voice soft, but pitched to let him know she wasn't in a mood to put up with any nonsense.

He turned to face her.

"Father Bernard called me this afternoon," she said.

Jared shrugged. "So?"

" 'So'? " Janet echoed. "Is that all you can say?"

"What do you want me to say?" Jared demanded. "Sister Clarence got pissed off at me, and so did Father Bernard, so I spent the afternoon cleaning the church. That's my problem, not yours."

Janet's eyes narrowed. "Your problems *are* my problems. I'm your mother."

Jared's eyes flashed with sudden fury. "Jeez, Mom! I'm not a little kid! I'm almost sixteen years old!"

"And until we came here, you've never gotten in trouble at school."

"I'd think you'd be proud of that, instead of climbing all over my back," Jared snapped, turning his back to her. "I'm going down to my room."

"Jared!" Janet exclaimed. "When I'm talking to you, I—" Catching sight of Molly, whose eyes were wide with worry over the anger in the voices she was hearing, Janet scooped the little girl into her arms. "It's all right, sweetheart," she crooned. "Mommy's not mad at you, and neither is Jared. Nobody's mad at you."

Taking the little girl by the hand, she led her into the library, which served Ted as a temporary office, and turned the little girl over to her father. "How about looking after Molly for a few minutes? I have to deal with Jared."

Ted stood up from the desk. "Maybe I should take care of it—" he began, but Janet shook her head.

"This is between him and me. Besides, I'm finally going to get a look at his room."

"Okay." Ted sighed, lifting Molly into his lap. "But I warn you— teenage boys' rooms can get pretty weird."

"Whatever I find, I'm sure I'll be able to cope with it," Janet replied. Unwilling to reopen any of the slowly healing wounds in her marriage, she resisted the urge to remind him that she'd been dealing with Jared pretty much by herself almost since the day he was born. Leaving Molly and Ted in the library, she headed for the basement.

She stopped at the top of the stairs, peering down into the shadows rendered deeper by the glare of the single naked bulb screwed into a socket in the wall halfway down. *Why would anyone want to live down here?* she wondered as she went down the creaking stairs. She tried to imagine what it must be like in the middle of the night, and shuddered at the thought of the spiders that must be creeping around. She paused at Jared's door, staring at the gleaming brass lock that she'd first noticed a few days ago. But at least there was no KEEP OUT sign, like the one he'd put on the door to his room when he was six. She reached for the doorknob, then changed her mind and knocked softly instead.

A moment later she heard Jared's voice, muffled by the door. "What?"

"May I come in?" she called.

A silence, then: "It's not locked."

Twisting the knob, she pushed the door open, stepped forward, then stopped short. Whatever she'd been expecting—and she wasn't sure if she'd been expecting anything in particular—it wasn't this.

For a single, utterly disorienting moment, Janet felt as if she'd stepped into a void. A wave of vertigo swept over her, and she instinctively put out a hand to steady herself. Then, as her eyes began to refocus, her brain to straighten out the signals it was receiving, the dizziness passed.

The room was painted black.

Not a glossy black, which might have created some interesting light patterns, but a dull, flat black that absorbed practically every ray of light the overhead lamp put out. The rafters that had been exposed the first time she'd been down here had disappeared: Jared—or, more likely, Ted—had filled the spaces between them with sound-deadening insulation, held in place by sheets of plywood painted the same flat black as the walls. The bulb that had once been suspended from a hanging wire was now screwed into a socket mounted on the ceiling, and it was covered by a shade. The shade, though, was nothing more than a red paper lantern, which only served to cast a fiery glow over the room. "Is that thing safe?" Janet heard herself ask, and immediately wished she could retract the words.

Too late.

"It's not gonna burn the house down," Jared said sullenly. "I checked it out with Dad."

As if he'd know, Janet thought, and then felt guilty about the disloyal thought. In truth, Ted had learned a lot more about reconstruction since they'd moved to St. Albans than she would have thought possible. There didn't seem to be a single question about wiring, plumbing, heating, or anything else relating to the house that he didn't have an answer for. So far, every one of his answers had proved to be correct.

Janet's eyes swept the rest of the room. There was a bed in one corner—at least most of a bed, for Jared hadn't bothered to put a frame under the box springs and mattress he and Luke had dragged down from the second floor. There were a couple of other mattresses—apparently rescued from the attic, or some part of the huge basement she herself hadn't yet explored—that were half folded up the walls to form rudimentary sofas.

There was a large table, and Jared had built what looked like some kind of workbench along the wall opposite the windows.

Against another wall stood an armoire that Janet remembered from one of the second-floor bedrooms, and a chest of drawers she couldn't recall having seen before.

The windows were covered with black paper.

How can he stand it? she wondered. *No light, no air, a musty odor.* But she checked herself, remembering her purpose.

She scanned the room again, searching for something—anything— she could relate to, finally fixing on the desk lamp that stood on the table next to Jared's backpack, and on a floor lamp next to the bed.

"Well, at least you can still find enough light to read," she said as brightly as she could.

Jared, sprawled out on the bed with his arms crossed on his chest, glared at her. "I like it, okay?" he said. "And Dad said I could do anything with it I wanted to, as long as you couldn't hear my music upstairs."

"But I'm sure he didn't mean—"

"Can you hear anything?" Jared interrupted. "Do I bother you?"

"No, but—"

"Then what's wrong with it?" he demanded.

Other than the fact that I can't see, I can't breathe, and I feel as if the walls are closing in around me, I suppose there's nothing wrong with it, Janet said to herself. Then she remembered what Ted had told her before she came down. *"Teenage boys' rooms can get pretty weird."* It wasn't as if she hadn't been warned. "I guess nothing's wrong with it," she finally replied. She took a tentative step toward him. "Truce, okay? I'm just worried about you, that's all. It seems like ever since we came here, you've . . ." She searched for the right word, but couldn't find anything better than the one already in her mind. "It just seems as though you're different, that's all. And I'm worried about you."

For several seconds Jared said nothing. When he finally looked at her, Janet saw the same fury glittering in his eyes as she'd seen upstairs. "Just leave me alone," he said. "Okay, Ma? Just leave me alone!"

A painful memory broke into Janet's consciousness. *His father*, she thought. *He sounds just like his father!* But it was more than the words Jared had spoken, which she must have heard a thousand times—*ten* thousand times—from Ted. It even went beyond the dark blaze in his eyes. It was an aura that seemed to have gathered around him; the same kind of impenetrable miasma that had surrounded Ted when he was drinking, making it impossible for her to reach him. Instinctively, she took a step toward Jared, but quickly stopped herself, remembering all the rebuffs from Ted over the years.

Was it possible Jared had begun drinking? She tried to reject the thought even as it popped into her head, but scanned the room once more, this time searching for a bottle or a glass.

Drugs?

She sniffed the air, searching for any sign of the sweet pungency of marijuana. All she smelled was the stale, musty odor that permeated the basement. But Jared wouldn't take drugs.

Would he?

Certainly she wouldn't have thought so a few weeks ago; in fact, if anyone had even suggested the possibility, she would have rejected it out of hand. Jared had lived through his father's drinking, and—

—and the children of alcoholics were far more likely to fall victim to the disease than those who hadn't grown up with it.

Not Jared, she prayed silently. *Oh, God, please don't let it happen to Jared.*

She wanted to reach out to her son, to hold him, to tell him that they could deal with whatever was going on inside him. But once again she saw the fury glowing in his eyes, and the impenetrable mask his face had become. Right now, she knew, there was no use trying to talk to him. Right now, he was his father's son. "Okay," she said. "I'll call you when supper's ready."

She backed out of the room, closed the door, and started up the stairs. She was halfway up when she heard the sound of the lock clicking.

Locking me out, she thought bleakly. *Locking me out of his life.*

* * *

Supper that evening turned into an eerie echo of all the suppers the Conways had survived when Ted was drinking. Though it was something none of them mentioned—as if they'd reached a silent understanding that by not talking about it they didn't have to admit it existed—Janet, Jared, and Kim had all felt a sense of reprieve, if not relief, when Ted didn't come home for supper, for when he did, the tension that hung over the table was often so thick that even one of the steak knives wouldn't have cut it. Even Molly had always sensed it, and no matter how hard Jared and Kim tried to keep their baby sister distracted, she invariably wound up fussing or making enough of a mess that Ted would demand she be taken away from the table. Recently, though, Molly's favorite place had become the spot just to the right of her father, who seemed to have tapped into an apparently inexhaustible well of patience that none of his children had seen before, and that Janet herself assumed had dried up years earlier.

But now all the old tension was back, except that instead of hanging like a dark curtain between Janet and Ted, the strain had fallen over Kim and Jared. Ever since the twins had first begun to talk, the supper table was their favorite place to recount the events of their day, each of them finishing the other's sentences, each picking up on his or her sibling's thoughts. Now, though, a silence hung over them. It wasn't the kind of comfortable lag in the conversation that used to occur when both of them seemed to run out of things to say at the same moment. Rather, the silence felt like the uneasy quiet of nighttime on a battlefield.

Janet felt as if she and Kim were crouched low in a foxhole, listening for something that might betray the approach of some enemy that neither of them could quite see but both of them knew was there. Now and then they would exchange a wary glance, and Janet could see the worry in her daughter's eyes.

Jared had been the last to arrive at the table, and then he'd hardly spoken, barely even acknowledging Molly's loud greeting. Instead, he sank into his chair and began eating, stolidly moving the food from his plate to his mouth.

Molly, picking up on the mood at the table, quickly began fussing. Then, halfway through the meal, she picked up a fistful of mashed potatoes and hurled it at her brother.

Janet and Kim both froze, their eyes meeting.

For a split second Jared seemed not to notice the wad of potatoes and gravy oozing down his chin, but then he looked up at his baby sister. Molly, pleased finally to be capturing her brother's attention, smiled happily and waited to see what Jared would do. But as Kim and Janet watched—and Jared's eyes fixed on his baby sister—the smile faded from Molly's face, and then she began screaming.

It was a high-pitched wail, the kind of sound a cornered animal might make just before a predator leaps upon it and tears it to shreds.

Janet rose from her chair to pick the child up. But before she could get to Molly, Ted had boosted the little girl out of the high chair and was cradling her against his chest. Molly's arms were coiled around his neck as she clung to him, her face buried in his shoulder as her body quivered with frightened sobs.

"There there, sweetheart," Ted crooned. "It's okay, Molly. Daddy's here, and nothing's going to hurt you."

As Molly settled down, Janet turned furiously on Jared. "What did you do?" she demanded. "What did you do that made her start screaming like that?"

"Me?" Jared shot back. "I didn't do anything! She's the one who threw the food. Why don't you get mad at her?" Standing, he wiped the last of the gravy from his cheek, crushed his napkin, and hurled it onto the table. As he stalked out of the kitchen, Scout, who was curled up on his blanket in the corner, tensed, then snarled at Jared.

"Shut up," Jared told the dog as he passed by. "Don't even think about it!"

Scout cowered back as if he'd been struck, his snarl dying away to a whimper.

When Jared was gone, Janet turned to Kim, whose face was ashen, her eyes wide. "What was it?" Janet asked. "Did you see what happened?"

"I—I don't know," Kim breathed, her voice shaking. "It was—I don't know. It was just the way he looked at Molly." Her eyes met her mother's, and Janet could see the fear in them. "Mom, it was awful. It was . . ." She paused as if trying to find the right words, then shook her head helplessly. "He looked like he wanted to kill her, Mom." Tears were running down Kim's face now. She slid her chair back and fled from the kitchen.

Janet turned to her husband. Ted, still rocking Molly in his arms and crooning softly into her ear, seemed not to even notice that his two older children had left the room. Suddenly, her worries about Jared's sullen behavior coalesced into anger. How could Ted simply ignore the scene Jared had caused? "Do you still think everything's just fine with Jared?" she demanded. "Or were you drunk for so many years that you don't even know how normal families behave anymore?" Regretting her words the moment she spoke them, Janet braced herself against the eruption of

Ted's temper she expected her words to trigger. But again no trace of the old Ted appeared. Instead, he offered her a sympathetic smile, and when he spoke, his tone was as soothing as the crooning he'd just used to calm Molly.

"Take it easy, hon. It was just a little squabble."

"Little squabble?" Janet echoed. "You call that a little squabble? Molly was scared to death!"

"And Jared was covered with potatoes and gravy," Ted reminded her.

"He wasn't *covered* at all," Janet objected. "He had a couple of blobs of—"

"All right, 'a couple of blobs,' " Ted agreed. He transferred Molly back into the high chair, ignoring the food stains that had spread across his own shirt as he'd held the little girl close and dabbed her tears away with a napkin. Then he began spooning food into her mouth. "All Jared did was glare at her," he reminded Janet. The beginning of a grin played around the corners of his mouth. "Consider yourself lucky he didn't sling some peas back at her, or maybe an even bigger blob of potatoes. We could have had a major food fight on our hands."

"For God's sake, Ted!" Janet flared. "He terrified Molly! He even terrified Scout! And have you seen his room? What is he doing down there? It looks like—oh, God, I don't know what it looks like!"

Then Ted's arms were around her and he was cuddling her as gently as he'd held his baby daughter moments before. "Hey, take it easy," he said. He tipped her face up so she was looking into his eyes. "Nothing that terrible happened. It wasn't anything more than a little squabble, and it's over now." His eyes held hers, and the fears she felt for Jared began to melt away. "There's nothing wrong with Jared," Ted assured her again. "He's just a perfectly normal teenage boy. When you think about it, we've been incredibly lucky at just how normal he is." His finger stroked her cheek, and she felt a thrill run through her body. "When I think about the problems we could have had . . ." He let his voice trail off, and was just bending over to kiss her when there was a loud knocking at the back door. "Don't move," Ted whispered. "Just hold my place and I'll be right back."

Ted opened the door and saw Luke Roberts standing nervously on the porch. "Is Jared here?" the boy asked.

"Down in his room." Ted held the door wide open so Luke could come in. The boy hurried through the kitchen, barely nodding to Janet, and disappeared through the butler's pantry, toward the stairs to the basement. As soon as he was gone, Ted's arms were once more around his wife. "Told you I'd be right back," he murmured.

Janet looked worriedly up into his face. "After the trouble they got into at school, don't you think we ought to send Luke home? At least tonight?"

Once again Ted's eyes sought out her own and held them. "If we did, Jared would be gone in an hour," he told her. "Better to know where they are, don't you think?"

"But—" Janet began, but Ted didn't let her finish.

"No buts," he said. "Let's just clean up the kitchen, and put Molly to bed. And maybe," he said, putting on a wide smile, "I'll put you to bed, too."

As she and Ted set to work, all the worries—the fears—Janet had felt a few minutes earlier drained from her. By the time she and Ted went upstairs half an hour later, all she was thinking about was the way Ted had looked at her, and the feeling his touch—just his finger, stroking her cheek—had brought to her body.

Everything else was forgotten.

CHAPTER 24

Luke Roberts wasn't quite sure what was happening, but on the other hand, he didn't really care, either. At least he was out of his house—away from the sound of his mother's voice. Did she even know he was gone? Probably not. He'd left his door locked, then gone out the window, cutting through the backyards of the two houses between theirs and the corner. His mom might have knocked on his door, but when he didn't answer, she'd figure he was either asleep or pissed at her— which he was—and call Father MacNeill. But at least she wouldn't go around and try to look in the window to see if he was there. "You're thirteen now," she'd told him on his birthday two years ago. "You're growing up, and Father MacNeill says you should have some privacy."

Father MacNeill!

For as long as Luke could remember, his mom had acted as if the priest was his real father—in fact, when he was real little, he'd actually thought Father Mack *was* his real dad, until someone told him that the priest wasn't really anyone's father at all. Sometimes late at night, Luke still tried to picture what his father looked like, but no matter how hard he tried, the only image he could conjure was that of Father MacNeill. Which sort of figured, he decided, since his mother used to start almost every sentence with "Father says . . ." So even when she'd given him the "gift of privacy," as she'd called it—when all he'd really wanted was a dirt bike—she took half the gift away right off the bat by adding that "Father says you mustn't abuse the privilege." After taking a deep breath, her face turned beet red and she blurted the other thing Father MacNeill had said: "And you mustn't use the privilege to abuse yourself, either. That would be a mortal sin." He'd considered pretending that he didn't know what she was talking about, just to see how she'd explain it, but finally decided not to, figuring if she ever walked in and caught him, he could at least claim ignorance that he was committing a sin. Of course, then he'd have to go confess to Father MacNeill, since she'd be bound to tell him what she caught him doing. But at least she'd stuck by her promise not to come into his room unless he said it was okay. Father Mack had probably told her she'd go to Hell if she broke the promise. So after their fight tonight, he'd just gone out the window to hang out with Jared for a while. His mom would probably be on the phone with the priest for at least an hour anyway, and by the time he got home, she'd have either gone to bed or fallen asleep in front of the TV. Either way, she'd never even know he was gone.

When Luke arrived, Jared was taking a bunch of candles out of the big wooden cabinet they'd dragged down from the attic last week and setting them up on the workbench. Luke flopped down on one of the mattresses, dug into his pants for a joint, but only found a roach. He and Jared each took a hit or two while Luke told Jared about the fight he'd had with his mom, then they threw the butt through the grate that covered the sump in the middle of the floor. After that, Jared lit the candles—and some incense to cover the smell of the joint, just in case. He turned on some music and started fiddling with the lights, then the strobe came on, and Luke began to see strange patterns emerging from the blackness of the walls.

"Cool, man," he murmured. "How'd you do that?"

"Do what?" Jared countered.

"That stuff on the walls."

Jared looked at him. "What are you talking about? What stuff?"

Luke frowned, confused. Was Jared putting him on, or was he actually starting to see things?

"Tell me what you see," Jared said. Though his voice was barely audible above the pounding music, the words resonated in Luke's head with the authority of a command. "Tell me what you see," Jared repeated. "And tell me what you want."

Luke concentrated on the strange patterns that seemed to be floating in nothingness in front of the black wall. Fluorescent paint, he thought. He glanced around for the source of the black light that made the designs seem to glow with a luminescence of their own, but Jared had hidden it so well he couldn't see it at all.

Cool.

The patterns began moving, their colors—hot pinks and brilliant greens—transmuting before his eyes into a rainbow of hues in evershifting shapes. The fumes of the incense filled his nostrils, and he sucked them in, imagining that it was another joint.

The candles flared brighter, and the floating patterns took on a blinding brilliance.

"What's going on, man?" he asked. "Jeez, I can hardly see!"

"Watch," Jared commanded. "Keep watching, and think about what you want. Anything you want. Anything at all."

The patterns of color began to pulsate, swelling to fill the entire room with swirling light that now seemed to come from everywhere. A golden cross appeared above the workbench. It was blurry at first, as if out of focus, and as Luke concentrated on it, he realized it was spinning.

Spinning, and upside down.

And there was something on it—some figure he couldn't quite make out. He wished the cross were spinning slower so he could see more clearly.

Even as the thought formed in his mind, the spinning began to slow . . .

As he had almost every night since Ted Conway moved his family into the house where his mother had died, Jake Cumberland lurked in the protective shadows of the carriage house, blending so perfectly into the night that even someone passing within a few feet of him would not have sensed his presence.

The magic he had attempted with the cat—the magic he'd learned by watching his mama—had failed. The Conways were still here, and every night he could feel their evil growing and spreading—spreading like the kudzu that crept across the countryside so quickly you hardly knew it was there until one morning you woke up and the shrubs were covered with it, and the trees were choked with it, and it was too late to do anything about it.

And if the Conways stayed—

But they wouldn't stay, for he was there every night, working his mama's magic.

Now, as he sensed midnight coming on, he spread out his amulets and herbs and began muttering the incantations he'd heard from his mama's lips before she'd died. . . .

Weird, Jared thought. Where's it all coming from?

It wasn't the grass—there'd only been enough left of the joint for a

couple of quick hits, and he hadn't sucked it in the way you were supposed to. In fact, he didn't really like the drug much, since all it had done
the couple of times he actually tried it was make him feel like he was
going to throw up. He hadn't actually done it, but had to spend a couple
of hours concentrating on keeping peristalsis working in the right direction. Then he'd wondered if the rest of his autonomic systems—his
breathing, heartbeat, and everything else—was going to have to be con-
sciously controlled, too. That put him into a panic for a minute, and he
actually felt himself stop breathing. Once he'd gotten the panic under
control, though, everything was okay. But he hadn't been tempted to try
it a third time.

So if it wasn't the grass, where was it all coming from?

The light.

The sounds.

The voices.

None of it was real—it couldn't be. There wasn't anyplace in the
room the light could be coming from, since the one bulb hanging from the
ceiling wasn't even on. And there was no way the candles could be making the room look the way it did. Still, when he set up the candles, taking
them out of the armoire and arranging them on the workbench, he'd kept
changing them around. It was almost like there'd been something inside
his head, some pattern, telling him exactly how to set them up, and he
kept adjusting them, moving one and then another, until he knew—just
somehow *knew*—that they were right. Then he lit them and dropped down
onto the mattress. And it had all begun.

The music from his boom box had taken on a different sound, and
he heard things he'd never even imagined before—wailing notes that
sounded almost like human voices, but that he knew were not. And
although the candle flames hadn't actually seemed to change at all, weird
patterns started to emerge from the black walls, and a strange glow that
didn't look like any light he'd ever seen before began to suffuse the room.
It started as nothing more than a speck of light hovering in the center of
the room—right over the sump, in fact—which had slowly grown, swelling until it filled the space, then somehow kept on expanding. The walls
faded away, and it seemed he was in some kind of cathedral.

That was when he started hearing the voices.

It was just a babble at first, but after a while a couple of them were
clear enough to recognize.

Kim's voice.

She was calling out to him, but sounded so far away that he could
barely hear her.

Luke's voice was much closer, and when he concentrated on it,

Jared realized he could hear it as clearly as if Luke were talking right into his ear. But then, as he listened, he realized it wasn't actually Luke's voice he was hearing at all.

It was his *mind*.

Somehow, in some way he didn't understand, he was listening to Luke Roberts's thoughts.

Then, as he focused his mind on Luke, he began to see the things Luke was seeing.

And feel Luke's emotions.

Luke was angry.

Jared could feel his friend's fury—even see it. It looked like a bubbling pool of molten lava, glowing red, churning within the confines of Luke's subconscious.

But what was he angry about?

An image flashed into Jared's mind.

A woman.

Luke's mother!

But he'd never met Luke's mother. How did he know it was she he was seeing?

He knew. *Somehow, he knew.*

And as he saw what Luke was seeing, and felt what Luke was feeling, Luke's anger became his own. . . .

"**J**ared?" Kim called out, but even to herself, her voice sounded almost inaudible, as if coming from a great distance away. She called out again, louder this time, "Jared!"

Where was he?

Kim took a tentative step forward, searching for some sign of him, but she could barely see in the misty darkness that had closed around her.

Fog!

Of course! That was it. Fog had settled in, muffling her voice, and making it hard to see. "Jared," she cried out yet again. "Where are you?"

She listened, but heard nothing. Yet how was that possible? She was certain he'd been with her—right next to her—just a moment ago. But where could he have gone?

She shivered, although she didn't feel the least bit cold. What should she do?

Should she just wait for him to come back?

Should she try to find him?

The dark mist grew thicker, and as it swirled closer, wrapping Kim in a gauzy miasma, the uneasiness that had come over her when she first realized Jared was no longer by her side began to congeal into fear.

"No," she whispered. "I don't want to be alone, Jared. Don't leave me. Please?"

Where could he have gone?

He'd been there just a minute or so ago—she was sure of it. They'd been looking around the old house—exploring some of the rooms they'd never been in, and then suddenly he'd vanished.

A trick!

That was it—he was just playing a trick on her!

The grip of fear loosened slightly—enough to let Kim start moving again, but as soon as she did, she knew she was lost. Alone in a place she did not recognize. She'd fallen into some kind of vacuum, and everything she'd ever known seemed to have vanished.

Her heart began pounding as fear once more tightened its hold on her.

Move!

She had to move!

If she didn't, she might never escape from this terrible place where she could see nothing—hear nothing—*feel* nothing!

Finally, she forced herself to grope her way through the dark fog, her hands stretched out in front of her as she felt her way along.

Something brushed at her fingers, and she jerked them away.

She froze, straining her ears as she struggled to hear a sound that might betray the identity of the thing she'd touched, but all she could hear was the pounding of her own racing heart.

Then she felt the touch again, only this time it was her legs that the thing brushed against.

Stifling a scream, she shrank away from the strange sensation.

Why couldn't she see? Though there wasn't much light, there should have been enough for her to see something other than the swirling mist that floated around her.

She gasped as the thing that lurked just beyond her vision and just beyond her hearing brushed up against her again.

Then, as if from somewhere far in the distance, she heard a throbbing sound emerge from the mists, and for a moment she thought it must be the beating of her own heart. But as it grew louder, she realized that wherever it was coming from, it wasn't within her own body. Yet even as the sound swelled, it sounded oddly muffled, as if the mists surrounding her were smothering it as well.

Then something pressed against her legs.

Her heart racing, she instinctively reached down to shove whatever it was away.

A second later her fingers sank into—

Fur! The soft, wonderful feel of Scout's thick golden coat!

It was Scout she'd touched, Scout she'd felt brushing against her. Dropping to her knees, she put her arms around the dog and pulled him close, burying her face in his coat. "Where's Jared?" she whispered to the dog. "Where is he, Scout? Find him for me."

The dog stiffened, and twisted out of her arms, disappearing into the swirling mists.

Follow him! She had to follow him, or she'd be lost forever in the suffocating gray fog.

"Scout?" she called out. "Scout, where are you?"

She began moving again, forcing her legs to carry her forward, stretching her hands out to feel her way. A moment later she felt something, and began exploring it with her fingers.

A door!

She found the knob and pulled it open, stumbling through into a corridor.

The mists thinned, and finally she could see.

She wasn't in a corridor at all, but on the broad mezzanine that ringed the house's huge entry hall!

The stairs! There they were, off to the right!

And the music was louder now, and coming from somewhere below!

Downstairs. That must be where Scout had gone. Kim hurried to the top of the stairs and started down, quickly coming to the landing where they curved downward in the broad flight that would take her into the entry hall. She started down once again, but the stairs seemed to go on forever, stretching away from her in endless repetition. She hurried her pace, racing down the stairs, and finally came to the bottom.

The music was thundering in her ears now. It still seemed to be coming from everywhere and nowhere; it drew her forward until she stood at the top of the stairs leading to the basement.

She stared down into the dark abyss, seeing nothing but blackness.

Blackness, and a single pool of light that seemed to fade away into the distance even as she gazed down at it.

But that was where Jared had gone.

She knew it. She could feel it.

And if she wanted to find him, she had to go there, too.

Steeling herself, Kim started down into the darkness.

The music grew louder with each step, until it was throbbing painfully inside her head. But she kept going, for she was beginning to feel something else, too.

Jared.

He was here, close by.

She kept going, deeper into the blackness. With each step, the pool of light seemed to recede. Yet at the same time, it pulled her toward it like a moth. "Jared," she whispered, her voice lost in the throbbing of the music. "Jared, where are you?"

At last she came to a door. A closed door. She paused, part of her wanting to go through the door, while another part of her wanted to turn away, to flee back up the stairs through the darkness, even disappear back into the gray miasma in which she'd first found herself. But she reached out and took the knob.

And pushed the door open.

The music swelled, her head feeling as if it would burst, and the brilliant light that broke from beyond the door blinded her for a moment. But then her vision cleared, and she gazed into the space that opened before her.

The ceiling, which soared to a height that made her dizzy, was supported by huge black columns so large their mass threatened to overwhelm her. Indeed, the entire chamber seemed to be bearing down on her, and despite the vastness of the space, the walls felt as if they were closing in on her. Everywhere, strangely etched panels hung, and Kim's eyes, blinking in the brilliant glare, moved rapidly from one hanging to another, gazing at the figures depicted in them. There was something familiar about them, a flickering of recognition at the edges of her consciousness, but each time she focused on one of the great gleaming panels, the feeling of recognition retreated. Only when she saw what lay at the far end of the vast chamber did she realize what it was: some kind of cathedral. But a cathedral unlike any church she had ever entered, for instead of offering her peace and comfort, this vast emptiness was filled with a terrible despair that seemed to worm its way into the core of her being.

Then, at the far end of the cathedral, above an enormous altar, she saw the cross.

It hung upside down, and where the figure of Jesus should have been, Kim saw the form of a woman, hanging head downward, her face a visage of agony.

On the altar itself, another figure lay, stretched prone on its back, gazing up toward the vaulted ceiling. And in front of the altar, a third figure stood. A tall figure, its arms raised, and spread wide in a gesture of supplication.

Or of blessing.

Even though the figure's back was to her, Kim recognized it at once.

Jared!

She took a step toward him, calling out his name.

He turned.

His eyes met hers, and Kim realized it wasn't Jared at all.

The face was Jared's.

The hair.

The eyes.

The smile.

But it wasn't Jared, for from the familiar form of her twin brother radiated an aura of something so strong it was almost a physical force.

It was Evil.

An Evil so pure and unadulterated that for a moment Kim could do nothing more than stand paralyzed in the face of it. Suddenly she understood that it was the source of everything she'd seen and felt and heard.

The suffocating gray mist.

The force that guided her down the stairs and led her into the cathedral.

The throbbing music.

All of it was Evil, pure and simple.

And at the center of it was Jared.

Now it reached out to her. She could feel it creeping closer, stretching tentacles toward her. Tentacles that—if she allowed them to touch her at all—would never release her from their grip.

She heard her name whispered in the shimmering light: "Kiiim . . ."

Part of her wanted to answer the siren call, wanted to reach out to the blinding light, be absorbed into it.

"Kiiimmmm . . ."

The whisper came again. The Evil drew closer.

And before her eyes, everything began to change. The light turned gray and cold, and now she could see that the great pillars soaring to the ceiling were made of bones. The images in the shimmering windows were visages of death. A terrible, paralyzing cold gripped Kim. Then, as if of its own volition, her right hand came up to close on the tiny golden cross, her aunt's deathbed gift. In an instant, the cold released her and she turned, fleeing from the temple of death, plunging back into the darkness, stumbling up the stairs.

Her heart pounding, her breath coming in labored gasps, Kim raced through the house and started up the great staircase in the entry hall. The gray fog closed around her again, wrapping her once more in its asphyxiating bonds, and then she could neither see nor hear.

As the breath went out of her, and the gray faded to black, she uttered a single, silent scream.

Then she gave herself up to the mists and the darkness.

She deserves it.
She really deserves it.

Luke Roberts repeated the phrase over and over as he watched the face of the woman suspended head down on the inverted cross that floated above the shimmering altar.

His mother's face.

He'd watched in fascination as the spinning cross slowed to a stop, but even when he finally got a clear look at the face of the woman, he hadn't recognized it right away. All he'd seen was the pain in it—the agony. The mouth was open but no scream emerged; the eyes were stretched into horrified orbs, but no tears ran from beneath the lids. Everything about the face was distorted, but slowly—so slowly Luke was barely aware of it—he began to recognize his mother.

As her features came into focus, so also did all the angry memories—memories that, until this moment, he hadn't even known existed.

Her fault!

Everything was her fault!

Her fault that they never had any money.

Her fault that no matter what he did, Father MacNeill always found out about it.

It was probably even her fault that his father was dead!

But now she was finally getting what she deserved.

His eyes met hers then, and he felt her silent accusation:

Why are you doing this to me?

All the fury he'd felt that evening when he got home from cleaning the church came flooding back to him. What was she doing, getting all over his back? He hadn't done anything! So he'd been a couple of minutes late getting back from lunch. Big fuckin' deal! Who cared, except her and all those priests? As his anger grew, he watched his mother writhe on the inverted cross, watched blood begin to ooze from the pores of her face.

Don't you like it? he silently taunted. *Well, now you know how I feel when you're always picking at me!*

His rage—a rage far stronger than he'd ever felt before—continued to grow, until he was on his feet, moving toward the altar. Drawing closer to the cross, his arm outstretched, he pointed directly at his mother's pain-ridden face with a quivering finger.

"Die!" he hissed. Then his voice rose. "Die," he shouted. "God damn you! Just die!" His voice cracked, and he dropped to his knees. "Die!" he breathed once more. His rage spent, his head dropped forward onto his chest and his eyes closed.

Luke's whole body trembled, then stilled, and finally, depleted, he opened his eyes again.

The candles Jared had arranged on the workbench were guttering—one of them had already gone out.

The visions he'd seen—the hallucinations of the glorious cathedral—had vanished, leaving only the black-painted reality of the basement room. Luke's heart was hammering, his whole body was covered with a sticky sheen of sweat, and his breath came in panting gasps. His legs feeling as if they'd barely support him, he moved back to the mattress, letting himself sink into its softness, lying back against the wall as his respiration and his pulse slowly returned to normal.

He felt both exhausted and exhilarated, and as the minutes crept by, he listened to the discordant sounds of the music that still blared from Jared's boom box. As the last chords faded away, he finally spoke. "Jeez," he whispered, turning to gaze at Jared in the flickering light of the few candles that were still burning. "Where'd all that come from?"

"Where'd what come from?" Jared asked.

Luke frowned uncertainly. "D-Didn't you see it?" he stammered. "It was like—like some kind of huge church or something. And there was a cross." Haltingly, he tried to describe what he'd seen, what he'd felt, but even as he spoke, the details began to fade from his consciousness, until all that remained was the memory of his exhilaration.

And the anger.

Then he looked at his watch.

One o'clock.

It wasn't possible! He'd only gotten here a little while ago—it couldn't have been more than an hour.

Could it?

He looked again—the numbers on the face of his watch hadn't changed. And he felt exhausted. His muscles all hurt—even his bones seemed to be aching.

The church! That must be it—he must finally be feeling the effects of the hours he and Jared had spent cleaning the church that afternoon. "I—I better get outta here," he mumbled, scrambling to his feet. "My mom's gonna kill—" The words died on his lips as a flicker of a memory rose in his mind, then vanished so quickly he wasn't even certain what it was he'd remembered.

Something about his mom, and—

—and what?

Nothing. Whatever it was, it was gone. "Better get goin'," he muttered.

J ared waited until Luke was gone, then relit the candles on the workbench. Every detail of what Luke had seen was still etched sharply in his mind, as was every word Luke had uttered as he'd stood pointing an accusing finger at his mother's image.

Luke himself might not remember what he'd said, but Jared did.

"Die, God damn you! Just die!"

Then he heard another voice—a voice so faint he could barely make out the words at all.

"No," Kim's voice whispered. "No, Jared, don't . . ."

Jared hesitated, the match in his hand flickering above the only unlit candle on the workbench.

"Don't," Kim's voice whispered once more, but so faintly now that her words were easy to ignore. "Don't do it, Jared. Please don't do it . . ."

Jared lowered the match to the wick.

The flame shrank, nearly dying away.

But then the wick glowed red, caught fire, and flared up.

The memory of Kim's softly whispered words was lost as the blinding light expanded once more to fill the room.

"No, Jared! No!"

Kim's own shriek jerked her awake, and she sat bolt upright. A flash of terror came over her—a terror such as she'd never felt before. Then, just as quickly, it was gone.

A dream! It had been nothing but a dream!

The mists she'd been lost in, the darkness she descended into, the vast cathedral she'd seen—all of it had been a dream!

And the figure she'd seen, the evil figure she'd recognized as Jared—nothing but a nightmare.

She sat in the darkness. Though the night was warm and unseasonably humid and her face was sticky with sweat, she felt chilled as well, almost feverish. She got out of bed, pulled on her robe, and went into the bathroom. She flicked on the light, turned on the tap, then washed her face with cool water, rinsing the salty perspiration away from her skin. Finally she looked at herself in the mirror.

She looked exhausted, as if she hadn't slept at all. But the clock on her nightstand said it was after one, so she must have been asleep. Her complexion looked pasty and her hair hung in lank strings around her face. As she reached up to comb it back with her fingers, the mirror reflected a flicker of movement from behind her, and she whirled around, scanning the room.

Nothing!

It must have been her imagin—

And then she saw it.

A rat—the biggest rat she'd ever seen—was climbing out of the toilet, its wet fur matted down. As Kim screamed, the rat bared its teeth, hissing at her. Then another rat climbed out of the bowl, and another.

As Kim screamed in horror she jerked the bathroom door. The latch stuck.

Trapped!

More and more rats erupted from the toilet as Kim's heart raced. They were coming toward her, skittering across the floor toward her bare feet—

"NOOOO!" As the terrified shriek rose from her throat, Kim yanked at the door one last time and it flew open. Sobbing, she stumbled out into the hall just as her parents came through the doorway to their own room at the far end of the mezzanine.

"Kim?" her mother called. "Kim, honey, what is it?"

She hurled herself into her mother's arms, shaking, unable to speak. She pointed toward the bathroom door, which she'd jerked closed behind her.

Her father started toward the closed door, but she reached out, clutching at him. "No," she croaked. "D-Don't. Don't go in there."

Ted looked at her. "Don't go in? Why?"

Kim struggled to speak. She could still see the rats boiling up out of the toilet, their teeth—hundreds of needle-sharp fangs—bared, hissing furiously as they swarmed toward her. "R-Rats," she finally stammered, her voice quavering, her body still trembling at the memory. She began sobbing again. "They were coming out of the toilet, Daddy."

Janet's arms tightened around her weeping daughter. "Call someone, Ted," she said, her own voice shaking now.

But Ted was moving toward the closed bathroom door again.

"Don't!" Kim wailed as his hand closed on the knob and he started to turn it. "Oh, God, Daddy—"

But it was too late. The latch clicked open, and the door swung inward. Gasping, Kim's arms tightened around her mother and she shrank away from the terror about to emerge from the bathroom.

Silence hung over them as Ted pushed the door wider and stepped inside.

Then he was back and looking worriedly at his older daughter. "Honey, there's nothing there," he said softly.

Kim huddled deeper in her mother's arms. "No," she said. "I saw them. I know I saw them."

Ted spread his arms helplessly. "Take a look," he said, stepping away from the door. When Kim made no move, he came back and took her hand. "It's all right, Kim. Just look. I'll be right beside you."

Her heart racing, Kim let go of her mother and let her father lead her toward the open door. At the threshold she tried to pull away, the memory of what she'd seen still vivid. Yet now, as she peered into the brightly lit room, she heard nothing, saw nothing.

Warily, her fingers clutching her father's hand, she edged closer.

Behind the door! That was it—they were hiding behind the door, and as soon as she was inside they would swarm over her.

Her father seemed to read her mind. With his free hand he reached out and pushed the door open until it struck the wall behind it. "See?" he said, stepping inside the room and gently drawing Kim along with him. "Nothing."

She gazed around.

Her father was right.

The water in the toilet was still, and there was no sign of the swarming rats she'd seen a few moments ago.

"A dream," her father told her. "It must have been a dream."

Saying nothing, Kim let her parents lead her back to bed, let her mother tuck her in as if she were a little girl. But after her mother kissed her good night and reached for the light, Kim stopped her. "Leave it on," she whispered. "Please leave it on."

Janet hesitated, then smiled reassuringly at her daughter. "All right," she said. "But just remember, darling—it was only a dream. Just a terrible dream. There's nothing here that can hurt you." She kissed Kim once more, then slipped out of the room, pulling the door closed behind her. "She'll be all right," she told Ted as they returned to their own room. "She's just leaving the light on for a few minutes."

But it wasn't for just a few minutes.

It was for the rest of the night.

And even with the light on, Kim could still see the rats, hissing at her, snarling at her, waiting for her to turn off the light so they could sink their teeth into her.

Not until dawn, when the rising sun finally washed the images away, did Kim fall into a restless sleep.

CHAPTER 25

Sandy Engstrom felt her nerve slipping away when she was still a block away from the Conway house. All week, ever since Kim had invited her to sleep over tonight, all the stories she'd heard while she was growing up had been creeping back out of her memory. Nor had it helped that most of the other kids she knew thought she was crazy even to think about spending a night in the Conway house. Jolene Simmons hadn't even bothered to try and be polite. "You'll be lucky if you don't get killed!" she said. "Everyone knows all the Conways are crazy! That's why Father Mack's going to make sure they can't open a hotel. In fact, I hear he's planning to make them move right out of town!"

"How's he going to do that?" Sandy countered. She put on her bravest face, but knew she sounded more anxious than scornful.

"Well, if you didn't spend all your time with that Kim person, you'd know, wouldn't you?" Jolene glanced around to see who might be listening, and her voice dropped. "There's going to be a meeting on Saturday night, and Father Mack's going to make sure they don't give Mr. Conway a permit. He's going to make sure everybody from St. Ignatius is there, and everyone's going to tell your father he can't give Mr. Conway the permit."

"It's not my dad who decides," Sandy said. "It's the whole council."

Jolene groaned. "Well, what*ever*. It won't make any difference who decides, because everybody in town is going to talk against Mr. Conway. I mean, everybody knows all the things that have happened in that house!"

"Nobody knows anything," Sandy protested, but even she could hear the uncertainty in her voice. After the conversation with Jolene, she told her mother she'd changed her mind about the sleep-over, but her mother shook her head.

"If you don't go to Kim's Friday night, everyone will think we believe all that dreadful gossip. And that won't be good for your father at the meeting on Saturday. He intends to help Ted Conway get his permits."

And that, Sandy knew, was that. The Engstroms would put up a solid front, no matter how Sandy might feel. Sandy had almost demanded to know why what she did would make any difference, but she already knew. As long as she could remember, she'd lived by a single rule: whatever she did reflected on her father; therefore it was most important never to embarrass him in public, or contradict him. And that meant that no matter how frightened of the Conway house she might be, there was no way to cancel the sleep-over.

And, of course, it was Jared's house, too. Sandy had been very, very careful not to mention her crush on Jared to anyone, but all through the week, the thought of Jared's gorgeous blue eyes sent small, delicious shivers of excitement racing through her.

Now, though, as she turned onto Pontchartrain Street, all the fears rushed back. *It's just because it's almost Halloween,* she told herself, but as she glanced around at the glowing jack-o'-lanterns that grinned and leered from every porch, she felt no reassurance.

Her step slowed. She could see the house at the far end of the street, off by itself, looming against the starry sky, casting an enormous shadow in the moonlight. She felt a chill. Most of the second floor was dark, and even on the first floor, only a few lights were lit. The porch lights were on, one on each of the columns that flanked the front door, but even they looked dim, as if the house were swallowing up the light itself. Too late to go back home. Reluctantly, she stepped onto the broad porch and rang the bell. But as she waited for the door to open, she felt eyes—unseen eyes—watching her.

But that was silly! It was nothing more than the jack-o'-lanterns on the porches and the stories that had been tumbling through her mind that were spooking her. Still, the sense of someone watching remained. Cautiously, she looked around into the gathering darkness.

Was that a flicker of movement, over near the carriage house?

Sandy strained her eyes, peering into the shadows that surrounded the building, but she could see nothing.

Every shadow seemed to hold some unseen menace. Suddenly, all she wanted was to be safely inside the house. Then, just as she reached for the bell again, Kim opened the door. Relief flooding over her, Sandy quickly stepped inside.

* * *

Jake Cumberland waited in the shadows until the door closed behind Sandy Engstrom. Then he began his nightly ritual . . .

The first surprise came as Sandy peered into the huge entry hall. A great gleaming brass chandelier hung from the soaring ceiling, flooding the space with enough light to drive every shadow away. The floor, intricately inlaid with half a dozen different kinds of wood, looked as if it had been installed only a few days ago, instead of more than a century earlier. The space was freshly painted in a bright off-white, and she gazed in wonder at the soaring staircase at the far end of the hall.

"It's really beautiful," she said in an awed whisper, looking around in wonder. "Is it all like this?"

Kim shook her head. "It's just getting started. Some of the rooms upstairs are still really creepy."

The eager light in Sandy's eyes faded. She glanced around uneasily. "Where's Jared?" she asked.

"He's not here," Kim said. "Dad gave him enough money so he and Luke could go to the movies, and told him not to come home until at least eleven. Want to see the living room?" Concealing her disappointment at Jared's banishment to the movies, Sandy followed Kim toward the set of doors leading to the living room. As they were crossing the entry hall, Kim's parents came down the stairs.

"We'll be with Sandy's folks," Janet said, "and we should be home by ten-thirty. Molly's sound asleep, and I don't think she'll wake up. But if she does—"

"I'll give her a bottle of juice," Kim finished. She looked anxiously at her father. "You told Jared he can't bring Luke home, didn't you?"

"I told him he couldn't bring Luke home unless we were here," her father told her. "But I couldn't very well forbid him to bring his friend home at all, could I?"

Kim shrugged in reluctant acquiescence. "I guess."

"Okay. And remember, if you need anything, just call us at Sandy's house."

A minute later they were gone, and with the departure of the adults, Sandy's carefully controlled fears threatened to break free of the restraints she'd barely managed to put on them. At Kim's next words, her nerves frayed even more.

"Let's go upstairs," her friend said. "I'll show you some of the rooms."

Kim led Sandy up the stairs, but before taking her into any of the ruined rooms her father hadn't yet gotten to, she took her to her own room, which looked nothing like it had a few weeks earlier. Kim explained how her dad had stripped the rotting wallpaper away, repaired the plaster, and put on new paper in a bright flowered pattern that matched the bedspread on the huge four-poster bed as well as the curtains. A thick carpet covered the floor, and a chandelier, glittering with crystal, was suspended from a gilded medallion in the center of the ceiling.

"It's really nice." In the bright light of Kim's bedroom, Sandy's fears began to ease. "Are all the rooms like this?"

"Dad's going to make them all different," Kim said. She led her friend down the hall toward the room two doors down. But ten feet away, Sandy stopped short.

Something—some image she couldn't quite make out—seemed to have flickered in front of the door for an instant. She rubbed her arms as a chill came over her.

"I don't want to go in there," she announced.

Kim eyed her curiously, her head cocked. "It's just a room."

Sandy shook her head. "It doesn't feel right," she insisted.

"What do you mean?" Now, as she remembered the terrors she'd experienced a few nights before, her own heart began beating faster. But her terrors had been caused by nothing more than nightmares. "How does it feel?"

Sandy hesitated. The chill had passed as quickly as it had come. The door looked just like all the other doors that opened off the mezzanine. "I—I don't know," she stammered. "I just thought—" She stopped, embarrassed. "I'm okay," she said.

Kim opened the door and they stepped into a room lit only by the glow of moonlight coming in through the window. Even in the shadowy light, Sandy could see that it had once been a nursery. An ancient-looking crib stood near the window, and though the wallpaper was faded, she could still make out a pattern of teddy bears dancing across the walls. But the room felt strange.

Unlived-in.

She remembered the story she'd heard so many times while she was growing up, of the baby that George Conway's wife had given birth to, but who had never been found.

And then Sandy knew.

This was the room intended for that baby.

Sandy heard a sound, but it was so faint that for a second she wasn't sure she'd heard it at all. "Listen!" she said, her voice low. "What was that?"

THE RIGHT HAND OF EVIL

"What was what?" Kim asked.

"Shhh!" Sandy hissed. "I heard something! Just listen!"

Both girls were silent, then Sandy heard it again. A baby crying! "There!" she exclaimed. "Didn't you hear that?" Kim shook her head. "It was a baby! I heard a baby crying!"

"Maybe it was Molly," Kim suggested.

Relief made Sandy's knees go weak. Of course it was Molly! How stupid could she get? If she wasn't such a fraidy cat, she would have known right away that it had to be Kim's baby sister crying. She followed Kim into the little room that adjoined the master bedroom, where a soft nightlight glowed next to Molly's crib. The two girls leaned over the crib and peered down at the sleeping child. Sandy started to speak, but Kim held her finger to her lips. "If she wakes up, she'll never go back to sleep," she whispered. They tiptoed back out, and Kim gently closed the door behind her. "Well, I guess whatever you heard wasn't Molly."

A tendril of panic flicked out and tried to grasp Sandy, but this time she refused to let herself give in to it. "It probably wasn't anything. Let's go down and watch the movies we rented. Then at least I'll really have something to be scared about." As they started down the stairs, Sandy glanced once more at the closed door to the old nursery. No matter what Kim said, she'd heard something.

She'd heard a baby, and the baby had been crying.

And it had been in that room.

Sandy wished she hadn't come over here at all.

Janet Conway felt as if she'd somehow slipped into another world. A parallel world that looked, sounded, and felt so perfectly familiar that it was hard to believe it wasn't the same world in which she'd been living her entire life. In the two hours since she and Ted had arrived at the Engstroms' it seemed she'd skidded into the Twilight Zone as she listened to Marge's summary of the rumors flying through the town over the last few weeks—tales involving the killing of babies and the seduction and slaying of a servant girl. It wasn't as if she'd never heard the rumors before—in the few weeks since the first time they had been to the Engstroms' for dinner, she must have heard every one of them. But tonight, hearing all the threads woven together, they took on a surreal quality. Janet was barely able to believe people would repeat such things, let alone accept them as true.

There had apparently even been whispers of Devil worship.

Devil worship?

In *her* family?

"Where on earth could such stories be coming from?" she wanted to know, her voice shaking with outrage. She searched her mind for something to explain the terrible stories, but there was nothing. Nothing any of them had done. There'd been the problem with Jared being late getting back from lunch, but the school had dealt with that. Then she remembered a moment in the cemetery, at Aunt Cora's funeral, and she heard Ted saying, *"I just don't hold with religion,"* despite her own silent wish that he would keep his opinion to himself. But he hadn't: *"Never have. I don't mind my kids going to your school, but don't count on any of us showing up for church on Sundays."*

Father MacNeill? But could that brief conversation have been enough to make the priest try to drive them out of town?

"Might just be," Phil Engstrom mused when she repeated the incident. "Father Mack don't take lightly to people not holdin' with his religion. Don't take lightly to it at all." His eyes shifted from Janet to Ted, then back to Janet. "Anything else happen that day? If we're gonna beat this opposition tomorrow night, I better know ezactly what we're up agin'."

Janet, about to shake her head, was stopped by another memory rising up like a cobra uncoiling. "Jake Cumberland," she said. "He was there, too. He just stood outside the fence, glowering at us." There had been something strange, even eerie, about the man, and Janet shuddered, recalling his mute, angry stare. Then she herself grew angry that their hope for a new life was threatened by something so trivial as rumors spread by an angry priest and the antipathy of a slightly deranged trapper who apparently held Ted responsible for something that might have happened to his mother forty years earlier.

"There has to be something we can do," she said, still searching for a solution as the evening came to an end. "Maybe we should sue Father MacNeill, or—"

"We're not going to sue anyone," Ted interrupted.

Janet sighed. "But it just seems so unfair—"

"It is unfair," Ted agreed. "But we'll get through it. We'll just have to go to the meeting tomorrow, and convince everyone that even if everything they've heard is true, it doesn't have anything to do with us. I'll just have to bring them around, that's all."

As they were driving home later, Janet found herself looking at the houses they passed. On most of the porches, the jack-o'-lanterns were still flickering, as if winking mockingly at her. Hadn't she read somewhere about a movement to ban Halloween on the grounds that the celebration might have some connection to Satanism? A month or two ago, the notion would have struck her as ludicrous. Now, as she looked at the leering faces of the carved pumpkins, she found herself wondering how many of the people behind those jack-o'-lanterns had been listening to the rumors about Ted's family, believing them, and passing them on.

Hypocrites! she thought bitterly. *They're all a bunch of hypocrites.*

"Looks so peaceful, you'd never know what's going on, doesn't it?" Ted asked, seeming to read her mind.

She reached over and slipped her hand into his. "Do you really think it will all blow over?"

"Sure it will." Ted braked the car to a stop. "Maybe when people find out tomorrow that nothing terrible happened to Sandy when she spent the night at our place, things will start dying down." He grinned. "I mean, wouldn't you think if we were such monsters—or even if the house really is haunted—that something awful would happen to her?"

"Don't say that," Janet protested, shuddering. "Don't even think it!"

Yet the words were already spoken, hanging in the air. As she put her key in the lock of the front door, Janet had a terrible premonition about what she might find inside the house.

She pushed the door open and stepped inside, Ted right behind her.

The lights in the entry hall were off.

The house was silent.

Then she heard something.

A door, creaking open.

Her pulse quickened, and a chill passed through her.

Then, as the unseen door creaked once more, the quiet of the house was shattered by a scream.

"Kim?" Janet shouted, switching on the chandelier and flooding the entry hall with light. "KIM!"

There was a silence—a terrifying silence that froze Janet's blood—until she heard her daughter's voice.

"In the library!" Kim called out. "We're watching a movie."

From behind her, Janet heard Ted snicker, and turned to glare at him. "Don't you tell her," she warned. "Not a single word."

"Please?" Ted begged. "You looked so scared."

"And you weren't?" Janet countered.

Ted hesitated, then nodded. "Well, maybe just a little bit," he agreed. "Come on, let's go take a head count and make sure the right number of bodies are here."

Together, they went into the library, where the two girls were stretched out on the floor watching a movie. On the screen, a masked figure held one of the nastiest-looking knives Janet had ever seen, about to plunge it into a terrified victim. "How can you watch that?" she asked. "I'd be scared out of my wits."

"It's fun," Kim told her.

"It's creepy," Sandy declared.

Kim rolled her eyes at her friend's nervousness. "It's only a movie. We can shut it off anytime we want."

Janet glanced pointedly at the clock. "Well, just make sure it's off by midnight, okay?"

Ten minutes later Janet and Ted were in their room. Molly was still sound asleep in her crib, and there'd been no sign of Jared all evening. "See? I told you there was nothing to worry about," Ted said as he slid into bed. "Now, why don't you come join me?"

"Ted! Kim and Sandy are right downstairs!"

"They won't hear a thing," Ted assured her. "Come here."

As Ted wrapped his arms around her and began covering her with kisses, Janet felt the tension of the evening finally slipping away.

"It'll be all right," Ted whispered in her ear. "Don't worry, sweetheart, I'll make it all right."

Then his mouth covered hers, and she gratefully gave in to the pleasures of their bodies.

CHAPTER 26

T he touch was as gentle on her skin as the caress of a summer breeze, so light that at first Sandy was hardly even aware of it. All she knew was that a slight thrill had run through her, disappearing so quickly that she wasn't quite sure she'd felt it.

Yet something *had* happened.

Something she wanted more of.

She stretched her body languidly, but didn't open her eyes for fear of losing the last faint vestiges of the elusive pleasure.

The touch came again, as soft and soothing as the fur of a kitten, but now she could hear something, too.

A strange sound, not quite a voice, but not quite music. The sound reached deep within her, resonating inside her.

The touch was stronger now, like gentle fingers against her skin, and once more she stretched her body, as if reaching out to the source of the caress.

The sound—the odd not-quite-music—was forming into a whispered voice, drawing each syllable of her name into a sigh of longing: "Saann . . . deee . . ."

Then again: "Saann . . . deee . . ."

"Yes," Sandy whispered. "Oh, yes . . ."

Now, lying in the darkness, the soothing sounds washing over her, she felt soft lips touch her own, and the gentle touch grew more bold.

Hands slipped beneath her blouse, and the nipples on her breasts hardened while at the same time a great lassitude spread over her.

She wanted nothing more than to lie where she was, surrounded by the protective darkness, thrilling to the touch, yet calmed by the soothing sounds.

She shivered with pleasure, straining closer to the touch.

And in the instant she responded to it, it vanished.

Sandy's breath caught, and she felt a terrible sense of disappointment.

Of loss.

"Nooo," she whimpered so softly the word was barely spoken. "Noooo . . ."

She reached out, searching in the darkness for the source of the touch, silently pleading for its return.

And in the darkness she felt something. Her fingers closed on a strong hand, and a moment later she felt herself being drawn to her feet.

"Come," a whispered voice instructed. "Come with me. . . ."

Sandy let herself be led through the darkness, afraid to open her eyes lest the magical touch and voice prove to be as ephemeral as a dream, vanishing as she came wide-awake.

She had no sense of where she might be going, where the pleasure might lead her, but it didn't matter. All she wanted was to follow.

Slowly the darkness around her began to change. Her whole being felt suffused with a growing light, and the hands that guided her now lay her gently on a surface so soft it felt as if it must be nothing more than a cloud. Sighing in contentment, Sandy let herself sink into the softness.

The suffusing light brightened into a golden glow swirling with a rainbow of colors, and once again she heard the strange sounds—not quite voices, but not quite music—pulsing in her head, wrapping her whole body in its throbbing rhythms. Then, from somewhere just beneath her consciousness, a voice whispered to her.

"Open your eyes, Sandy. Don't just feel me and hear me. See me, too . . ."

Obeying the voice, Sandy slowly opened her eyes. She was blinded by the golden luminescence and flow of color, but then an image began to take form.

A face—the most beautiful face she'd ever seen—loomed a few inches above her own. Eyes the color of sapphires gazed into her own; full lips hovered close to hers, smiling. The jaw was strong, the chin slightly cleft. The cheekbones and forehead were high, and framed by waves of chestnut hair.

It was exactly the face that until now she'd seen only in her fantasies, coming to her during the daydreams in which she imagined the man who would someday sweep her into his arms and carry her away.

As if in answer to every craving she'd ever felt, the face above her came closer. She felt the lips brush her own. She tried to raise her arms, to pull herself closer to the object of her dreams, but somehow her limbs refused to obey.

She lay helpless in the vision's thrall, craving every touch, moaning softly.

She felt the tip of a tongue prod gently at her lips, and opened her mouth to accept it. Then, once again, she felt the caressing fingers stroking her body.

The buttons of her blouse opened; her jeans slid down her hips.

The fingers were everywhere now—hundreds of them—tracing intricate patterns on her skin, brushing over her breasts and hips, stroking her thighs.

Her legs spread, and her breath turned ragged as the electricity of the vision's touch streamed through her.

The rhythms of the music intensified; the throbbing grew more urgent.

Sandy felt herself writhing now, straining upward against the bonds that seemed to bind her to the cloud, every nerve in her responding to the magical touch. Her skin felt damp with sweat, and then she felt a tongue—no, dozens of tongues—licking it all away. Her own moans mixed with the pulsing rhythms and she felt as if she might pass out as wave after wave of pleasure washed over her.

"Yes . . ." she whispered once again. "Oh, God, yes . . ."

Then, as she gave herself over completely to the sensations of her body, another sound broke through the unearthly music in her head.

It was the sound of laughter—laughter that mocked her.

For an instant she tried to pull away, tried to extricate herself from the maelstrom of pleasure in which she wallowed, but it was far too late.

Moaning one last time, she submitted herself to the pleasure.

And the laughter grew.

No! Not again! Don't let it be happening again!

But instead of instantly passing, leaving her with the eerie feeling that she'd just reexperienced something that had happened before, the déjà vu only deepened its grip on Kim.

It was happening all over again.

Once again she was lost in the house, racing through an endless maze of corridors that branched off, then branched again and again, forcing her to make a choice at every juncture.

Once more she could sense some unseen menace closing in on her, toying with her, circling her, never quite visible, but always drawing closer and closer.

When she came to the top of the flight of stairs with the barely visible pinpoint of light at the bottom, she wanted to turn back, knowing what she would find when she finally came to the bottom of the stairs and entered the light.

Jared.

But not Jared.

Someone else, someone who looked like Jared but wasn't.

She tried to turn away from the stairs, but now she could hear the music, too, faintly throbbing rhythms that, though barely audible, insinuated themselves inside her like tentacles wrapping around every nerve in her body, taking over control so that she had no choice but to take that first step down into the abyss.

Kim's heart pounded with terrible anticipation as she descended the endless staircase, and when she finally came to the bottom, it felt as if all the energy had been drained from her body, and along with her energy, her will to resist had been sapped as well.

The music was louder now, and its hold on her stronger. The point of light stood in the darkness like a beacon, and despite her exhaustion, Kim moved toward it. After what seemed an eternity, she stood before the final door.

Don't, she told herself. *Don't go through the door.*

But even as the thought formed in her mind, her hand went to the knob, turned it, and slowly pushed the door open. It swung silently inward on its hinges, moving as easily as if it were floating weightlessly in the air. And as it opened, the strange cathedral appeared before her, its roof soaring so high it was all but invisible. Candles—millions of them—flickered everywhere, suffusing the vast chamber with a shadowless glow, and filling it with a sweet pungency that made Kim feel lightheaded. Straight ahead of her the altar was all but lost in the swirling smoke of the candles, but even from the doors she could see that something—something familiar—lay at the foot of the inverted cross that hung above the altar itself.

As the doors slammed shut behind her, the light of the candles faded into a stark white glare punctuated by pools of darkness, a darkness so black that Kim shivered with visions of the terrors those shadows might hide.

She wanted to turn, wanted to flee, but her will was not her own.

Slowly, inexorably, she began to walk down the aisle.

Like a bride. The manic thought seemed to come out of nowhere. That thought was followed by another: *If I'm a bride, where is my groom?*

And suddenly she saw him.

A tall figure, clad in a flowing robe of scarlet—the only splash of color in the surreal scene—appeared in front of the altar, facing her, one hand outstretched. As she moved down the cathedral's broad aisle, the face of the waiting figure came into focus. His features were strong and even; his eyes seemed to hold her own, drawing her toward him like a moth to a beacon of light.

Then she recognized him.

The figure was Jared.

Jared? she thought. *It can't be Jared—you can't marry your own brother.*

The figure drew closer.

No, not Jared. It couldn't *be Jared. It had to be someone who looked just like him.* Had *to be!*

The music, a cacophony of discordant shrieking, battered at Kim's ears as she approached the altar. The red-robed figure reached for her hand, and Kim watched helplessly as her own hand seemed to rise against her will to slip into his. Just as their fingers were about to touch, the face before her changed.

The skin, smooth and milky white only a moment before, turned scaly.

Pustules erupted from the suddenly sunken cheeks.

The clear eyes began to run with cloudy mucus, and the mouth opened to reveal a long, sharply pointed tongue that darted toward her, splitting in two, with each of the two points morphing into the twin heads of a pair of serpents whose mouths gaped open as they hung before her, their fangs dripping with venom, their forked tongues lashing out at her.

Her whole body spasming with terror, Kim jerked her hand back, and her fingers closed on the golden cross that still hung suspended on her breast where her great-aunt had placed it.

The face before her contorted with fury, and the figure twisted aside, screaming in rage, phlegm and bile erupting from its gaping mouth.

Sickened, Kim reeled away. As she turned to flee back up the aisle, she saw Luke Roberts.

Naked, he lay before one end of the altar, sprawled atop Sandy Engstrom, whose arms and legs were wrapped around his glistening torso as she writhed ecstatically beneath him. Stunned into frozen immobility, Kim stood rooted to the spot as her brother's best friend and her own twisted and flailed on the floor before the altar. Then, as if feeling her watching him, Luke looked up, and his eyes locked on hers.

He smiled.

Once again Kim saw the face of the demon—eyes running with mucus, skin turned into a reptilian hide erupting with pustules. Now the twin serpents burst forth from his mouth, along with a terrible, high-pitched laugh that crashed against Kim like shattering glass.

Her gorge rising, her throat filling with the burning fire of vomit, Kim turned away from the grotesque scene on the floor, and now the grinning visage of the demon loomed above her once more, both his hands outstretched, his fingers growing into curving talons that dripped with blood. Just as the creature's claws were about to sink into her flesh, she turned one last time and raced back up the aisle of the cathedral. The aisle seemed to stretch away from her as she ran. The taunting laughter she'd heard boiling from Luke's throat was joined now by other cackling voices, the peals striking her back like the stinging tips of a lash, driving her on despite the exhaustion that threatened to overwhelm her.

Finally she came to the doors and burst through, pulling them closed behind her. In an instant she was plunged into darkness, but she bolted ahead and a moment later stumbled headlong into the bottom of the stairs.

Screaming, she threw her hands out to break her fall and—

Kim jerked awake, a scream still rising in her throat. She choked it back just before it could smash the silence of the night, and then she lay still, her heart pounding, her mind reeling as the last fragments of the nightmare faded away.

She became aware of the faint throbbing of music then, and a glowing point of light in the darkness surrounding her.

Oh, God, was she still caught up in the nightmare?

But no—she couldn't be. If she were still in the clutches of the dream, would she even be wondering if it was a dream?

She must be awake!

She willed her pounding heart to slow, and as her pulse eased, so also the terror that gripped her began to ebb. Disoriented, she looked around.

The library! That's where she was! And the glowing point of light was nothing more than the stand-by indicator on the television set!

She sat up. "S-Sandy?" she stammered.

Silence, save for the muted rhythms of the music.

The music from the dream?

She got up and switched on the floor lamp at the end of the sofa on which Sandy Engstrom had been sprawled while they watched the movie.

The sofa was empty; Sandy wasn't there.

The details of the dream loomed once more in her mind, and she whimpered softly as she saw again the vision of her friend, her body glistening in the candlelight, her limbs entwined around—

No!

It hadn't happened! She hadn't seen it! It had only been a dream.

Then where was Sandy?

The question hanging in her mind, Kim moved out of the library and through the living room to the entry hall. The house seemed to have grown in the gloom; the huge rooms appeared more immense than ever. She crossed the entry hall, moved into the parlor and the dining room.

Nothing.

She was passing the door to the basement stairs when she paused. The music—the music she had thought was only another vestige of the nightmare—was louder now.

Her terror mounting once again, and wishing she could just turn away, Kim reached out and pulled open the door.

The music blared.

She stepped through the door so she was standing on the landing at the top of the stairs, gazing down into the darkness.

The darkness, and the faint point of light that leaked through the keyhole of the door to Jared's room.

Just like in the dream . . .

Don't, Kim told herself. *Just don't go down there.*

But even as the words filled her mind, her feet began carrying her down the staircase. With each step she took, the rhythms of the music reached deeper into her, and the point of light drew her steadily onward. At the bottom of the stairs she stood before the door to Jared's room.

She paused, listening.

Now she could hear more than just the music itself.

Whispered voices, and faint, mocking laughter.

And moans.

Moans of ecstasy.

She was in Jared's room! Sandy was in Jared's room!

Kim's hand reached for the knob, but she stopped herself as the memory of the pagan cathedral she'd seen in her dream—the cathedral that had turned into a chamber of horror—rose in her mind. What if it wasn't a dream? What if everything she'd seen were somehow real? What if Sandy really was—

Unable to finish the thought, Kim turned away from the door and hurried back up the stairs, then shut the basement door behind her and leaned against it.

What should she do?

Should she wake up her parents?

Sandy would never forgive her!

But if she was with Jared and Luke—

Kim felt as if she were caught in another nightmare, but this time she knew it wasn't a dream. This time it was real. From behind her the music reached through the door, and she could almost feel its tentacles sinking into her once again, as it had in the nightmare, trying to draw her back down into the basement.

Just as in her dream, her fingers closed on her aunt's tiny cross, and as she felt it in her hand, her resolve strengthened. She left the door to the basement and made her way back to the entry hall.

As she started up the great staircase toward the second floor, the waves of music receded, loosening their grip on her.

At her parents' door, she hesitated.

Whatever was going on in Jared's room wasn't any of her business. No one had forced Sandy to go down there.

And if she told on her, Sandy would never speak to her again.

Silently, Kim made her way around the mezzanine to her own room, easing her door open just far enough to slip inside, praying it wouldn't creak. Just as she was closing it behind her, she realized her room wasn't empty.

Kim froze, listening.

Breathing! She could hear the sound of breathing!

Once again her heart began to race, but even as her fear built, she moved her hand slowly toward the light switch on the wall. When she finally felt it beneath her fingers, she drew in her breath and held it.

She flipped the switch, and the chandelier in the middle of the ceiling glared into brilliant light, washing the darkness from the room.

Sandy Engstrom sat bolt upright in Kim's bed, clutching the sheets around her neck. For a long second the two girls stared at each other in shock, then Sandy collapsed back against the pillows, giggling. "What are you doing?" she asked when she finally subsided. "You scared me half to death!"

"I didn't even know you were up here," Kim began. "I thought—" She was about to blurt out the truth when she caught herself. "I woke up, and you were gone, and I thought you must have gone home or something. How come you didn't wake me up?"

Sandy rolled her eyes exactly as Kim had when she herself had been frightened by watching *Scream*. "I tried," she said. "When the movie ended, I tried to wake you up, but finally I just gave up and came up and went to bed." She looked at the clock. It was just past three A.M. "Do you always sleep that hard?"

Kim shook her head. "I thought—" She hesitated, then shrugged helplessly. "I don't know what I thought," she finally finished.

She got undressed and slid into bed next to her friend.

Should she tell Sandy about the nightmare?

No. She didn't even want to remember it herself.

But long after Sandy had fallen back to sleep, Kim lay awake as the details of the dream came back to hang in the darkness in front of her.

Over and over, she witnessed the wanton scene on the bloody altar, saw over and over again the face of the demon that had reached out to her. As the night crept on, she tried to banish the visions, but failed.

It was only as the rising sun drove back the dark that the demons finally released Kim from their grip and let her sleep.

Even then she could still feel the throbbing rhythms from the basement as the tentacles of Jared's music reached out to ensnare her.

She slept, but she didn't rest.

CHAPTER 27

It was a dream.

It had to have been a dream. Yet even now, with the morning sun flooding through the windows, Kim could remember every detail. She lay staring up at the ceiling while the horrifying images—the impossible images—she'd seen last night recurred in her mind like some insanely repeating videotape, endlessly replaying the same sequence.

Beside her, Sandy Engstrom stirred, then sat up, rubbing her eyes. Seeing Kim was awake, she pulled her knees up to her chest, wrapped her arms around them, then eyed Kim warily. "If I tell you about a dream I had, will you promise not to tell anybody?" she asked, her voice dropping to a conspiratorial whisper. "I mean, not a soul!"

A flicker of foreboding flashed through Kim, but she nodded.

Sandy's eyes gleamed, and even in the warmth of the morning she shivered with remembered pleasure. "It was about Jared."

Kim's stomach knotted as she was consumed by a terrible feeling that she didn't want to hear what Sandy was about to tell her. But she heard herself say, "I promise. I won't tell a soul."

Sandy hugged her legs more tightly to her chest and sighed. "It was really weird," she began. "I was sound asleep, and then I started to wake up. I could feel someone touching me, but I wasn't scared at all. It felt really wonderful. And when I was wide awake, he took me somewhere. It was the most beautiful place I've ever seen. Oh, God, Kim, you should have seen it! It looked kind of like a church, but a lot more beautiful than any church I've ever been in!"

No! Kim thought. *It's not possible!*

As she listened to Sandy, Kim recalled the details of her own dream, in which she'd watched Luke making love to her friend.

Could it be that she hadn't been dreaming at all? Her mind reeled as she tried to make sense of the possibility that it had all really happened. But that made no sense, either. The house was big, but none of the rooms was anywhere near as large as the one Sandy described.

The one she herself had seen in her own dream.

Could she have been sleepwalking? Had it been some strange hypnotic state? If not a dream, then what?

"Kim?" Sandy said. "Kim, what's wrong? You look white as a ghost. Are you okay?"

Jerked out of her maelstrom of thoughts, Kim nodded mutely. Should she tell Sandy they'd both had the same dream—*exactly* the same dream?

No way. Sandy would think she was crazy. Besides, they couldn't possibly have had exactly the same dream, so there must be some other explanation.

Something that made sense.

"I—I'm fine," she stammered at last. "I just didn't sleep very well, that's all."

Sandy cocked her head, and for a second Kim had the strange feeling that somehow Sandy was looking right into her. But then the color drained from Sandy's face, and she scrambled out of bed and hurried toward the door.

"Sandy? What is it?"

"S-Sick," Sandy blurted, clapping her hand over her mouth as she rushed out into the hall. Moments later Kim heard the muffled sounds of Sandy throwing up in the bathroom next door.

Getting out of bed, Kim hurried toward the bathroom, where her friend was kneeling on the floor in front of the toilet. A racking seizure hit Sandy, and she retched into the toilet, a blackish fluid spewing from her mouth.

As Kim ran cold water in the sink, soaked a hand towel and pressed it against Sandy's forehead, another spume of vomit burst from Sandy's mouth into the toilet bowl.

When the seizure passed, Sandy took the wet towel from Kim and eased away from the toilet. Not trusting herself to stand, she leaned against the wall and wiped her face with the towel.

"I'll get my mom," Kim said, then flushed the toilet and opened the bathroom window to let the rancid odor escape.

"Don't," Sandy said, pushing off from the wall and steadying herself against the sink. "I—I think I'm okay now. I don't want my mother to know."

"But if you're sick—" Kim began, but Sandy didn't let her finish.

"So I got sick! Remember what I ate last night?" She groaned just thinking about the pizza, potato chips, Fritos, cookies, ice cream, and Cokes they'd consumed. "I'm okay," she said. "Really, just let me take a shower, and I'll be fine."

But Kim wondered. She'd eaten nearly as much as Sandy. If it was the food, why wasn't she sick, too?

Kim stood at the top of the basement stairs, staring down at the closed door to Jared's room. Jared had left half an hour ago, so the room was empty.

Should she take a look at it? But how could it possibly look like what she'd seen in her dream, and what Sandy Engstrom had described?

But even as she argued with herself, Kim moved down the steep flight of stairs to Jared's door.

Don't do it, she told herself as her hand went to the doorknob. *It's his room. Whatever he's got in there isn't any of your business.*

She turned the knob and pushed the door open.

Inside, she saw nothing more than the four black-painted walls, the workbench, Jared's bed, and the mattresses that served as furniture.

No altar.

No stained-glass windows.

Nothing.

A dream, Kim repeated to herself as she went back upstairs.

It was just a dream.

But she didn't believe it.

Something had happened last night.

Something terrible.

CHAPTER 28

Ellie Roberts eyed her own image worriedly. The mirror on the back of her closet door was so old the silvering was flaking away, but despite the mottled look of her reflection, she knew something was wrong. Maybe she shouldn't go. Maybe she should just take off the dress—her best one, the one she only wore to mass on special holidays—and stay home. But she'd promised Father MacNeill, and a promise was a promise, especially to the man to whom she owed so much. When he'd mentioned the town meeting, it hadn't seemed so much to ask. Ellie knew practically everyone in town, especially the Catholics. She'd grown up with them—known them her whole life. But on the evening Father Mack had asked her, she'd had a bad dream about it, a horrible dream that woke her up in a cold sweat in the middle of the night. Ellie knew what was causing her bad dreams.

Speaking at the meeting.

She had almost gone to Father MacNeill the next morning and told him she'd changed her mind, that she just couldn't do it, couldn't get up in front of the whole town to speak. But she'd put it off all day, and the next day, too, and every day since then. And every night, she woke up with her skin clammy and covered with goose bumps, and a feeling of dread.

And now the night was here and there was no turning back.

Her eyes shifted from the burning face in the mirror to the sparse contents of the closet. Just as she decided her best dress was too dressy and reached for the dark blue outfit she often wore on Sundays, the doorbell rang. Luke called out to her, "Mom! Father MacNeill's here!"

Too late to change.

Her stomach churning, Ellie turned away from the closet, patted her hair nervously as she checked herself out in the mirror one last time, then went out to greet the priest.

"Ellie, you look lovely," Father MacNeill said, reaching out to take both her hands in his own. "I swear, if I weren't a priest you could positively turn my head!"

Ellie felt a flush rise on her face, but pleasure turned to embarrassment as her son spoke.

"What's going on?" Luke demanded. "How come you're all dressed up?"

Before she could reply, Father MacNeill turned to Luke. "We're going to the meeting. Perhaps you'd like to come along."

Luke's eyes narrowed suspiciously. "What meeting?"

"To protest the permit the council's considering issuing to convert the old Conway house into an inn."

Luke's expression hardened as his gaze swung accusingly back to his mother. "That's a bunch of crap!"

Ellie's shocked eyes flicked toward Father MacNeill. "Luke! Don't use that kind of language in front of—"

"I'll say whatever I want," Luke declared, his voice rising, his eyes flashing angrily. "Just because you don't like Jared is no reason to—"

"It doesn't have anything to do with Jared Conway," Father MacNeill broke in. Luke swung around to glower at him.

"Bullshit!" he said. "You got it in for Jared same way as Mom does. What the hell's going on?"

"That will be enough, Luke!" Ellie's cheeks burned with shame. "How dare you speak that way to Father MacNeill?" She turned to the priest, her hands playing nervously at the buttons of her dress. "I'm sorry, Father. Ever since he started hanging around with this Jared person—"

"He's not 'this Jared person'!" Luke broke in, his voice trembling with anger. "You don't even know him!"

"I don't have to know him," Ellie said, doing her best to keep her own voice under control. "I know he's a bad influence on you, and that ever since he came to town, you haven't been the boy I raised!"

"Maybe I don't want to be 'the boy you raised,'" Luke shot back, his voice mocking his mother's words with mimicry. "Maybe I want to be whoever I am! Did you ever think of that?"

"I just want you to be the best person you can—"

"No you don't!" Luke flared. "You want me to be whoever Father MacNeill thinks I ought to be. You think I don't see how he runs us? All I ever hear is Father Mack says this and Father Mack says that! So now you're gonna go down and make a jerk out of yourself in front of the whole town, just 'cause Father Mack says so? Jesus!"

"How dare you?" Ellie flared. Her temper snapping, she took a step toward Luke and struck him across the face.

The sound of the slap silenced the room like a shot, and for a moment not even a breath was drawn. Ellie, her hand stinging, froze, and her eyes flicked toward the priest.

Luke's eyes narrowed to slits as he took in his mother's glance, his fingers touching his face where the mark of her hand was already starting to show.

Father MacNeill instinctively took a step back, as if somehow to distance himself from what had just happened.

"That's right, Ma," Luke said, his voice so low it was no more than a rasping whisper. "Hit me. Hit me, then look at Father Mack to see if it's okay." His eyes fixed balefully on the priest. "What about it, Father?" he asked, his voice injecting venom into the priest's appellation. "Did she do all right? Did she do what you wanted her to?"

"I'm sure I can't countenance violence under any circum—" the priest began, but Luke didn't let him finish.

"Don't give me that! You think I don't know what's going on around here? It's Jared! You don't like him, and Ma doesn't like him, and Sister Clarence doesn't like him, and Father Bernard hates his guts. You think I don't know that? You think Jared doesn't know it? Well, guess what, *Father*? Jared's not going anywhere!"

"This has nothing to do with Jared," Father MacNeill replied. The careful neutrality he always tried to maintain when talking to any of his flock had started to crack under Luke's onslaught, and his voice took on a chilly edge. "Although it's obvious his influence on you has not been a positive one. And it isn't just your mother and I who object to the Conway house being turned into a hotel. There are many people who agree with us."

"Not 'us'!" Luke hissed. "You! And I'll bet every single person who agrees with you goes to St. Ignoramus, right?"

"Luke!" Ellie cried, again stepping toward her son, her right hand rising reflexively.

"Don't!" Luke told her. His body quivered with fury as he glowered at her. "Don't you dare hit me again. And don't you go to that meeting, either! You hear what I'm saying?"

"Your mother is free to go anywhere she wishes, young man," Father MacNeill admonished Luke. "And I will not tolerate your speaking that way to her. 'Honor thy father and thy mother that their days may be long'!"

"I don't have a father!" Luke raged. "My father's dead, remember? You're not him." He wheeled on his mother once more. "If you go to that meeting, I hope you get hit by a truck!" Turning away, he stormed toward the front door.

The silence that fell in the living room as Luke slammed the door behind him lasted longer than the one that had followed Ellie's slap.

"He didn't mean it," Ellie finally breathed. "He didn't mean it at all."

Father MacNeill, though, wasn't so sure. To him, it had sounded as if Luke Roberts meant every angry word he'd uttered.

Every single one of them.

"**M**ommy! Wanta see!"

Janet lifted Molly out of the stroller and held her up so she could see the people milling around in front of Town Hall. Why had she let Ted talk her into bringing Molly? What possible interest could a meeting to discuss a zoning variance have for a sixteen-month-old? Still, what choice had there been? She'd called five possible baby-sitters, but by the time she talked to the fourth one, she knew the search was futile. Two of the girls hung up when she told them who she was, and the other two had excuses that sounded so flimsy, she was sure they'd made them up on the spot. Only the last one had been honest enough to admit that there wasn't enough money in the world to get her to spend even a few hours alone with a small child in "that creepy old house."

"Jared can take care of her," Ted suggested, but Janet shook her head, surprising herself at how quickly she'd dismissed the suggestion. And she stuck to her position, despite Ted's arguments, though she could not bring herself to voice her growing mistrust of her own son.

Mistrust.

How could it be that in the few short weeks since they'd moved to St. Albans, the implicit trust she'd always had in Jared—the certainty that she could always count on him, even when Ted had been at his absolute worst—had completely eroded? And yet there it was. So many little things, slowly accumulating like the tiny trickles of water that eventually merge together to form a mighty river. None of them particularly serious taken individually, and all of them easily explainable. Certainly Ted had explained them to her over and over, reminding her that Jared was almost sixteen and starting to stretch his wings.

Of course he wouldn't spend nearly as much time with his sister as he used to. Of course he'd value the privacy of his room in the basement. All boys his age start testing the limits of authority at school. And at home. Janet had listened, unable to argue, since everything Ted said made complete sense. Yet nothing he'd said, none of the reassurances he'd given her, had counteracted the cumulative effect of all the small changes in Jared's personality.

She no longer trusted him.

Where once she'd felt nothing but a mother's normal surge of love when he came near her, now her guard went up and she felt herself tense. *The same way it used to be with Ted.*

She stopped short, realizing that it was a perfect description of how she felt. It was as if all the traits she'd hated in Ted—which had vanished since they moved to St. Albans—had transferred themselves to Jared!

"Honey?" Ted said. "You okay? Want me to take Molly?"

Jerked from her reverie, Janet let Ted lift Molly out of her arms, and as the little girl clung to her father's neck, Janet tried to dismiss the strange idea that had just occurred to her. Yet as Molly snuggled contentedly against her father's chest, burying her face in his shoulder exactly as she used to do with her big brother, the idea only set its roots more deeply in Janet's mind.

"Maybe I should wait outside with Molly," Kim suggested.

With the warmth of Molly's body suddenly gone, Janet felt the fall chill. It was late October, after all. She buttoned her sweater. "I don't think so," she replied. "But if you don't want to go in—"

"I was hoping the whole family would be here," Ted said.

"Then how come you didn't make Jared come?" Kim countered.

Ted smiled sympathetically at his older daughter. "I know it doesn't seem real fair, but I'd sure appreciate it if you'd come in with us. If they see the whole family, how can they turn us down?"

"If they haven't already made up their minds," Janet fretted.

"I'm sure some of them have," Ted agreed. "But as Phil Engstrom told us, we've got a better than fifty-fifty shot. You heard what he said— if they get to know all of us, he doesn't think they'll turn us down."

Then maybe it's a good thing Jared's not *here,* Kim thought. All through supper that night, she'd tried to ignore the argument between her father and her brother, but from the moment it began, a hard knot formed in her stomach, and she'd only been able to pick at her food. What troubled Kim most, though—even scared her—was the way she hadn't been able to pick up anything from Jared. Always before, she could glean at least some hint of his feelings, some sensed understanding of what was going on with him, almost if she could share in his emotions, at least a little bit.

But not anymore.

Tonight, though she'd heard him getting angrier, she hadn't felt anything at all. At first she wondered if he was even really angry, or just acting. But as Jared continued to argue with their father, she could hear the fury in his voice. She could see it in his face, too. But she couldn't feel it. And when he finally left, storming away from the table and out of the house just like their father used to do, all she'd felt was relief that he was gone.

Relief!

Was that how her mother had felt all those years, when it had been so bad with her father? Relief when he left the house, and anxiety when he came back?

Just the thought of it made Kim shudder.

She heard someone calling her name. Sandy Engstrom was waving to her from across the street, showing no sign of the sickness that had seized her that morning.

"Kim!" Sandy called. "Dad says you should all sit with us!"

Abandoning any thought of skipping the meeting, Kim was about to start across the street toward the small crowd in front of Town Hall when a horn blared, startling her. As her father's hand closed on her arm to pull her back onto the sidewalk, she looked up, then froze in horror at what she saw.

It happened so fast that she knew there was nothing that could have been done to stop it. Not by her—not by anyone.

The car was coming around the corner, and the woman was already in front of it by the time anyone saw her. Time seemed to stand still as Kim gazed at the terrible scene. The woman seemed frozen to the spot, her head turned toward the car that was about to strike her, her purse clutched in her right hand, her left arm outstretched as if to fend off the vehicle.

Then she turned.

Now it seemed to Kim as if she were watching through a telescope. Though the woman was half a block away, Kim could see her face as clearly as if they were only a foot apart.

The woman's eyes were wide with terror.

Her mouth was agape, though no sound was coming out of it.

And Kim recognized her.

It was the woman she'd seen in her nightmare the night she'd imagined the rats crawling up out of the toilet.

The woman who'd been suspended upside down from the cross in the strange cathedral.

But how could that be?

Yet now, as she stared in mute horror at the woman, Kim had no idea who she might be.

Then the horrifying tableau came to life.

The car's horn blasted again. The woman screamed.

The scream was cut off by a terrible thumping sound.

The woman's body was lifted into the air, and a second later it dropped back, falling onto the hood of the car, where it glanced off the windshield and was hurled to the street.

There was a screech of brakes, nearly lost in the screams of the crowd. In an instant the woman on the street was surrounded. Kim could hear someone shouting for a doctor.

Then she saw a priest—Father MacNeill—kneel down by the woman and begin to pray.

Kim's father and mother started to move toward the fallen woman, and she moved along with them. But then something, some force, made her pause.

Jared!

She could feel him!

She could actually feel him again!

But where was he?

Stopping, Kim scanned the area and saw nothing except the quickly growing crowd around the injured woman, who was now moaning and reaching up for help.

Then she spotted him.

Her brother was standing in the square, perhaps fifty feet away. He was not looking at her. He was looking at the woman who'd just been struck by the car.

Looking at her, and smiling.

She opened her mouth to call Jared. Before his name left her lips, however, he turned and looked at her, as if she'd actually called to him.

The smile—the strange grimace of pleasure that had twisted his lips as he gazed at the accident victim—was gone.

Instead, Kim saw him glaring at her. Glaring at her angrily, as if he'd just been—

Kim stopped short, unwilling even to think the word she'd been about to use. But as she watched her brother, she knew there was no other way to describe his expression.

He looked guilty.

He looked as if he was doing something wrong, and he knew it.

He looked as if he'd just been caught.

CHAPTER 29

Phil Engstrom banged the gavel to bring the meeting to order exactly one hour after it had originally been scheduled. He struck the podium again and again, but the murmur refused to die away as the crowd that had turned out for the meeting continued to whisper among themselves about the accident.

An ambulance had arrived from the fire station around the corner less than a minute after the car struck Ellie Roberts, and she was rushed to the hospital no more than five minutes after she fell to the pavement. Phil himself had seen the accident from start to finish, and in his eyes it had been quite simple: Ellie stepped out from between two cars to cross the street at exactly the same time that Clarie Van Waters turned the corner. To Phil, the accident had been an unfortunate confluence of Ellie not watching where she was going and eighty-year-old Clarie insisting on driving her ancient DeSoto years after her license should have been lifted.

Nevertheless, the rumors began flying even before Ellie was taken to the hospital. The crux of the gossip was that since Ellie had been on her way to protest the variance Ted Conway wanted, Conway therefore must have had something to do with the accident. That Ted had been nowhere near either Ellie or the car and could in no way have been responsible seemed to cut no ice whatsoever. The problem, Phil thought, was that the accident and the talk that quickly accompanied it was enough to change the whole tenor of the meeting. Where an hour ago he had sensed that the town was fairly evenly split and a vote could go either way, now he could feel support swing toward Father MacNeill's opposition to the variance. He'd toyed briefly with postponing the meeting, but quickly abandoned that idea, knowing it would be interpreted—correctly—as a stalling device. So, even as he banged the gavel to bring the meeting to order, Phil Engstrom was wondering about how he and Ted might reverse the decision later.

"All right, everyone," he said. "If we don't want to be here all night, we better get started." He droned through the legalisms and rules of procedure, then decided to let Father MacNeill have his say first. Better to let Ted see what he was up against, he thought, and then decide how to handle it.

Father MacNeill moved to the podium slowly, his head bowed as if he were just now thinking about what he wanted to say. Even when he faced the crowd, he said nothing, fingers tented beneath his chin as if he were still deep in thought, or perhaps even seeking divine guidance. But when he finally spoke, he never mentioned God or the Church. The Catholics in the room, Phil Engstrom knew, were mostly already convinced. Instead, Father MacNeill talked about the history of the town, about its stability, about its continuity. Phil Engstrom didn't even need to look at the approving nods coming from every part of the room to sense which way the wind was blowing.

"Here in St. Albans," the priest said, moving into his summation, "there has always been a place for everything, and everything has always been in its place. Certainly, none of us can have any objection to a new inn opening in our town. I, for one, would support it. But the Conway house stands in a residential area—a *family* area—and to invite strangers into the very heart of our neighborhood strikes me as folly." His eyes moved from face to face. "The place for strangers—and whatever pleasures they might seek—does not lie in the area in which our children play." A murmur of approval rippled over the room, and Phil Engstrom knew it was all over. The priest's invocation of the specter of child molestation—although he hadn't quite said it—would be enough.

As Father MacNeill moved back to his seat, pausing every few steps to accept the murmured praise of his parishioners, Phil turned the podium over to Ted Conway. "Good luck," he muttered under the rustle of the audience readjusting themselves on the hard benches, though he didn't see how Ted was going to turn this around. Right now, he didn't think Conway would get more than ten votes out of the whole lot of them.

Ted stood at the podium, gazing out at the sea of faces that filled the auditorium. Throughout the priest's speech, he had felt the mood of the room harden, sensed that what little support he'd had left when the meeting opened was washing away under the cleric's river of words.

But Ted had also noticed that as Father MacNeill scanned the audience, addressing himself first to one person, then to another, meeting the eyes of nearly everyone in the room, he'd never looked at him.

Not once.

Now, Ted's own eyes sought out the priest, who was sitting next to Father Bernard with his head bowed while his fingers manipulated his rosary beads. Ted willed him to look up, to meet his gaze.

Though Father MacNeill continued to pray, Ted was certain he saw the line of the priest's jaw harden.

He can feel me, Ted thought. *He knows I want him to look at me, and he won't do it.* His eyes shifted away from Father MacNeill, and once more he scanned the room.

A month ago he would have been feeling the thirst for a drink— indeed, he wouldn't have come to the meeting at all without at least a couple of belts of scotch to bolster his courage. But not tonight. Tonight, as he gazed out at the hostile eyes fixed on him, he felt no desire for a drink.

Nor any fear that he would fail.

Ted picked a man in the fourth row whose eyes were already smoldering, although he had yet to utter a word.

"My family has been in St. Albans as long as St. Albans has existed," he said. "I know it. You know it." He focused on the angry-looking man. "We've all heard the stories, and I'm not going to deny them." The man frowned, looking less certain. "But I'm not going to talk about those old stories. Instead, I'm going to talk about myself, and my wife, and my three children, and the dream I have."

The audience stirred once again, and Ted saw that it wasn't only the man in the fourth row who now looked uncertain; he saw hostility dissolving into curiosity throughout the room. When he resumed speaking, his voice was as low as Father MacNeill's had been, but commanded every bit as much attention as the priest's. Slowly, his eyes moving from one face to another, he told the story of how he had come to bring his family to St. Albans.

It's not possible, Janet thought. Though she couldn't see the audience from her place in the front row, she could sense the change in the atmosphere of the room. Even Molly, who wriggled in her lap all through Father Mac-Neill's speech, had settled down, as if the sound of her father's voice was enough to calm her. Where did he learn to do this? Janet wondered as she watched Ted speak to the crowd. Soon after he began to speak, his eyes met her own for a moment. In that instant, as he talked about what their life had been like only a few weeks ago, she felt a sense of empathy so great—a certainty that he not only understood exactly how she had felt, but that there was nothing he wouldn't do to make up for it—that tears came to her eyes. His gaze shifted from her, releasing her from the grip of his own emotions just as she was on the verge of crying. "It's going to be okay, Mom," she heard Kim whisper. "Daddy's going to make it all right." Janet could only nod, not trusting herself to speak.

*H*e's all right, Beau Simmons found himself thinking in his seat in the fourth row. Maybe Father MacNeill just didn't know him very well. And the Church never wanted anything to change. Jeez, if he and Sue Ellen had listened to him, he'd be trying to support ten kids by now! And if he hadn't paid attention to what Father MacNeill said about birth control, why should he listen to what he thought about Ted Conway? The hostility he'd initially felt toward Ted Conway melting away, Beau Simmons sat back on the bench and listened intently to every word Ted spoke.

*H*oly Mary, Mother of God, pray for us sinners now and at the hour of our death . . .
Father MacNeill's fingers tightened on the beads. He'd gone through the rosary twice already, concentrating only on the words he silently spoke to God, shutting out the ones Ted Conway was addressing to the townspeople around him. But no matter how hard he concentrated, he could feel the change in the room.
The mood of the crowd—the mood that he himself had created so carefully over the last few weeks—was rapidly changing.
The Devil take him! the priest silently cursed, then instantly begged forgiveness for his blasphemy. But what was he going to do? Should he rise to his feet once again, as soon as Conway was done, and try to undo the damage?
No.
The man would only take a second turn himself, spinning out the same silken net that was falling over the crowd right now.
Better to ignore it and seek guidance from a higher source.
Once again closing his ears to the sound of Ted Conway's voice, Father MacNeill returned to his prayers.

"*F*or as long as St. Albans has existed, my family has been here," Ted Conway finished a little over an hour later. His voice, showing no sign of strain after the long speech, reached out across the room, touching everyone there. "All I'm asking is that you let me and my family be part of this community. I promise you'll never regret it." As the audience gazed silently at him, Ted left the podium, shook Phil Engstrom's hand, and returned to his seat.

"Well," the mayor said, gazing out over the room and reading the shift in its mood as clearly as Father MacNeill and everyone else who had heard Ted speak, "I think we might as well take the vote." He read the variance one more time, then looked at the crowd. "All those in favor?"

For a moment no one moved, and Phil wondered if he'd completely misgauged the effect of Ted Conway's speech. But then there was a stir of movement in the fourth row as Beau Simmons raised his hand. A moment later three more hands went up, then another dozen, and soon Phil Engstrom was gazing out at a sea of waving hands. "Contra-minded?" he asked, making no effort to hide his pleased smile as he saw the scope of the victory.

Father MacNeill, Father Bernard, Sister Clarence, and two other nuns raised their hands.

"Well, then I think that's that," the mayor announced. "Congratula-tions, Ted. You have your variance."

A smattering of applause was interrupted when a figure rose at the back of the room.

"The work of the Devil!" Jake Cumberland proclaimed, his arm raised, his shaking finger pointing directly at Ted Conway. "I'm tellin' you, this is the work of the Devil!"

The townspeople turned to the source of the outburst. "Oh, for God's sake," Beau Simmons hooted when he recognized Jake. "Who let you in?"

The tension broken, a wave of laughter broke over the room, and suddenly they were all on their feet, crowding around Ted and Janet, offering congratulations. As the crowd pressed in, Molly began to cry, and Kim took her from her mother's hands and quickly moved through the crowd and outside.

Standing on the steps in the cool and quiet of the night, Kim could see Father MacNeill and Father Bernard, together with the three nuns who had accompanied them, making their way across the square. She also saw Jake Cumberland. He stood beneath a streetlight, staring at her, and for a moment her eyes met his. Then he turned away, shaking his head as he started down the street. But even as he retreated, she heard him talking to himself, and the words rang in Kim's ears and made her hold Molly close.

"The Devil's work," he said once again. "It's all the Devil's work."

* * *

"**S**he's been like this since a little after she arrived." Sue Ellen Simmons nervously twisted one of the buttons on the blouse of her nurse's uniform as she looked down at Ellie Roberts's face. Her complexion was ashen, and her eyes seemed to be focused on something off in the distance, as if she were gazing at something far beyond the unadorned wall six feet beyond the end of the hospital bed in which she lay. Her right arm was in a cast, and there were a few abrasions on her face, but other than that, she was uninjured. "I just don't understand it," Sue Ellen fretted. "She was in shock when she came in, of course, but who wouldn't be? And she was talking—asking about Luke, asking where he was. But when we asked what happened—just whatever she remembered, you know?—she got this look on her face and she hasn't said a word since. Not one word."

"What does the doctor say?" Father MacNeill asked.

"When she first came in, I figured she'd be on her way home within an hour," Sue Ellen replied. "But Doctor might keep her overnight."

The meeting at Town Hall had ended half an hour ago. Father MacNeill hadn't even taken the time to stop at the rectory before coming to the hospital to see Ellie, and when he'd told Sue Ellen that even her husband had voted for Ted Conway, she'd clucked her tongue.

"Something's going on," she'd said. "Beau told me himself there was no way he was voting for that variance. He said everyone knows Ted Conway's an alcoholic, and there's nothing Beau hates worse than a drunk." She shook her head sadly. "His pa used to beat him, you know."

"I'd like to talk to her alone," Father MacNeill said now. "If you don't mind?"

"That might be the best thing for her," Sue Ellen replied. "If you need anything, I'll be right down the hall."

He waited until the nurse was gone, then pulled a chair close to Ellie Roberts's bed. Taking her left hand in his, he patted it gently. "Ellie? Ellie, it's Father MacNeill. Can you hear me?"

For nearly a minute there was no reaction from Ellie. Just as Father MacNeill was about to speak again, he felt a slight pressure on his hand and saw a flicker of movement in Ellie's eyes. Then he heard her voice, so faint it was all but inaudible.

"Father, forgive me," she whispered, her lips barely moving, "for I have sinned. . . ." She trailed off into silence. Father MacNeill waited. When Ellie said nothing more, he reached out and gently stroked her forehead.

"I don't believe that, Ellie," he said. "Whatever happened, it was only an accident. You didn't sin, and you weren't being punished."

Another long silence fell over the room. Ellie didn't seem to react to his words, but Father MacNeill sensed that she'd heard them.

He waited.

It was nearly five minutes before Ellie's head turned just enough so her eyes could gaze into his. When their eyes met, Father MacNeill knew there was something different about her, that something deep inside her had changed.

"What is it?" he asked. "What happened, Ellie?"

Her fingers tightened painfully on the priest's hands. When she finally spoke, her voice trembled and her eyes filled with terror. "Evil," Ellie whispered. "I've seen the face of Evil, Father."

Father MacNeill felt a chill, but did his best to slough it off. "It was only an accident, Ellie," he soothed.

Ellie shook her head. "No!" Her voice took on a harsh intensity as her fingers clamped the priest's more tightly. "No, you don't understand, Father. It wasn't an accident!"

Father MacNeill felt the icy mantle of foreboding close around him. "Tell me," he whispered, his voice trembling. "Tell me exactly what happened."

Ellie Roberts tensed. She didn't want to tell the priest what she'd seen, didn't want to remember it at all. Yet since Sue Ellen Simmons had asked her about the accident, she'd been fixated on the image that had seared her mind the instant before Clarie Van Waters's car struck her.

There'd been nothing wrong. Nothing at all. She was waiting to cross the street, and no matter what anyone said, she hadn't been careless. She looked both ways, just as she always did, and saw Clarie's car coming around the corner. She could still remember it perfectly; even remember the exact words that had gone through her mind: *Uh-oh, here comes Clarie—better stay on the curb until she's gone all the way past.*

But for some reason, which she hadn't understood, she found herself stepping off the curb between two of the cars parked across the street from Town Hall.

She'd seen Clarie bearing down on her. Even now she could watch it like a movie running in her head. Clarie's car was coming around the corner and heading right toward her. If she didn't stop, didn't stay where she was, safely tucked between the red Taurus and the white minivan, there would be no way Clarie could avoid hitting her.

But she didn't stop.

Couldn't stop.

It was as if some force—some unseen power—had taken control of her and pushed her out from between the cars, impelling her to step in front of Clarie's old DeSoto just as if she hadn't seen it.

At the last second she tried to turn away from the force, to rip herself loose from its grip. Twisting around, her eyes hunted for the source of the power that held her, and then she saw it.

Jared Conway!

He was standing only a few yards from her, and looking right at her.

But how did she know it was him? She'd never seen him before—she was sure of it.

Yet the moment her eyes met his, she knew who he was.

And then, as Clarie's car bore down on her, he smiled.

But it wasn't a smile; not really. Rather, it was a cruel twisting of his lips, as if he was anticipating what was about to happen to her, and relishing the pain she was about to feel.

Then, in an instant, his face changed.

His lips twisted and stretched, and she saw sharp fangs jutting from bloodied gums. Saliva dripped from his mouth, and when his tongue flicked out, she could feel the sting of its forked tip, even though he stood less than ten yards away.

Everything about him changed in that instant. His ears grew pointed, and his skin red and scaly. His body swelled, and his clothes fell away, revealing skin that was a tissue of suppurating, festering boils oozing pus that clung to him in reeking globules. His eyes narrowed to glowing slits, and his fingers lengthened into viciously taloned claws that stretched toward her.

The single scream she uttered, the one cut off by the impact of Clarie's car, had less to do with her fear of the oncoming car than her shock and terror at the visage she beheld. For in that single instant before she was lifted off the street and tossed from the hood of the DeSoto, she recognized the face of evil.

"The Devil," she whispered now as she clung to Father MacNeill's hand, which had turned cold and clammy as he listened. "That's what I saw, Father. The Devil himself." But then a glint of triumph flickered in Ellie Roberts's eyes. "He didn't get me, though. He tried, but I'm still here. And tomorrow morning I'll be in church, just like always."

"You don't have to do that, Ellie," Father MacNeill told her, but she shook her head.

"I do," she whispered. "I've looked on the Devil himself, and now I need to look to God. I'll be there."

As Ellie Roberts dropped back against the pillow, exhausted after recounting what she'd seen, a series of images flicked through Father MacNeill's mind.

Beau Simmons, whose innate stubbornness had evaporated in the face of Ted Conway's mesmerizing speech in Town Hall. His opinion, usually so stubbornly held that no logic in the world could change his mind once he'd made it up, had bent to Ted Conway's will that night like a reed bowing to the wind.

Jake Cumberland, rising at the back of the room to point an accusing finger at all of them, his voice nearly echoing what Ellie Roberts had just told him: *"The work of the Devil! I'm telling you, this is the work of the Devil!"*

Releasing Ellie's hand, he rose from the hard chair and went to the window. The moon, nearly full, was high in the sky, bathing the town in silvery light.

Was it possible?

Surely it had to be something else.

Jake was a superstitious man whose mother had filled his imagination with all kinds of tales as he'd grown up.

Beau Simmons, for once in his life, might simply have changed his mind. Even he himself, Father MacNeill recalled, had felt his resolve weakening in the face of Ted Conway's spellbinding speech. And if he could be swayed, who in the hall that night could not have been?

And Ellie Roberts? Who knew what aberrations the shock and pain of the accident might have caused in her mind? She might easily have blacked out, even for a few seconds, and seen some fragment of a nightmare left over from her childhood. But to have seen the Devil in the body of a fifteen-year-old boy? Surely it was impossible.

And yet, deep inside, Father MacNeill knew he was lying to himself.

He knew that at the core of his being, in the place where his faith and his religion resided, he believed every word she'd told him.

She'd seen the Devil.

He was right here, in the heart of St. Albans.

Just as he'd always been.

It was well past midnight—long after the hour that normally found Monsignor Devlin whispering the last prayers of the evening before offering his arthritic bones the respite of his bed. On this night, though, he was aware of neither the hour nor the pain in his body, so consumed was he with the final pages of the Bible that Cora Conway had entrusted to his care. For a quarter of a century after Bessie Delacourt's scrawled entry, no one had written in the Bible at all, but then Abigail Smithers Conway had taken up a pen and continued the account of the Conway family. Abigail's hand was far more sure than Bessie's had been, but the story she had slowly unfolded was so painful that the old priest had been able to read only small pieces of it at a time.

Tonight, though, he went back and read it through from the beginning . . .

15 May 1937

Today I opened this Bible for the first time. My purpose was only to record the death of my husband, Francis Conway, three days ago. I had not wished to read these pages, for I am afraid I have always been something of an ostrich—I prefer not to see things as they truly are. But Frank is gone and I must now face the truth of the last twenty-five years.

Though I would not let myself even think it, I believe I must have known that Bessie Delacourt did not leave my husband's house the night before our wedding to go to Atlanta, as he always told me. I chose to believe him that day, and in making that choice I condemned myself to accept whatever he told me during all the years of our marriage. It seems that a lie must become the truth if one is to live with it throughout one's life.

Believing Frank, though, did not mean I was deaf to the whispers that have swirled like dead leaves around this house for all the years I have lived in it, and though I tried not to, I always heard Bessie's voice in my mind, telling me that I would know when it was time to read these pages.

Frank killed Bessie.

I believe that, just as I believe he killed Francesca's sister—his own daughter!

I thought—hoped?—that all the terrible things I have dreamed over the years were only nightmares filled with demons and rituals from which I would awaken screaming.

After my nightmares I would hear the rumors, though no one ever spoke them to my face.

So many babies—little girls all—vanishing in the night without a trace.

I always told myself the children never came to play with Phillip and George because of other things, but after reading these pages, I know the truth.

My sons had no friends because the other children's parents were afraid for them.

It seems that they were right.

Phillip must have known, too, for he left when he was fifteen and has not come back—I fear I shall never see him again.

I do not know what the future holds, though I am sure that I, like Francesca and her little daughter Eulalie, will never be able to escape this place. I do not know about Francy's husband. Abraham Lincoln Cumberland seems a good man, but surely he must hate all of us.

1 November 1937

Abe Cumberland was hanged last night. The men came for him at midnight, wrapped in sheets, their torches filling the air with smoke. It was like one of my nightmares come to life, and when George pointed to the rooms above the carriage house where Abe and Francy live with their little Eulalie, I screamed and screamed, hoping to wake up.

I did not.

Instead I was condemned to watch little Eulalie—who is only five—as my own son helped the mob to lynch her father.

They said Abe had stolen a baby, and killed her.

I do not believe it, for I saw that infant die in one of my dreams, and I saw my son holding the knife above her little breast. But even now I cannot bring myself to speak any of it aloud.

22 January 1950

Eulalie Cumberland's child will be born soon. If it is a girl, I fear for what my son might do. I—

AS THE PAIN STRUCK HER CHEST, THE PEN IN ABIGAIL CONWAY'S HAND SKIDDED ACROSS THE PAGE, LEAVING A JAGGED LINE THAT WOULD BE THE LAST MARK SHE MADE IN THE WORLD. SHE CRIED OUT AS THE SECOND STAB OF PAIN LASHED THROUGH HER, SHOOTING DOWN HER LEFT ARM INTO HER FINGERTIPS. AS THE AGONY MOMENTARILY RECEDED, THE DOOR TO HER ROOM OPENED AND HER DAUGHTER-IN-LAW HURRIED IN.

"MOTHER CONWAY?" CORA ASKED ANXIOUSLY. "WHAT IS IT? ARE YOU ALL RIGHT?"

ABIGAIL STRUGGLED AGAINST THE SURGE OF PAIN, AND SHOOK HER HEAD. HER HANDS TREMBLING, SHE CLOSED THE BIBLE THAT LAY OPEN ON THE DESK IN FRONT OF HER, AND REPEATED THE SAME WORDS TO CORA THAT BESSIE DELACOURT HAD SPOKEN TO HER THIRTY-EIGHT YEARS EARLIER. "YOU'LL KNOW WHEN TO READ IT," SHE WHISPERED AS ONCE AGAIN THE HOT KNIVES SLICED HER. "YOU'LL KNOW."

AS CORA CONWAY RELIEVED HER OF THE BURDEN OF THE BIBLE, ABIGAIL SLUMPED IN THE CHAIR. DARKNESS CLOSED AROUND HER AND SHE WAS FINALLY RELEASED FROM THE AGONY OF HER RUPTURING

HEART, AND THE TERROR THAT HAD RULED HER LIFE. SHE DESERTED HER BODY GRATEFULLY; WHATEVER ETERNITY HELD FOR HER COULD NOT BE AS TERRIBLE AS THE YEARS SHE HAD SPENT IN THE CONWAY HOUSE.

"So much evil," Monsignor Devlin muttered as he finished the last entry, which had been written by Cora Conway a few days before her husband hanged himself, and her baby—along with Eulalie Cumberland—had vanished. Cora herself had done little more than describe Abigail's last moments, and add a few cryptic words of her own:

Perhaps Eulalie's magic can end the evil of the Conways. I doubt it, though, for I often wonder if it is not the Conways who are evil, but this house itself.

And that was the end. Except for the missing pages, the dark history of the family was complete.

As he closed the Bible, Monsignor Devlin felt someone behind him, and turned to find Father MacNeill standing close to his chair.

"So Jake is one of them," the younger priest said softly. "It's no wonder he hates them, is it?"

Monsignor Devlin shook his head. "Nor can we blame him, can we?" Not waiting for any reply, he went on, "But we still don't know how it started—where it began."

Father MacNeill was silent for a moment, and when he spoke, his voice was grim. " 'The work of the Devil,' " he said. "That's what Jake called it tonight at the meeting. 'The work of the Devil.' Maybe he's right."

Monsignor Devlin sighed, wishing he could argue with Father Mac-Neill. But he could not, for every syllable the younger man had spoken rang with truth.

Halloween

CHAPTER 30

Father MacNeill barely slept. When the first light of the sun crept through the window of his small room on the second floor of the rectory, he wished he could pull his single thin blanket over his head and hide from the day. But he resisted temptation, despite his certainty that he would find no more rest in the brilliance of the morning than in the darkness of the night that had finally passed, so upset had he been by the last entries he and Monsignor Devlin had read in the Bible Cora Conway had entrusted to her last confessor.

The Bible that was itself a confession of the sins of the Conways.

But more than those chronicles of ancient wrongs had kept him awake. Through those early hours when sleep refused to come, he'd also had the uneasy sense that somewhere beyond the walls of the rectory, evil was afoot. He tried to tell himself it was nothing more than a reaction to the horrors of which he'd read, but the feeling stayed with him. Several times he left his bed to peer out into the darkness, searching for the source of the unease that kept him from sleep.

There had been nothing.

Nothing, at least, that he could see or hear, save for the flickering of a few jack-o'-lanterns left lit on porches or in darkened windows, and the plaintive hooting of an owl hunting in the darkness.

Yet he'd known that somewhere, concealed in the blackness, some evil was hidden. Each time he turned away from the window, he dropped to his knees in prayer—prayer that brought him no comfort. The hours seemed to stretch on forever in an endless cycle of searching, praying, and tossing restlessly on the thin pallet that was all he allowed himself for a mattress.

Now, he rose, stretched the knots of tension from his arms, pulled on his clothes, and went down to the kitchen. Putting on a pot of coffee, he went to the front door, where the Sunday newspaper would be waiting. As he was bending down to pick up the paper, something in the periphery of his vision caught his attention. The unease of the last hours flooding back to him, Father MacNeill straightened up, scanning the gardens around the rectory, the churchyard, and the cemetery. Nothing seemed amiss. But as he looked at the cemetery a second time, he saw it.

One of the mausoleums—one whose very presence had always offended him—didn't look quite right.

From where he stood on the porch of the rectory, staring at it, he could see that the door of the crypt was slightly ajar. It was the narrow shadow cast by the open door, he realized, that had caught his attention as he bent down to pick up the paper.

Going back into the rectory, Father MacNeill called the police department, and was relieved when one of his own parishioners answered the telephone. As he sat down to await the arrival of Ray Beckwith—who had spent his entire career as one-quarter of the town's tiny police force—his fingers counted the beads of his rosary. His lips moved rapidly as he silently spoke the words of his prayers, repeating them until his orisons were interrupted by the chime of the doorbell. As he opened the door, the look of mild curiosity on Sheriff Beckwith's face turned to one of concern.

"Are you all right, Father Mack?" the officer asked. "You look like you've seen a ghost."

"I didn't sleep well last night," the priest confessed. "I had a sort of—well, I suppose you could call it a premonition. And I'm afraid it might have come true."

Beckwith's brows knit into a worried frown. "What's going on?"

"I'm not sure yet," Father MacNeill said. "But something happened in the cemetery last night, and I called you right away. I didn't want to run the risk of disturbing anything."

"Disturbing anything? You mean like one of the graves?"

"One of the crypts," MacNeill told him. "Let me show you."

Together, the two men made their way through the cemetery until they were standing in front of the mausoleum. Now, though, they could see that it wasn't simply that the door had been opened.

It had been defaced, as well: above the door, staining the white marble, was a bloodred pentagram.

"Oh, Jesus," Ray said softly. "Who'd want to do a thing like that?"

The priest gazed at the pentagram in silence, and then the inscription beneath the crypt's door:

> GEORGE CONWAY
> BORN JULY 29, 1916
> DIED JUNE 4, 1959

"I'm afraid I can think of a lot of people who might want to do something like that," the priest said, his voice grim. He shook his head. "I still don't understand why they let him be buried here. He died in sin."

Beckwith's lips pursed. "That's why they deconsecrated this part of the cemetery. That's how come the fence is around the mausoleum."

Father MacNeill shook his head. "It's still within the grounds of the church," he insisted, his agitation rising. "It should never have been done."

Beckwith sighed, unwilling to argue with the priest. "Not much anybody can do about it now. Do you want to take a look at the coffin?"

"Don't you need to find out if there are fingerprints?" the priest countered.

Beckwith shook his head. "Everything's so weathered and rough, nothing would show." He glanced around at the empty streets. "But if you want to have a look inside, we better do it now, while there's no one around. Otherwise the whole town'll be talking. Let's just not touch anything more'n we absolutely have to."

Together the two men slid the coffin just far enough out of the crypt to reveal its broken latches. As Beckwith supported the weight of the coffin, Father MacNeill carefully lifted the lid open and peered down into the moldering face of George Conway.

The man's eyes had sunk so deep into their sockets they had almost vanished, and his skin, no doubt initially treated with embalming fluid, had dried and stretched over the years, until now it was a transparent sheath over the skull itself. The teeth showed clearly, and the flesh of the neck, though still showing the abrasion of the noose that had killed him, had desiccated to the point that it seemed the black suit George Conway had been buried in had been put on nothing more than a skeleton.

The priest leaned closer. As his eyes fell on the hands that had been crossed over Conway's chest, he gasped.

The right hand was missing, severed at the wrist.

When the priest gasped, Ray Beckwith struggled to peer around the open lid, and finally worked his way far enough around the end to afford a clear view. "Oh, Christ," he whispered. "What in hell is going on?" Then, remembering to whom he was talking, he quickly apologized. Holding his breath against the odor of ancient death drifting out of the open casket, Beckwith bent to examine the corpse. The cut in the leathery skin looked fresh, and there was a clean nick in the end of one of the arm bones.

"It was done last night," the priest said softly. "I'm sure of it."

"Okay," Beckwith said. "Let's just close it up for now. I'll get a crew out here later on to examine the area more closely. Let's just have us a look around the rest of the cemetery and see if they did anything else."

Sliding the coffin back into the crypt, they closed the door as carefully as they'd handled the coffin itself, then walked through the cemetery, looking for any other signs of vandalism.

The graveyard appeared undisturbed, until they came to the grave of Cora Conway.

On a tree next to her grave, held in place by the sharpened end of a crucifix, was the skin of a dead cat, complete except for its head.

But it wasn't the grizzly hide of the cat upon which Father Mac-Neill's eyes instantly fixed, but the profaned crucifix.

He recognized it immediately.

It had come from inside his own church.

He turned to face the policeman.

"We're going to find out who did this," he said, his voice unsteady. "We're going to find out, or I fear all our souls will burn in Hell. Every single one of us."

CHAPTER 31

"**B**ut what will Father MacNeill say?"

Marge Engstrom waited for her words to have their expected effect on her daughter. But when Sandy announced that she didn't care what Father MacNeill said, she was too tired to go to church that morning, Marge's brow creased in frustration. "I don't know what's gotten into you, Sandra Anne," she declared, using her daughter's full name, which she only did when seriously annoyed. "You know perfectly well that after last night—"

"After last night, why would it matter if any of us go?" Sandy protested. "Father MacNeill's already mad at us, isn't he? I don't see how me going to church is going to make any difference!"

"He's not angry at *us*," Marge explained with a note of exaggerated patience that only made Sandy want to dig her heels in and stick to her position. "It wasn't your father who swayed the meeting last night—it was Ted Conway. But if we don't go to church this morning, Father MacNeill might very well assume that we've taken a position against him."

"Well, haven't we?" Sandy demanded.

Marge pursed her lips. "As mayor, your father didn't vote last night, and though you may not have noticed, neither did I. Your father wants to maintain a position of neutrality, for the good of the entire community."

"You mean he wants to be reelected," Sandy said, and saw by her mother's wince that she was right.

Marge Engstrom recovered quickly. "Your father is a very good mayor, and part of the reason he's a good mayor is that he maintains bridges to every part of our community. If you look at the votes two years ago—"

Sandy rolled her eyes. "I read Dad's campaign brochure, Mom. I even wrote part of it, remember? And I'm still not going to church!"

Marge eyed Sandy carefully, wondering yet again if perhaps it had been a mistake to let her spend the night at the Conways'. It was a thought that had occurred to her when Sandy came home looking like death warmed over. Her face had been sallow, and her eyes so dark that Marge didn't think she could have slept at all. What on earth had she and Kim Conway been up to?

"Nothing," Sandy had insisted. "All we did was watch a couple of horror movies and go to bed."

"Well, no wonder you look so terrible," Marge had replied. "I swear, I don't know why they let them make those terrible movies. All that blood and violence! Why can't you and your friends watch nice movies? I'll bet you didn't sleep a wink. Not a single wink."

By yesterday afternoon, after Sandy had a long nap, she'd seemed fine. But this morning she looked pale again.

The argument over church had been going on for half an hour. Now, with only fifteen minutes left before mass, Marge gave up. "Well, I guess I can't force you," she told Sandy, making one last effort, "but you're the one who'll have to answer to your father. He'll be very disappointed in you. It's very important to him that the family be together on Sunday morning."

It's important for us to be seen *together,* Sandy silently corrected, certain her mother knew as well as she did that if her father really wanted them all to be together, he wouldn't go off to play golf every Sunday morning, and meet them at church just in time for them to walk down the aisle together. Did he really think he was fooling anybody? "Maybe I'll go later," she offered, but knew she wouldn't.

The moment she woke up that morning, she knew she couldn't sit through one of Father MacNeill's masses today. Just the thought of it made her feel almost as sick as she'd been yesterday morning at Kim's. But now that she'd gotten out of church, she was starting to feel better. Maybe, after her mother left, she'd just go back to bed for another hour.

W hen Marge Engstrom stepped out into the bright fall morning a few minutes later, she decided that if Sandy didn't want to go to church, it was her daughter's loss, not her own. Besides, Sandy didn't look well, and perhaps just this once it really would be better for her to lie down for a while. Surely Phil—and God—would forgive her this once!

Marge set out toward St. Ignatius briskly, nodding to everyone she met. Birds were chirping, and there wasn't a cloud in the sky, and by the time she was across the street from St. Ignatius, even her concern about

Sandy had all but vanished. Then she saw the activity in the graveyard, and stopped short.

Had someone died?

But no—surely she would have heard about it!

Marge hurried her step. "What's happened?" she asked Corinne Beckwith, who was standing just inside the cemetery gate, whispering to Sister Clarence.

"It's terrible." Corinne glanced around to be certain no one else was listening, though Marge suspected that whatever Corinne was about to reveal had already been repeated—in strictest confidence—to everyone Corinne had talked to already. "Ray told me this in the strictest confidence, so you have to promise not to breathe a word to anyone. Not anyone!" Then, without waiting for the demanded promise to be tendered, she plunged on. "Someone opened up George Conway's coffin last night, and cut off his right hand. Can you imagine such a thing? Just cut it off! What kind of person would do such a thing! Well, of course it's the fault of those Conways. Everything was fine until they came to town. Now the church has been vandalized, and people's pets are being slaughtered, and . . ."

But Marge had stopped listening, her attention drawn to the cat that was pinned to the tree with the broken crucifix. For some reason, what kept running through her mind over and over like a stuck record were the words Jake Cumberland had spoken at the meeting last night: *"The work of the Devil! I'm tellin' you, this is the work of the Devil!"*

For the first time in years, Marge Engstrom didn't wait for Phil to arrive before going into the church. With all the tales she'd heard since she was a little girl, all the whisperings about the things that had supposedly gone on in the Conway house spinning anew through her head, she dipped her fingers in the font, made her genuflection, and slipped into her regular pew. When her husband sat down at her side a few minutes later, she slid her hand into his. "There's going to be trouble," she whispered. "I can feel it."

Then she began to pray. But this morning, her prayers went far beyond her regular pleadings for her husband and daughter.

This morning she prayed for the souls of every single person in St. Albans.

Father MacNeill dressed for mass with deliberation. Slipping first into the finely woven linen alb—pressed perfectly wrinkle-free by his housekeeper, Sister Margaret Michael—he fastened the cincture around his waist, then added a stole. Finally he put on the chasuble, then gazed at himself in the mirror. Beyond the closed door of the vestry he could hear the murmuring of the crowd gathering in the sanctuary, but instead of the usual soft, almost chanting rhythms of prayer, this morning he heard the excited buzz of gossip winging through the church.

Of course, he had no one to blame but himself—he should never have called the police, at least not until he'd investigated the vandalism in the cemetery himself. It might even have been all right if they'd sent someone other than Ray Beckwith; he should have realized that Ray would be unable to hold anything back from Corinne, and everyone in St. Albans knew that if you wanted a piece of news spread as rapidly as possible, you simply told Corinne Beckwith, first swearing her to absolute secrecy and making her promise not to mention it in the newspaper.

And he was certain where they would place the blame: after Ted Conway's performance last night, he had gained the support of much of the town—even of the St. Ignatius congregation. So it was hardly likely blame would fall where Father MacNeill was already certain it belonged. No, much more likely they would turn their wrath on Jake Cumberland. Poor, ignorant Jake, who had stood at the back of Town Hall last night, denouncing Ted Conway as a tool of the Devil.

And why wouldn't they turn on him? After the accusation he'd made, wouldn't it be logical to assume he'd also desecrated the corpse of the man he'd always held responsible for the death of his own mother?

"Best them Conways don't come back here ever again," Jake had told him not too many weeks ago, when Cora Conway lay dying at the Willows. *"They come here, they'll have me to deal with. And I know what to do, too. Don't think I don't!"*

Father MacNeill had known Jake was speaking of the voodoo crafts he'd learned from his mother so many years ago. He hadn't bothered to argue—the priest had always understood that one man's faith is another man's superstition, and that trying to destroy Jake's belief in his mother's religion would be as useless as trying to destroy his own faith in the living Christ.

As the church bell tolled the hour, Father MacNeill smoothed the chasuble one last time, picked up his breviary, opened the vestry door, and stepped into the sanctuary. For a moment the murmuring went on uninterrupted, but as first one person and then another realized their priest now stood before them, the tenor of the buzzing changed, and finally died away.

Father MacNeill scanned the congregation. The church was crowded this morning, though he suspected that had more to do with the news of the desecration in the cemetery than it did with his own powers to preach.

Even Corinne Beckwith, whom he was certain accompanied her

husband to church only to keep Ray happy, was paying attention this morning. Father MacNeill wondered if she had her tape recorder going, or would be content taking notes with a pen and paper. But like nearly everyone else in the sanctuary, she obviously was expecting him to say something, to explain to them what had happened last night. How, though, could he point an accusing finger until he was certain he knew the culprit's identity?

As he was still trying to decide what, if anything, to say, the door at the back of the church opened and he saw three figures silhouetted against the brilliant morning light. They stepped forward, the door closed, and for a moment they were lost in the shadows of the vestibule.

Then Janet Conway, holding the hand of her little daughter, Molly, stepped forward, dipped her fingers in the font, and dropped into a quick genuflection. Straightening, she searched the church for an empty pew.

A moment later Kim repeated the ritual her mother had just performed.

Then Ted Conway stepped forward, slipping his arms almost protectively around his wife and older daughter.

Father MacNeill found himself holding his breath as he waited to see if Jared Conway would also appear in the church. The seconds crept by, as heads turned to see at whom their priest was staring. When Jared didn't appear, Father MacNeill finally let out his breath and waited to see what the Conways would do.

Phil Engstrom rose from his seat in the first pew, as if to leave. His wife was beside him, though Father MacNeill didn't see Sandy. The mayor's gaze locked on Father MacNeill's, and the priest saw that even the mayor had finally rejoined the ranks of the righteous, abandoning his support of the Conways. Then Phil turned and looked directly at Ted Conway, and as the two men's eyes met, the priest saw something change. Phil Engstrom appeared uncertain for a moment, and then his face cleared and he smiled at Conway. "There's plenty of room here, Ted," he declared. "Come and sit with us."

Stunned by the change in the town's mayor, Father MacNeill watched as the Conways made their way down the aisle, every eye in the church tracking them. Only as they edged into the Engstroms' pew did anyone speak.

"If there's room in this church for them, then there isn't for me," Ellie Roberts declared. Rising from her seat, her right arm in a sling, she stepped out into the aisle and, limping heavily, left the church.

Father MacNeill waited. No one else left.

Then he turned his back to the congregation and began celebrating the mass in the old tradition: facing the altar and intoning the words in the ancient language of the Church. The Latin phrases rolled from his tongue in fulsome cadences, and when he finally turned to face the congregation, every one of them had closed their eyes as he recited the final benediction.

Every one of them, except for one.

Ted Conway's eyes were wide open.

And they were blazing with undisguised hatred.

Janet glanced at the clock on the wall of the big reception room in the parish hall. Its hands seemed not to have moved since the last time she'd looked. The mass had ended an hour ago, but Ted insisted they stay for the hospitality hour. Every minute had seemed like an hour as she stood with Marge Engstrom, pretending she didn't notice how few people approached them, or see the hostile clutches of parishioners whispering to each other while pretending not to glance her way. Worst of all were those who spoke to Marge but ignored Janet and her family completely, acting as if they simply weren't there. And everywhere she looked, Ellie Roberts was there, whispering to one group after another. All the goodwill Janet had felt after the town meeting had evaporated; if the meeting were to be held again tonight, she was sure there wouldn't be a single person in the room who would vote with them. "It's like they think *we* had something to do with what happened last night," she said as Ted and Phil finally came over to join them.

Shortly after mass was over, the Conways heard about the desecration of their uncle's tomb, and the grisly object pinned to the tree. Though Kim refused even to look at the cat's hide, Janet and Ted identified it as Muffin's. Tears had streaked Kim's face when she learned the fate of her pet, but she wiped them away, refusing to expose her pain to a town that had suddenly turned so hostile.

Ted shook his head. "It's not that so much as Ellie Roberts—she's telling everyone that Jared made her walk in front of that car."

"But that's stupid!" Kim burst out, breaking out of her grief over her pet to defend her brother. "I saw Jared, and he wasn't anywhere near Mrs. Roberts!" As almost everyone in the room turned to stare at her, she flushed with embarrassment. "Can't we go home, Daddy?" she begged. "Please?"

For a moment Janet thought Ted was going to argue with Kim, but instead he nodded. "Sure. I don't think we're going to be able to bring any of these people around right now, anyway." Saying goodbye to Phil and Marge Engstrom, they stepped out into the bright sunlight.

Just being outside of the parish hall—and away from the hostility she'd felt radiating from nearly everyone in it—Janet began to relax. But when Ray Beckwith stopped them before they'd even reached the sidewalk, her anxiety came rolling back.

"Do you know where your son was last night, Mr. Conway?" Beckwith asked.

Ted's eyes fixed angrily on the officer. "He was at home. Why?"

"Now, don't get all het up," Beckwith said quickly. "I have a job to do here, and all I'm trying to do is—"

"All you're trying to do is blame my son for vandalizing my uncle's mausoleum?" Ted demanded. "Why shouldn't I get 'het up,' as you so picturesquely put it?"

"I'm not saying he did it—" Beckwith began again, but once more Ted didn't let him finish.

"You're damned right you're not! And if you do, I'll slap a lawsuit on your ass so fast it will make your head spin!"

Ray Beckwith's face reddened. "Now you just hold your horses, here, Conway—"

"Hold your own damned horses," Ted shot back. His voice dropped to a menacing growl. "I'm fed up with what's going on in this town. Since the moment we arrived, it seems like a lot of people have been trying to get us to go away. For starters, there's Jake Cumberland, right? Where was he last night? The last time I saw him was at the town meeting, where he was pointing at me and ranting about the Devil! So before you go accusing my son, why don't you check out Cumberland?" His gaze shifted toward the church. "And speaking of the Devil, why don't we talk about the church, too! It was Father MacNeill who was talking against me at that meeting, wasn't it? In fact, the last few weeks he's talked to practically everyone in town, trying to get them to vote against letting me open a business. And now there's been vandalism in the cemetery next to his church, but it was *my* uncle's crypt that was vandalized. So if I were you, Sheriff, I wouldn't be talking to me about this. I'd get my ass in there and start asking Father MacNeill and everyone else who's been whispering about us all morning what they know about this!"

Ray Beckwith, his ruddy face paling in the wake of Ted's torrent of words, stepped back. "Yes, sir, Mr. Conway," he said, his voice suddenly drained of the anger he'd shown a moment before. "I can certainly understand your feelings. And I'll certainly look into every possibility."

Again Ted fixed his gaze on the policeman. "You see that you do." He turned to Janet. "Let's go home."

Father MacNeill fairly trembled with rage. "He actually suggested you investigate *me*? And you took him seriously?"

Ray Beckwith quailed before the priest's anger, wondering what he'd done to deserve the bad luck to catch the call that morning when the vandalism had been discovered. They were seated in the priest's small office, where Father Bernard had joined them as Beckwith attempted to piece together the sequence of events. It had been discovered that the cross used to pin the cat's hide to the tree came from the side chapel in St. Ignatius. But the church had been locked last night—Father MacNeill had unlocked it himself before mass that morning. A few other people had keys, but none of them would have given a key to Jared Conway, or Jake Cumberland, for that matter.

Jared Conway, Beckwith ascertained, had in fact been inside the church, unsupervised. Hadn't Father Bernard checked on the work the boys had done? And if he had, how had he failed to notice that missing cross right away?

A vein in Father Bernard's forehead throbbed as he admitted he hadn't actually examined the boys' work that afternoon. Beckwith turned to Father MacNeill. "Seems to me at least one of you might've noticed if that cross had been missing since the boys cleaned the church."

That was when Father MacNeill started getting angry. "I'm in and out of the church a hundred times a week. I can't possibly notice everything that's wrong."

"But you noticed the crypt in the Conway mausoleum was open," Ray reminded him. "It wasn't open more than an inch. But you noticed."

That tore it. Father MacNeill's face hardened into an angry mask. "Are you suggesting I might have vandalized the cemetery myself?" he said in a tone calculated to make Ray back down.

But Ray stuck to his guns. "I'm just doing my job. I talked to Mr. Conway, just like you wanted me to, and now I'm talking to you just like he—" He caught himself too late. The priest leaped on it immediately.

"Well?" Father MacNeill demanded when Ray didn't answer his question right away. "Did Ted Conway tell you to investigate me or not? It's a simple enough question."

"I told you, Father MacNeill. I'm doing my job, and my job is to investigate what happened last night. It's not to decide who did it, then go about making everything fit."

Father MacNeill glared furiously at the policeman. What on earth could make Ray Beckwith, who until this very afternoon had never failed to treat him with the respect his position deserved, suddenly speak to him as if he were a common criminal?

Then he remembered glancing out the window of the parish hall just after Ted Conway led his family out. He'd seen Ray talking to Conway, but mostly he'd seen Conway talking to Ray. Talking to him the same way he'd addressed the whole town at the meeting? Of course. And Ray, obviously, had fallen victim to the man's charm as easily as everyone at the meeting had.

It's time for me to talk to that man myself, Father MacNeill decided.

"Very well," the priest said aloud. "I wouldn't want to interfere with you performing your job, Raymond. And I'm sure when you're done, you'll have discovered the truth. But I'm telling you right now—if you think anyone here had anything to do with this terrible criminal act, you're wrong. Perhaps mortally wrong."

Leaving the threat to the future of Ray Beckwith's soul hanging in the air, Father MacNeill turned his back on the policeman and left the room.

"**P**erhaps we ought to wait until tomorrow morning," Father Bernard fretted. The afternoon had turned warm, but not nearly warm enough to warrant the perspiration dripping down his arms and back. No, his sweating wasn't caused by the heat, but by his nerves. And to what purpose? Tomorrow morning he could call Jared Conway and Luke Roberts into his office at school and get the truth out of them very quickly, indeed. In his office, Father Bernard was in charge. Outside his office, it was another matter entirely. From the time he'd first arrived at St. Ignatius, he'd been the leader in the school; in the rectory, however, it was the force of Father MacNeill's personality that held sway. Which was how it happened that he was now walking along Pontchartrain Street toward the Conway house, with sweat trickling down his back, staining the sleeves of his cassock.

"There's no reason to wait until tomorrow," Father MacNeill shot back. "If Ray Beckwith won't do his job, we shall simply do it for him." He paused a moment, gazing down the street at the Conway house. This afternoon, with the sun shining on its new coat of paint, the house had finally lost its look of a crumbling derelict. The missing slate on its roof had been replaced; somehow Ted Conway had even managed to find new trim to replace the fancywork that had rotted and broken over the years the house sat empty and untended. The last of the overgrowth crowding the grounds had been stripped away, and only a few strands of dying kudzu still clung to the great spreading magnolia from which George Conway had hanged himself so many years ago. Indeed, the disrepair that had given the house its darkly foreboding look was gone, so much so that for a moment Father MacNeill wondered if it was possible that everything he'd ever heard about the house—everything Monsignor Devlin had shown him in the Conway Bible—had been untrue.

But an instant later, as he started across the street, he felt it. It was as if an evil force was emanating from the house itself. He tried to ignore it, but even as he neared the door, he felt it.

A chill.

And something else.

It was as if something unseen—unseeable—was waiting for him. Preparing to attack him.

As he drew closer, every nerve in his body began tingling, and a wave of panic rose inside him. He forced it down, though, and with Father Bernard trailing after him, made himself stride up the walk, mount the steps, and ring the bell. From somewhere deep inside the house a chime sounded, and then a dog began barking.

The priest was about to press the bell a second time when Janet Conway opened the door. She was bent down, clutching at the collar of a large golden retriever. The dog was still barking, but its tail was wagging furiously as it attempted to scramble out. "I'm sorry," Janet blurted, "I'm afraid—" Her words died on her lips as she recognized Father MacNeill. An uncertain frown appeared as she straightened up. "I'm afraid Scout isn't much of a watchdog," she finished. Tightening her grip on the dog's collar, she pulled the door open farther.

A wave of cold rolled through the gap. Father MacNeill took an involuntary step back.

"Is there something I can do for you?" Janet asked, keeping her tone neutral, but with difficulty.

"I wanted to have a few words with you," Father MacNeill began. "And your son, too." As he uttered the words, the priest felt a wave of pure emotion break over him, an emotion he recognized at once.

Hatred.

Something—or someone—in this house hated him with an intensity he'd never felt before. A hatred so strong that once again he lurched back a step. Under his cassock, his body was suddenly slick with sweat, and the panic he'd only barely managed to control a few moments ago was again threatening to overwhelm him.

Janet's frown deepened as the priest staggered backward. "Are you all right?" she asked anxiously, opening the door still farther. "Would you like to come in for a moment?"

Father MacNeill struggled to control the panic that had seized him. He tried to take a step forward, but could not. It was as if a wall—a physical wall—blocked him. When he tried to speak, his voice was constricted, as though a rope was tightening around his throat. "I—wanted a word with—" His breath caught for a moment, then he managed to finish his sentence: "—with Jared," he stammered.

Once again he tried to take a step toward the open front door, but it was no use.

He couldn't enter the house, couldn't so much as set foot across the threshold.

"Jared?" Janet repeated. Her eyes flicked from Father MacNeill to Father Bernard. Both priests were sweating, and their faces were ashen. Before she could say anything else, Ted appeared behind her.

"Is there something we can do for you?" he asked coldly, his eyes fixed on Father MacNeill.

Once again the priest took an involuntary step backward. "If we could just have a few words with Jared," he repeated.

Ted Conway's eyes bored into the priest's. "About?" he demanded.

"Is he here?" the priest countered, his voice trembling despite his efforts to control it.

Janet, still struggling with Scout, looked uncertainly to her husband. "Should I call him?"

Molly peeped around the edge of the door. She gazed out at the two priests, then suddenly began crying and reached for her father. Ted swung the little girl up into his arms. "We might do better to call the police," Ted said as he jiggled Molly and she calmed down.

Janet glanced from her husband to the priest, then back to her husband. "I—I'll just call Jared," she stammered. If she didn't do something to break the tension between Ted and the priest, one of them very well might call the police. "He didn't have anything to do with what happened last night, so what can it possibly hurt?"

Without waiting for a reply from Ted, she hurried through the dining room and opened the door to the basement. "Jared?" she called. "Jared!" When there was no response, she went down the steep flight of stairs and rapped on the closed door to his room. A moment later the door opened a crack, and she could smell the musty odor of the fumes that constantly drifted up from the sump in the middle of the room. "Father MacNeill and Father Bernard are here. They want to talk to you."

Jared's expression clouded. "What about?"

"Something happened at the cemetery last night, and for some reason Father MacNeill thinks you might have something to do with it. All you have to do is tell him you didn't, and that will be the end of it."

When Jared said nothing, Janet felt her stomach tighten. If Jared refused to talk to the priest, MacNeill would assume the worst. But then Jared shrugged. "Sure," he said. "I'll be up in a minute."

By the time Janet got back to the front door, Kim was standing at the bottom of the stairs. "What do they want?" she asked, anxiously eyeing the two priests who waited on the porch.

"It's all right," Janet assured her. "They just want to talk to Jared. They'll be gone in a minute."

Then Jared appeared, and as Father MacNeill looked at the boy, a single thought—a single concept—came into his mind.

Death.

Then, for just the barest fraction of an instant, he saw a change in Jared Conway's face.

The boy's eyes seemed to turn to slits, and his nostrils flared. It was more than an expression of anger; it was as if the boy's physiognomy had begun to transform itself into something inhuman.

But as quickly as it appeared, the vision was gone. It happened so fast that a second later the priest was no longer sure of what he'd seen.

But he could no longer look at Jared.

He shivered, trying to shake off the horrible chill that had seized him, then steeled himself and once more forced his gaze to meet the boy's. He spoke deliberately. "You took a cross from the church," he said. "You vandalized your uncle's tomb, and you pinned the skin of a dead cat to a tree with the cross."

"No!" Kim cried out, her voice breaking. "Don't you dare say that! Jared would never have hurt—"

Before she could finish, though, Jared himself spoke. "Go to hell," he said softly. His eyes remained on the priest, and Father MacNeill felt an outpouring of hatred wash over him. He felt as if he couldn't breathe, and his heart began to pound. "You don't know anything about what I did last night," Jared went on. "Stay away from here. Stay away, or maybe you'll wind up with one of your precious crosses shoved right up your—"

"Jared!" Janet cut in. "Don't you dare talk to Father MacNeill like that!"

"I'll talk to him any way I want!" Jared shot back.

Molly began to scream, and Janet quickly took her from Ted. "I'm sorry," she blurted to the two priests. "I can't imagine—"

"Don't apologize!" Jared burst out. "You said he wanted to ask me some questions. So, did you hear any questions?" His eyes fixed once more on the priest, and his voice turned venomous. "You think you know what's going on around here? Well, you're wrong! You don't have a clue what's going on!" He moved forward, raising his hand to point a finger at the priest, and Father MacNeill stumbled backward, barely catching himself against one of the columns that supported the roof. "Get away from here!" Jared screamed. "Get out of my house!"

Suddenly, the finger turned into a talon, and the priest jerked away as it slashed out at him. Once again he saw the demon he'd caught a glimpse of only moments ago, but this time it was leering at him, its fangs bared, its tongue flicking toward him like a snake's, its eyes glowing with evil fury. His hands clutched at the crucifix hanging from his waist, and as he raised it, he heard a rasping voice emerge from the throat of the beast before him.

"Next time, I'll drive the cross through your heart, priest!"

Father MacNeill's nostrils filled with the sour stench of vomit, and his own gorge rose. Then, with a howling cackle of harsh laughter, the vision vanished.

"Just get out of our house," he heard Jared say again. The boy turned away and disappeared back inside.

"I—I'm so sorry," Janet stammered. "I don't know what would make him say any of that. Jared isn't like that. He—He's—" She shook her head helplessly as she tried to soothe Molly, who was crying again.

Father MacNeill barely heard her. The cold was finally releasing him from its terrible grip, and his heartbeat was starting to slow. As his breathing returned to normal, he swallowed the bile that had risen in his throat. Finally, he was able to look at Ted. "I think I know what I came to find out," he said softly.

Ted's gaze never wavered. "You didn't come to find out anything. You think you already know. But you're wrong, Father. You don't know anything." Taking Janet's elbow, he gently steered her back into the house and closed the door.

Father MacNeill stared at the closed door, but instead of seeing the great oaken panel, he saw instead the demon face he'd beheld a moment ago. "Did you see it?" he asked Father Bernard. "Did you feel it?"

Father Bernard looked at him uncertainly. "I'm not sure I—"

"Evil," Father MacNeill breathed. "You can see it. You can feel it." He moved unsteadily off the porch and down the path to the sidewalk. Only when they had crossed the street and walked some distance away, did he finally turn back to look again at the house.

"Evil," he whispered. Then, with Father Bernard beside him, he began the long walk back to the rectory.

Ray Beckwith pulled his squad car up in front of Jake's weather-beaten cabin out by the lake. The rowboat was hauled up onto the narrow strip of muddy beach, and Jake's dog was chained outside. As the hound began baying, Jake opened the door and stepped out onto the porch.

"Hey there, Jake," Ray called out as he got out of the car. Jake nodded, but said nothing. "How's it going? Nice afternoon, huh?"

Jake's face was an impassive mask. "Don't think you came out here to talk about the weather. What d'you want?"

"Just got a couple of questions, that's all," Ray replied. He nervously eyed the hound, which was straining at the end of its chain. "Okay if I come up on the porch?"

Jake shrugged. "Suit yourself."

He made no move to quiet the dog, so Ray circled carefully around, staying well out of reach of the animal's snapping jaws. "I just wondered what you were doing last night, Jake," he said as he stepped up onto the porch.

"Figured," Jake replied. "You're wantin' to know if I had anything to do with what happened down at the cemetery last night."

"You heard about it?"

Jake shrugged and countered, "Know anybody who didn't?"

"So where were you last night?" Ray asked.

"I was out tendin' my traps. Me and Lucky took off 'bout ten. Didn't get home till near dawn."

Ray nodded as if he were no longer listening, but when he spoke again, he watched Jake's reaction to his question. "Mind if I show you something?"

"Don't mind at all," Jake replied. If he was worried, it didn't show in his face.

Ray went back to the squad car and returned a moment later, carrying a package wrapped in black plastic. As the dog strained at its chain, Ray glanced at the open front door of the cabin. "Maybe we should go inside?"

Jake shrugged and led Ray into the tiny cabin. The officer laid the package on the table and opened it, exposing the cat's hide that had been found pinned to the tree over Cora Conway's grave. As he pulled away the last piece of plastic, Ray kept his eyes on Jake Cumberland.

The trapper winced as he saw the skin.

"You've seen it before," Ray said.

Jake Cumberland's mind felt numb as he stared at the skin of the cat. He could still remember snatching the cat up the night the Conways moved into the house, skinning it on this very table, then taking the hide back to the Conways. The last time he'd seen the cat skin was when he'd left it nailed to the back of the carriage house as a warning to the Conways to go away.

They hadn't heeded his warning, but they hadn't gone to the police, either. If they had, Ray Beckwith would have been out here long ago. *What'll I do, Mama?* he silently asked. *What should I say?* And as clearly as if she'd been standing right there next to him, Jake heard his mama's voice: *He don't know nothin', Jake. He don't know nothin' at all.*

"Don't reckon I have seen it before," Jake said, his gaze shifting from the cat skin back to Ray Beckwith. "Don't reckon I've ever seen that before in my life."

The two men eyed each other, the unspoken challenge hanging in the air.

"Then you won't mind if I have a look around, will you?" Ray said softly.

Again Jake shrugged. "Don't make no never mind," he said softly. "Take a look, if you want."

As Jake watched, Ray Beckwith searched the cabin. He checked the garbage first, poking through a bucket of food scraps mixed with the entrails from some animal Jake had caught last night.

Nothing.

He moved on, opening and closing the few drawers and cupboards that hung around Jake's sink. Finally his eyes fell on the trunk.

"That locked?" he asked.

Jake shook his head. "Nothin' much in it 'cept for my mama's stuff."

"Voodoo stuff?" Ray asked.

The muscles in Jake's jaw tightened, but he said nothing, and when Ray knelt down to open the trunk, he made no move to stop him. Lifting the lid, Ray stared down at the collection of oddments that filled the compartments of the tray, then lifted the tray itself out of the trunk. Beneath it he saw a folded tablecloth, and beneath that a jumble of what looked like clothes. He was about to replace the tray when he suddenly changed his mind and plunged his hands into the tangle of material.

His fingers brushed against something.

Something furry.

He closed his fingers on the object and lifted it out of the trunk.

Rising to his feet, Ray turned to face Jake Cumberland. The trapper's eyes were fixed on the cat's head as if he were looking at a ghost.

"I don't know how that got in there," he said, his voice rising. "I swear I don't."

Ray wordlessly laid the cat head on the table next to the hide. The color match was perfect, as was the cut where the head had been separated from the hide. He faced Jake. "You want to tell me about it?" he asked.

But Jake's expression had gone as flat as when he'd first appeared on the porch. "Nothin' to tell," he replied. "I was out tendin' my traps last night. Anybody at all could've snuck in here and put that in Mama's trunk."

Ray pursed his lips, nodding. "I guess that's true," he said. "But I guess you could've put it in there, too, now couldn't you?" Without waiting for an answer, he went on, "I'm gonna have to take you in, Jake. Folks are pretty upset about what happened last night." But it still didn't quite make sense to Beckwith. If Jake had put the cat's hide on the tree, why had he been so surprised to see it? What else could he have expected to be confronted with? "You knew what had to be in that package the minute I got it out of my car, didn't you, Jake? Didn't you think it had to be the skin from the cemetery?"

Jake nodded. "Figured it was."

"Then why did you look surprised when you saw it?" Ray pressed. "I know you weren't faking it—you recognized that skin, but you weren't expecting to see it." Ray took a deep breath. "What's going on, Jake? Isn't there anything else you want to tell me?"

Jake shook his head. "Don't think so," he said softly. "Besides, who knows? If everyone's as upset as you say they are, maybe I'll be better off in jail."

He followed Beckwith out to the squad car. Then, as Ray was about to drive away, Jake Cumberland turned to take one more look at his cabin and his dog.

The dog stared back at him, sitting down and cocking its head, as if puzzled.

"Goodbye," Jake whispered.

As the car headed down the dirt road, he twisted around for one last glimpse of Lucky.

Jake knew he would never see his pet again.

CHAPTER 32

J anet stood back and eyed the mural critically. Maybe she shouldn't have tried to work tonight, but always before—back in the days when Ted was drinking—her painting had provided her with a refuge from the reality of her life. This evening, the magic hadn't worked, and she knew her lack of concentration showed in the results on the dining room wall. It was almost done—indeed, it might have been done tonight if she'd been able to stop thinking about Jared through the long afternoon and evening.

"Don't worry about him," Ted had advised her when she'd looked for Jared after the priests had left, and discovered he wasn't in the house. "He's pretty angry, and frankly, I don't blame him. If Father MacNeill had been accusing *me*, I think I might actually have thrown a punch at that sanctimonious bastard."

"Ted!"

"Oh, come on. Don't tell me you think MacNeill had a right to come around here acting like—"

"It's irrelevant what I think about Father MacNeill—I'm not his mother. But I *am* Jared's mother, and it doesn't matter how angry he was. I won't have him talking like that to anyone! And I won't have him simply walking in and out of the house anytime he feels like it, either! Especially not tonight. I don't want him out on Halloween! If there's any trouble—any trouble at all—everyone will blame Jared. I know it!"

"But there's not going to be any trouble," Ted had argued.

So far, he'd been right. As dusk came on, Janet readied a bowl of candy for the trick-or-treaters, but even as she placed it on a table near the front door, she wondered how many of the town's children would come to their house.

And how many would throw eggs, or leave burning bags of dog dung on the porch?

When there'd been no knocks at the door by eight-thirty, she understood that none of the children would come, but she still kept going to the window and peering out into the darkness, her nerves on edge.

Between trips to the window, she tried to concentrate on the mural, but failed. And now, as she gazed at the trompe l'oeil she'd created on the wall, she knew she shouldn't have tried to work at all, for the scene depicted beyond the faux French doors no longer seemed quite as real as it had this morning. Yet she couldn't put her finger on what was wrong— the perspective was right, and so was the lighting from the not-quite- visible moon. Maybe something in the shadowy areas at the far side of the garden? The clock in the living room struck eleven, and realizing how late it was, Janet abandoned her paints and went into the library. Ted was working at his desk, studying the bids for the construction of a reception desk in the foyer. He looked up when she came in, his smile fading as he read the worry in her eyes.

"It's eleven o'clock," she said. "And Jared still isn't home." Ted stood up and came around the desk, slipping his arms around her.

"How about if I go have a look around and see if I can spot him?"

Janet looked anxiously into his eyes. "Will you? I keep thinking I ought to call the police, or the hospital."

"Not yet," Ted counseled. "It's Halloween, and I'll bet whatever he's doing, he's not planning to be back until midnight."

"Which is exactly why I want him home," Janet said. "Of all the nights for him to—"

"Tell you what," Ted broke in. "I'll go out and check the pizza parlor and the drive-in, and swing by Luke Roberts's house. If I don't find him, we'll call the hospital. In fact, I'll stop by there before I come home. But I'm sure he's okay. Try to take it easy, at least until I get back, okay?"

Janet slipped her arms around his neck and pressed herself close to him, but even the strength of his body did nothing to calm her edgy nerves. "I'll try," she agreed. "I don't think I'll be able to, but I'll try."

"And go to bed," Ted told her. "You've been working all afternoon and all evening, and you're exhausted. Just relax. I'll find him."

After Ted was gone, Janet returned to the dining room, looked once more at the mural, then cleaned her brushes, put away her palette, and started upstairs. She'd just come to the landing where the great staircase split when a wave of apprehension broke over her.

Something was wrong.

She held still, listening.

Silence.

Yet she still felt . . . what?

Stop it! she commanded herself. *It's nothing but nerves because it's Halloween, and Jared's not here, and suddenly everything seems to be going wrong again.* Yet before she continued up the stairs, she turned to gaze down into the great empty expanse of the entry hall. She'd turned most of the lights down, but now, as she peered down into the gloom below, she wished she hadn't. Somehow the cavernous room seemed to have grown even larger, its corners lost in shadowed darkness.

Unbidden, the memory of the night Kim had sworn she'd seen rats in the bathroom came to her, and Janet shuddered as she thought of what might be lurking in the dark corners of the house. *There's nothing,* she silently repeated. *Nothing.* But she hurried her step as she went up the short flight to the mezzanine.

As she came to Molly's door, she felt it.

It was as if a cold hand had been laid on her back, stopping her short. The chill intensified, wrapping around her like a shawl knitted of ice.

It had to be nothing more than a draft. But the door was shut tight, and even the crack beneath it wasn't wide enough to permit the kind of cold she was feeling to seep through.

Janet reached out, her hand closing on the glass knob of the nursery door. It was like holding an ice crystal in her hand.

She turned the knob and pushed the door open. It creaked softly, and she heard Molly stir.

She stepped inside the room, and the chill lost its edge. Hurrying to the crib, she bent over and peered down at her sleeping child. Molly's eyes opened a crack, glinting in the soft moonlight that filled the room, then she went back to sleep. Tucking the child's blanket close around her, Janet bent lower, her lips brushing Molly's forehead.

Molly sighed contentedly, then curled on her side, her right thumb sliding into her mouth.

Satisfied that her youngest child was sleeping peacefully, Janet tiptoed out of the room.

The chill had vanished as quickly as it came.

In the master bedroom she undressed, put on a nightgown and robe, and slid into bed. Switching on the lamp on the bedside table, she picked up a magazine. Maybe reading would keep her worries about Jared at bay, she thought, at least until Ted came home.

And then she heard it.

A sobbing sound, muffled and indistinct.

At first she thought she'd imagined it, but then she heard it again.

Molly?

Throwing the light cover aside, Janet got out of bed and went to the door that joined the master bedroom to Molly's room. She listened, heard nothing, and opened the door a crack.

Silence.

She closed the door again, and went to the other door—the one that led to the mezzanine—and listened.

There it was again, but louder now.

Janet's pulse quickened, but she steeled herself and pulled the door open.

The sobbing increased, swelling into an anguished moan.

A knot of fear formed in her stomach, but she pulled the robe tight around her, tied the belt, and stepped out onto the mezzanine.

Then she heard the cry: "No!"

The single word died away as quickly as it had come, but in the instant it hung in the air, Janet recognized Kim's voice. Racing to the far end of the hall, she twisted the knob of Kim's door, threw it open, and flicked on the lights. She was blinded by the sudden glare for a second, then saw Kim huddled on her bed, sobbing. Her arms went around her daughter, pulling her close.

"It's all right, Kimmie," she whispered, using the nickname her older daughter had shed five years ago, on her tenth birthday. "It was only a bad dream. I'm here."

"It was Jared," Kim cried. "Mom, it was awful! He—He killed Scout!"

"No," Janet soothed. "It was just a dream, Kim. It didn't really happen."

"What's doing it, Mom?" Kim sobbed. "What's making me have these terrible dreams about Jared?"

"What dreams?" Janet asked. Settling herself onto the bed next to Kim, she gently eased her daughter's head onto her lap. "Honey, what have you been dreaming?"

Kim hesitated, recalling images from her nightmares. Then, slowly, she began talking, telling her mother about the strange things she'd seen in her dreams, the terrible things she'd witnessed Jared doing. "But they weren't like real dreams at all, Mom," she finished. "They were so real, it seemed like it was all really happening! But it couldn't have happened, could it?"

"No, of course not," Janet soothed, stroking Kim's hair. "I know dreams can seem real, but they aren't. And you mustn't let them frighten you."

Sniffling, Kim sat up and wiped at her eyes with the sleeve of her nightgown. "It's just that Jared's changed," she said. "He isn't anything like he used to be." She looked bleakly at her mother. "You know how I used to know what Jared was thinking? What he was feeling?"

Janet smiled. "The Twin Thing."

Kim nodded. "It was like that tonight. It was like I knew exactly what he was doing. I could see it as clearly as if I were standing right next to him. He—He had a knife, and Scout was lying on a table, and—" Her voice broke into a choking sob.

"But it wasn't real," Janet assured her once again. She got off the bed and gently pulled Kim to her feet. "Come on. I'll show you. We'll go down to the kitchen and get Scout, and he can come up and sleep with you tonight. Okay?"

Nodding, Kim let Janet lead her out of her room, down the stairs, and into the kitchen.

"Scout?" Janet called out softly.

There was no welcoming thump of the big dog's tail banging against the wall as he wagged it. There was only silence.

Janet switched on the light.

Scout's bed was empty.

She frowned, trying to remember when she'd last seen the dog.

She wasn't sure. "He has to be here somewhere," she said. "Come on."

But fifteen minutes later, Janet and Kim both knew that Scout was gone. Nor did he come when they opened the back door and called him.

"It doesn't mean anything," Janet insisted as she and Kim climbed the stairs back up to the second floor. "He might have gone off with Jared this afternoon."

"He doesn't even like Jared anymore," Kim said, her voice wavering. "That's why he sleeps in the kitchen now!"

"Then maybe he went with your father," Janet said. But she'd watched Ted leave, and hadn't seen the dog go with him.

But there was something else that could have happened, something that she could see had already occurred to Kim: If Scout had vanished into the woods the same way Muffin had on the night they'd moved into the house, would he be found the same way the cat had?

Just the thought of it made Janet shudder, and as if by mutual consent, neither she nor Kim even mentioned that possibility.

* * *

The cabin lay dark and hushed beneath the pale silvery light of the moon. Jake Cumberland's hound was perfectly still, flattened against the ground beneath the cabin's floor. He'd neither moved nor made a single sound since he'd first scented the two figures stealing through the darkness toward the house. Had the chain not restrained him, he would have fled away through the covering darkness rather than slunk into the meager shelter provided by his master's house.

The night prowlers had gone silent; neither owls nor bats swooped and flitted in search of prey, for every creature they might have sought had vanished into burrows beneath the ground or hollows inside the trees.

No fish jumped in the lake, no frogs croaked along its bank; even the insects they hunted had ceased their nightly feeding and mating.

The quiet of death had fallen over the night. A dark cloud scudded over the moon as if to protect even it from bearing witness to the ceremony taking place within the cabin's walls, where five flickering candles on the table struggled to hold back the descending darkness.

Luke Roberts stood next to Jared Conway, his unblinking eyes fixed on the object that lay on the table in the center of the pentagram formed by the candles.

In his right hand, Jared held a knife—its cutting edge honed to razor sharpness by Jake Cumberland's own whetstone and strop. As he clutched its leather-bound haft, the instrument itself seemed to speak to him, whispering of the creatures it had disemboweled, the hides it had slit, the flesh it had slashed. Jared lowered the knife toward the offering on the table, but just before he drove the blade into the creature's breast, he gazed one last time into its eyes.

"Don't," he heard his sister's voice whisper inside his head. "Oh, God, Jared, please don't."

Jared hesitated as Kim's voice, only dimly heard, tugged at him, tried to restrain him. It was as if he stood on the edge of a dark and fathomless abyss, feeling inexorably drawn to it. Every fiber of his being wanted to step over the edge, to drop into the darkness below, plunge deep into whatever lay within the blackness that beckoned to him.

And only Kim's dimly heard voice held him back.

"Don't," her voice whispered again. "Please, Jared. Don't."

Jared's eyes moved from the body of the creature to its head.

Scout lay on his back, his legs splayed wide as if to expose his belly in submission to some far stronger creature than he. His head lolled to one side. His mouth lay open, his tongue hung out.

And one of his eyes—his soft, trusting brown eyes—seemed to gaze up at Jared, as if joining in Kim's whispered plea.

But it was already too late. He plunged the knife into the dog's heart and Scout's life ended with a silent spasm.

Now all that remained was to carry out the ceremony, to offer his pet to his new master.

Pulling the knife from the dog's corpse, he lowered its point until it just grazed the skin of Scout's belly.

Yet still he hesitated, looking one last time into Scout's eyes, hesitating as, fleetingly, a brief, flickering doubt entered his mind, as though something within was telling him to step back—step back from the edge of the abyss.

Too late. With Kim's pleading voice fading away, he felt himself slide into the darkness. As Luke watched, Jared slipped the point of the knife through the retriever's hide and ran its edge up the center of its belly and chest to its throat. Four more slits ran up each leg, and then he began peeling the skin away from the flesh below. He worked quickly, the blade seeming to guide his hands as if the knife itself had performed the work so often, it needed no aid from him.

Deftly, he sliced through the abdominal muscles, then cut away the creature's entrails.

He cut through the rib cage and laid open the animal's chest, exposing the lungs and heart.

Raising the knife high, Jared muttered a dedication of the blood offering he was about to make, then plunged the knife deep into the heart. Dropping the knife, he plunged his hands into the blood that oozed from the punctured heart into the chest cavity. With reddened fingers he anointed Luke's forehead.

Plunging his hands again into the gore within the slaughtered dog, he moved away from the table and began tracing patterns on the cabin's wall, intricate designs that rose out of some hidden place in his subconscious, flowing from his bloodied fingertips onto the ancient wood. And as he etched the design in blood, muttered imprecations—unintelligible curses condemning the man who had lived his entire life within the cabin's shelter—flowed from his lips.

Jake Cumberland's eyes flicked open in the darkness of his cell. He felt disoriented for a moment, but slowly his mind cleared and he remembered where he was. And why.

He wasn't going to get out of jail—he already knew that. His mama had explained it to him when he was small: *"Don't ever do nothin' that'll let 'em put you in jail,"* she'd told him. *" 'Cause once they gets you in, they ain't gonna be lettin' you out again. Not around here. Onliest way they ever gonna let you out is at the end of a rope. That's what they did to my daddy, Jake, when I was no bigger'n you. They came for him one night, and took him down and tied a rope around his neck, and after that I didn't have a daddy no more. So you watch yourself, hear?"*

Now, in the blackness of the Halloween midnight, he heard another voice. An evil voice, whispering inside his head.

Do it yourself, Jake, the voice said. *Don't wait, Jake. Don't wait for morning. Do it now.*

At first Jake tried to ignore the voice, but it wouldn't be put off, and as the seconds ticked by and turned into minutes, it grew stronger, more insistent.

Do it, Jake. You know you want to. Come on, Jake. Now, Jake. Now!

The voice took on a mesmerizing rhythm. Without thinking about it, Jake rose from the cot on which he lay and took off his pants. He began ripping at the denim, tearing the legs into strips.

You know what to do, Jake, the voice whispered. *Just do it. Do it now.*

Jake began braiding the strips of denim together, his fingers working the material as easily as they knotted together the twine for his snares. Soon he was done.

The rope was nearly six feet long, plenty long enough to do what had to be done.

Now, Jake, the voice whispered. *Do it now.*

Jake tied one end of the braided rope around his neck, then stood on the cot and reached up to the sprinkler pipe that ran across the cell's width.

He tied the free end of the rope around it and tested the knot. It was solid; it would hold.

Die! the voice commanded. *Die right now!*

Without another thought, Jake Cumberland stepped off the edge of the cot. He dropped a foot, and then the rope jerked tight.

His neck did not break, but the loop around his neck dug deep, closing his windpipe.

His body twitched, his feet kicked out.

Then, in the darkness, he saw his mama. She was at the end of a tunnel, and her hand was held out to him. As Jake began hurrying through the darkness toward his mother, the voice faded away.

Jake Cumberland was dead.

His incantations done, the inscriptions on the walls complete, Jared Conway severed the dog's head from the carcass and placed it inside the trunk where the night before he had hidden the head of the cat.

He cleaned the hide of the last remnants of flesh, rolled it tight, and slipped it into a plastic sack. As Luke carried the flesh, bones, and entrails outside, Jared blew the candles out, one by one. As the last candle flickered out, the room plunged into utter blackness.

Taking the skin of the slaughtered dog with him, Jared left the cabin, and as he and Luke disappeared into the darkness, the life of the night began again.

A trout broke the surface of the lake, snapping at a water bug.

An owl swept down from the trees, its talons closing on a mouse that had only a moment ago ventured forth from its burrow.

Bats flitted through the night sky, feeding on the gnats and mosquitoes that rose into the air from their hidden shelters in the grass and leaves.

And Jake Cumberland's hound crept out from beneath the cabin, sniffed at the pile of entrails left at the foot of the steps, and began devouring the unexpected feast.

Ted Conway slumped behind the wheel of the Toyota, waiting in the darkness. After leaving the house, he'd done exactly as he'd promised Janet he would—he'd driven past the Roberts house. It was dark and quiet.

He cruised around the square, slowing as he passed the pizza parlor but barely glancing through its brightly lit windows, certain the boys would not be there.

Then he came back, parking the car in the darkness well away from the house, waiting.

He heard the night fall silent, saw the cloud slide over the moon. Still he waited, knowing that soon his vigil would end.

Finally the sky cleared and the night sounds picked up again. Ted straightened in the seat, his senses sharpening, his eyes scanning the edge of the forest that lay beyond the grounds. The seconds ticked by, turning into minutes. Still he waited, until his patience was rewarded by a flicker of movement within the shadows. Two figures emerged from the trees and slipped as silently as phantoms across the grounds toward the house. Starting the engine of the Toyota, Ted shifted it into gear, switched on the headlights, and drove down the street to the driveway. He pulled close to the carriage house, then shut off the engine, got out, and slammed the car door behind him. Entering the house through the back door, he paused at the door to the basement, listening.

The sound of discordant music boiled up the stairs and filtered through the door.

Satisfied, he climbed the stairs to the second floor and went into the master bedroom where his wife and older daughter waited.

"Found him," he said, smiling at the relief that came into Janet's face. "He was at the pizza parlor with Luke. I dropped Luke off at his house and had a long talk with Jared on the way home."

"I think maybe I'll have a talk with him myself," Janet said, starting to get out of bed.

"And I think maybe you should just stay where you are," Ted told her, gently pushing her back into the bed. "Believe me, he's stinging bad enough after what I had to say to him. Anything you want to add can wait until morning." He shifted his attention to Kim. "And tomorrow's a school day. You should be in bed, too."

"What about Scout?" Kim asked. "Was he with Jared?"

Ted's eyes clouded. "I don't think so. Isn't he here?"

Kim shook her head.

"Well, if he's not back by morning, I'll go look for him, too. He's probably just out doing what dogs do."

"But after what happened to Muffin—" Kim began, but her father didn't let her finish.

"It's not the same thing," he assured her. "But Scout will be back— I guarantee it. And now it's time for you to go to bed."

Kissing his daughter good night, Ted watched her circle around the landing and disappear back into her room. When her door was closed, he went back into the bedroom, undressed, and got into bed next to Janet.

"You okay now?" he whispered, taking her in his arms and nuzzling at her ear.

Janet pulled away from him. Should she tell him about the terrible cold that had come over her in front of Molly's room? Or would he just laugh at her, and accuse her of listening to the ghost stories people told about the house? And what about Kim's nightmares?

Feeling the tension in her body, Ted propped himself up on one elbow. "Something's wrong," he said. "Tell me about it."

Still Janet hesitated, not sure where to begin. Ted gently turned her face so she was looking into his eyes.

"Tell me," he whispered. "Tell me what's wrong."

"It was when I was coming up the stairs," Janet began. But as she was about to describe the chill she'd felt, she realized how foolish it would sound. In fact, now that he was back and caressing her cheek, it seemed that nothing unusual had occurred.

She'd felt a draft, which she exaggerated in her own mind simply because of the vastness of the house and the lateness of the hour.

Kim had had a nightmare.

And Scout, like any normal dog, had taken off into the night.

The important thing was that Jared was safely back home, and so was Ted. She turned to face him, snuggling close. "It's all right," she murmured. "Nothing happened at all."

Then, as Ted's fingers crept beneath her nightgown and began tracing patterns on her naked skin, the last of the fears she'd felt that night drained away.

It was nearing midnight, but neither Monsignor Devlin nor Father MacNeill was ready to give up their vigil.

"It's Halloween," Father MacNeill had said as they'd eaten their supper earlier. "And something's going to happen. I can feel it."

"Perhaps you're wrong," the older priest had cautioned. "Perhaps we're both wrong." He rested a bony hand on the old Bible that Cora Conway had entrusted to him the day she died. "Perhaps none of this means anything. Perhaps it's nothing more than the ramblings of unhappy women."

"You know that isn't true," Father MacNeill replied. "And we haven't read it all. If we could find the missing pages—"

"They're gone," Devlin sighed. "I've already examined every page of the Bible twice. They simply aren't there."

After their evening prayers, the two priests had retired to Monsignor Devlin's small room, where Father MacNeill had searched the entire Bible one more time, carefully turning each page. He could almost feel the missing leaves. So certain was he that he would find them that it wasn't until he'd turned the very last page and even carefully examined the binding itself that he made himself admit they weren't there. Sighing heavily, he pushed the Bible away, as if to distance himself from the source of his disappointment. As the book slid across the table, there was a crash as the small box behind it fell to the floor.

His disappointment giving way to regret, he reached down and picked up the music box. "I'm so sorry," he said. "How could I have been so clumsy?"

"It's all right," Monsignor Devlin assured him. "It doesn't work anyway."

Frowning, Father MacNeill opened the lid of the music box. There was a faint click as the mechanism engaged, but no music played.

"When I bought it, it played a truly frightening rendition of Ave Maria." Devlin chuckled. "I suspect Cora broke it deliberately."

"Cora?" MacNeill echoed. "Cora Conway?" When Devlin nodded, Father MacNeill turned the box over and examined its bottom. A winding key protruded through a brass plate held in place by four small screws. His pulse quickening, the priest hurried downstairs, returning a few minutes later with a battered metal tool box. Sorting through the jumble inside, he finally came up with a screwdriver small enough to fit the screws on the music box.

A minute later he carefully lifted the brass plate. And there, carefully folded, were the missing pages. His hands trembling, he unfolded them, smoothed them on the table, and began reading Loretta Villiers Conway's perfect script . . .

October 31, 1875——

It is my wedding day.

I had not expected ever to have a wedding, so ill have I been, and even today I am not certain it would not have been better for me to have died. But I know I must marry Monsignor Melchior Conway, or suffer eternal damnation, for that is what both my father and the Monsignor have told me.

The Monsignor came from Philadelphia three months ago. Our own priest asked him to come, so certain was he that I was possessed of the Devil. I do not remember the Monsignor's arrival, for it was during the time when I was confined to my bedroom, of which I remember very little. What I do remember I now record here.

I was in the cellar of our little house when I noticed a strange mist rising from a hole in the earthen floor. As I breathed the mist, everything in the basement changed. All became golden, and images appeared before me——beautiful images. A being appeared, and touched me in a way I should not have permitted.

I became ill the next day, and cannot bring myself to write the things they say I have done. They say I have been a wanton, and committed mortal sins, which is why the Monsignor came from Philadelphia.

At our first meeting——of which I have no clear memory——I took the Monsignor to the place where my illness began. I do not know how long we prayed in the cellar that night, but it cannot have been long enough, for the Monsignor insisted we go back the next night, and the night after that.

My illness soon began to retreat in response to the Monsignor's prayers, but I am told that my health now depends on him. He will give up his religious vocation to marry me, which father says I must do, though to marry a priest seems to me the gravest of blasphemies.

There was an inch of space in which nothing had been written, and then Loretta Villiers Conway's hand began again:

It is done.

I am married to the Monsignor by his own authority, for neither he nor Father were able to prevail upon our priest to marry us. Sister Mary Anthony came to our house after supper, and though she would not set foot indoors, she gave me a gift of two small crosses made of pure gold, which she said could protect me, and one of my children as well. Then she begged God to forgive me my sins.

I suspect that He will not.

Nor will He forgive Monsignor Melchior, for I believe I know the truth of what lies in our cellar. It is Evil itself that resides deep within that hole, and I fear the Monsignor has become its Servant.

I have this day married the right hand of Evil.

The Monsignor has ceded himself—and the eldest sons of all the generations to come—to the Evil that dwells beneath this house, and I know we shall prosper on this Earth, but I know also that we are damned—damned for all Eternity.

The silence in the little room on the second floor of the rectory was complete as Father MacNeill finished reading the pages that Cora Conway had cut from the Bible and hidden in the music box. But why these pages? Why hadn't Cora cut from the Bible all the pages detailing the sins of the Conways? Even as he posed the question in his mind, he knew the answer: in Cora's mind, it was only this darkest secret that must be kept; all the rest might have been attributed to madness, but these first entries—the ones she'd hidden—proved the damnation of all the Conways' souls.

It was finally Monsignor Devlin who spoke. His voice quavered, as if the burdens of his years had suddenly grown heavier: "An exorcism," he breathed. "So that's how it started—an exorcism."

"A failed exorcism," Father MacNeill corrected. "He came to banish Satan, but gave up his soul instead."

Through the open window, the bells of St. Ignatius began to toll the darkest hour. Both priests shivered. An evil had been unleashed on St.

Albans on a Halloween more than a century earlier. Now, on this Halloween midnight, had it spread over the town once more?

"Kimmie? Kimmie, come on!"

It was Jared's voice calling her name, and at first she didn't see him.
Then she spotted him, fifty yards ahead of her, beckoning to her. They
were in a meadow, and he was running toward a lake, and in a few seconds they would both plunge into the cool water, popping through the surface a moment later, laughing and splashing. She broke into a run, doing
her best to keep up with him, but Jared was faster than she, and plunged
into the lake before she could even get to the shore. She stopped at the
edge of the water, watching to see where he'd come up, her eyes looking
first one way, then another.

But he didn't come up.

"Jared!" she called out. Then again: "Jared?" When her brother still
didn't appear, she ran a few yards along the lake's edge, first in one direction, then in the other.

"Mommy!" she called out. "Mommy, help! Jared's gone!"

But when she looked around, her mother was nowhere to be seen.

Then, as clearly as if she'd heard him shouting the words, Jared
called to her again.

"Help me, Kimmie! Help me!"

With no thought but to save her brother, Kim dove into the water,
plunging deep as she searched for her drowning twin. At first she saw
nothing except sunlight filtering through the clear water, but as she
plunged deeper and the light faded, she caught a glimpse of him.

He was far below, looking up at her, his hand extended as if reaching out to her. But as she watched, he sank deeper into the watery darkness, until she could hardly see him. She tried to dive faster, kicking as
hard as she could, but no matter how fast she swam downward, Jared was
always just a little beyond her reach. The water seemed to be turning to
jelly around her now, and she struggled against it, straining to reach her
brother before he disappeared completely. Then, for one fleeting moment,
the tips of her fingers touched his. She tried to clutch at his hand, but he
fell away into the blackness, disappearing.

Kim stopped swimming and let herself drift in the darkness. A great
emptiness—as dark as the water surrounding her—yawned within her,
and as she slowly let herself sink into it, the pain of not having been able
to save her brother began to ease.

The darkness deepened.

Then, somewhere in the darkness, a point of light appeared. As Kim

watched it, it slowly grew brighter. At first she thought she must be floating back toward the lake's surface. But when she finally opened her eyes,
the water was gone.

She was back in the great cathedral-like chamber, which had somehow grown even vaster than before. Tonight there was no trace of the
shimmering light she'd first seen here; tonight she felt as if she were
utterly lost in the shadows that filled the huge space. Then, far ahead of
her, she once again beheld the inverted cross, suspended in the shadowy
light as if by some unseen force. Mesmerized, Kim moved toward it. As
she did, the candles spread on the altar beneath the cross burst into flame.
As the light grew, Kim saw the eviscerated body of an animal on the altar,
a dagger plunged though its heart, its blood dripping into a silver chalice.

Two robed and hooded figures appeared at either end of the altar.
They moved closer together, and for a moment her view of the altar—and
the cross—was blocked. The two figures bent over, and a terrible feeling
of apprehension came over Kim.

She tried to back away, but some unseen force held her in place.

Then the two hooded figures stepped aside and she once again
beheld the cross.

A tiny figure, its face contorted in pain, was affixed to it.

Silver spikes had been driven through each wrist.

A third punctured the child's feet.

Blood dripped from a wound in the child's chest, oozing down the
neck and face to mat into the already reddish hair.

Molly!

Kim screamed out loud, and in an instant that seared itself into her
mind, the two robed figures whirled around.

Her father and her brother stood glowering at her, their faces contorted with hatred.

She screamed again, and jerked awake.

For a moment her head swam with the dying remnants of the dream.
Her heart was pounding so hard she could hear it, and her skin was
clammy with sweat.

A dream! she told herself. *It was only a dream!*

She eased herself back down onto the pillow and tried to erase the last
fragments of the dream from her memory, but the faces of her father and
brother kept looming up in the darkness, leering at her, almost taunting her.

She turned over in bed, but still the dream stayed with her, only now
it was the twisted face of her baby sister she saw, hanging upside down
from the inverted cross, impaled by the nails, her life slowly ebbing away.

Then the earlier dream came back to haunt her, the dream in which
she'd seen Jared killing Scout.

She had convinced herself that it, too, had been just a dream. But when they'd gone to find Scout, he'd vanished from the house.

As the first faint light of dawn etched the sky with silver, Kim got up from her bed and tiptoed out onto the landing. The great house lay silent around her, and as she made her way around to Molly's room, she had the eerie feeling of unseen eyes following her.

She paused before the door, shivering in a sudden chill that seemed to come out of nowhere.

Finally, her hand trembling, she reached for the knob, twisted it, and slowly pushed the door open.

The chill reached deeper into her, touching her soul.

She stepped into the room, straining to catch a glimpse of her sister in the gray light of dawn, but all she saw was a mass of rumpled bedding.

"Molly?" she whispered, edging closer to the child's crib. "Molly? Are you okay?"

There was no movement at all from the crib. Kim, standing by its side, looked down at the tangle of sheets and blankets. *Please,* she prayed silently. *Please let her be all right.*

She reached out, took the edge of the blanket, and pulled it aside.

And there lay Molly, sound asleep, her thumb tucked in her mouth.

Choking back a sob of relief, Kim bent down, gently kissed the sleeping child, and tucked the blanket back around her.

All Souls' Day

CHAPTER 33

Jake Cumberland's cabin looked peaceful enough when Corinne Beckwith pulled into the little clearing next to the lake. Jake's hound was lying in the dust, and he sat up when she got out of the car, cocking his head as if trying to decide whether to sound an alarm. "It's okay," she said soothingly, moving slowly toward the dog with one hand extended. The dog stood up and edged closer to her, and Corinne made certain to stay just beyond the reach of his chain until he'd sniffed at her fingers, whimpered softly, then extended his tongue to have a lick. "Good boy," she said, bending down to scratch his ears as she gazed at the house. "I bet you're hungry, aren't you? Well, that's why I'm here. First we'll find you something to eat, then we'll start thinking about where you're going to live from now on." Though Corinne was certain the dog couldn't understand her words, something in her tone must have told him that his master wasn't coming back. Whining, the dog dropped down into the dust, and Corinne crouched beside him. "I know, boy," she said, stroking his coat. "You're going to miss him, aren't you?" Patting him once more, she stood up and turned toward the cabin. It looked utterly deserted this morning, as if it, too, knew that its sole occupant had abandoned it forever. Corinne took a step toward it, but then the dog was back on its feet, growling.

"Are you going to let me take a look, or are you going to try to rip my throat out?" Corinne asked. As she reached out to him again, the dog pressed himself against her legs, looked at her through bloodshot eyes. "Guess you're not going for the throat, huh?"

Corinne straightened up once more and continued toward the cabin, and the hound followed her. When she moved up onto the porch, though, he yelped, and when she reached for the doorknob, he barked loudly.

Corinne eyed the dog speculatively, uncertain whether the bark was a warning or the animal was merely eager to get inside. Unwilling to risk arousing the dog's guarding instincts, she moved to the window, shaded her eyes against the glare of the morning sun, and peered inside. As her eyes adjusted to the relative gloom inside, she saw the strange designs that had been smeared on the cabin's wall with some kind of rust-colored paint.

Paint . . . or blood?

Feeling queasy, Corinne stepped back from the window. Her hand dropped to the hound's head. "Who was it?" she asked. "Who was here?" She stepped off the porch, fished in her purse for her cell phone, and a moment later was talking to her husband. "You better get out here, Ray," she told him. "Something terrible went on in Jake's cabin last night, and after what happened in the jail, no one's going to be able to blame this mess on him."

T wenty minutes later Ray Beckwith stood with Corinne in the center of Jake's shack, his expression grim as he studied the strange and bloody symbols that stained the walls.

"Looks to me like someone was out here doin' more of Jake's voodoo stuff last night."

Corinne nodded. The first thought that had come to her when Ray had told her of Jake's death was that someone had turned Jake's own magic against him. Though Corinne had no more faith in voodoo than in any other religion, she knew that for followers of voodoo, the knowledge that someone was casting a spell had sometimes resulted in the sickness—or even death—of the victim.

The power of suggestion: if you believed you could be killed by magic, then you could be.

And if someone had let Jake know what kind of ritual would be performed, and when . . .

Corinne could almost see Jake awaiting the hour in his cell, feeling the power of the voodoo "magic" surround him. His belief alone could have made him hang himself. But as she scanned the pentagrams and symbols on the walls, her eyes kept going back to a cross whose transverse bar was far below the midpoint.

A Christian cross, inverted?

"What about Satanists?" she asked.

Ray Beckwith groaned out loud. "Now you're starting to sound like Father MacNeill. Next thing, you'll be trying to blame this on the Conways, just like he did with the cemetery yesterday morning." He started toward the door.

"Where are you going? You haven't even searched the cabin."

"Gonna get the dog," Beckwith replied. "Maybe he can lead us right to whoever was here."

The hound made no objection as Beckwith replaced its chain a few minutes later with a strong leather lead he kept in the trunk of the squad car. But when he tried to coax it into the cabin, the animal turned recalcitrant, pulling and tugging at the leash as Beckwith tried to pull him through the front door. When the officer kept tugging, the hound snarled and snapped at him.

"Jesus!" Beckwith snatched his hand back just in time and glared at the dog. "What's going on with him?" he asked. "He musta been in here a million times before."

"Well, he's not going in now, and he didn't want me going in earlier," Corinne told him. "The question is, what does that mean?"

Beckwith scowled. "It means Jake had a stupid, stubborn good-for-nothin' animal here, that's what it means!"

"Or it means whatever happened in here last night scared him so much he doesn't want to go near the cabin," Corinne said.

Rechaining the dog, they went back into the cabin. As Corinne watched, her husband repeated the search he'd carried out the afternoon before.

Two minutes after he began, he lifted Scout's severed head from the trunk. "Oh, Jesus," he whispered. "Look at this."

As Corinne Beckwith's stomach threatened to betray her, she forced herself to look at the grisly object in her husband's hands. "I know that dog," she whispered. "It belonged to Jared Conway."

CHAPTER 34

Morning did nothing to dispel the terrors Kim had felt the night before. As she came downstairs, fingers of panic still reached out to her. Although everything in the cavernous entry hall looked exactly as it had yesterday, it felt strangely ominous even in the morning light. Pausing at the bottom of the stairs, Kim found herself shivering, as if the terrible chill she'd felt at the door to Molly's room as dawn was beginning to break had now spread down the stairs. As she passed through the dining room on her way to the kitchen, she stopped to gaze at the trompe l'oeil mural her mother was painting on the wall opposite the windows. The perfectly executed French doors, the faux terrace, even the balustrade outside, looked exactly as they had yesterday afternoon, but now, with the sun flooding in the windows opposite, it looked as if her mother had done something to the garden beyond the terrace. Kim studied the mural for several minutes before she realized what had changed.

The garden seemed to be dying.

The flowers that appeared so perfectly fresh and lifelike only yesterday looked this morning as if they were starting to wilt, and the green of the trees seemed to have faded, as if the painted foliage were somehow starting to turn brown. But why would her mother have done it? Kim moved closer to the wall, to see if some kind of wash had been applied to the whole garden, but it was almost as if each flower, each leaf, had taken on a faintly unhealthy cast. The mural, which a day earlier had given the whole dining room a bright and cheerful feel, now sent a somber mood over the room.

Kim turned away.

As she pushed open the kitchen door, she unconsciously braced herself against Scout's enthusiastic morning greeting. In the fraction of a second it took for her to remember that Scout was no longer in the house, the strange feeling of unease she'd had as she came downstairs notched up. Turning on the stove and setting a pot of water to boil, she went to the back door, stepped out onto the porch, and called out to Scout. As she waited for the dog to respond, she sucked the morning air deep into her lungs, and felt some of the tension that had been building inside her start to abate. She called out to Scout three more times, and when the big retriever didn't appear, she went back into the house.

Her father and brother were in the kitchen now, standing at the counter, their backs to her. The memory of the two robed and hooded figures she'd seen in her dream came to mind, and when first Jared, then her father, turned to look at her, another memory snapped into focus. The expression she'd seen in their eyes—the terrible look of hatred—recurred to her.

The terrible vision dissolved as quickly as it had come as she realized that the "hooded robes" of her dream were this morning nothing more than the same bathrobes they wore practically every day.

"Where's Mom?" she asked.

"I told her to sleep in this morning," her father said.

Had a look passed between her father and Jared? She wasn't sure. She cocked her head, frowning uncertainly. "Is something going on? Something I don't know about?"

This time she was certain that Jared glanced at his father. Then he grinned at her. Not the friendly grin he used to give her, when they'd still been so close. This morning the grin had an edge to it.

"Going paranoid on us?" he asked.

Kim felt herself blushing. "I'm not paranoid," she said, too quickly. "I just—I don't know. Something just doesn't feel right."

"That sure sounds like paranoia to me, doesn't it, Dad?"

Kim's unease hardened into anger. Since when had Jared and their father gotten so buddy-buddy? Especially since Jared was supposed to have gotten a chewing out last night!

"I better go up and get Molly," she said, suddenly wanting to get out of the kitchen.

"She's still asleep, too," Ted said softly, in a tone of voice that stopped Kim short. She turned to look at him. Her father's eyes locked on hers. "You'd better just get ready for school, Kim," he said quietly. "If you don't hurry, you're going to be late." His eyes held hers a few seconds longer, then he smiled. "All right?"

Kim nodded silently and left the kitchen. As she went upstairs to get

dressed, she had a vague feeling that there was something else she'd
intended to do before she realized how late it was and that if she didn't
hurry she wouldn't make it to school by the first bell. She dressed, still
trying to remember what it might have been, but as she combed her hair,
then gathered up her books, she decided that whatever it was, it couldn't
have been important.

It wasn't until she was a block away from the house that she remembered Molly and the dream she'd had last night. She wondered if maybe
she shouldn't go back to the house.

Just to be sure.

But if she did, she would surely be late to her first class.

And besides, the dream she'd had last night was only that—just a
dream.

Wasn't it?

The two cars pulled to a stop in front of the Conway house, and both
drivers got out. But as Corinne Beckwith started to follow Ray across the
lawn toward the columned porch fronting the house, her husband held up a
hand as if he were controlling traffic. "This isn't exactly a committee we've
got here," he reminded his wife. "I think I can deal with this one alone,
okay?"

Corinne glared at Ray. "If I hadn't gone out to Jake's to take care of
that dog this morn—" she began. But her words died on her lips because
something seemed off kilter. It was as if something were emanating from
the house, something that left her feeling she didn't want to be here, after
all. *It's just the light,* she told herself, peering into the shadows that darkened the porch. But it wasn't just a trick of the light; it was as if the entire
house had taken on a dark cast; as if it held something unknown that even
the structure's massive walls couldn't quite contain.

Why would anyone want to live in this place? Corinne wondered as
she let her husband continue—alone, and with no further argument—up
to the porch. For some reason, just looking at the Conway house this
morning made her shudder.

Ray Beckwith pressed the doorbell, and heard the sound of a muffled
chime drift through the thick wood of the doors. He shifted his weight nervously from one foot to the other as he waited for the door to open. As the
edginess that had come over him as he approached the house became more
pronounced, he reminded himself that he was here on legitimate business; he
had no cause to feel uneasy.

And yet, inexplicably, he did.

So far, he hadn't had a bad experience with Ted Conway. Sure, the man had been a little angry yesterday, but why wouldn't he be, with Father MacNeill practically accusing his son of defacing his own uncle's tomb? And when he'd gone out to Jake Cumberland's, Conway's idea had panned out, though he did still have some doubts about that. Now that Jake was dead, however, and if Corinne was right that the dog whose head they'd just found had belonged to the Conway boy—

His thoughts were interrupted when the door opened and Ted Conway appeared. For a moment Ray had the feeling Conway hadn't recognized him, but then the man smiled.

A smile that lit up his face, and made Ray Beckwith's nervousness evaporate.

"Hey, Ray, how's it going?" he asked. Then he spotted Corinne standing on the sidewalk. "May I assume by the presence of the press that this isn't purely a social call? Don't tell me you and Corinne have let Father MacNeill convince you that Jared's up to something!" The dazzling smile returned. Then he winked, as if the two of them were sharing a secret. "Or is it me again? Please don't tell me someone's cooked up some list of ordinances I've already violated. We're not even open yet! Won't be for months."

"Actually, it's a little more serious than that. Somethin' happened out at Jake Cumberland's last night." He told Ted what had happened to Jake last night, and what he and Corinne Beckwith had found in Jake's trunk. "And when Corinne said you have a golden retriever, I figured I better come over here."

Ted Conway gazed steadily at the policeman. "So you think Jared took his own dog out to Jake's place and killed it." He shook his head almost sadly. "You sure you haven't been talking to Father MacNeill? It sounds exactly like the kind of thing he'd come up with." His voice hardened. "But it doesn't really make much sense, does it?" A frown creased his brow. "Except, of course, that Scout *is* missing. Jared let him out right after he got home last night, and he didn't come back in." He shrugged helplessly. "We figured there must be a bitch in heat somewhere in the neighborhood, and you know how dogs are. Once they get that scent, there's no stopping them, is there?"

Ray Beckwith shook his head. "No way," he agreed. "Sometimes they can be worse'n tomcats." He pulled a small notebook out of his jacket pocket. "You say it was Jared that let him out?"

"That's right," Ted replied. "In fact, I was with him. We were both in the kitchen. The minute Jared opened the door, Scout was off like a rocket."

"And what about your boy? He go out again?"

Ted shook his head. "It was already pretty late, and it was a school night, too. Besides, he wasn't feeling well—went right to bed after we gave up trying to get the dog back. Still feeling kind of flu-ish this morning, so we're keeping him home from school. But I'll tell you what—how about if I have him give you a call once he's feeling a little better? Then you can ask him anything you want."

Ray Beckwith closed the notebook and tucked it back into his pocket. "Don't really see that that'll be necessary," he said. "Seems like you've pretty much told me what I need to know. Sounds like someone came across the dog and took him out to Jake's. Used it for some kind of voodoo ceremony. I guess someone really had it in for Jake—"

"Or for us," Ted Conway interjected. "Maybe whoever did it used Scout for a reason." His eyes fixed on Beckwith.

The sheriff frowned as he turned Ted Conway's words over in his mind. Then he thought he understood what the other man meant. "You mean Father Mack?" he asked.

Ted Conway shrugged again. "You said that, Ray," he said softly. "Not me."

As Ted Conway's eyes remained steadily on him, Ray Beckwith wondered why he'd let Corinne talk him into coming over here. It was suddenly so obvious that the Conways didn't have anything to do with the vandalism, he felt he was just wasting time. "No sir, Mr. Conway," he said. "I'm sure not gonna let that happen." Shaking hands with Ted, he strode off the porch.

"Well?" Corinne asked anxiously. "Was it their dog?"

Ray nodded. "But none of them had anything to do with it, babe. The dog took off last night, and the boy was in bed, sick. Still is."

Corinne's lips pursed suspiciously. "Did you see him?"

"I didn't need to see him," Beckwith shot back. "You've been married to me long enough to know I can tell when someone's lying to me. Ted Conway wasn't lying."

Corinne's gaze shifted back to the house. Ted Conway was still standing on the porch, and as his eyes met hers, Corinne felt as if a wave of hatred had broken over her.

Suddenly, all Corinne Beckwith wanted was to get away.

As far away as she could.

CHAPTER 35

K im sat through the first hour of classes barely hearing a word that Sister Clarence said. She continually glanced out the window, hoping to see Jared coming across the square toward the school, but by the time the class was half over, she knew he wasn't coming. Even then she couldn't concentrate. From the moment she'd seen Sandy Engstrom, she knew something was wrong. Sandy arrived at school just as the bell rang, and when she rushed by her, Kim assumed Sandy was trying to get to her locker while she still had time. But when Sandy finally arrived in class—two minutes late—her friend hadn't taken her regular seat right next to her.

Instead, she slid into an empty desk at the back of the classroom.

Sister Clarence had gone silent when Sandy entered the room, and Kim expected her friend to be sent directly to Father Bernard's office. But after fixing Sandy with a stern glare, Sister Clarence's face took on a look of concern. "Sandra? Are you all right?"

Every head in the class turned to gaze at Sandy. She was wearing more makeup than Kim had ever seen on her before, but even the makeup couldn't cover the pallor of her complexion.

"I'm fine, Sister Clarence," she announced in a challenging tone that made Kim brace herself for her immediate banishment to Father Bernard's office. The whole class held its collective breath, waiting. But for the first time in anyone's memory, Sister Clarence backed down.

"Very well," she said. "But I won't tolerate your being late again."

For the rest of the hour Kim kept stealing peeks at her friend, but Sandy never looked back at her. When the bell rang, Sandy was out the door before Kim had even finished packing her books into her bag. She hurried after Sandy, threading her way through the crowded corridor toward the lockers, where the two girls had fallen into the habit of meeting between classes.

Sandy was nowhere to be seen.

Sandy hadn't been in church yesterday.

Sandy hadn't called her yesterday, either.

And now, this morning, she hadn't even spoken to her.

Kim was just starting back toward her own locker when she caught a glimpse of Sandy through the glass of the school's front door. She glanced at the big clock on the wall above the door, and saw that she still had five minutes before her next class. Working her way through her milling classmates, she pushed the front door open and went out onto the sidewalk.

Sandy was deep in conversation with Luke Roberts. As Kim approached them, both teenagers fell silent.

"Sandy?" Kim asked uncertainly. "What's going on?"

Sandy turned to gaze at her. As Kim met Sandy's eyes—which seemed to have sunk within her skull—she saw it.

The same look she'd seen in her brother's eyes this morning. And her father's.

Then Luke turned to look at her, and there it was in his eyes, too.

Kim's pulse raced as an image rose in her mind, from the nightmare she'd had, when she saw Sandy and Luke writhing in front of that strange candlelit altar with the inverted cross.

Then Sandy spoke, in an angry, hissing voice Kim had never heard from her before. "Leave us alone, you stupid bitch!"

Kim's eyes widened in shock, but even as the words battered her, another memory rose in her mind.

Sandy sounded like Jared! Just like Jared when Father MacNeill had come to the house yesterday afternoon!

She took a step toward her friend. Without warning, Sandy spat at her, sending a great wad of greenish phlegm oozing down the front of Kim's blouse. Kim stared at the mess in shock, then, as peals of ugly laughter erupted from Luke and Sandy, she turned and fled back into the school. Tears of pain and humiliation streamed down her cheeks, and the crowd, already thinning as the students drained into the classrooms, parted to make way for her as she lurched toward the girls' room. She dropped her book bag on the floor and stared at herself in the mirror. Her face looked almost as pale as Sandy's, and as more images and memories tumbled through her mind—some of them dreamed, some of them real, all of them terrifying—confusion and terror overwhelmed her.

She ran the water in the sink, splashed some on her face, then gingerly scraped the wad of phlegm from her blouse. Sandy had *spit* at her! Actually *spit* at her! How could she have—

Her thought died as her eye caught something in the mirror. She looked down, and where the phlegm had been, there was now a small hole in her blouse.

A hole with blackened edges, as if it had been burned.

A whimper escaped Kim's lips. She rubbed harder at her blouse, as if trying not only to erase the charring from the material, but the hole as well. She was still working at it when she heard her name.

"Kimmie? Kimmie!"

Jumping, she glanced in the mirror, and there he was.

Jared!

She whirled around.

The girls' room was empty; she was alone.

"Kimmie!"

She whirled around again, but this time the mirror was as empty as the room behind her.

"Kimmie, help me!"

Jared's voice had a plaintive note to it now, and she remembered the dream she'd had this morning, when Jared was drowning and she tried to reach him but couldn't.

"Jared?" she whispered, but even the barely spoken word echoed in the emptiness of the room. "Oh, God, Jared, what's happening to us?"

A moment later she heard him calling to her again, but now his voice seemed to be coming from beyond the room. Leaving her book bag where it lay, Kim stumbled out of the bathroom.

The hallway outside was empty.

Still she heard Jared's voice, calling out to her.

She followed the voice, moving down the corridor, then turning into another.

Then up some stairs.

Down another corridor.

More memories tumbled through her mind, images of the corridors through which the unseen menace of her nightmares had pursued her, but still she kept going, following Jared's ever fainter voice.

Then, at last, she came to a closed door. She stood paralyzed with a terrible certainty that she knew what lay beyond.

The obscene cathedral, where she'd witnessed all the worst horrors of her nightmares.

Where only this morning she'd seen little Molly, suspended upside down from the cross above the altar, the candles flickering in front of her tortured face.

Then, barely audible through the confusion in her mind, she heard Jared's voice once more. "Kiiimmmm . . ."

Steeling herself, Kim pulled the door open.

Not the cathedral.

The biology lab, with zinc-topped worktables laid out in neat rows, each of them equipped with a sink.

And on the walls, shelf after shelf of specimens, the dissected carcasses of frogs and mice, the organs of larger creatures, all of them floating in sealed jars of formaldehyde. As she stared at the jars, she saw that they were now filled with blood—overflowing with blood. And in every one of them was some fragment of Molly's body.

A little foot in one, a leg in another. Another jar held a hand. In the largest jar was her baby sister's head.

Molly's eyes were wide open, and her mouth was stretched into a grimace of agony. She seemed to be staring through the haze of blood right at Kim, and as she looked into Molly's twisted face, Kim felt every bit of pain Molly must have felt as—

Screaming, Kim cut off the thought, unable to bear it. But no matter where she turned, there were more jars and still more jars, and from every one of them, Molly stared at her.

Kim kept screaming, and finally, her mind no longer able to cope with the images that churned through it, she collapsed to the floor, sobbing and moaning.

"No," she whimpered. "Oh, no . . . please, no . . ."

CHAPTER 36

J anet woke slowly, luxuriating in the sunlight streaming through the window and in the memory of the night before, when Ted had taken her in his arms.

It was like being on their honeymoon all over again, before Ted's drinking had taken over their lives. Strange how it had crept over every part of their existence so slowly that she hadn't truly realized quite how bad the problem was. But now that it was over—now that the Ted Conway she'd first fallen in love with was back—she could see exactly how it had happened, how she'd let Ted's alcohol nibble away at her marriage. The thing of it was—as she could now see—it had never taken a big enough bite all at once to force her into facing the true reality of it. Not, anyway, until that last night, when Ted stayed up drinking long after their fight, only to come at last to the realization that she would finally leave him.

She stretched languidly, once again feeling Ted's hands on her body, his mouth on hers, his strength as he made love to her. Her reverie was interrupted by the faint sound of the clock tolling the hour in the living room below her. When it reached seven, she threw back the sheet—if she didn't hurry, she wouldn't have time to fix breakfast for Jared and Kim.

The clock struck twice more.

Nine?

But it couldn't be—she never slept past seven, and most mornings was up by six. A glance at the clock by her bedside confirmed how much she'd overslept. Why hadn't anyone wakened her? Why hadn't—

And then she knew. Ted had known how tired she was, and how

worried about Jared. Even after they made love, she'd lain awake until, finally, Ted made her talk it out. It had been hard—she'd become so used to dealing with her problems by herself that she'd almost forgotten how to talk to Ted, but he'd drawn it all out of her, even agreed with her that Jared wasn't just "stretching his wings," but that something more was going on. Only after he promised to help her deal with the problem had she fallen asleep.

In his arms, feeling safe, and comforted, and loved.

And this morning he'd obviously decided to let her sleep in and take care of the kids himself. She pulled on a thin robe and went to the nursery, half expecting to find her youngest daughter awake and playing in her crib. But Molly was gone, her bedding straightened up and tucked in, exactly the way she herself always did it. Sighing contentedly, she moved out onto the landing.

And instantly knew that something was wrong.

She peered down into the yawning entry hall as she moved toward the top of the stairs. Was it something about the light?

She looked up at the skylight, but it looked the same as it had the day Ted cleaned it. Yet when she looked down once again, she realized that there was, indeed, something odd, as if a slight haziness was hanging over everything. Janet blinked a couple of times and rubbed her eyes, but the haziness remained. Then, when she started down the stairs, she felt it.

There was a chill in the air, as though it were the middle of winter and a freak cold snap had struck. But the night had been warm enough to leave the windows open, and a single thin blanket had been sufficient. At some point—probably early this morning when the sun began flooding in—she'd kicked that away, too. Yet as she descended the stairs the air grew colder, until, by the time she reached the first floor, gooseflesh was creeping over her skin.

She paused at the bottom of the stairs. The haze had thickened, and though she smelled nothing unusual, the atmosphere seemed heavy and hard to breathe.

Fumes of some kind?

That must be it—Ted must be painting, or cleaning something, or— Molly!

Where was Molly? If she were breathing these fumes—

Janet quickened her step, moving out of the entry hall into the dining room, hurrying toward the kitchen. Then something caught her eye, and turning, she stared at the mural on the wall, the mural she'd been working on only last night.

The marble tile of the terrace she had so carefully textured, so you might expect it to be smooth and cold to the touch, looked old and stained.

The balustrade appeared chipped and battered.

And beyond the balustrade, the garden she'd created, painstakingly drawing and coloring every leaf and blossom, had died.

The leaves were gone, only bare limbs and twigs remaining. Even the silvery glow of moonlight had been mottled, and the sky was tinged with green as if a terrible storm were about to break.

It wasn't possible, she thought. No one could have repainted the whole wall during the few hours she'd been asleep!

That was it! It *had* to be.

She must still be asleep, and this was a nightmare from which she'd awaken in a minute or two. She'd be back in her bed, and it would take a few seconds before she realized that her work—the best work she'd ever done—had not really been ruined.

But she didn't awaken.

Instead, the mural itself seemed to come to life. The clouds in the sky darkened, and then the branches of the trees began to move, bending forward, reaching, their twigs stretching like skeletal fingers, straining toward her. Then talons appeared at the ends of the twigs, and as one of the branches lashed toward her, Janet reflexively turned away, stumbling toward the kitchen.

Then she heard it.

A soft cry, muffled, almost inaudible.

She stopped short, one hand on the kitchen door, listening.

It came again.

A baby?

Molly?

Pushing the door open, she strode into the kitchen, her eyes going to Molly's playpen, over in the corner, safely away from the stove.

Empty!

Her mind raced. The car was outside, so Ted hadn't gone somewhere and taken Molly with him. Where was she? Where was *he*?

The carriage house?

No! The cry she'd heard—and now she was almost certain it had been Molly—had come from somewhere inside the house! Turning away from the back door, she went back to the dining room.

The sound she heard this time was so low it was almost inaudible. Janet held her breath, wishing there were some way to silence the pounding of her own heart.

There!

A low, throbbing sound, so low she wasn't quite certain whether she'd heard it or simply *felt* it. It could have come from the floor itself, up through her feet and body, and only then into her consciousness.

The basement.

It was coming from the basement.

As she pulled the door to the basement open, she heard the muffled cry of the baby again. But it was much clearer now. She groped for the light switch. Flipped it.

"Molly?"

No answer.

"Molly!" Then: "Ted? Are you down there?"

There was still no answer, and she started down the steep flight of stairs.

As she did, the cold deepened, its icy grip closing around her.

As a thick haze appeared out of nowhere, the glare of the naked bulb that lit the stairs was muted to a pallid silver glow that barely held the shadows at bay. The bulb itself appeared to be suspended in nothing but the gathering mist.

The throbbing sound was louder with every step she took, but so also was the sound of the crying baby.

Nor was there any longer any question that the bawling child was Molly.

Janet came at last to the bottom of the stairs, and the closed door to Jared's room. The pulsing rhythm was all around her now, drowning out even the pounding of her heart, but still she could hear Molly crying out. She put her hand on the doorknob to Jared's room and paused, a terrible feeling of foreboding passing over her. Suddenly, she wanted to turn away from the closed door, to escape the throbbing beat of the music and the terrible cold.

But she couldn't.

Not until she'd found Molly.

The doorknob was so cold it numbed her fingers, and when she tried to turn it, she thought at first that it might be locked.

Then the knob turned.

The light above her blinked out.

Janet froze in the darkness.

The bulb. It was only the bulb. No one was above her; no one had turned the light out. Yet all around her—everywhere and nowhere—hidden in the darkness, she could feel a presence.

The blackness held her to the spot where she stood like an insect pinned in a display case. She had a terrible sense of being watched, as if some unseen being were above the case, peering down at her as if at some strange species.

A feeling of utter helplessness came over her. The throbbing rhythm grew stronger still. The cold and darkness threatened to strangle her. With

THE RIGHT HAND OF EVIL

every fiber of her being she tried to free herself so she could flee back up the stairs and escape from the horror that held her in its thrall.

Then, once again, Molly cried out.

This time her voice was filled with terror. In an instant all of Janet's maternal instincts rose within her. Her own fears vanished and she threw off the bonds of the cold and blackness. She pressed against the door.

It opened a crack and a flickering light crept through.

Janet pushed the door harder, and it swung open.

As she saw what lay beyond, a terror beyond anything she'd ever felt before gripped Janet.

She began to scream.

And scream.

And scream . . .

The sound of her name was so faint that at first Kim barely heard it. But then she heard it again: "Kiiiimmm"—the single syllable drawn out as if whoever was calling out to her had almost despaired of her responding. Then, as the cry came a third time, it seemed suddenly sharper.

"Kim? Kim! Kim, can you hear me?"

Hands gently shook her. She opened her eyes and looked up. Three faces loomed above her, but their features were lost in the glare of the bright light behind them. Then, as her eyes adjusted to the light, the faces came into focus.

Sister Clarence. Father Bernard. Father MacNeill.

But where was she? She'd been in the lake, trying to save Jared, but—

She tried to sit up, but Sister Clarence's hand held her back.

"It's all right, Kim. Don't try to get up. Just try to tell us what happened."

"Jared!" Kim blurted. "He needs me! He's—" But then, before she finished the sentence, her mind began to clear. "Molly!" she cried out. She pressed her hands against her eyes and shook her head as if trying to deny even the memory of what she'd seen. "They cut her up! They cut her up, and put her in jars, and—" Now her sobbing did overtake her, and a moment later she felt Sister Clarence's arms go around her. The nun's hand gently stroked her hair.

"It's all right, Kim. We're here. Nothing's going to happen to you. Just try to tell us what you saw."

A kaleidoscope of images was tumbling through her mind, and she instinctively clutched at the tiny golden cross her aunt had given her. "What is it?" she whispered. "What's happening to Jared? He—"

"Hush, child," Sister Clarence soothed. "You're safe with us. Everything will be all right." But even as the nun spoke, Kim knew that Sister Clarence didn't believe her own words.

"Just tell us," Father MacNeill told her. "Don't worry if none of it makes sense. But you have to tell us everything."

Kim's voice choked as a sob rose in her throat. "Mommy says it's just dreams, and—" She broke off again, remembering the terrible scene of Sandy and Luke making love in front of the candlelit altar. "I can't," she whispered. "It's . . . it's . . ."

"I know," Father MacNeill said. He reached out and laid his fingers on her forehead, as if baptizing her. "But no matter how terrible it seems to you, you can tell us. You can tell us. You can trust us."

As the priest's cool fingers continued to stroke her brow, Kim felt the terror inside her begin to lose its grip. Slowly, she began relating all the nightmares she'd had since she and her family moved into the old house on the edge of the town. She told them about Muffin's disappearance, then Scout's, and about the humiliation of Sandy spitting at her. "And then later this morning," she concluded, her voice breaking as she choked back her tears, "I—I thought—oh, God, I thought Jared and my father were killing my baby sister!" Her eyes fixed on Father MacNeill. "I was in the biology lab, and I saw—"

She faltered as another sob threatened to choke her, then went on. "I saw Molly. She was all cut up, and they'd put her into jars of—of—" She gazed beseechingly at the priest. "What is it, Father? What is it?"

Instead of answering Kim's question, Father MacNeill's hand covered Kim's as she clutched the cross. "Where did this come from?" he asked.

Kim frowned. "M-My aunt," she said uncertainly. "Aunt Cora gave it to me just before she died."

The priest nodded. "And there's another one, isn't there?" he asked.

Kim started to shake her head, but then the scene in her aunt's room at the Willows came back to her, and she nodded. "It was for Molly," she breathed. "My mother took it."

Now Father MacNeill took both of Kim's hands in his own and looked into her eyes. "I want you to think carefully," he said. "Did your mother put the cross on Molly?"

Kim shook her head. "She said she'd keep it until Molly got older."

"But it's in the house?" Father MacNeill pressed.

Kim nodded. "It's probably in Mom's jewelry box."

"And just now you heard Jared calling you, is that right?"

Once again Kim nodded. "But it wasn't really him, was it?" she said. "I mean, wasn't it you who was calling my name, trying to wake me up?"

The priest's hands tightened on Kim's. He looked straight into her eyes. "I'm going to tell you something, Kim." The timbre of his voice brought all of Kim's terrors flooding back as the priest continued to squeeze her hands. "You have to be strong, Kim," he went on. "Can you do that?"

Kim hesitated, then forced herself to nod.

"They weren't dreams, Kim," Father MacNeill said. "None of it. Everything you saw—everything you thought you dreamed—really happened. All of it."

CHAPTER 37

*I*t wasn't possible.

None of what she was seeing could possibly be happening.

Janet's last scream hung in the air, fading away, only to build once again, as if somehow the vast chamber into which she'd stumbled were amplifying it and reamplifying it.

Every muscle in her body had gone flaccid, and for a moment that went on forever, she thought she would collapse to the floor.

Her mind cast out in every direction, seeking something, anything, that would make sense of what she was experiencing.

A nightmare?

But she was awake! She knew she was awake.

An hallucination. That had to be it—everything she'd seen, the strange look to the house, the bizarre alterations to her trompe l'oeil, none of it could be anything but an hallucination.

Her eyes flicked over the impossible vision before her. Jared's room, that musty, black-walled chamber, had vanished. But what had taken its place couldn't exist. As the door had swung open, the piercing light from within blinded her for a second, but then her vision had cleared and she'd seen it: a space so vast it seemed to go on forever, its farthest reaches lost in shadows so black they devoured the harsh, cold light that seemed to come from everywhere—and nowhere. But what had made her scream—the image that had ripped an anguished howl of pure horror from her throat—was the altar that loomed in the distance, dominating the entire space, although it appeared so far away as to be unreachable.

Bones. The whole thing was made of human bones—thousands of

them. The altar was covered with flickering candles from which the scent of burning flesh billowed into the thick, smoke-filled atmosphere. On the altar lay the desiccated remains of a hand.

A human hand.

A right hand.

Its nails split with age, its rotted skin falling away, its forefinger curled as if beckoning to her. She knew instinctively where it had come from: the desecrated tomb of George Conway. Even as its image burned into her mind, Janet forced herself to look away, only to be faced with something else. It, too, she recognized in a flash: the severed right fore-paw of her son's pet, Scout. Next to it lay the foot of another animal, but that one, blessedly, she did not recognize.

Nauseated, she tore her eyes from the grisly objects, only to face an even more horrifying vision: above the altar, floating unsupported by any-thing she could see, was an inverted cross.

From the cross was suspended a figure, held to it with a single spike piercing both feet, its head dangling down. Two more spikes pierced the figure's wrists, pinning them to the transverse of the cross.

A great gash was torn in the figure's right side, and blood oozed from the wound. Blood, and something else as well.

A squirming, roiling mass of maggots, erupting from the great wound.

At last her eyes fastened on the figure's face, and her screams built until her own voice filled the vast space, then buffeted back at her, per-verted into taunting laughter. For it was her own features she beheld above the altar, twisted in anguish, blood dripping down the planes of her face to mat her hair.

She felt the pain now. Her feet and wrists throbbed with agony, and the wound, churning with the ravenous maggots, burned unbearably in her side. She could feel the heat of blood streaming from the gash, and her nos-trils filled with its coppery odor. She tried to take a step forward, collapsed to her knees and screamed again as her bloodied hands struck the floor.

Drugs!

That was it! Somehow, she had to have been drugged. But even that made no sense, for she could remember everything perfectly clearly, from the moment Ted came home last night.

Their lovemaking.

Falling asleep in his arms.

Waking up, filled with a sense of well-being and contentment.

She'd eaten nothing—drunk nothing.

Then how . . . ? But the question was never completed, for even as it formed, two new figures appeared. Although their backs were toward her, she recognized them immediately.

Her husband.

And her son.

Together, they placed a bundle on the altar, something she couldn't quite see, for it was wrapped in some kind of animal skin.

A skin covered with golden fur.

Then, even before realizing what the skin must be, she knew with terrible certainty what was inside it.

"Molly!" she screamed.

Ignoring the agony in her feet and wrists, Janet raced toward the grotesque altar. From out of nowhere, a terrible peal of laughter rolled over her, and both Ted and Jared turned to gaze at her.

Ted raised his finger to point at her, and she felt a stab of heat lash into her, as if she'd been struck by a laser. Still she lurched toward the altar, her arms outstretched, her baby daughter's name shrieking from her lips. "Molly . . . Molly . . . Molly . . . Molly . . ."

The howls of mocking laughter swelled, and over and over again she felt the whiplike flick of the unseen force emanating from Ted's hand. Then, when she was still ten yards from the altar, Ted spoke.

"Stop her!"

Jared, a glittering dagger clutched in his right hand, started toward his mother.

CHAPTER 38

Father MacNeill held Kim's hands in his and looked deep into her eyes. He could still see the terror that had taken root inside her, but now there was something else as well: a look of resolve was displacing the fear. As they stood in front of the house, the girl's determination was overcoming the paralyzing panic that had overpowered her in the biology lab at school. "You can do it, Kimberley," he said quietly. "Just remember, your aunt was right. The cross will protect you. You're going to see more frightening things than you can even imagine, but as long as you wear the cross, you will be safe. Do you understand that?"

Kim hesitated only a fraction of a second before nodding. *Safe,* she whispered to herself. The word had become a mantra, which she kept silently repeating as her fingers constantly went to the cross suspended from her neck on the thin gold chain: *Safe . . . Safe . . . Safe . . .* But what if the chain broke? What if the cross fell away and—

"Kim . . . Kiiimmmmm . . ."

Jared's voice again! But it sounded weaker, as if he were sinking farther into the depths she'd seen in her dreams, sinking beyond her reach. "Now," she whispered, almost as much to herself as to the two priests who flanked her. Leaving them on the sidewalk, she started toward the house.

"We can't let her go in there by herself," Father Bernard said as she moved across the lawn.

Father MacNeill said nothing until Kim mounted the steps to the porch. Even from here he could feel the icy chill emanating from the structure, almost see the heavy aura of evil that hung over it. "We don't have a choice," he finally replied. "Neither you nor I could even cross the threshold. We don't have the strength."

As Kimberley Conway slowly opened the front door, stepped through it, then closed it behind her, the two priests began to pray.

As it echoed through the vast emptiness of the house, the sound of the door closing behind Kim had a terrible finality to it. She stood perfectly still. Everything about the house had changed; the icy chill was all-pervasive now, and Kim knew there was nothing she could do to protect herself from it. The air had taken on a heaviness that made it difficult to breathe, and every instinct within Kim told her to leave.

To leave now, before it was too late.

But even as her instincts tried to force her to turn away, she started toward the stairs.

A rat came out of nowhere, darting toward her. Kim reflexively flinched backward, a shriek of revulsion rising in her throat.

Not real!

The words rose in her mind as her right hand clutched the cross around her neck.

The rat vanished.

Vanished, or only veered away to disappear through the open doors of the dining room?

Steeling herself against the panic the rat's appearance had brought on, Kim continued toward the stairs. The atmosphere grew even heavier, and her feet seemed mired in quicksand, as if she were caught up in a terrible nightmare.

She came to the bottom of the stairs, but even as she set foot on the first tread, the staircase itself came alive with snakes. They were everywhere, writhing among themselves, then rising up, their heads swaying as their tongues flicked out at her.

Kim's fingers tightened on the cross, and she took a second step, then a third.

The serpents parted before her.

As she came to the landing, a high-pitched shriek rent the silence of the house, and Kim whirled around, but saw nothing.

Another shriek, once again behind her.

She spun around again, but again saw nothing. Now the shrieking built to a howl, and Kim covered her ears, bolting up the flight to the mezzanine. A moment later she stood in front of the door to her parents' room, and as she reached for the knob, she tried to prepare herself for whatever might wait within.

She turned the knob, pushed the door open.

The corpse, naked, hung from the chandelier, a thick rope knotted around its neck.

The mouth hung open, the tongue lolled out.

The empty, dead eyes fixed on Kim.

It was her mother.

Once again a scream boiled up in Kim's throat; once again the voice inside spoke as her fingers tightened on her cross: *Not real!*

Her mother's lifeless arm came up; her finger pointed accusingly at her. "Your fault!" The words croaked from her mother's constricted throat, dribbled from lips grayed with death.

Kim's heart thudded, her legs went weak. Hysteria threatened to overwhelm her. But then, from somewhere deep within, she heard her aunt's voice whispering. "It will protect you. The cross will protect you." Forcing back the hysteria that threatened to paralyze her, Kim turned away from the specter hanging from the chandelier, and went to the small dresser on which her mother's jewelry box sat. Opening the lid, she began searching, hunting for the second cross. The top tray was filled with a tangle of necklaces and a few inexpensive rings, but there was no sign of the cross. Kim lifted out the tray. Beneath it was another compartment, in which lay three boxes. The first one contained a single strand of pearls; the second an ornately carved jade pendant Kim hadn't seen since her grandmother had died a dozen years earlier. Attached to the pendant's chain was a small tag, with a message written in her grandmother's shaky hand: *For Kim on her 21st birthday.* She clutched the pendant for a moment, then put it back and opened the third box.

The second gold cross glittered brightly. As Kim lifted it out of the box, a scream of agony erupted behind her. She whirled around to see her mother's corpse twitching at the end of the rope; both hands were now stretched toward Kim as greedy fingers tried to snatch away the cross.

"No!" Kim breathed. "Never!"

The specter screamed again, the dead features of the face contorting with rage. The arms stretched toward her until the fingers almost touched Kim's flesh.

Her courage teetered as her heart pounded. But she didn't flinch away.

With one final howl of enraged frustration, the terrible specter of her mother's corpse dropped away.

The chain wrapped around Kim's fingers, the cross itself clutched tightly in her left hand, she returned to the bedroom door and paused, listening. Through the door's thick panels she could hear something—

something that sounded faintly familiar, but that she couldn't quite put a name to.

She opened the door a crack, and instantly the sound threatened to deafen her.

Wasps!

Millions of them, swirling in a cloud so thick she almost couldn't see across to the opposite side of the hall. All her instincts told her to slam the door closed again, to cower in the safety of the bedroom until the stinging horde was gone. But once again she forced her instincts aside and threw the door wide.

The wasps swirled around her head.

Steadily, Kim began walking toward the head of the stairs, her skin crawling with the anticipation of millions of tiny feet clinging to her, thousands of stingers plunging into her body. She broke into a run, pounded down the stairs, then through the doors into the dining room. She slammed the dining room doors closed. Instantly, the droning of the insects died away.

As she moved toward the door to the basement stairs, she tried not to even glance at her mother's mural, terrified of what she might now see there. But her eyes were drawn to it, and her breath caught in her throat as she gazed into a blazing inferno beyond the French doors she had watched her mother draw. Flames were everywhere; the trees bore limbs of fire, and clouds of smoke hung in the sky. Burning figures whirled and spun across the fiery lawn. The cacophonic moans of a thousand tortured souls rolled out of the scene, and Kim felt an unbearable hopelessness pervade her.

Then a longing seized her—a terrible longing to banish the cold that had enveloped her the moment she'd entered the house by stepping into the blaze. Abruptly, the French doors were no longer painted on the wall, and she knew all she had to do was step through them and she would be warmed by the fires.

The fires of Hell.

She took a step toward the doors; they opened of their own volition, as if to welcome her.

Another step.

Then another.

Only one more, and—

Seizing control of herself, Kim turned away from the flaming eternity beyond the doors and moved instead to the door that led to the basement.

A door that slammed behind her, plunging her into inky blackness.

The cross clutched in her hand, she began descending the stairs.

* * *

Janet felt the tip of the dagger at her throat, but even the threat of its plunging deep into her neck would not have stopped her had she been able to force her body to obey her will. But instead of responding to the commands of her mind, everything below her neck had gone numb. It was as if some alien force had wrested control from her, compelling her to stand where she was and watch.

Ted had by now opened the skin of the dog, unwrapping Molly, who now lay naked upon the altar.

Molly, too, seemed in the grip of the same force that had paralyzed Janet, for she made no move to escape. But she was crying, and Janet could hear her terror.

Ted had lain the child on her back, and she looked utterly helpless in the candlelight. Her eyes were fastened on the image on the cross— Janet's own image—and Janet was certain Molly thought that what she was seeing was real.

"Stop," she begged Ted. "For the love of God, Ted! What are you doing?"

Ted turned to face her. Though she still recognized him, his handsome features were bloated, his skin blotched and mottled. Sores and pustules were erupting on every part of him that she could see, and as he turned to her, his robe fell open.

His skin was rippling strangely, and then Janet saw the source of the rippling as swarms of maggots began to break through his skin, wriggling free, dropping off him to creep across the floor toward her.

She sobbed, and with every cry that emerged from her throat, a hideous peal of cruel laughter boiled from her husband's mouth.

His glittering eyes flicked toward her as the knife in Jared's hand moved. Janet felt the point slip through her skin.

"Wait!" Ted commanded.

Jared froze. The knife stayed, quivering, its point still in her flesh.

"Molly," Ted whispered. "Molly first, and then your mother."

"No," Janet whispered. It was a nightmare—it had to be! And yet, despite its impossibility, Janet knew it wasn't a dream. "Oh, please . . ." she moaned, her voice breaking.

The point of the knife withdrew as Jared moved away from her, leaving a bead of blood on her neck. But still Janet was held in the thrall of the unseen force, and could do nothing to save her youngest child. As she watched helplessly, Jared approached the altar until he stood above Molly, the dagger poised above her naked belly.

"Do it, Jared," Ted's menacing voice whispered. "You know you have to, Jared. You know you want to! Serve your master, Jared! Serve him as I promised you would!"

An explosion of pure rage erupted from Janet. "What!" she demanded. What master? What did you promise? "Tell me what you did!"

Ted's glittering eyes fixed on her. "I did what I had to do," he spat. "I did what I needed to do for me, and for you, too!"

Janet gazed bleakly at him, her mind reeling, trying to grasp what he was saying. But nothing made any sense. Everything she was seeing, everything she was hearing—all of it was impossible. Yet deep inside, she knew it wasn't impossible. Deep inside—in some way she would never be able to fathom—she knew what Ted had done.

He had given up his soul.

And his son's soul, too.

Not *his* son! *Their* son! "No," she screamed. "You can't do it. You can't give Jared away! He's not yours, Ted!"

"Isn't he?" Ted taunted. "Watch him! Just watch him. He'll do exactly as he's told." He turned away from Janet to face the altar, and raised his arms.

Before her the inverted cross—and the agonized image of Janet herself—disappeared. In its place a visage of pure evil materialized, a face with features torn from a nightmare. The eyes, sunk deep within suppurating sockets, glittered in the hard, cold light. They were fixed on Janet, and she could feel them boring into her, searching deep within her, looking for—what?

Weakness!

What do you want? Though the question was spoken silently, Janet could hear the menacing—yet somehow seductive—voice as clearly as if it had spoken directly into her ear. *You can have it. You can have anything you want.*

Now the image began to change, the vile face softening until she was looking at Ted.

But not Ted the way he was.

Ted the way he'd been, many years ago.

Except even that wasn't true. The Ted she now beheld hovering above the altar wasn't Ted as he'd ever been; he was the Ted she'd always dreamed of.

Perfect in every way, his features handsome and even, his eyes clear.

Everything about him idealized.

The image of Ted smiled at her. It spoke again with Ted's voice, caressing her, soothing her.

Promising her.

"Anything, Janet. You can have anything you want. Your life can be as perfect as you've ever dreamed . . ." The voice went on, whispering, murmuring, reaching deep within.

"No," she whispered, but this time it was more a plea than a command, and as the voice continued its siren song, the image's perfect eyes fixed on her. She felt the deep pull of temptation. "Please," she begged. "Don't do this to me . . . please don't do this. . . ."

But now she was feeling Ted, too, feeling his hands on her body, his warm fingers exploring every part of her, touching her, stroking her. She felt a surge of warmth grow in her groin and begin spreading through her, and her words turned to soft moans of ecstasy.

"You want it, Janet," the voice purred. "You know you want it. Anything and everything. Just give yourself to me, Janet. Open yourself. Let me in. Let me possess you. Let me—"

Suddenly, a single word resounded through the vast cathedral, shattering the seduction. "NOOOooo . . . !"

For a moment Janet had no idea where the sound had come from, but then she heard it again, from behind her. Tearing her eyes loose from the perfect image of Ted that hung suspended above the candlelit altar, she twisted around.

She saw her elder daughter coming toward her. Kim's face was ashen, her eyes wide with a combination of terror and wonder. Her right hand was clutching the cross that hung from a golden chain around her neck. Her left arm was extended straight out before her, and from her fingers hung the second cross, the one Janet herself had put away for Molly. As Kim drew near, Janet reached out to take the cross, but Kim passed by her, her eyes never wavering from—

—the image above the altar! Kim was gazing at it, and the expression on her face was enough to tell Janet that it wasn't she to whom Kim would offer the golden cross, but to the terrible being floating over the glowing candles. Then, as Janet watched, the visage of a perfect Ted changed again, mutating into something else, something with eyes that glittered with hatred. The soft skin that had been so perfect a second earlier turned red and scaly, and Ted's full lips thinned and hardened until Janet was staring at the mouth of a reptile.

The mouth opened, and a two-headed serpent shot out, each of the serpents writhing individually, each of their maws gaping wide to exhibit venom-dripping fangs.

Whimpering with terror, Janet cowered back from the terrible being.

Kim, though, walked steadily forward.

Both Jared and Ted stood before the altar now, the image of their god looming above them. The dagger vibrated in Jared's right hand, a few inches above Molly's naked breast, and as Kim drew closer, Ted's voice echoed through the chamber.

"Do it," he commanded once more. "Do it now!"

Jared's hand moved, and the dagger's point touched Molly's skin.

"DO IT!" Ted screamed. "Make your sacrifice!"

Not real!

Kim repeated the words over and over again as she moved toward the altar. She tried not to look at the terrifying being that floated above the altar, concentrating instead on forcing her feet to obey the will of her mind instead of the power of her fear.

Not real, she told herself again.

But this time she knew it was real, that what she was seeing was the very source of evil itself, and not merely an image conjured up in some underworld to frighten her away.

She could still hear Jared's voice calling to her, but it was weaker now. She was close enough to feel his mind, and she could sense him weakening as their father railed at him. In another moment or two it would be too late.

The twin serpents flicked toward her once again, their fangs bared, their slitted eyes glowing, but when she moved the cross in her left hand toward them, they veered away, hissing like water splashed on a sizzling griddle.

She moved closer, and now the evil image itself was screaming, bellowing in rage as she drew nearer, then nearer still, until she was next to Jared, standing before the altar, gazing into her brother's face in the light of the flickering candles that lit the area above the altar. The tip of the dagger still rested on Molly's breast. Molly herself was crying, and wailing for her mother.

"Do it, damn you!" she heard her father command, and saw Jared's knuckles turn white as his fingers tightened on the haft of the dagger.

He raised it, ready to plunge it deep into his little sister's chest.

Kim reached out and dropped the chain over Jared's head. The cross fell to his chest.

In the instant the cross touched him, Jared's face contorted with rage, and he lifted the dagger higher. His mouth opened and a screech of fury burst from his throat. A moment later the dagger flashed downward.

And plunged to the hilt into Ted Conway's chest.

Ted staggered, then sank to his knees. Jared, the dagger still clutched in his hand, pulled it loose. Ted gazed up at Jared, his eyes filled with shock, color draining from his face. He opened his mouth as if to speak, but Jared thrust the dagger into his father's gaping face, ramming it through the roof of his father's mouth to sink it deep into the core of his brain.

His life already ended, blood still gurgling from his wounds, Ted crumpled to the floor in front of the altar.

"Get Molly," Jared whispered, but even though his words were barely audible, Kim heard them directly from his mind. "Get Mom. Get out. For God's sake, get out."

Lifting Molly off the altar, Kim turned and ran up the aisle, calling out to her mother to follow her. A moment later they burst through the doors.

And back into the darkness of the staircase.

As the terrible nightmare released her from its grip, Janet stopped short. "I—I don't understand—" she stammered. "What—"

But Kim, still carrying Molly, pushed her up the stairs. "Get out!" she said. "Jared says we have to get out. Now!"

Something in her daughter's voice penetrated the confusion that surrounded Janet, and, taking Molly from Kim's arms, she stumbled up the stairs, through the dining room and entry hall, and out onto the front porch.

The sun was shining brightly, and a faint breeze played in the air.

Janet was back in the perfect morning to which she had awakened.

CHAPTER 39

Father MacNeill's prayers died on his lips as the front door of the house flew open. When Kim burst out onto the porch, no more than ten minutes after she'd gone into the house, he was certain she'd failed. Either she hadn't found the second cross, or, more likely, she had lost her nerve.

He didn't want even to think about the worst possibility, that somehow she had lost the cross that had been hanging around her neck.

When Janet Conway appeared with Molly in her arms, however, he released the breath he'd unconsciously been holding and took a step toward the house. But as he moved off the sidewalk and onto the Conway property itself, the chill of evil fell over him, and he knew that the terrible confrontation inside had not yet ended.

Kim, exhausted by what she'd been through, collapsed into his supporting arms. He held her for a moment, feeling her heart pounding, her body trembling. "It's all right," he told her. "You're going to be all right." Eventually, the throbbing of her heart began to slow, her trembling to ease. "Where is your brother?" he asked, then more urgently: "Where is he?"

Kim raised her face—streaked with tears she could no longer keep under control—and looked beseechingly into the priest's eyes. "He stayed," she whispered. "He told me to leave, but he stayed."

"And your father?" the priest went on.

Kim's voice wavered as she struggled against the sob that threatened to choke her. "He—He's dead," she stammered. "Jared—"

Father MacNeill pressed the forefinger of his right hand against her lips to silence her before she could finish. "Not Jared," he said quietly.

"Jared did nothing." His eyes fixed on Kim's. "Do you understand that? It was never your brother. Never."

Janet, her strength ebbing away, sank onto the narrow strip of lawn between the sidewalk and the street. Hugging Molly close—as much for her own comfort as for her child's—she tried to grasp what had just happened. But she couldn't. Nothing—not one single thing since she woke up that morning—made any sense. And yet as she listened to Father MacNeill talking to Kim, it sounded as though both of them not only knew about the nightmare she'd just been through, but somehow understood it. Her eyes drifted to the house, but all she could see was the terrible image of her son, a knife—glistening with blood—gripped tightly in his hand as he stood above his father.

Above *Ted*—

No, *not* Ted.

Someone—some*thing*—else. But not Ted.

Not Jared—

No, it had to have been some kind of nightmare—it *had* to have been. . . .

Certain her sanity was collapsing, she summoned the last reserves of her strength. "Tell me," she pleaded, her voice breaking. "Someone, please—tell me what's happening to me. . . ."

Father MacNeill knelt beside her and placed a comforting arm around her shoulder. "Hell," he said softly. "You've just been to Hell, Janet. But you're back. It's over."

But still he felt the cold of evil spreading out from the house. Still, he knew it was not over.

Not yet.

CHAPTER 40

The vast space around him filled with a cacophony of rage that threatened to shatter Jared's mind. The dagger forgotten, he reflexively clamped his hands over his ears to shut out the anguished shrieks of the damned souls whose wailing agonies resounded around him.

The knife, its blade still smeared with Ted Conway's blood, had fallen only a fraction of an inch from Ted's lifeless hand. As Jared turned away from the altar, his foot touched the haft and it swung around, brushing against the fingers of its victim.

As metal touched flesh, the finger twitched as if shocked by electricity. Then, instead of relaxing back into the stillness of death, Ted's fingers closed on the dagger. The blood on its blade faded as if sucked back into the body from which it had spurted only moments before. A guttural sound spewed from Ted's throat, and he sat up, then staggered to his feet, bracing himself against the altar. His eyes burned into the retreating back of his son with such intensity that Jared, feeling the fury of his father's gaze, turned back.

His father's mouth opened. Jared could see the wound in its roof, and when his father spoke, the words were muddied as they crossed the tear the dagger had opened.

"No," Ted gasped. "Not this way." He tried to straighten his back, and took a lurching step toward Jared. "This isn't how it ends." He reached out, beseeching Jared. "Not like this."

Jared took a step forward, ready to take his father's outstretched hand, but a second before their fingers touched, an image rose out of his subconscious.

* * *

*N*ight.

Asleep in his room.

Then awake, uncertain what had called him out of sleep.

A voice—his father's—calling to him.

Rising from his bed, following his father's voice down the stairs, through the dining room, then down into the basement.

A door.

He opened it.

Beyond the door, a heavy mist, but through the mist, he'd seen his father reaching out to him. "Help me, Jared," he'd heard his father say. "I need you to help me."

He moved forward through the mist, and his father's hand—icy cold—closed on his. And in that moment when his father's fingers clamped on his own, a terrible feeling of desolation fell over Jared.

He felt lost; abandoned.

Fear entered his soul, a terror of what his father was about to do, but that he had no power to resist.

His father led him through the fog, and they came at last to a golden, jeweled altar, glowing as if lit from within. Above the altar, he had seen an inverted cross, and in front of the cross hung a visage of pure evil.

Jared felt his soul shriveling as he beheld the image. He tried to turn away, but the eyes of the image held him. The eyes were hungry, and even before his father spoke again, Jared knew what it was the evil image craved.

And he knew he was lost.

"You are my son and my firstborn," he heard his father say. "You will obey me." Unable to resist his father, Jared gazed upon the face of evil.

"I give you my son," Jared heard his father say.

The face of evil smiled, and then Jared heard another voice, which seemed to come from everywhere and nowhere. It penetrated into the deepest part of his mind and soul, and Jared listened.

He had no choice.

"You belong to me, Jared," the voice whispered. "Your father has given you to me, and now you are mine."

Jared nodded.

"You will serve me and only me. You will build me a cathedral, and bring me others. You will feed me. You will worship me. You will destroy my enemies." The voice whispered on, instructing Jared in the depravities he would commit, the sacrifices he would make.

And then, before even the first flicker of dawn began to break, he had returned to his room, to his bed, to his sleep.

When he woke up again, he knew it was not a dream, and that very day he went to the basement and began.

Began doing everything the voice of evil had instructed him to do.

Powerless to resist, he called out to Kim, begging her to help him, and several times she'd come.

She'd seen what was happening, seen what he was doing, but she hadn't understood, hadn't helped him.

Until today.

Jared's hand was only a fraction of an inch from his father's reach when he pulled it away, and instead of his fingers closing on his father's, they closed instead on the gold cross his sister had hung around his neck. He felt his soul expanding within him, felt the cold and loneliness in which he'd been living begin to dissipate. As the grip of evil lost its strength, the intensity of the howls that filled the cathedral grew. But it was no longer the lost souls of Hell crying out. Rather, it was Evil itself, raging at the escape of its victim but powerless to stop it.

Jared's eyes rose once more to the evil image floating before the inverted cross, then returned to his father. "You gave me to him," he said softly. "You gave your own son to the Devil." Stepping past his father, who had already collapsed back to his knees, Jared swept the candles from the altar.

In an instant, flames spread through the profane cathedral, and once more the voice of evil screamed with rage. Jared ignored it, turning away to stride to the door.

"No!" his father screamed. "NOOoooo!"

As his father's scream died away, Jared turned to look at him one last time. The flames were everywhere now, and his father, his wounds once more streaming with blood, was spinning among them, turning first one way, then another, searching for an escape.

But there was no escape.

There would never be an escape.

Jared, his lips forming the first words of a prayer he hadn't uttered since he entered this house, turned and walked through the doors.

"Holy Mary, Mother of God, pray for us sinners now and at the hour of our death . . ."

"What do you think they're going to do with her?" Luke Roberts asked Sandy Engstrom.

Sandy shrugged indifferently. "They can lock her up and throw away the key, for all I care." Though it was still an hour before noon, they were sitting in the pizza parlor, where they'd been ever since Father Mac-Neill and Father Bernard had taken Kim Conway out of the biology lab. As they finished their second Cokes, they decided that if any of the nuns gave them any grief when they went back to school tomorrow, they'd just say they were so upset by what happened to Kim that they couldn't bear to stay at school.

Luke's lip curled into a smirk. "I thought Kim was your best friend."

"Melissa Parker was my best friend," Sandy retorted. "Kim's way too goody-goody." Cocking her head, she eyed Luke. "Did you and Melissa ever do it?"

Luke's laugh was harsh. "Are you kidding? She was just as bad as Kim! You'd think she was gonna be a nun or something."

Sandy opened her mouth to reply, but suddenly she felt something deep inside her letting go.

Something she hadn't even known was gripping her.

For a moment—a moment that passed in the blink of an eye—she had a terrible feeling that she was going to start vomiting again, as she had every morning since the night she'd spent at Kim's, but that sensation passed, too.

She shook her head, blinking. She felt utterly disoriented. What was she doing sitting in the pizza parlor at eleven in the morning? Sister Clarence would kill her!

And sitting across from her was Luke Roberts! Luke Roberts, whom she'd never planned to speak to again. She was just about to scramble out of the booth when Luke stood up.

"Jeez!" he said. "What am I doing here? Father Bernard and Father Mack are really gonna kill me this time!" Without so much as a goodbye, he dashed out the door and ran toward the school, a block away.

Sandy left enough money on the table to pay for her Coke and Luke's, too.

She slid out of the booth to start back to school, her mind wiped clean of everything that had happened to her since she'd first entered the Conway house.

Still praying, Jared Conway walked through the dining room and entry hall to the front door. He could feel the house throbbing with the evil it contained, and as he neared the front door, he felt it reaching out to him, still trying to ensnare him, to pull him back into the realm of darkness.

He opened the front door and stepped out onto the broad porch.

As he pulled the door closed behind him, he thought he heard his father's voice calling out to him one last time.

This time, he didn't listen.

As he stepped off the porch and started across the lawn toward his mother and sisters, the house burst into flames.

They were flames, Jared knew, that could never be completely put out.

Standing with his arms around his mother and twin sister, he watched the fire for a long time, but at last, as the frame of the house gave way and the structure collapsed into the conflagration, he turned away.

For him, it was finally over.